LIGHT
ON FIRE
ISLAND

LIGHT ON FIRE ISLAND

A NOVEL BY

MARLENE BATEMAN

Covenant Communications, Inc.

Cover image *Shining Beacon* © Juuce, courtesy istockphoto.com.

Cover design copyrighted 2009 by Covenant Communications, Inc.

Published by Covenant Communications, Inc.
American Fork, Utah

Printed in USA
First Printing: February 2010

15 14 13 12 11 10   10 9 8 7 6 5 4 3 2 1

ISBN-13 978-1-59811-552-9
ISBN-10 1-59811-552-9

To Josh, whom I love dearly

ACKNOWLEDGMENTS

Much gratitude and appreciation goes to my husband, Kelly, who is always supportive and who offered a number of helpful suggestions after reading the manuscript. Thanks also to proofreaders Barbara Roberts, Howard Roberts, and Holly Horton. Finally, thanks to the experts at the Fire Island Lighthouse who patiently answered my many questions: Dave Griese, administrator of the Fire Island Lighthouse Preservations Society, Inc., and Lynn Dunlop, program coordinator at the Fire Island Lighthouse Preservation Society, Inc.

ONE

Sitting in the plush Long Island Railroad car, Celena tried to sit placidly, one gloved hand laid atop the other. But the tightening and clenching of fingers betrayed her. To curb her anxiety, she focused on the landscape, which appeared, in the tender light of late April, to be a river of pale green flowing by. The only splashes of color came from the red tulips, purple Johnny-jump-ups, and yellow crocuses she saw dotting the grass near stations along the railway line.

The afternoon ride could have been relaxing, but Celena had the uncomfortable sensation that she had leaped off the very edge of the world and was falling free in blue space. It seemed impossible that only that morning she had donned her red jacket and navy skirt and left her grandparents' home in Maryland. That comfortable, safe world now felt far away. At Bellerose, Mineola, Bethpage, and other stops along the way, she had to resist the impulse to jump off and buy a return ticket. But even though the clatter of the train's wheels matched the churning in her stomach, Celena resolutely removed her gloves and set her mind to going back to Fire Island. She could not turn back now. Joshua had seen to that.

Her eleven-year-old brother had been nearly inconsolable when he'd called two nights ago, so agitated that he could hardly speak. He'd finally managed some disjointed phrases such as "fell," "the bosun's chair," "in the hospital," and "take care of the light." He had eventually regained a small portion of his composure, but the situation was still daunting. Even now, Celena could still remember the sweeping, empty wind of terror she had felt as Joshua begged, "Celena, please come back! With Father hurt, you *have* to help me!"

Despite an inner voice warning her that what her brother asked was too much given the five years that had passed, she'd impulsively assured him that she would come and take care of everything. She would have pulled down the moon if that would have taken the wretchedness from his voice. Rueben Wyatt had taken the phone then, assuring her that her father's injuries were not life-threatening. Rueben and his wife, Tana, still lived in Saltaire where Celena had grown up, and though a fisherman by trade, he had been her father's backup at the lighthouse for many years.

It had been beyond belief that her father had fallen while painting. "How did it happen?" she'd asked.

Rueben's reply was slow. "Matthew was painting, and . . . it seems the rope gave way."

Celena gasped, horrified. When she was old enough, her father had let her help paint the lighthouse. She'd never had any fear of heights, which was a good thing as she dangled far above the ground in the little bosun's chair, swabbing on paint. She waited for further comment, but Rueben was uncharacteristically reticent. Usually the only way to get him to stop talking was to gag him. Celena prodded for more details, but he remained tight-lipped. Suddenly an uncomfortable shiver ran down her spine. What was he holding back? After a few more tries she gave up and moved on to other matters. "Can Joshua stay with you tonight?"

"Of course." Rueben paused. "So, will you come home?"

There'd been no other alternative, especially with Rueben's mysterious silence. "I'll come," Celena had said with only a slight catch in her throat.

That night, she'd lain awake a long time. Even when she did fall asleep, it was only to waken suddenly from another dream about her mother. With a light dew of perspiration on her forehead, Celena had put on a robe and begun pacing. The wooden floor was cool under her bare feet as she told herself that she'd done all that was possible under the circumstances. Still . . .

Her mother had only been sick a few months before it was discovered her illness was not something the doctors could cure. As the amount of morphine used to control the pain increased, her mother's moments of lucidity decreased. So Elizabeth Jackson had used a few precious minutes of clarity to extract a double-pronged promise from her daughter. One was to ask Celena to watch over Joshua and teach him the gospel. The second had to do with Celena's father, and although at the moment it had seemed far beyond her ability to accomplish, Celena had promised.

The memory had made her turn to her mother's photograph, framed in pewter on the bedside table. Celena had inherited her mother's large brown eyes as well as her thick hair, although Celena's had a touch of red. Her nose was her father's, as was her firm chin and high forehead. At times, she fancied that a sense of disappointment lurked behind her mother's somber expression. Feeling a pang, Celena had turned away. Her mother had courage aplenty—enough to stand up to haughty parents and marry the man she loved, and years later, to tell her husband she wanted to be baptized into a church he openly reviled.

Celena had sighed, hoping she'd inherited some of her mother's courage, for she needed a good supply to go back to Fire Island. Perhaps no one ever really lost the person they once were. Celena worried about the little girl who might still be hiding inside the woman she was now. Would seeing her father set her free from the pain she had buried under layers of years, or exacerbate it? It was a fair question, for sometimes instead of cooling with age, the hurt seemed to fester inside like a red carbuncle. She was left feeling that if she misstepped now, she would fall forever.

That must not happen, Celena thought resolutely. She would not let it. While she would not have chosen to return, circumstances were pulling her back and she would look at this as an opportunity rather than an ordeal—a chance to make good on promises made long ago.

Celena remembered that night of questions, and now each mile that took her closer to Fire Island increased her sense of purpose. When the conductor called out, "Bay Shore Station," Celena rose determinedly, pulling on her gloves. It was 1926—five years since she'd last been here, and she was a grown woman—able to courageously face whatever lay ahead.

A cabbie took her bags, and Celena directed him to Babylon, where she would catch the Bay Shore Ferry. As he drove, Celena began to feel surprisingly eager. Peering through the thick fringe of red cedars and post oak, she occasionally caught a glimpse of the glittering blue line that was Great South Bay.

Once on the ferry, she had to shade her eyes against the diamond-edged glitter of light that danced across the water. Standing at the railing, Celena looked across the bay to Fire Island, its thirty-two mile length stretched out long and narrow and familiar. The black-and-white banded lighthouse was just as majestic as always, cutting across the horizon, seeming to tie the sky and the sea together. Inexplicably, Celena shivered.

A pleasant male voice broke her reverie. "Well, well, well. If it isn't little Celena Jackson." She turned to see Clint Paxton moving toward her with leonine grace. In his late thirties, Clint was fit and trim, with the look of someone who spent most of his time outdoors. His dark blond hair was lightened by the sun, and his eyes widened appreciably as he approached. "You've certainly grown up."

She smiled, pleased at the warmth in his gray eyes. Deeply tanned and handsome, he took as little notice of the flutter he caused in most every woman—young and old—as the air he breathed. It seemed impossible, but somehow he had become even more good-looking. "How is the ferry business?" she asked in reply.

"Booming, as you can see," he said, waving a hand at the crowd on the gleaming white deck. "Fire Island is becoming known as a bohemian retreat. We've got a premier resort, called Clearwater, opening in just a month. I'm not sure if you remember my cousin, Gerald Roberts, but he's the manager. He used to live on the island but moved when he got married. He's been divorced a number of years now." He looked at Celena admiringly and changed the topic. "Forgive my saying it, but seems like yesterday you were in pigtails, and now you're a beautiful woman."

Celena felt herself blushing. "You're still the mayor, aren't you? I don't know how you do that and run the ferry too."

"My mayoral duties are supposed to be part-time work, but they've never been that. It takes time to keep everyone happy. In the end, it always comes down to doing what's best for the greatest number of people—while considering the future of the island." Clint rubbed the back of his neck. "Unfortunately, just when one issue gets settled, another turns up with people ready to do battle. I've often thought I ought to have boxing gloves on hand at our council meetings."

"Last one left standing wins?"

He laughed. "Exactly!"

Just then a young boy approached them. "Mr. Paxton, sir? My friend over there says that he's seen lights on the beach at night, floating like ghosts. He says the lighthouse is haunted. Is that true, sir?"

Celena was surprised by the question, and Clint seemed even more so—uncomfortable even. But it was only for a moment; then, with a quick wink at Celena, Clint spoke in a conspiratorial whisper. "Not many know it, but people have seen ghosts. You've heard about the mooncussers who used to roam the beaches waiting for ships to wreck, haven't you? You never know when they're going to show up."

The boy's eyes were large and afraid, but there was excitement in them too.

"I'd advise you to stay far away from the lighthouse," Clint counseled solemnly.

As the boy ran off, Celena looked at Clint curiously, but he merely grinned. "Thought I'd liven up his visit!" Then his face sobered. "I wanted to tell you how sorry I was to hear about your father. He came over on the ferry this morning, well sedated, with a nurse who said he was going to Bay Haven."

"Helen's going to take care of him at the boardinghouse. Joshua and I are going to stay there too."

"He'll be in good hands then." Clint looked reassured. "Helen's an excellent nurse. I moved there myself a few years ago. It's a lot easier to let someone else do the cooking and cleaning."

Celena nodded. Helen Montgomery was a prim, straightlaced woman who had worked as a nurse before her marriage and occasionally took in patients who needed light nursing. Her husband, Bernard, was home only infrequently and seemed to have no interests beyond the ocean and his ship.

"Is Ethan still helping Helen around Bay Haven?"

"Most people think Helen's the one helping her brother by keeping him busy. Poor man isn't much good at anything."

Celena's voice grew chilly. "On the contrary. If Ethan's still doing all the repairs and yard work, I'd say he was quite good at a lot of things."

Clint grinned. "You're right. I'd forgotten that you and he were friends. Probably the only one Ethan ever had, next to his wife, God bless her soul. Say, you'll be happy to know Lydia is here. You two used to be friends, as I recall." It had been some time since Celena had thought of Lydia Montgomery. Lydia was Helen's only child and was as vivacious and outgoing as her mother was cool and self-contained. She and Celena had been best friends when children, but in their teens, the two began to go their separate ways.

There was a change in the sound of the motor and Clint nodded toward the island. "We'll be there in just a few minutes." Celena looked toward the lighthouse that was drawing steadily nearer. When she was younger, it had always been a source of pride to know that her father was the lighthouse keeper and that she lived in the home connected to it. "I guess the Bureau of Lighthouses will be sending someone out to watch the light," Clint commented idly.

"I suppose so. Rueben's taking care of it right now."

"Rueben? He's a little old for that, isn't he? If he needs help, have him call me. Rueben's had me substitute for him a few times, so I'm thoroughly trained." Clint paused. "Are you going to stay with us for a while?"

Celena hesitated. She knew that many people in Saltaire would assume she'd come back to stay and take care of her father, but that was out of the question. "Just a short visit, I'm afraid."

Clint nodded. "That's understandable. You've made a life for yourself and will need to be getting back. No one can blame you for that. In fact, it's admirable that you came back at all."

Celena shot a quick glance at him, but he kept his gaze on the gulls wheeling overhead. He knew all about it, of course. Everybody knew everyone else's business in Saltaire, and the conflict between herself and her father had gone on too long to remain a secret. But Celena would not think of it now.

Directly ahead of them was Saltaire, a bustling place compared to the other nearby towns. Saltaire was the widest town on the island too, at half a mile across. The area was lush with tall pine, maple, and ash trees, which, on the outskirts of town, were home to white-tailed deer. Though she had left with bitterness, she had sorely missed Fire Island. As she thought of the place with fondness, the ferry cut its speed again and began angling itself into position beside the dock.

"I'd better get below," Clint said. "I'll see you soon." On either side of the ferry's dock were other docks used for fishing boats, sailboats, dories, and yachts. A man came out of a plywood shack and caught the ropes that were tossed to him, fastening the ferry to the moorings. Celena waited impatiently until her bags were brought out, then turned when she heard a shout to see Joshua racing toward her. He was tall for his age, and skinny, with tousled blond hair and a deep tan that bespoke long hours in the sun. He had fine features, with a nose that turned up slightly. She noticed that his hair was too long, hanging practically in his eyes, and chalked up one more mark against her father. She held out her arms and braced herself but still swayed backward as he ran into her.

Clasping him tightly, Celena murmured, "Oh, how I've missed you!"

Joshua had on a wide smile. "It's great you're here. Now everything will be all right."

His confidence in her brought an exhilarating surge of pride and happiness. She had passed the test. Celena put her hands on his shoulders. "Of course it will." She inclined her head toward the luggage. "How about helping me with those?" Her brother picked them both up, the muscles on his thin arms straining. Celena wanted to giggle but held it back, reaching out to take one of the grips. Joshua scurried away sideways like a horseshoe crab, half dragging, half carrying the bags.

"Hey! Come back here! If you carry those all the way to Bay Haven, your knuckles will be dragging on the ground." He made a face and kept going. "I've got an idea," she called after him. "Why don't you carry those bags all the way to Ocean Bay Park, maybe even the Sunken Forest; then I can take you around the country and sell tickets. I bet a lot of people will pay to see a boy with arms as long as a gorilla's."

That did it. Joshua started laughing and had to stop. As she snatched one of the bags, Joshua asked, "Can we go out to the lighthouse now?"

"I haven't even unpacked! We can save that for another day, don't you think?"

He frowned, and in a voice that was all business said, "If we're going to be running it together, we ought to make sure everything's okay." Celena jolted to a stop. There was a loud thump as she dropped her bag, which fell onto its side.

Her brother looked at her with some concern as Celena spluttered, "Is . . . is that why you wanted me to come back? To run the lighthouse?"

"Well, sure." Joshua looked surprised that she might think anything else.

"I thought Rueben was going to run it!"

"Rueben's old," Joshua explained patiently, as though he were the twenty-four-year-old and she eleven. "He has a hard time getting up all the stairs. I counted them once. Did you know there are one hundred and ninety-two?" He went on with the kind of optimism that was particular to youth. "I wanted to start tonight, but Rueben said you needed time to settle in. We can start Thursday."

"Rueben was in on this?" Celena was incensed. "I'll kill him." She took a deep breath, but it didn't help. "Joshua, did it ever occur to you to *ask* if I'd be willing to run the lighthouse?"

Her brother looked puzzled. "I did!" When Celena stared at him, a defensive note crept into his voice. "I asked you to help and you said you would!" It was an open-and-shut case to him.

"Just asking me to come back and help is not the same thing as asking me to take over the light! I thought I was coming back to . . . to . . ."

"Run the lighthouse," Joshua said, trying to be helpful.

Celena closed her eyes. He had a fatally one-track mind. She had to derail this before it spoiled their reunion. "Look, I obviously misunderstood, but let's talk about this later. What do you say we go get some ice cream?"

"Yeah!"

They went down the wide, wooden boardwalks that crisscrossed the town, crossing Bay Promenade to reach Broadway, the main street the village was centered around. Across the street was Tillman's general store. In front, several old men were playing checkers on top of a barrel head. Joshua went ahead of her into Bigelow's Drugstore, and they sat on slick red stools to eat ice-cream sundaes. Behind the counter were large glass mirrors and big colored signs for Coca-Cola, Fletcher's Castoria, and McKesson and Robbins liniment.

They had finished their treats and were headed to Bay Haven when Doc Harrison's son Zach—Joshua had written that they were best friends—pulled over on his bike. He was a husky boy with short brown hair and mischievous dark eyes.

"Hello, Zach," Celena said. "You and Joshua must be having a growing contest. I'm not sure which one of you is taller!"

Joshua pulled himself up straight. "I am!"

Finding his friend's claim difficult to dispute while straddling his bike, Zach chose to ignore it. "Teacher gave us some Latin homework after you left."

Celena glanced at her watch. "Why don't you two go on over to Zach's and do your homework. Zach, do you think you two can be done by dinnertime?"

"Yes, ma'am."

Celena gave her brother a big hug. "I'll see you back at the boardinghouse, then." She watched after him a moment or two, then went on, stopping when she reached Bay Haven. Setting her bags on the sidewalk, she looked at the square, white-frame house with black shutters. After five long years of silence, she was going to see her father again. Facing the boardinghouse, Celena had the uncanny feeling that she was standing before a chasm with nothing on the other side.

TWO

The boardinghouse was large by Fire Island's standards. At the top was the captain's walk—its white railing looking like a crown. In the late 1800s, people often salvaged goods from shipwrecks, so they went regularly to the captain's walk to watch the sea during stormy weather. A veranda ran the full length of the house and held assorted chairs and a porch swing. The latticework below the railing was hung with shaggy wisteria vines whose leaves were just beginning to unfurl and which would soon cover the brown shoots in a profusion of foliage and lavender flowers. Fanciful scalloping along the eaves had recently been painted. Ethan's work, no doubt. Celena wondered how he was coping with his wife's death. It was hard to think that Sarina, who had been so full of life, had been dead for two years, leaving the island as unexpectedly as she had arrived.

From the beginning, they had been an unlikely pair—the fiery, outspoken Sarina and the slow, reclusive Ethan. It was a favorite topic of speculation as to why a spirited woman like Sarina, who was a gypsy and used to living a nomadic life, would settle down and marry someone who was, as Rueben put it, "about as bright as Alaska in January." But no one dared question proud Sarina with her flashing eyes, or Helen, who would freeze anyone with an icy stare if they dared ask questions about her brother. And one might get more coherent answers out of a fence post than from Ethan.

As Celena climbed the wide, board steps, anxiety again curled itself like a snake inside her stomach. She paused; then, with a resolute lift of her shoulders, she stepped into the spacious foyer, setting her bags on the rose-patterned rug. She remembered the uncomfortable horsehair chairs and the highboy with shining brass pulls against the west wall. Across the room were stairs going to the second level and doors to the kitchen and the dining room.

She also remembered the faded wallpaper, with its sprigs of violets and twining ivy, from the days when she used to come and play with Lydia. Helen Montgomery's world revolved around her only child, and although Celena and Lydia did everything together, Helen always overlooked Lydia's shortcomings and complained that *Celena* was the one laughing too loud and that it was *Celena's* running through the halls that disturbed the guests.

How long ago it seemed when she would meet Lydia on Sundays at the small white Baptist church where their families attended services. The years had passed quickly, and Lydia had been nineteen and Celena seventeen in 1919—the year missionaries from The Church of Jesus Christ of Latter-day Saints had come to Fire Island. Proselytizing elders had come before, but this was the first time their families had attended their meetings. Lydia soon lost interest, but Celena continued to go, along with her parents, Joshua, Rueben, and Tana. A few months later, Celena's mother had become ill, and although Elizabeth still attended when she could, Matthew stopped going. At the same time, Lydia began gravitating toward a different group of friends. There had been rumors that Lydia was behind a series of shoplifting incidents from Tillman's when she had suddenly disappeared. Helen would say nothing beyond that Lydia had decided to go to Chicago to live with her aunt.

Celena was wondering how business was when Helen walked in. Helen Montgomery must have been a beauty when she was younger, for even though she was in her late forties, she was attractive, with pale blue eyes and fine features that could have been sculpted from marble—cool and aloof. She was tall and, though no longer slender, had appealing curves. Her brown hair was streaked with gray and worn in a loose chignon at the back of her head. Today, she wore a long-sleeved dress of dark blue with tiny white flowers.

Helen gave a small, polite smile. "So, you've finally come back."

It almost seemed a rebuke, but Celena chose to ignore it. "Thank you for making room for me."

"It's early in the season. Not many people are here," Helen said ungraciously. "How long are you planning on staying? I suppose you have to get back to whatever it is you do. Cleaning offices, wasn't it?"

Celena's back stiffened. Although it was 1926, few women had jobs outside the home, and those that did often had low-paying ones. "I work in a *law office,*" Celena corrected. "As a *secretary* for Weatherby and Winston."

Helen's face showed little change. "It's a mistake for you to come back," she stated baldly. "Your father doesn't need any more turmoil in his life. He's been through enough." Her lips were set in a thin line of disapproval as though Celena herself had caused the accident.

"The last thing I want to do is upset him," Celena replied coldly.

Helen regarded the younger woman doubtfully, then stepped behind the L-shaped counter in the corner. She reached into one of the cubbyholes, then handed a key to Celena.

"Which room is my father in?"

"He's at the end of the hall, but don't go in and disturb him," Helen replied, sounding very much in charge. "The trip from the hospital was hard, and someone from the Lighthouse Bureau has already been in to see him. He needs to rest now. You can see him after dinner."

Celena flinched slightly at such high-handedness but asked, "How is Ethan?"

Helen's face relaxed slightly. "He's fine. I talked him into living here a few years ago. He put in an entrance to his room around back, so he could have his privacy." That was a tactful way to put it. It would have been closer to the truth to say Ethan wanted to hide from people. From Joshua's reports, he'd become even worse in this respect since Sarina's death.

As Celena unlocked her door, she glanced at the end of the hall. It was ironic to have left the island because of her father and now to return for the same reason. But pushing the thought aside, she entered her own room. The large room was spare but spotless. The bed on the right was obviously Joshua's, with a blue quilt pulled up unevenly to the wrought-iron headboard. On the chest of drawers was a large conch shell, assorted books, and a handful of marbles. She put her suitcase on the second bed, which was topped with a white quilt. A movable screen for privacy stood nearby.

Celena pushed the window open. The fresh, salty tang of the air brought back a flood of childhood memories. Days spent wandering the beach collecting shells, exploring tide pools, or picking the wild blueberries that grew everywhere. Sometimes her mother would pack books and a jug of lemonade, and the two of them would find a shady thicket of pitch pine and red cedar where they could read. Celena kept her thoughts away from the memories that followed, those of her last year here, because they were full of pain and bitterness. But all would be well. Soon she would be going back to Maryland.

She changed into trousers and, stepping to the bathroom, bathed her face, smoothing back her hair with wet fingers. When she straightened to her full height of five feet, three inches, her reflection was squarely in the middle of the mirror. She checked to make sure her auburn hair was still held in a smooth twist at the back of her head and her fringe of bangs lay straight. Her large, light brown eyes were serious today beneath thick lashes, betraying her inner feelings.

Uncertainty engulfed her. Had she done the right thing in coming back? Suddenly she thought of Sam. How odd that his face still appeared when she least expected it. Perhaps the time had come not only to fulfill her promises to her mother but to free herself from the memory of Sam McCain.

There was a knock. She was halfway to the door when it opened and a lively voice said, "Hello, Celena, mind if I come in?" Before she could respond, Lydia strode in, sure of a welcome. Lydia was long-limbed and curvaceous. Her hair had been dyed blond and was cut short in a shingle that just reached her chin. "It's been much too long—it's wonderful to see you," she gushed sweetly. "You're as pretty as ever," Lydia added in a slightly surprised tone, giving her a hug.

Celena wasn't sure what to make of Lydia's overly warm greeting, but returned the hug and responded, "I'm glad to see you, too."

Lydia dropped down on a bed. "Are you still working for those stiffs in Maryland? Sounds dreadfully dull."

"I enjoy the work. It's not dull at all."

"I bet." Lydia grinned. "Bunch of potbellied old men, dusty files, boring work."

"It's not like that," Celena protested. "Anyhow, what about you? I thought you were in Chicago."

Lydia pouted, pursing lips that were outlined in bright pink. "I was, but there was a little misunderstanding with Auntie Rose about a necklace. But it's so boring here. You're lucky you don't have to live here anymore."

"Joshua wants me to stay and help run the light until Father gets better."

Lydia's green eyes widened. "You're not going to, are you? Not after your father kicked you out?" The words, spoken out loud, still caused a pang, even after all this time. "There's no need to stay anyway, since the lighthouse is going to be sold." Lydia idly held out her hands, admiring her brightly painted fingernails.

Celena's jaw dropped. "What are you talking about?"

"Sorry to shock you, dear-heart," Lydia said, looking anything but apologetic. "But surely you know the Lighthouse Bureau is closing down a bunch of lighthouses."

Feeling a qualm, Celena replied carefully, "I read in the newspaper that they were closing some, but they'd never close Fire Island." Her suspicions rose. "What's it to you, anyway?"

"Mother's decided to buy the lighthouse." Celena must have looked shocked, for Lydia said, "You weren't planning on staying, anyway, so why the face?"

"Joshua would have told me if the light was for sale," Celena said flatly.

"It's not for sale yet," Lydia admitted grudgingly, "but it will be soon."

"But why would your mother want the light?"

"It'll make a great tourist attraction and pull in scads of new customers for Bay Haven. I'm all for that. Have you priced clothes lately?" She looked Celena up and down with a tinkling laugh. "I guess not." She leaned closer. "You ought to try my rouge—you look like you've seen a ghost. And you haven't even been out at the lighthouse yet."

"What do you mean?"

"The ghost at the lighthouse, silly."

When Celena narrowed her eyes, Lydia blurted, "No, no. This is legit, I swear. The lighthouse really *is* haunted. It started a few years ago. I'd avoid it if I were you, but then, you're the dutiful daughter, aren't you? You'll see when you're out there—all alone."

Celena frowned as her old friend stood.

"Great chatting with you," Lydia said. "See you at dinner."

* * *

Some time later, Helen knocked to say Celena had a visitor. In the foyer, Rueben Wyatt's whiskery face lit up when he saw her. He had faded blue eyes in a fisherman's face—a thousand dark wrinkles etched around his mouth and eyes from squinting into the sun every day. Despite his age, Rueben still had a thatch of iron-gray hair that matched his bushy eyebrows. His stomach protruded far over the belt that sat low on his hips. As Celena hugged him, she breathed in the faint smell of fish clinging to his coat.

"I need to get to the light but wanted to welcome you home." He eyed Celena. "Look at you now. I bet you have to beat the men off with a stick, even if you are wearing pants like a man."

She grinned. "You haven't changed at all."

"Hmm. And I always thought you were honest."

She looked at his cane. "That's new."

"You can blame Tana for that," he stated. "I do. She bought the blasted thing. Hated it at first, but I have to admit it beats falling down." As they walked to a sofa in a nook by the fireplace, Rueben's cane thumped across the bare oak floor. "Satisfying sound, that," he remarked, settling into a corner. "Makes people sit up and pay attention." Celena glanced at him from under lowered lids. She'd always pictured him as strong and vital, but now it was clear she'd been patching the past onto the present—allowing memory to obscure reality.

He caught her looking. "Getting older isn't any picnic. The only good thing about it is that wrinkles don't hurt. Now, are you settling in all right?"

She narrowed her eyes. "I found out Joshua's expecting me to run the light. I can't believe you didn't tell me."

He looked bewildered. "But Joshua asked you to help. The night we called."

"Men," Celena sighed. "Young or old, you're all alike."

Rueben was concerned. "If you can't run it, Clint and I can handle it."

"Joshua's so set on running it that I told him I'd do it while I'm here."

"Good. I already asked Clint to run it for me Friday night, but I'll tell him you're going to do it. You can start Thursday. I'll drop by to make sure you've still got the hang of things."

"Will you be all right running it for a couple of nights?" There was worry in her voice.

Rueben raised shaggy brows. "I must look older than I feel. Don't worry. I can run that lighthouse as easy as I can land a tuna. Bad knees are what handrails and canes are for, and I'll have both at the light. Now, have you seen your father?"

She glanced over to where Helen was registering a guest. "Helen wanted him to rest."

"Old barracuda," Rueben growled with a glance at Helen. "Anyway, when you do see him, don't expect too much. You know your father. By the way, I found out that someone called the Lighthouse Bureau and told them Matthew was going to be permanently disabled."

Celena was astonished. "But I spoke with Doc Harrison before coming out. He said he didn't know yet if Father's injuries were permanent or not! Who called?"

"Wish I knew." Rueben shook his head. "Since I'm your father's assistant, I called to report Matthew's accident. When they told me that, I set them straight. Told them not to jump the gun on getting a new keeper." He looked sober. "That sure was a bad fall your father took."

"Was anyone around when it happened?"

The old man rubbed his chin. "That's a good question."

"What do you mean?" Celena asked in surprise.

"There's something mighty peculiar about that," Rueben began. "You see, I knew your father was painting that day, so when I was done fishing I went out to the light. I was just going round the last bend when I saw—"

Rueben stopped abruptly as Lydia, carrying a pile of folded linen, came down the stairs, smiling brightly at a couple of men who were in the foyer.

"Never mind." Rueben leaned back. "I'll talk to you tomorrow."

Celena was mystified. "I still don't understand how Father fell."

"You and me both." Grunting slightly, Rueben stood up. In a low voice he said, "Right now there's too many ears around, and if there's one thing I've learned, it's that letting the cat out of the bag is a whole lot easier than putting it back in."

Celena didn't press. They walked to the front porch, where the sunset had begun to gild the glowing sky, sending wide streamers of gold across the horizon. "Tana said she'll be expecting a visit from you tomorrow." He paused. "Celena, I'm glad you're back. Your father needs you."

"He's never needed anyone!" Celena's response was short and bitter.

Rueben regarded her contemplatively. "He's an independent cuss, I know, but it's a shame you don't know him better than that. See you tomorrow."

Celena stood there long after the tapping of Rueben's cane had faded. Then she went to her room. She was unpacking when the door flung open and hit the wall with a bang.

"That stupid Zach!" Joshua cried, outrage contorting his face. "When I told him you were going to run the light, he said they were going to turn the light over to someone else—that there's something wrong with Father's leg and he can't run it anymore." He took a deep breath. "But that's a lie. Father told me he was going to be okay. Celena, you have to stay and run the light until he gets better. If they give it to someone else, I'll never get to be the next keeper! Zach even said so."

Celena knew that now was not the time to point out that Joshua had scornfully discounted his friend's opinion then accepted it as gospel fact in virtually the same breath. Neither was it the time to tell him she was only going to stay a few days—the time necessary to arrange to take her father and Joshua back to Maryland. Instead, she said feebly, "It's been a long time since I ran the light."

"But Celena, no one else knows how to run it except Rueben and Clint! Rueben's too old, and Clint already has a job. Father said he'd run it until I got to be eighteen. Then he's going to turn it over to me."

"It might take a long time until Father gets better," she tried. Joshua stared blankly, unable to see what a lengthy recovery had to do with Celena staying. She tried another tack. "Besides, women don't run lighthouses by themselves."

Joshua ran to the dresser and, looking jubilant, returned with a book, which he opened briskly, jabbing his finger triumphantly at a page. It was a list—a lengthy one—of women lighthouse keepers. Abbie Burgess Grant, Matinicus Rock Lighthouse, 1853–1872; Lucy J. Baxter, Sandy Neck Lighthouse, 1862–1867; Ann Davis, Point Lookout Lighthouse, 1830–1847—the list went on and on.

"Impressive," she admitted, "but all of these were a long time ago."

"And things are easier now!" Joshua had a pleading look on his face.

"Look, Joshua, I know you wanted to be the next keeper, but . . ."

Sensing a refusal, Joshua looked at her defiantly, his thin chest rising and falling heavily. "You *said* you were going to come back and help me! They're going to take the lighthouse away and you don't even care!" His eyes filled with accusing tears, twisting Celena's heart. She reached out for him but he sidestepped, staring at her balefully. Celena hadn't realized that the lighthouse that dominated Fire Island was such an integral part of Joshua's world. It was going to take more time than she had thought to convince Joshua that the best thing for all of them was to go to Maryland.

"I did come back to help," Celena assented as she randomly selected a dress to wear to dinner. "Look, I'll run it for a little while, but I need to talk with the doctor and find out how long it will take Father to recover enough for him to take over."

Joshua's face relaxed a little but remained somewhat mutinous.

"Go and wash up now for dinner," she said. "We don't want to be late."

As they walked into the dining room, Helen was sitting at the head of the table. The seven men at the long table rose, while Helen and two silver-haired ladies smiled and remained seated. Clint Paxton nearly took her breath away when he gave her a smile. He introduced her to Gerald Roberts, a portly man in his late fifties who had a florid complexion, heavy jowls, and a pleasant, cheerful expression. He wore expensive clothes and his hair, mostly gray, gave him a distinguished look.

"You probably don't remember me," he boomed in a rather loud voice, "but I grew up here. Left when you were just a little thing. I came back every once in a while to visit my cousin, Clint." Celena sat in the chair Clint held out, and Joshua took his place beside her. Gerald continued. "I always did love it here. Didn't imagine I'd ever have the good fortune to return, but like I always say, things have a way of working out. I'm the manager of the new Clearwater Resort that will be opening soon." At this pronouncement, he swelled with importance.

Helen quickly introduced the others: a mixture of tourists, construction workers, and a drummer—a salesman who would set up his merchandise in the lobby, stay a few days to show his wares, then move on. As Helen ladled oyster stew into bowls from a large white soup tureen, Gerald took the bowls and passed them around the table.

When he handed Celena hers, she asked, "When did you come back to Fire Island?"

"About two years ago," Gerald replied. "I wanted to watch over the construction process. I've enjoyed staying at Bay Haven, but Clearwater should be finished around the first of June, so my son and I will be moving in then." Minerva, the round, pleasant-faced cook and housekeeper, came in carrying two heaping baskets of rolls. She smiled at everyone before returning to the kitchen.

"You just missed Nathan Gibbs," Helen commented. "He's the contractor who's building Clearwater. Since the resort is nearly done, he went to check on another project, but he'll be back in a few weeks."

As Celena unrolled her napkin, Perry said, "I'm sorry about your father. I saw him today and he's having a tough go of it, I must say." Celena stole a look at Helen. So, she had allowed others, even a traveling drummer, to see her father.

Celena didn't think she had much of an appetite, but the creamy stew was perfect—with the oysters barely curled at their edges. Then, Lydia swept into the room. Celena wondered if Lydia had arrived late just so she could make a dramatic entrance. Although her friend had always been unconventional, Celena couldn't help but stare. Lydia had changed and was dressed as a flapper, one of a growing group of rebellious young women who liked to live fast and enjoy the new freedom the twenties offered. Her dress was cut in the new style with the waist dropped to the hips. She wore rayon stockings, shiny pumps, and her hemline was shockingly high, coming just below the knee. Her bobbed blond hair was striking, with a large curl slicked down on each side of her face. Aware that every eye in the room was on her, Lydia sashayed in, setting the fringe on her skirt dancing about her knees. She came to hug Celena, kissing the air by her ear.

"Don't want to waste lipstick on *you*, love," she whispered impishly before smiling widely at everyone, including her mother, who was watching stony-faced. Shaking out her napkin, Lydia cooed to Celena, "I'm glad you changed; you look fabulous!"

"And you look just—" Celena struggled to find words.

Lydia finished her sentence. "Positively scandalous! I know!" She laughed gaily, then leaned over the table and in a false whisper that was loud enough for everyone to hear, said, "You should have *seen* the look on Mother's face when she first saw me in this!" Helen's head was bowed as she concentrated on her soup. There were two spots of pink high on her cheekbones. "I suppose you've already met everyone," Lydia said, her green eyes bright. "Wait a minute. Where are you hiding that handsome son of yours, Gerald?"

"Oh, he had some business to take care of," Gerald said, then explained to Celena, "My son came out to Fire Island a couple of months ago. He's a bookkeeper and has been helping me out until we hire someone."

"He works too hard." Lydia's mouth was in a pout.

Celena said to Gerald, "Clint tells me Fire Island is becoming very popular with tourists."

"And rumrunners," Lydia broke in.

"Rumrunners?" Celena was surprised. "You mean people are smuggling liquor here on Fire Island?"

A number of the men guffawed, and Lydia gave a tinkling laugh. "Dear-heart, where do you think it all comes from? A cabbage patch?" She stopped short, and in an exaggerated tone, added, "Oh, I forgot! You're one of those odd people that don't drink."

One of the construction workers spoke up authoritatively. "Being so close to New York, Fire Island is one of the best spots on the East Coast to run in bootleg liquor."

"There's smugglers all along the coast—from Maine on down to Florida," added another muscular worker, sounding very sure.

A genial older man nodded. "The Coast Guard may try, but stopping rumrunners is like trying to wipe out a plague of locusts with a flyswatter."

"Ah, well, enough of that," Gerald said jovially, spreading a roll thickly with butter. "You'll have to come over and see Clearwater. I put in a big dance hall. We'll have live entertainment every weekend. There'll also be a first-class restaurant, though I have to admit that I like Bay Haven's homemade touch." Gerald threw a meaningful glance toward Helen, a gesture she studiously ignored.

One of the elderly women spoke up in a querulous voice. "But won't Bay Haven and Clearwater be competing for business?"

Clint answered smoothly, "Clearwater will have a completely different clientele. People who like a slower, more low-key atmosphere will still come here."

"That's right," Gerald broke in, looking at Helen anxiously. "Clearwater will attract a lot of people, but once they find out about Bay Haven, I'm afraid we'll lose them all."

Helen took a sip of water, giving Clint, then Gerald, an unreadable look over the top of her glass. There were hard lines in her face, and Celena wondered if—despite the mayor's assurances—Helen *was* worried that Clearwater would shrink her business. There were undercurrents here Celena didn't fully understand.

"How long are you planning on being with us, Celena?" Gerald asked.

"I'm not certain."

Joshua's head jerked toward her. "You said you were going to help me run the light."

Celena laid a reassuring hand on her brother's arm. "I am, but a lot depends on how long it will take Father to recuperate."

Clint's gray eyes were sympathetic. "You've got a lot on your plate right now, with your father and the light. Just remember that I'll be glad to run it for you until your father recovers. Everyone knows you have a job you need to get back to."

Celena murmured her thanks, then said to Helen, "I thought Ethan would be here tonight."

"He rarely eats with us."

"Ethan doesn't like to be around people, no sir," Gerald stated in his loud voice. "I've got him doing odd jobs around the resort, and once I've told him what to do, I don't see him again. Ethan's a good worker, but with him being the way he is, I don't hold him to set hours."

Talk turned to other things, and the rest of the meal passed pleasantly. Joshua took a tray to his father's room while Celena and Lydia carried dishes to the kitchen, where Minerva had a sink full of soapy water ready. Lydia excused herself, saying she was going out for the evening. Helen gravely thanked Celena for her help but informed her that paying guests weren't expected to assist, making sure their relationship stayed on a business level.

Back in her room, Celena busied herself unpacking. After a time, Joshua opened the door. "Father wants to see you now," he announced.

Celena felt a sudden tension. After all these years, the time had finally arrived. She shook out the dress she was holding. "Thanks, Joshua. I'll go when I'm done here."

"Father wants to see you *now*."

Celena tried to mask her irritation. Her father had not changed. He was just as authoritative and domineering as ever.

"All right. At least I've got one bag emptied." Celena stepped over to the dresser to check her appearance. Her eyes, she noted with regret, were already snapping. She smoothed her hair, which was swept up and fastened in back with a tortoiseshell comb. Turning, she held out her hand to Joshua. "Let's go."

Joshua stood motionless. "Father said he wanted to talk to you alone."

Inwardly, Celena fumed. Having Joshua present might have made the initial meeting less awkward. But of course, what she wanted didn't matter to her father.

"Okay." She tried to smile. "I shouldn't be long." Going down the hallway, her heart began to pound. Celena stopped in front of the door, which was open a few inches, to tell herself she was no longer a young, frightened girl. Still, he had wounded her heart deeply, possibly beyond repair, and now he was right there, on the other side of that door. Celena took several deep breaths. Then she smiled and, when her face didn't break into pieces, knocked.

THREE

At Celena's knock, a weak but gruff voice called out impatiently, "Come in! Anybody can see the door's open." Hearing that imperious tone made Celena feel suddenly confined in a tight cage of hostility. The room was comfortably furnished, though one wall was curiously bare except for a nail, and rose-quartz sconces on the wall bathed the room in a faint pinkish glow.

A sheet topped by a green chenille spread was pulled away from Matthew's left leg, showing the white cast which ran from his thigh to his toes. His pajama top was unbuttoned, revealing the white bandages around his chest. It was evident from the outline of Matthew's body that he was as lean and sinewy as ever, but her father's face seemed shrunken from what she remembered—pinched and a bit gray under the deep tan that had come from years of living beside the ocean. His normally clear blue eyes were dark and sunken under level gray brows. His grayish-brown hair had thinned, and his hairline had receded since she had seen him last. Matthew's stern chin bristled with stubble, and there were creases in his narrow face—the kind pain often left.

It was hard not to think about the last time Celena had seen him. The harsh words and angry recriminations of that day were a culmination of a year's worth of quarrels that had begun before her mother's death and long before Matthew had become so bitter toward the Church. During that year, he had taken every opportunity to disparage the Church, and Celena, filled with righteous indignation, refused to let any scornful comment pass without a stout and spirited defense. Arguments multiplied, and their relationship spiraled downward until the day it finally shattered—when Matthew had erupted in blind fury over what he saw as his daughter's mulish stubbornness in refusing to cut her ties with the Mormons.

It was a moment that had taken her breath away—when he had ordered her to renounce her beliefs or leave his house. Celena remembered that moment as if it had happened yesterday. It seemed his decree had gone right through her vitals, paralyzing her, and Celena had stood very still, as if she had no power to speak, move, or even blink her eyes. Then she had staggered slightly, as if gravity had slipped away from her and she could not repossess it.

Suddenly, all those old, bitter feelings returned, telescoping until Celena had to put a hand on a chair until the room could settle. She had known this feeling would come, but had underestimated its intensity. Celena went to the window to wait until the feeling passed.

Bay Haven was built on a small rise, and when she opened the curtains, the rhythmic flash of the lighthouse beacon swept through the room with its set flash-and-eclipse pattern. Celena looked out at a blowing world where the moon sailed between jagged clouds and white birches bent in the wind. Off to the west, a great purple thunderhead spread like an anvil, with lightning shooting out and forking silently to earth. There was a faint mutter of thunder in the background. The power in it gave her courage. She went back to stand ramrod straight on the rag rug beside her father's bed.

Her tone was wooden as she said dutifully, "Hello, Father. How are you feeling?"

"How do you think I'm feeling," he growled, "with my leg in plaster, my chest wrapped so tight I can't breath, and feeling like somebody took a hickory stick to me?"

"You don't need to snap at me," Celena retorted. "*I* didn't take a stick to you!"

Matthew's breathing was shallow to ease the pain from his broken ribs. "I know, but from the look on your face, you'd like to. Never mind. I just hate being trussed up like a mummy."

"Can I get you anything?"

"Aye. A new leg." If he'd hoped to lighten the mood, the effort fell flat. "Still haven't forgiven me, have you?" Matthew spoke carelessly, making it clear that whether she had or hadn't made no difference to him.

Celena's eyes flashed at the taunting. "I don't recall you ever asking to be forgiven."

A hint of amusement touched the corners of his mouth. "True," he acknowledged. "But I thought all you religious fanatics were supposed to forgive no matter what." Anger bit at her like the stinging of an insect. It was strange how emotions could not be buried by words but could easily be aroused by them.

The past exploded into the present, and, forgetting that she had resolved beforehand not to argue or defend, she blurted, "I'm *not* a religious fanatic! And what you did *was* unforgivable."

She was unable to read the strange expression on his face. "Why did you come back?" he asked.

"Because Joshua asked me."

"That's what I thought," he said flatly. The look on his face changed, hardened ever so slightly. "I suppose you hurried out here before the receiver was even cold. You always did rush into things without thinking them through."

Celena flushed, realizing he was referring to her decision to be baptized a member of the Church. He meant his words to sting, and because they did, it was an effort to keep her emotions in check. Anger steadied itself into a silvery shimmer, a cold flame that enveloped her. He went on. "You didn't need to come. Joshua and Rueben can handle the light."

Was he mad? Celena's skin prickled with exasperation, and she spoke slowly, as if talking to someone feeble-minded. "Joshua—is—a—little—boy. He's only eleven."

"That's old enough," Matthew asserted, plucking at the sheet. His voice was beginning to sound drained. "Why, when I was his age, I got up at sunrise and put in a full day's work."

Please don't tell me how you rowed your dinghy through a snowstorm to get to school on Long Island, Celena thought impatiently. Out loud she said, "Joshua has to go to school."

"Aye, but Rueben can—"

Celena cut him off. "No, Rueben *can't!* He's too old and Joshua's too young. You've made plans to suit yourself without considering others, as usual. You need to give up the light. You're over sixty and just had a serious accident. I want you and Joshua to come and live with me and Grandma and Grandpa." She'd meant to break into that slowly, but it was out now.

Matthew's voice was coldly brittle. "I'll never give up the light or leave Fire Island. Neither will Joshua. You're acting pretty high-and-mighty to come back and tell me what I need to do."

"And where did I get that from?" Celena replied tartly. "Besides, maybe Joshua's not as set on staying as you think." Even as the words left her mouth, Celena knew they weren't true but were coming from some strange, cold desire to wound. "Did it ever occur to you that Joshua might have dreams other than the ones *you* want him to have?"

"I know right enough what Joshua wants, and that's to stay here." Matthew's voice was like steel. "I'll thank you not to upset Joshua with your harebrained notions about leaving."

It was too much. "You didn't care about upsetting *me* five years ago when you told me to leave. And how do you know what Joshua wants? Do you ever listen to him? You never did to me!" Her words were like tiny glittering knives and poured out so easily that they might have been springing from some untapped well. "You've never cared about hurting people before. Sometimes I think hurting people is what you do best. After all, look at what you did to me. And to Mother."

The silence that descended was stifling and surreal. Her father's face went very gray and still. Celena hated how her words lingered in the air, refusing to diffuse. Someone down the hall opened a door. Outside, in the distance, a dog barked. There was a rumble of heavy thunder. There did not seem to be enough air in her lungs, and when the silence got bigger than anything the room could contain, Celena turned in one sharp, fluid movement and ran. Clattering down the porch steps, she collapsed onto a wrought-iron bench in a corner of the yard.

With trembling hands, Celena covered her face. How could she have spoken so? She thought the past had been buried, but apparently it had lain in too shallow a grave. Those cutting words had shot out so unexpectedly that Celena knew they had volcanoed from some uncharted and unplumbed depth of old grief. Her body began to shake with muffled sobs. Perhaps she should go away sooner than she'd intended. But then, what about her promise and those times she had felt the quiet spirit of her mother prompting her to live up to her word?

She'd done her best to fulfill the first part of the promise about Joshua, writing to him after she'd left, but Celena was still confused about the part to do with her father. What did her mother have in mind when she made Celena promise to have empathy? In frustration, Celena had even looked up the word in a dictionary, finding that it required her to be aware of, sensitive to, and vicariously experience other people's feelings. In regards to her father, not only did that seem a hard thing to ask, it was nigh impossible. Also, it smacked too closely of forgiveness, and that was one thing her father did not deserve.

As the wind prowled high above and lightning flashed in low clouds, Celena gulped for air, wondering dimly where all the tears were coming from. It felt like she cried for everything—for when she had been forced to leave Fire Island, and for all the times since, when she'd felt alone and miserable. She even cried for more recent hurts, including the injuries Sam had dealt her, until it seemed impossible for her slender body to shed any more tears.

Finally Celena raised her head and through a sheen of tears saw the lighthouse flash its great silver beam—one flash followed by nearly a minute of darkness. The air was thick with the scent of lilacs as she watched the shaft of light swing over the yard, then disappear. Sadness washed over her like a long, slow wave as she thought of Sam. At least the hurt there was nearly gone, as it should be after a year. Yet she still missed him at times. The bond that had tied them had been real, and Celena had expected their love to last.

Unlike her father, Sam was not afraid to show emotion. He had charmed her with his boyish enthusiasm and dark good looks. After seven months, they had begun to talk about a future together. Then, one night during a romantic dinner, Sam had knelt and presented her with a ring. Other diners had applauded as Celena slipped the diamond on her finger and hugged Sam tightly. Had it really all happened?

She was suddenly and powerfully tired. Slipping back to her room, Celena saw that Joshua was fast asleep. She changed behind the screen and slipped to her knees on the rag rug to pray for strength. Although she was aware of a need to forgive, it seemed so far beyond her capabilities that all she could do was pray for the next best thing: the desire to forgive. When she rose, her knees were stiff, and as she slipped between the cold sheets, Celena shivered before pulling up the quilt.

* * *

The next morning, Celena woke to find Joshua tugging at her arm. It had been a restless night, one she'd spent listening to the rain as it peppered the roof and sang through the tops of the sassafras trees. And now she'd gone and overslept. Yet there was an unusual clearness in her head—a lighter feeling, though Celena had difficulty knowing why. It was as if last night's tears had washed clean some old wound. And something else had come clear through the long storm of weeping and the protracted prayer—a feeling that the time had come to fulfill her promise, whether here or in Maryland. For too long, she'd disregarded the second part, and Celena had the shivery feeling that if she did so again, she might squander her last hope of fulfilling it.

After breakfast, Celena sent Joshua to get his books while she went onto the porch. There was a sheen on everything that came from the dazzling sun shining on the residual wetness of the storm. Celena kept her arms folded against the cool air until Joshua ran out, schoolbooks dangling from a strap. She hugged him fiercely before he bounded down the stairs and out to the road where Zach was waiting. Joshua waved as they ran for the school bus at the corner.

Briefly, she thought about going and seeing her father, but a gust of air, as if from the north, caused her to button her sweater and run lightly down the sidewalk. The houses on Neptune Walk were fairly close together, with most of them painted white or brown, although there was an occasional burst of color in pink or green. It was enjoyable walking along, listening to snatches of birdsong and hearing children's voices. Two brown pelicans went by, flapping their wings, and Celena felt a small surge of delight.

But when she recalled Lydia talking about lighthouse closures, Celena felt chilled. She had read about radar and knew that in time it would diminish ships' dependence on lighthouses, forcing more lights to close, but that was still far in the future. Although Celena knew the Lighthouse Bureau was closing down a few lighthouses, she had assumed the decommissioned lights were ancient, crumbling relics. It had never entered her mind that Fire Island could be one of those shut down. Still, if the light were to close, wouldn't that simplify everything? So why this odd sense of violation? And why did she feel so disturbed at Helen wanting the light? How would Joshua react to such news? And her father, did he know?

She looked up to realize she had reached her destination. Tana and Rueben Wyatt lived in a sturdy foursquare house on the corner. Set well back from the water, it was close to the road and surrounded by clusters of pin oaks. At Celena's knock, Tana opened the door wearing a brightly-flowered dress. Her face was cheerful and kind, and her eyes were like brown pebbles behind wire-rimmed glasses. Tana's white hair was cut short in soft waves, and when they hugged, Celena was now at least a head taller.

"I'm so glad to see you!" Tana cried. "Come in, come in. I've got a few minutes before I have to go open the post office." Tana Wyatt had been the postmistress of Saltaire for years. In many small towns the post office was located in a person's home, but in Saltaire it had been elevated to a higher status, being installed inside Tillman's general store. "Rueben will be back soon," Tana continued, ushering her into the front parlor. Sunshine streamed in through the windows, making the polished oak floor gleam. They sat near the fireplace, where a small fire had been kindled to take the chill off the spring morning. Celena picked a chair that let her look through the windows to the beige dunes and rippling ocean.

"Last night Rueben told me that you wanted to talk to me. Am I in trouble?" Celena asked with mock concern, a smile tugging at her lips.

"Oh, for heaven's sake," Tana spluttered as she gathered up her knitting. "I only wanted to find out what you thought of Joshua's idea."

"So you knew he wanted me to run the lighthouse too!" Celena sardonically added, "I suppose Joshua's informed everyone on the island."

"I don't believe the tourists who came over on last night's ferry know yet," Tana replied dryly. She tossed her ball of yarn into a bowl near her feet, and her needles began clicking.

"I guess I'm the last to know Joshua's been expecting me to run it."

"That's children for you," Tana said candidly. "They think nothing of asking for the world, then act surprised when you don't hand it to them gift-wrapped. I expect Joshua sees you as a knight in shining armor, riding in to save the day."

"My armor's a little rusty," Celena admitted glumly. "I told Joshua I needed to talk with the doctor to see how long it will take Father to recover."

"It was a miracle Matthew survived at all," Tana said, shaking her head. "It'll be a long time before he'll be able to climb all those stairs again. Doc Harrison said it was a terrible break."

"Joshua's afraid the Lighthouse Bureau might assign someone else permanently unless I take over as keeper."

"You *are* going to run it, aren't you?" Tana stopped knitting. "I was hoping you'd work things out with your father and stay for good. He's still crusty, but I think you'll find that he's changed since you left. Besides, I know how much you love Fire Island. You used to say that you were never going to move away."

"I didn't want to," Celena said bluntly. "I was forced to."

Tana looked at her sadly. The fire muttered as a log crumbled into itself. Then the front door opened and Rueben came in. He hung his overcoat on a wooden peg, revealing coveralls and a faded cotton shirt. "Good to see you, Celena," Rueben said, pulling a chair over to the fire.

"I was just telling Celena that she ought to stay," Tana said.

"I've got a job to get back to," Celena reminded her.

Tana rocked gently, her feet barely meeting the floor. "That's just an excuse. Besides, there are lots of jobs here on the island."

"Like rum-running," Rueben said with a wink. "It certainly pays well." When his wife raised her eyebrows, he hastily added, "Or so I've heard."

"Does it pay enough so I can afford to bail you out of jail?" Tana challenged.

"Now who said I was doing anything of the sort?" Rueben made a face. "Besides, no one takes rum-running seriously."

"The Coast Guard does," Tana stated soberly. "I know you're thinking of William, but you'll do nothing of the sort."

When Celena glanced at Rueben, she was surprised to see a look on his face that she had never seen before. Almost defiant. For a few moments, the only sound was the occasional crackle of the fire. An uneasy prickling stirred at the back of her neck.

"We have a grandson who is very sick," Tana explained, her needles moving deftly. "You remember Hannah."

Celena nodded.

"Will is Hannah and John's youngest son. He's only six. We've been trying to help with medical expenses, but everything costs so much . . ."

"Doctors! Hospitals!" Rueben snorted. "Bloodsuckers is what they are. And prices on fish are way down. There's got to be some way—"

"Let's not get into that," Tana implored. Turning to Celena, she changed the subject. "I meant to ask you earlier. How is your father doing today?"

"I . . . I didn't see him this morning."

Tana and Rueben threw quick glances at one another. "What about last night?" Rueben asked. Celena shrugged noncommittally, then held her hands out to the fire even though she wasn't cold. "So it's like that, is it?" he said. "Who lost their temper first, you or him?"

"Me," Celena said grimly. "But I was provoked."

"Oh, I don't doubt that." Rueben chuckled. "There are times when Matthew could rile the Pope. Though I must say, before you left, it didn't take much for your father to provoke you—not with that chip the size of Vermont you were carrying on your shoulder." Rueben ignored her indignant glare and asked, "Have you thought any more about running the lighthouse?"

"I've already decided to take Father and Joshua to Maryland. Father can recuperate there." She heard Tana's small gasp.

"So that's your plan, is it?" Rueben boomed. "Well, you were always one for doing things your way. Did you tell your father? Is that what started the fight?"

"It wasn't a fight," she said irritably. "Besides, it's just until he recovers!"

"And you don't think he will, do you?"

"I don't know what to think," Celena said miserably. "But it will be a lot easier for me to take care of him in Maryland, where my job is. Besides, if the accident *has* caused permanent damage, Father won't be able to run the light anyway. There aren't a lot of choices."

Rueben shook his head. "Maybe you don't see any, but I bet Matthew will come up with a few."

"Why don't you want to stay?" Tana asked frankly. "Is it because you're afraid?"

Celena was taken aback. "I'm not afraid. If anything, I'm angry."

"Sometimes anger is just another way of being afraid," Tana said. "And I think you're afraid of him hurting you again."

Celena had no reply.

"Have you talked to Joshua about this?" Rueben asked.

"I told him I'd run the light for a while. I didn't tell him I'd stay until Father got better."

Rueben looked at Celena sharply. "You may not have said it, but sure as there's fish in the sea, that's what he's expecting. Joshua's counting on having the lighthouse passed on down to him, just like your granddaddy passed it to your father."

"Joshua will adjust. It's not like keeping the lighthouse is a matter of life and death."

"It is to him." Rueben's voice was brusque. "Think how terrible you felt about leaving the island. How would you have felt if you'd been eleven?"

The question was unanswerable.

"Is it true that the Lighthouse Bureau is shutting down lighthouses? Lydia says they might close Fire Island," Celena said.

"Hogwash," Rueben declared. "I'm not sure why you're worried, but I've got a friend who works at the bureau. I can give him a call. He'll give it to me straight."

She suddenly recalled their conversation the previous evening. "Rueben, what was it you started to tell me last night?"

He put a finger to his lips to shush her, pulling it down instantly when Tana looked up. Her brown eyes were curious. "What about last night?"

Rueben looked confused. "I can't rightly recall. We talked about a lot of things."

Tana shook her head. "I swear, Celena, not only does Rueben's mind wander, sometimes it leaves completely." Putting her knitting aside, she added, "I hate to leave, but I've got to open the post office."

She gave Celena a hug. "It's good to see you, dear. You come and visit again real soon." She collected her handbag, then paused at the door to look at them sternly. "You two behave now, but if it comes to bloodshed, you know where the bandages are."

After the door closed, Celena asked, "Why didn't you want to talk in front of her?"

"Because I'm too young to die. Besides, it's probably nothing. But for some reason it's been preying on my mind. Just before your father's accident, I saw someone walking away from the lighthouse."

"Who was it?"

"I was too far away to see. Whoever it was went across the dunes and down along the beach. I didn't think anything of it at the time. I then stopped at the generator building to do a little work. Matthew said he'd been having some trouble with the generator. When I heard a car, I went out and it was Doc Harrison. He told me Gerald—the mayor's cousin—had called and that there'd been an accident."

"It must have been Gerald you saw."

"Couldn't have been. He was at the light when I got there. And if it was someone going for help, they certainly wouldn't go along the beach," Rueben said firmly. "They'd head for the Coast Guard station, or Kismet. It just strikes me as mighty peculiar that no one has said anything about being at the lighthouse that morning." His face was grim. "No one I know would be able to stop talking about how they were the last one to see Matthew before he nearly got himself killed!"

"Maybe it was Ethan. He likes to walk along the beach."

"It wasn't him."

"How can you be sure? You said you were too far away to tell who it was."

"I was close enough to know it was a woman. Unless Ethan's taken to wearing a dress, it wasn't him."

"A woman!" Celena exclaimed. She furrowed her brow and then asked, "What was Gerald doing at the light, anyway?"

"I didn't ask. Too busy helping the doc."

Rueben stood up and stretched. "Anyway, I'm going to go out and fish a while. Want to come?"

"I'd like to, but I have to be back in time for lunch. Catch me a big one!"

"You betcha."

* * *

The sign over the store read, GENERAL MERCHANDISE, MR. PAUL TILLMAN, PROPRIETOR. A couple of men in Coast Guard uniforms stood talking nearby. They were a common fixture in town ever since the Coast Guard had opened a station west of the light. Three old men in chairs sat talking out front.

"No wonder smuggling's become big business," the barrel-shaped man with a shock of white hair was saying. "The government is making honest men into thieves. If a man can't make a living from the sea fishing or lobstering, he's got to do *something* to make money."

His friend concurred. "I hear rumrunners can make profits up to seven hundred percent for the right brand of scotch or cognac."

"All you have to do is take your boat out to those big ships moored offshore, load up, and avoid the Coast Guard when you come back," added the third man, pushing his thick glasses back up the bridge of his nose. There was hidden delight in his voice as he added, "No way to stop them either. The nights are too dark and the seas too big for the Coast Guard to get them all. Besides, even when rumrunners do get caught, they almost always get off with probation. Hardly any of them are convicted and put in jail."

The conversation intrigued her, but Celena pulled herself away. Inside the store, Elaine Tillman, a short, square woman in her thirties, was at the counter with a customer. Her plain face beamed when she recognized Celena. "As I live and breathe!" she squealed. "It's been a long time! I'll be right with you."

"No hurry," Celena replied. The store looked the same. There were several women at a counter looking at the mail-order catalogues. Near them were bolts of fabric and sewing supplies. Behind the counter were bins with sugar, flour, and coffee, and molasses in a barrel. Meandering, Celena turned a corner and almost fell over a man who was hunkered down, examining items on the bottom shelf.

"Oh, I'm sorry," she said, reaching out a hand to steady herself.

The man's light brown eyes were startled as he pulled out a tin of black shoe polish and rose quickly. "No, it's my fault," he said. "I didn't mean to be a human obstacle course." His dark hair was a bit longer than most men wore it, but it suited him. Celena judged him to be a few years older than she was. Solidly built with nice features, his square face was tanned and smooth. "I'm still rather new here, so if you don't mind my asking, are you from these parts or just here on vacation?" he asked congenially.

"Neither, really. I have a little business to take care of."

"Business?" His look was inquiring.

"Umm, I guess you could call it rescue work."

He grinned engagingly. "And who do you rescue?"

"Boys. Stubborn old men." She smiled slightly. "And if I get real lucky, myself."

His eyes were lively. "Do you ever rescue young men?"

"Never."

"Too bad," he said, putting on a face of mock disappointment. "Are you going to be on Fire Island long?"

"I hope not."

He looked surprised. "Most people love it here and stay as long as they can."

"Not me," she said firmly.

"Well, I hope you enjoy your stay, however long it lasts."

"Thanks. You too."

The man excused himself. Then Celena selected a writing tablet, pencils, and a packet of bobby pins. She arrived at the counter just as he was laying out his purchases.

"We meet again," he said with that pleasant smile. "If you'd like, you can go first."

Celena shook her head. "No, you go ahead."

Behind the cash register, Elaine had a big smile pasted on as she looked up at him. "Did you find everything you needed?"

"Yes, thank you."

"If you ever need any help, I'd be happy to assist," she assured him while ringing up his purchases. Celena looked harder at Elaine. Had she really batted her eyes at him? He took his sack, then paused to look at the display of postcards as Celena rang up her purchases. Elaine kept throwing him happy little glances, but her smile disappeared when he followed Celena out.

Celena stopped on the sidewalk and looked toward the light-house. The man stopped beside her and extended his hand. "I should have introduced myself earlier. My name is Daniel."

Celena smiled and shook his hand. "I'm Celena."

"Pleased to meet you," he replied. Nodding toward the lighthouse, he added, "Quite a sight, isn't it?"

"Yes it is," she agreed, sounding slightly surprised. "I'd forgotten how beautiful it is."

"So you've been here before."

"A long time ago." Celena continued to look toward the light, then remarked absentmindedly, "This is actually the second light. The first one was only eighty-nine feet—not nearly tall enough. Did you know this one has one hundred and ninety-two steps to the top?"

Daniel whistled. "That's quite a climb."

"Yes. And it's a long way to carry kerosene every night. Most everyone on the island gets their electricity from generators, but the lighthouse still runs on kerosene."

"Wow, you sure know a lot about the lighthouse! Since you seem so well informed, maybe you can satisfy my curiosity on another point. Why do they call this place Fire Island?"

"That depends on who you talk to." Celena smiled. "There are several theories. The first is that it started with a simple spelling error. You see, there were four or five islands in the 1700s, and some think the Dutch word *fier,* meaning "four," or *fieve,* for "five," was misspelled on early maps as "fire." However, folklore suggests the name came from land-based pirates or "wreckers," who built beach fires at night to lure cargo ships into becoming shipwrecked. The last theory is that it was named for poison ivy—either for its red leaves in autumn or its fiery itch."

"That's very interesting." Daniel smiled easily. "At least I'll know who to ask if I have any more questions." He glanced at his watch. "I'm supposed to meet my father now, but perhaps I'll see you again before you go. I hope you're successful with your rescues."

Celena smiled and thanked him, then turned toward Bay Haven. *If I am,* she thought, *I'll be pulling off the trick of the century.*

FOUR

When Celena woke the next morning, she thought back to the day before. After returning home from Tillman's, Celena had gone to see her father to apologize for her sharp words, but when she began, he'd cut her off, telling her brusquely that he didn't want to hear it. The rest of their visit had been decidedly stilted. After dinner, Celena had gone to check on her father, but he'd been sound asleep, lying in a rosy circle of light cast by the twin sconces.

Celena breakfasted with Joshua and waved him off to school, then went to see Matthew again, who was more affable than the day before but seemed very tired. When he drifted off to sleep, Celena set off for her father's home at the lighthouse to pick up her bike. Joshua said he had readied it so Celena could use it to ride to and from the light-house. She'd left her hair down today, and the breeze lifted it gently as she walked. Spring was here, with greening stubble in the fields and most trees in early leaf, although a few had leaf buds that were still close-furled nubs along dry branches.

As she approached the lofty lighthouse, a sense of pride rose within her; tonight *she* would be the one keeping the beacon going— protecting the lives of people as they sailed in schooners, trawlers, ocean liners, freighters, and frigates. In her daydreams, she had imagined showing Sam the tall, graceful tower. The fact that he had never come tugged at her heart.

The roar of ocean surf increased, the wild, rushing sound familiar and beautiful as Celena reached the flagged walk that led to the two-storied dwelling. The stone house was actually a duplex, with wings jutting out on either side, enabling it to house a keeper's family as well as an assistant keeper. Built in 1859, it had a high-pitched roof above the front door, with a hipped roofline on the sides of the building. There were two chimneys and a round window above the front door on the second story.

Celena recalled when she, Joshua, and her parents would sit out on the veranda during early summer evenings. Sometimes Joshua would curl up in his father's lap on the swing, his mother sitting contentedly beside them. Celena would sprawl on the top step, lean against a turned post, and listen to the swing's slow creaking. There was a fenced garden nearby where she had planted and picked vegetables. Celena remembered how hard her father had worked in order to pass the quarterly inspections. The outbuildings had to be constantly scraped and repainted—as the salty air and winter wind wreaked havoc on paint. There were always repairs: shingles that needed replacing, window frames rotting through, or a chimney crumbling. When she was older, Celena had helped keep the daily log and maintain an accurate inventory.

She thought momentarily about going inside but decided it would just bring back feelings of anger mixed with sorrow. For too long, when it came to her father, those two emotions had gone hand in hand. Her bike was leaning against the wall of the storage shed. True to his word, Joshua had made sure the tires were in good repair. Taking one last, long look at the house, Celena mounted the bike and pedaled away briskly, her auburn hair waving behind her, gleaming in the sun.

* * *

In the kitchen at Bay Haven, yellow curtains were tied back to invite the sun, and copper-bottomed pots caught the sunlight, adding a luster to the room. The air was fragrant with cinnamon as Helen pulled two peach cobblers out of the oven.

"Your father asked about you this morning." Helen's eyes were cool, blue stones. "Apparently you had more important things to do than be with him. Also, the doctor came by. He was surprised that you were off gallivanting when your father is lying here badly injured."

Celena wanted to grab the peach cobbler and dump it over Helen's head. She was sure Doc Harrison had said nothing of the sort. Minerva gave her a sympathetic look as she carried a load of dishes to the dining room.

"I'll eat in the dining room after I take Father's tray in," Celena called after her.

Helen opened a cupboard and pulled out a wooden tray. "Matthew could use some company during mealtimes if you ask me." Her tone was reproving. "Especially from his own daughter."

"Excuse me for saying so," Celena replied, working to keep her tone pleasant, "but I *didn't* ask you." Helen stood very still for few moments, her hands gripping the tray tightly. Despite the tension, Celena had a few questions she wanted to ask. "Lydia told me that you wanted to buy the lighthouse if the bureau decides to close it down."

Helen answered curtly, "That's right."

"But you've got your own business. Why would you want the light?"

"To bring in more tourists." Helen's tone indicated the answer would have been obvious to anyone with half a brain. "Plus, I'd open a gift shop and charge for tours. I've been assured it's a good investment. So when the Lighthouse Bureau decides to sell it, I intend to be first in line."

Even though she felt reassured by Rueben's claim that the bureau had no intention of closing the light, Celena felt her spine stiffen. She decided to change the subject. "Where is Ethan? I was hoping to see him."

"He doesn't check in with me." Helen's voice was still tight as she dished up stewed tomatoes.

He needs someone to check in with, Celena thought, feeling again that Helen was saying what suited her, rather than what was true. Helen Montgomery had always kept a tight watch on her brother, displaying a loyalty that was topped only by her fierce devotion to Lydia. Unfortunately, Helen's loyalty had never extended far enough to include Ethan's wife. While she had not openly shunned Sarina, Helen had paid her little attention ever since Ethan had married her so unexpectedly six years ago.

Every summer, Ethan went to Pennsylvania to work on a large farm owned by Shane Paxton, Clint's brother, who hired a few extra men to harrow fields, rebuild fences, and brand cattle. Clint had arranged it, explaining to Shane that while Ethan was mentally slow, his back was as strong as anyone's. One fall, Ethan had surprised them all by returning with a bride—a gypsy with flashing dark eyes and long black hair. It became a favorite topic of conversation in Saltaire as to why this lively, energetic woman with bright skirts and clusters of bracelets had married the slow and reclusive Ethan. Some speculated that Sarina found out Ethan had been squirreling away most of his wages for years. Others predicted a baby before winter's end. But Ethan and Sarina spent several years at their small cottage near the beach, and there was no baby.

With Sarina beside him keeping a keen eye on those who might otherwise act differently, people began treating Ethan in a new, more respectful manner. Sarina chattered away so easily that people unacquainted with Ethan could be excused for thinking he remained quiet because he couldn't get a word in edgewise. When he did speak, Sarina finished his half sentences, adding a word here and there so that the gaps were scarcely noticeable. Before his marriage, he'd had such a hard time speaking that it was difficult for strangers to tell if he was even possessed of a functioning intelligence. But it was not so with Sarina beside him.

After a few months, Sarina had decided Celena was a loyal enough friend to tell her how she and Ethan had met and how she had decided Ethan was the one for her. Brains were not everything, Sarina insisted. Besides, she was bright enough for the two of them! At that, Sarina had thrown back her head with that cascading dark hair and laughed.

As Sarina talked about her gypsy past, she had painted a picture so vivid that Celena could almost see the brightly painted wagons with their little curtained windows and the horses decorated with tassels and silver beads. Sarina told how her family and others in the caravan had told fortunes, sold lace, traded horses and mules, and worked at odd jobs. Sometimes her brothers had done things that were not right, Sarina had admitted. But they had only been following the orders of a devious man, someone of importance. At this, Sarina had looked at Celena as if willing her to question her about that. When Celena did not, Sarina moved on, and with an impish tilt of her head, finished back where she'd started, saying simply that Ethan had won her over with kindness. It had not been much of a trick to get Ethan to marry her, Sarina said—all she had to do was ask!

With a snap of her ringed fingers, she let Celena know what she thought of the townspeople's gossip. "Let them talk," she said defiantly, tossing her fine, black hair over her shoulder like a stallion tosses its mane. "What do I care? I have my home. I have my Ethan." From outward appearances, they had seemed happy, and it was a shock when Sarina had drowned in Great South Bay two years ago. When she'd heard the news, Celena thought sadly that life had been terribly unfair to Ethan.

Sighing at the memory of the tragedy while carrying the tray for her father, Celena entered his room without bothering to knock. Matthew was asleep, and his face had a waxy cast. Today, she felt none of the corked tension that had overwhelmed her before. When Celena cleared her throat, Matthew's eyelids fluttered open.

"I've brought your lunch." He looked at the food as if unsure what to do with it, and his blue eyes were so disoriented that she asked, "Do you want me to feed you?"

It was clear that Matthew understood when his brows lowered. "I'm not an invalid!" he snapped. Still, the furrow between his brows bespoke pain, and his eyes were cloudy as he ate in silence. Patches of clouds took turns shutting out the sunlight and letting it through the windows. When the sun was able to spill in, it rippled across the floor, as tentative and tenuous as Celena's relationship with her father. Celena noticed the bare wall again and wondered briefly where the picture had gone.

"I saw Rueben and Tana yesterday," she said, trying to make conversation.

"How is he doing with the light?"

"Fine, but Joshua and I are going to run it tonight. Rueben's coming over to make sure I haven't forgotten anything."

He grunted as if that was unlikely, and she went on. "I've heard that the Lighthouse Bureau has sold some lighthouses."

"Aye, a few of the older ones." Matthew's face was grave and level, as it almost always was, but not particularly concerned.

"Helen wants to buy the Fire Island Light."

Matthew almost spewed out his last bite. "She'll be waiting a long time, then. They'll never close Fire Island. It's one of the first lights transatlantic steamers see when they're bound for New York."

Celena pulled her chair closer and changed the subject quickly. "I was wondering about your accident. How did you fall?"

Looking pensive, Matthew said, "The last thing I remember is taking paint up to the lantern room. Next thing I knew, Doc Harrison was bending over me."

"Did anyone visit you that morning?"

He pondered that for almost a full minute before saying tentatively, "No." When Celena looked at him, Matthew added, "I thought I saw someone, but it was just because I hit my head."

"Who?"

Matthew was clearly reluctant to say. Lying back, he closed his eyes. She'd almost given up on him answering when he whispered, "Elizabeth."

Celena caught her breath. Of course, the doctor *had* said he'd suffered a concussion. Still, a covey of goose bumps went up her arms when she imagined her mother being there at the time of the accident. When she could talk without a tremor in her voice, Celena asked, "Do you remember Gerald finding you?"

"No." His voice was weak now, and strained.

"Did you check all the straps, ropes, and pulleys before going out on the bosun's chair?"

His eyes opened and he answered gruffly, "I told you I can't remember, but I always check everything. Can't figure it out." His eyes closed again, and he didn't stir when Celena left.

* * *

Celena was on her way to post a letter to her grandparents when Gerald came out of Tillman's. He was followed closely by Daniel, the man she had seen there the day before. The two men were nearly the same height, but Gerald was much broader. There was a certain ruggedness about the younger man, a muscular breadth to his shoulders that marked him for a man of action. He noticed her immediately and flashed that engaging smile.

His eyes flicked to the letter in her hand. "Doing some long-distance rescue work?"

She waved the envelope. "Top secret."

There was a friendly, relaxed way about him that Celena was drawn to. Here was someone at ease with himself. Gerald looked at them both. "So, you two have met, eh?"

"We ran into each other yesterday—quite literally, I'm afraid," Celena replied.

"You would have met at dinner your first night here, but Daniel had to work late," Gerald said. "Since it sounds like you haven't been properly introduced, let me do so. Celena, this is my son, Daniel Roberts. Daniel, meet Celena Jackson." Celena noticed now that his eyes were the same as Gerald's—light brown, open, and interested in everything.

Daniel asked, "You're staying at Bay Haven?"

Gerald answered for her. "Of course! So she can be near her father."

Daniel blinked. "Jackson. You're Matthew Jackson's daughter?"

"Oh, ho!" Gerald laughed heartily. "So, *this* is the girl you told me about—the one who knew so much about the lighthouse? And she never told you she grew up there? Oh, Celena, you sure pulled a fast one on him!"

Daniel looked at her long and warily. "I thought you'd just read some tourist guidebook, the way you went on about the lighthouse. Why didn't you tell me?"

Why indeed? she wondered. Because she'd been lost in some kind of melancholy fog? What *had* she been thinking?

Daniel's face became set. Gerald noticed and rushed on. "Now, don't take it so hard. She was just having a bit of fun with you."

It was the wrong thing to say. Chagrined at the look on Daniel's face, Celena blurted, "I wasn't trying to be secretive."

Gerald could not resist speaking for her. "Of course you weren't," he assured Celena. "Say, what we need is a chance to get to know each other better! Celena, why don't you come to Clearwater day after tomorrow? It's quite the place I've built. I'd love to show you around."

"Thank you," Celena replied a bit uncomfortably, "but you must be very busy, and I wanted to spend some time with Joshua since I'm not sure how long I'll be staying."

"Bring him along!" Gerald said in his booming voice. "We'd love to have you both." There were no words of welcome from Daniel. Still, what did that matter? She hadn't intended to offend him, and she would be leaving soon.

"I planned to spend the day working on your books," Daniel told his father evenly.

"You work too much," Gerald replied breezily. "Take an hour off. It'll do you good." Then he turned back to her. "I'll look forward to seeing you, Celena. Perhaps we can discuss my plans for the lighthouse."

Celena was puzzled. "Plans?"

"My plans to buy it." With that, Gerald tipped his hat and walked away, leaving Celena standing with her mouth open. Looking dismayed, Daniel gave a short, helpless shrug, then with long strides caught up with Gerald, bending his head toward him in earnest conversation.

* * *

Celena was just going up the steps to Bay Haven when Lydia opened the door. Over her smooth blond hair she wore a green scarf that brought out the color of her eyes. Her movements were airy as she floated onto the porch. "What's wrong? Someone kick your dog?"

"Gerald Roberts just told me he wants to buy the lighthouse." When Lydia didn't look surprised, Celena said slowly, "You knew."

"Gerald stole the idea from Mother," Lydia said sourly. "He's sneaky, that one. Acts friendly and concerned, but underneath he's something different altogether."

"Is he nuts?" Celena cried, flinging out her hands. "What could Gerald want with it?"

Lydia looked at her as if she were a child. "What do you think? The same thing as Mother—to bring in more tourists, because having more business results in more money. He knows that having the light would be a huge draw for his resort."

Celena had been thinking. "Gerald might be able to get financing to buy the light, using Clearwater as collateral, but what about your parents? Bay Haven must be doing very well."

"No concerns there." Lydia's voice was bright, but there was a flicker of something on her face. It made Celena suspicious.

"Does your father approve of this?"

Lydia wriggled away from the question. "Never mind that. Besides, I doubt that Gerald and Mother are the only ones who want the light."

"Tell me you're joking."

Lydia's smile was bright with mischief. "I bet rumrunners would love to have it."

"What would they do with it?" Celena's head was spinning.

Lydia laughed raucously. "Celena, you are so naïve! Dear-heart, picture this: It's a dark night. Men are sitting out in the Atlantic, their boats loaded with cases of liquor, but they need to know if the Coast Guard is around or not. Can you imagine a better signal than a flash or two from the lighthouse to let them know it's clear to come in?"

"But the Lighthouse Bureau would never sell the light to people like that."

"Oh, Celena. Sweet, sweet, Celena." Lydia's laughter was mocking. "Do you really think they'd send one of the ruffians who do the actual hauling? Their buyer is going to wear a fancy suit, black-and-white wing tips, and have a legitimate address on Fifth Avenue."

"It's not possible."

"I know." Lydia grinned wickedly. "I just wanted to see your reaction. It was even better than I'd hoped." She tilted back her head and laughed gaily. "I'm sorry, but that was too much fun to pass up. Actually, I really do think mother's going to get it. She's got a cousin who works for the Lighthouse Bureau. He'll be sure and swing things her way."

Celena was speechless.

"So are you ready to run the light tonight?"

When Celena nodded guardedly, Lydia teased maliciously, "Remember to watch out for the ghost."

Thoroughly annoyed, Celena started past her into the house. "If I do see a ghost, I'll tell him you said hello."

* * *

Minerva had Matthew's dinner tray ready, and Celena balanced it as she pushed his door open. Because of the large windows, the light in her father's room was always liquid amber, the shadows strange and soft. Tonight, there were dark circles under Matthew's eyes, and the lines on his face seemed deeper. He ate very little but seemed watchful.

When he put down his fork, Matthew asked, "Is something wrong?"

Celena had been thinking about Helen and Gerald, wondering if her father knew they both wanted the light. Startled, she replied, "I think I'm a little tired, that's all."

"Let's change places, then. You stay here. I'll go run the light." The bravado of his words contrasted with the fragility of his voice, and she smiled. Even if her father didn't have a cast, he looked too worn out to even make it to the door. Celena decided not to stay long. She had the feeling that she and her father were strangers reaching out just a little, and for the moment, that was enough. She didn't want to spoil the tranquility with talk of others' plans for the lighthouse.

Celena wasn't hungry, so in the kitchen, she put some cheese, bread, and two apples in a sack for later. Unfortunately, when Joshua found she wasn't going to dinner, he wanted to skip it as well. After a few attempts to dissuade him, Celena declared, "I'll not be trapped in a lighthouse with a starving boy. The sooner you eat, the sooner we can leave." He marched out and was back in a startlingly short time, cheeks bulging. Shaking her head, Celena led the way to their father's room.

Joshua had chewed sufficiently to announce proudly, "We're going to the light now!"

Celena tried not to notice how Matthew's face softened. She didn't want to be disarmed—weakened. Then suddenly, he scowled at Joshua. "What about our nightly game of chess? You're not forgetting that, are you?" For a split second, Joshua looked stricken. Celena was ready to make a sharp comment when she noticed the slight twinkle in her father's eye. Joshua saw it too and grinned, embarrassed at having been taken in by his father's teasing.

"Maybe we can play afternoons instead," Matthew suggested, his voice worn and tired.

Joshua noticed. "Are you okay?"

"Aye," Matthew mumbled, reaching over to pick up a large key that had a leather loop through the top. Joshua took the key, looking at it almost reverently. "Don't lose that," his father admonished. "I've only got two."

Clutching the key, Joshua started off. "Come on, Celena, we need to get to the lighthouse before it gets dark." She glanced at the window where the sun was still streaming in.

One corner of Matthew's mouth turned up slightly. "Get out of here so I can get some rest," he ordered.

By the time Celena got her bicycle, Joshua had already hopped on his rusted blue one and was at the road. By the time she reached the outskirts of town, her brother was out of sight. When Celena drew up to the keeper's cottage, the lighthouse was casting a long shadow over the beach. The boom of the surf sounded in the background as Joshua waited impatiently at the generator building. He held the can while she filled it with kerosene. She paused for a moment by the side of the lighthouse, standing at the bottom of walls that were almost eleven feet thick. Celena tilted her head back so far it hurt and found that gazing up at the top—something she had often done as a child—still caused a feeling of wonder. Somehow it was comforting to find that it did even now. Joshua unlocked the door ceremoniously.

The interior was cool and pleasant, smelling of wax, soap, and paint—a mixture of odors that told of ceaseless attention and care. The room to the left was the keeper's quarters, and the one on the right was the assistant keeper's quarters. Since there had been no live-in assistant for years, Matthew used it as an office. Joshua locked the door, hung the key on a hook, and ran down the short hall to a door that led to the enclosed corridor that connected the keeper's cottage to the lighthouse.

Before starting to climb the circling iron steps, Joshua paused to give his sister a wide grin so overflowing with excitement and pride that Celena was touched. With the jug of kerosene in one hand, he held on to the iron railing with the other and vaulted himself upward. Celena followed, looking up occasionally through the wire-mesh stairs to catch a glimpse of his shoes.

Occasionally the gloom of the curving staircase was relieved by light streaming in through small rectangular windows set in the thick stone walls. There were nine landings, and after the fourth, Celena stopped to look out to where the late evening sun was lighting up the island in a meld of gold and green. Her legs were aching when she made it to the service room, the second-to-the-highest level. Joshua was indignant when Celena started to explain how to check the kerosene level.

"I already know how to do that!" he retorted, then settled down when she let him fill the tank. The only solid floor in the lighthouse was the one above them, the lantern room. To get there, Joshua pushed a small trapdoor open and scrambled through. After Celena climbed up, she let the trapdoor down with a rope that was knotted at the end.

The Fresnel lens sat in the middle of the lantern room, looking for all the world like a giant glass beehive. When lit, prisms focused the bull's-eye lens into a single powerful beam that warned ships of the dangerous shoals lying just off the coast. There were glass windows all around, with a door on the north side that led onto the catwalk—a three-foot-wide walk that ran about the tower. Some visitors hesitated to go out on the catwalk, feeling exposed and unprotected one hundred and eighty feet above the ground. But ringed in by the iron railing, Celena had never been frightened by the height, even though she stood so high that birds flew below her. Sometimes, Celena felt so exhilarated out there that she almost felt like she could launch out into space and be scooped up by the wind.

Celena tugged at the door and, after slipping through, let the wind slam it shut. She and Joshua stood side by side—a slim, auburn-haired young woman and a tanned, blond boy that came up to her shoulder—looking out at the surf that flickered white on the distant reefs below.

Joshua pointed out at the ocean. "Two months ago I saw a whale, and last week there was a pod of dolphins!"

They watched a huge cruiser go by, the distance making it look like a toy ship. The entire island was visible before them: the meandering shoreline on the south; the western tip, where the island narrowed down to nothing; the lush greenness that extended eastward; and finally the blue waters of Great South Bay on the north. Celena noticed someone walking toward the light.

"Rueben's coming!" Joshua shouted. In a moment he was clattering down the stairs. He was back soon, but it took a moment for the older man to squeeze his bulk through the trapdoor.

"Doggone thing keeps shrinking," Rueben complained, straightening his suspenders that had gone askew. Joshua was dancing in his eagerness to start the light, but Rueben told him to wait. It wouldn't do to waste the fuel, which was strictly accounted for.

Finally Celena pronounced it countdown time. "Do you know all the steps?" she asked.

"Sure, I've helped Father lots of times," Joshua replied.

When Joshua crowded Celena as she inspected the mantle, she admonished, "Give me room to breathe!" But he continued to hang over her shoulder as she trimmed the wicks and recorded the weather in the logbook. In the service room, Rueben watched Celena show Joshua how to pump air until there was enough pressure to feed the mantle in the lantern room above. Next, Celena had her brother crank a clockwork mechanism that raised a sixty-pound weight on a wire rope. It turned the giant lens as it descended. They went back up and Celena lit an alcohol-spirit lamp to vaporize the kerosene, then a long candle, which she handed to Joshua, who lit the kerosene-soaked mantle.

Last, Celena instructed her brother to activate the clockwork mechanism. As the glass lens began to turn, bright shafts turned with it, looking like the projecting spokes of a fiery wheel. The prisms transformed the light from the mantle into an intense cylindrical beam that shone once every minute, warning all ocean vessels away from deadly shoals. As the light began to flash, Celena flushed with a sense of accomplishment. As long as the keeper kept the light shining and the captains heeded the warning flashes, all ocean vessels would be safe.

"Don't look into the light, Celena," Joshua cautioned. "It'll blind you."

"I'll be careful," Celena said, careful to keep a straight face.

Rueben was satisfied. "You did fine, Celena. Didn't miss a thing. All that's left now is to wind the clockworks every four hours. Just remember, if you ever need a backup, I'm here."

"Clint told me you trained him to run the light," Celena said.

"He's been good to help out. Caught on real fast. Clint does a good job, but not as good as this guy here!" Rueben ruffled Joshua's hair, then pulled up a stool. "By the way, I found out who called the Lighthouse Bureau and told them they needed a new keeper."

Joshua was outraged. "Somebody did that?"

Celena frowned. "It was probably Helen. Lydia told me she wants to buy the light."

"It was Helen all right, stirring up trouble. Her cousin has told everyone that Matthew is permanently disabled and said that if they're going to close any lights, it ought to be Fire Island."

"But they can't close the light!" Joshua cried, looking to Rueben for confirmation.

"Not by a long shot," Rueben said reassuringly, but his tone held a note of concern. He said to Celena, "I told the bureau that Matthew's injury might not be permanent, but the fellow there said that if you don't run the light, the bureau has two options—either get a new keeper or sell the lighthouse. Another thing—someone in the Coast Guard has contacted the bureau and said he'd like to be appointed the new keeper, but only if it's a long-term position. Apparently he has a wife and children and doesn't want to uproot them for a temporary job."

"Celena's going to run the light," Joshua told Rueben as if that ended the matter.

Celena decided to quickly reroute *that* conversation. "Rueben, why don't you tell Joshua about the mooncussers?"

When Joshua nodded eagerly, Rueben began. "It all started with a bunch of rough men called wreckers. Oh, they were a tough bunch, living alone on the island and salvaging cargo that washed up whenever a ship wrecked. But then they got greedy. What do you think they did?"

Joshua answered quickly, "They lit fires on the shore or hung lanterns from a pole to make the ships think there was a lighthouse!"

"That's right. They wanted the captain to think he had a safe harbor. Oh, they lured many a ship to its doom. And why are they called 'mooncussers'?"

"Because their tricks would only work when it was dark!" Joshua exclaimed.

Celena enjoyed the story but had other things on her mind. "I think I'll go down to the beach for a while."

"Ah, we've given her ideas, now," Rueben whispered conspiratorially to Joshua. "She's going to light a torch and try her luck!" As she went through the trap door, Rueben shouted dramatically, "Don't do it, Celena!"

She paused. "How's a girl supposed to have any fun, then?"

Joshua's laughter followed her down the stairs. It was a glorious night. The Milky Way was like a silver river meandering across the heavens. The moon was a bright yellow crescent, and looked so close that a long-armed man might think to touch it. A light fog was just beginning to roll in close to the ground, with a few wisps curling and swirling in the darkness.

Celena had always loved walking along the beach. Tonight she wanted to sit and listen to the waves and clear the cobwebs from her mind. She was disturbed by the exhilaration she'd felt at being in charge of the light, and she felt moved by the depth of her brother's passion for it. As she slid down the dunes, Celena suddenly remembered Lydia's talk of a ghost. But then, Lydia had only been trying to upset her. The air was thick and her soft-soled shoes made no sound as she passed a storage shed on her way to her favorite spot—a collection of boulders where she loved to sit and watch the waves undulate toward shore. As she walked, it was as if the night and faint moonlight were seeping through her skin into her bloodstream.

The outline of Clearwater was visible. It was an imposing building, with fanciful turrets and spires, and Celena looked forward to seeing it close up. She looked back to where the lighthouse stood like a sentinel, its piercing bright light flashing once every sixty seconds. Each lighthouse had its own unique flash pattern, enabling a seaman to know where he was by the pattern of flashes.

As Celena turned back toward her destination, she pulled up short. There was something ahead of her—no more than thirty yards away, near the cluster of boulders. When the tendrils of fog shifted, Celena thought she saw a human profile. But the body was so shapeless, the person had to be wearing a cloak or blanket. Could this be the ghost Lydia had mentioned? Just then, the faceless figure, still shrouded in the darkness and the mist, turned its black gaze in her direction. The person seemed as sensitive to the presence of another human as a deer would be, for Celena had been—and remained—soundless. Celena held her breath until the figure's head drooped. Cautiously, she took a step backward, then another, but on the third, there was a slight snap as she stepped on a stick. The head raised, swiveling toward her.

As the figure stood, Celena turned and ran. Sounds from behind told her that she was being followed. Going around the far side of the storage shed, Celena stopped, her back flat against the building. All was silent. The person was waiting for her to make a move. Her only chance was to go straight out as quietly as possible and run for the light. Celena had taken no more than five steps when a man came around the corner after her, a huge presence in a formless overcoat. He was fleeter than Celena. When he caught up, she thrust out her arms to ward him off. A strangled cry burst from her throat as she was enveloped in strong arms that squeezed her, forcing the air from her lungs.

FIVE

"Celena!" The deep, masculine voice held a note of joy. Because of its familiarity, she stopped struggling. The man was tall and broad, with hair everywhere—from his bushy beard to his heavy eyebrows to his long, straggly hair whipping around his shoulders in the brisk wind. He still had a pleasant, blunt-featured face and curiously innocent eyes. As his powerful grip relaxed, Celena balled up her fists and beat furiously at his chest. It was like hitting the side of a boulder.

"Ethan! Why didn't you tell me it was you? How could you scare me like that?"

Looking puzzled, Ethan dropped his arms. His mouth pulled down at the corners like a scolded child. "I—I thought you knew it was me."

"It's dark, Ethan! How was I supposed to know?" He hung his head and Celena remembered how childlike he was—never stopping to think about the consequences of his actions. "Never mind. It's all right." She took a deep breath. "Where have you been?"

"I came here to wait for you."

"Oh, Ethan," Celena said softly. He knew the cluster of boulders was her favorite spot on the beach. It was the perfect place to curl up, hidden away from the eyes of anyone passing nearby. "You could have seen me at Bay Haven," Celena reminded him.

"I knew you'd come to watch," Ethan replied enigmatically. Overhead, ragged bits of fog raced, allowing touches of faint moonlight to break through.

"It's rather dark to look at the ocean. I just wanted to sit and think."

"You need to watch," Ethan said firmly, looking around as if someone was listening. It was a mannerism she remembered well. Ethan always thought people were watching him. It came, she supposed, from being tormented unmercifully by other children while growing up.

Their own friendship had begun unexpectedly when Celena had gone to her favorite spot and found Ethan there. With her footsteps muffled by the sand and crash of the waves, he hadn't heard her approach. Standing behind him, Celena had been surprised to see him studying an old first-grade reader. It was well known that Ethan had not attended school past the third grade. Six years older than Celena, he had grown in size but not in achievement and had never learned to read. When he had finally noticed her, Ethan had scrambled to his feet, ready to flee as though he were five instead of eighteen.

"Don't go!" she'd cried. When he held his ground, Celena had reached out for the book, asking mildly, "Do you want me to read it to you?" Without waiting for an answer, she'd pointed at a spot beside her and commanded, "Sit here." Celena began to read, and slowly, Ethan lowered himself, eyes on the book. When she had finished, Celena handed it to him. Ethan had turned to the first page and read it perfectly. Celena had been astonished. He was halfway through when she had noticed he was one page off—moving his finger along one page while reciting the next.

"You're not reading at all," Celena had said in wonder. "You're just repeating." He had an amazing memory, a real gift, Celena had assured him, causing Ethan to beam with pleasure. Their friendship grew and they discovered they could talk to one another—plainly, simply, and without the subterfuge that one sometimes had to employ with other people. As the years passed, Celena had learned how Ethan ached to be accepted, to be like everyone else. In return, Ethan sympathized with Celena over losing her mother and let her talk through her anger when her father refused to let her live her religion. Their trials were eerily the same today—and the basis for their mutual understanding remained in place.

Tonight, Ethan's voice was soft, almost tremulous. "You've been gone a long time. May 8, 1921."

Celena smiled. "Five years. You always did have a tremendous memory."

"Now that you're back, you can help." His voice was eager.

"Help with what?"

"Watching the beach." Then, leaning closer as if afraid of being overhead, he whispered, "Those that die don't always leave, do they? Sometimes they stay because of love, sometimes because of hate." Ethan was doing his best to enlighten her, but she was still confused.

"What are you talking about?"

"Sarina. I know why she's staying." This was said with quiet intensity, like a confident student who knows the correct answer. "She's got things she wants done. Sarina told me that if she went away and didn't come back, I should watch the beach."

Celena's heart was heavy as she laid her hand gently on his arm. "I know you miss Sarina, but she's gone, Ethan. She's not going to come back."

Ethan smiled crookedly and shook his shaggy head. "You're wrong." His eyes scanned the misty landscape. "She's around. I know she is. She can't rest."

Tiny goose bumps pricked Celena's arms. "Why not?"

"People who die that way have to haunt those that killed them— until it's made right." He held a finger to his lips and looked over her shoulder with such a peculiar intensity that Celena wondered if there *was* someone standing out there, hidden behind the gossamer curtain of fog.

"But no one killed Sarina," Celena spoke carefully. "She drowned. It was an accident."

Ethan peered at her closely. "You don't believe me," he said sadly.

Celena shivered. "I'd better get back."

"I'll come so you're safe." As they walked, it was disconcerting how often Ethan swiveled his head to scan the beach. At the lighthouse, he nodded solemnly. "You'll be okay now." Then, quick as thought, he melted out of view.

* * *

The rest of the night was uneventful. When Celena woke her brother the next morning, he was groggy. He started to rebel when Celena told him that from now on, he'd have to start spending school nights at Bay Haven, but he perked up when she reminded him that since it was

Friday, he could come to the light that night. Once he left for school, Celena took a nap. Then she went to visit her father, who, despite looking drained and ill, wanted to hear every detail about the light. Afterward, Celena decided to go see Rueben.

Walking along with the wind singing over the tops of the trees, she thought of Sam. Sometimes Celena couldn't resist touching on old memories of him, in much the way the tongue seeks the hole from which a tooth has been pulled—even though it causes pain.

They'd made plans for a spring wedding. One day, Celena went on her lunch hour to order material for her dress. When it took less time than expected, she'd stopped at a nearby café. It took a few moments before she realized it actually *was* Sam sitting in a far booth. His arm was around a pretty little brunette who was looking up at him with the same look of adoration Celena knew she herself often wore. As Celena watched them bend their heads together to talk intimately, the noise in the restaurant seemed to undergo a distinct change. People's cutlery started to clatter and bang loudly. Glasses tinkled and seemed about to smash. Voices came and went in a roar. Somehow, her legs carried her over to them, and Celena found she had to hold onto the table to keep upright. After holding out her left hand so the girl could see the diamond solitaire, Celena wrenched the ring off and dropped it onto the table as the girl turned, bewildered, to Sam.

Nearing the docks, Celena pulled herself into the present, firmly putting Sam out of her mind. It helped to be distracted by the general air of activity—the unloading and loading of crates, longshoremen shouting, and fish and ice wagons rattling along the docks. The smell of waterlogged rope drying in the sun was strong as Celena walked past the line of plank shacks and festoons of nets that were laid out on wooden racks leading to the pier. There were the familiar sounds of masts creaking and dories knocking against each other. Although an assortment of boats were at their moorings, the late morning sun reflecting off their white hulls, Rueben's boat was not among them. Celena took a seat on a wooden bench, knowing he would be there soon.

The ferry was approaching. Squinting against the glare of sun on water, Celena watched the ferry's blunt prow kick up a sheet of water as it hit waves from a passing motorboat. She went over to the ferry's dock. When Clint saw her, he avoided the passengers crowding the ramp by vaulting over the side. His handsome face was alight.

"Dare I hope you were waiting for me?"

"Actually, I was waiting for Rueben."

"Oh! So you favor older men?" An elderly man in a shapeless cardigan going past overheard and gave Celena a wink.

"Clint, will you stop that!"

"I don't think so. You look too pretty when you blush."

Two young men from the Coast Guard strode past wearing smart, double-breasted service coats. The one with a Navy-style white duck hat gave Celena a polite nod.

"There they go," Clint said, "defenders of Prohibition, the most foolish amendment Congress has ever passed."

"Apparently you don't think much of the Coast Guard."

"On the contrary," Clint replied quickly. "I admire their work a great deal, but it's a waste of taxpayers' money to have the Coast Guard tracking down rumrunners when there are so many more important things they could be doing."

"But smuggling liquor is illegal," Celena countered primly.

"So is drinking. What are they going to do? Put three-fourths of America in jail?"

Rolling her eyes, Celena changed the subject. "Clint, you're the mayor. Have you heard anything about the Lighthouse Bureau selling the light?"

"Not a thing, though I know they've had to cut costs, like everyone else. However, I think they're more likely to close the Montak lighthouse than Fire Island's."

"It's just not right."

He looked at her curiously. "I guess it's hard for you to think about the light closing. After all, you did grow up there. I just hope Joshua doesn't make you feel guilty about leaving. You're a grown woman and have a right to live your own life. Just remember, I'd be glad to run the light until Matthew gets back on his feet, though I'd want your promise that you'd come back and visit us often." The warmth in his look was unmistakable. Celena dropped her eyes.

"I couldn't ask you to run it. You're overloaded as it is."

His gray eyes crinkled. "I'm fortunate to have a lot of good people working with me, both on the city council and the ferry. Besides, the ferry doesn't run at night, so I'd be free to take care of the light. By the way, how did things go last night?"

"Fine. Joshua was in heaven. Rueben came and told him stories."

"So you're allowing visitors? Would it be all right if I stopped by tonight?"

"We'd love to have some company."

The ferry was about ready to leave, so Celena watched Clint as he strode up the gangplank, looking younger than most of his crew. The ferry was still in sight when Rueben's boat finally approached, its motor gurgling. Celena took the rope he tossed and wrapped it around a post to hold the boat fast. Rueben stepped off and secured the other end.

"I wanted to talk to you. Do you have a few minutes?" Celena asked.

"I've got all day." Rueben's cane sounded loudly on the weathered dock as he followed Celena to an empty bench. "You know, I'm glad you came back," he said. "It was time, don't you think?"

She thought of her promise. "I suppose so." Celena remembered the day she'd left. As the ferry had pulled away that long-ago day, the low sky had begun to weep rain. She had stood at the railing, drinking in the sight of Fire Island through misty tears that obscured her vision.

"You left with a lot of wounds." Rueben's voice was low and somber.

Celena didn't like remembering the first days of her forced exile, when she'd seemed to be living a thin borderline of existence, no wider than a ray of late sun penetrating a slit in the blinds. Fastening her attention on a sailboat cutting across the bay, its white sails blown full by the wind, she said impassively, "I learned to live with them."

"You didn't have to *live* with them," the old man remonstrated gently. "You could have gotten *past* them. Your father never should have ordered you to leave, but trouble between parents and children is nothing new. Raising my boys was like trying to nail Jell-O to a tree. Now that they're grown, three of them remember the good times but the fourth is plenty bitter. Seems like memories can be like corks left out of bottles—they swell. How is it with you? Can you look beyond that last year and see further back to the good times? There were a few, I know."

"None of that matters now."

"It doesn't, eh?" His voice was skeptical. "Until you and your father can patch things up, there's always going to be something missing in your life."

The wooden pilings creaked and moaned as water slapped against them. Celena had been content in Maryland. She had. Yet it was like sitting out in a summer garden on a cloudy day—pleasant, but you knew it could be so much better. And whenever she thought the past had lost its power to hurt, pain would flare anew.

"It would break your mother's heart to know how long this has gone on," Rueben said.

Celena's mouth trembled with the unfairness of it. "And whose fault is that?" she cried, anger sticking to her like a burr. "*He's* the one that told me to get out and never come back! And don't you *dare* tell me I need to forgive!" she cried, fiercely annoyed.

"Ah, Celena, listen to yourself now, would you?" He gave her a look that went down to her marrow. "I'm not the one asking you to forgive. Somebody else did that." Underneath shaggy brows, Rueben's eyes were thoughtful. "I wish you'd stick it out for a bit. Your father's in a tight spot. If you leave, there's a good chance the Lighthouse Bureau will turn the light over to some young feller, maybe permanently. I'm not sure how Matthew would cope with that. Or Joshua either. I'd run it, but I've got to find something that pays better so I can help Will." As the sun played over the diamond surface of the bay, Celena again saw the pleading look on her little brother's face when he had asked her to stay and run the light.

The older man continued. "Running that lighthouse is not just a job to your father. It's a way of life. He grew up here, raised a family in its shadow. It'll be a hard thing if it's taken away."

Celena looked out at the glittering bay as if hoping to find an answer there. "But even if I did stay, he could lose it anyway—if his leg doesn't heal right. He has a long recovery ahead. That's why I think it would be best for everyone if I took him and Joshua back to Maryland."

Disapproval shone off of Rueben's face like steam off asphalt. "Best for *everyone*? Don't be fooling yourself, Celena. You're doing what's best for *you*. If you take them to Maryland, you'll be able to go on with your life just fine, but you'll be hurting them to no end."

Anger, red and bottomless, surged to the surface, making her feel like the dock was swaying under her feet. "And what did my father do to *my* life when he told me to leave?" she demanded. "Did *he* stop to think how I'd feel when he told me to take my things and get out?" Celena recalled how she'd left, crying and breathing hard and fast—feeling so alone that she was sure if she had shouted there would have been no echo.

As her voice rose now, the gulls that had been perched nearby took to the air in alarm. "I lost my family, my friends, and everything I knew because of my father!" Her words sprung from a grief so deep it was unfathomable. She had to stop to gulp air. Rueben did not—could not—know the full sum of hurt she felt. Not unless he could put on her bones and wear her skin would he ever know. It took an effort to collect herself. "I'm willing to see that he's taken care of—I'll even take care of him myself—but *only* in Maryland and only because of Mother. I'm not going to give up my life a second time."

Rueben bowed his gray head momentarily. "I don't blame you for feeling bitter. Still, I'd hoped things could have turned out differently." He tried again. "Have you thought about it from your father's perspective? Matthew was beside himself with Elizabeth being so sick and all. And then you two got mixed up in a strange new religion that he knew nothing about and trusted even less." He spoke carefully, as if explaining something to a child. "Your father wasn't himself. You've got to remember that he had just lost his wife."

Celena's voice was cold. "And I had just lost my mother."

"It was a bad time all the way around," Rueben said, looking at her steadily. "It's just that Joshua is as passionate about that lighthouse as your father, and as much as your brother idolizes you now, he'll not thank you for taking him away from everything he loves."

Celena had a scalding slash of intuition that what Rueben said was true. She looked toward the Fire Island lighthouse. It stood out against the horizon with a clarity she had never seen before. "I know Joshua loves the lighthouse, and I don't want him to lose it, but . . ."

"I know," Rueben said. "It would be a mighty big sacrifice and you'd have to ignore a lot of history to stay. But don't you think it's time to put the past behind you?"

When she replied it was in a small voice. "I don't know that I'm ready."

Rueben's gruff voice had a bit of a lash in it. "If you're not ready now, you're never going to *be* ready. And if that don't send a shiver down your back, it should." A flock of gulls swooped in low over the water, squawking raucously as a fisherman gutted his fish and threw the entrails into the water. Rueben spoke more gently. "Why don't you stay for a while, just until the doctor knows for sure whether his leg is going to heal up properly or not."

There was a sense of a net settling over her, entangling her in its folds. Celena had come to Fire Island with a clear plan for escape, but little by little she was getting entwined. She had to stand firm. "No, I'm going to take them back to Maryland."

"Headstrong as ever," Rueben muttered, rubbing his chin. A gull landed on the end of the dock, its head darting from side to side as it walked around, searching for a morsel to eat. Rueben stood and reached for his cane. "All right, I can see which way the wind blows. Where are you headed now? I thought I'd go see Matthew."

"I'm going back to Bay Haven myself. Doc Harrison is going to stop by."

"I'll go with you, then." He glanced down the dock at a lean man in coveralls. "Just let me ask Jimmy to unload my haul. He often helps if I give him a few fish for his trouble."

As they walked along, Rueben's cane beat a tattoo on the sidewalk. Forsythia was spilling its yellow spray in many yards, while enterprising tulips, pansies, and jonquils poked their heads through the bare earth. The day was so still and warm and tender that one could almost feel the leaves pushing out of their woody prisons and the first flowers stirring and fretting to be born.

"I'd forgotten how beautiful it is," Celena said, brushing back a few strands that had pulled loose from her ponytail.

"It is at that," Rueben acknowledged.

After a moment she said, "I asked Father if he saw anyone around the lighthouse, but he didn't remember anything about the accident. He did say though, that he saw my mother. At first I thought it was because of his concussion. Then I wondered if he had seen the woman you saw."

"Perhaps. Still, the thing that's got me flummoxed is that I can't imagine a woman in the entire U.S. of A. that would keep quiet about seeing Matthew just before he fell. Women are the gabbiest creatures on the planet."

"Is that so?" Celena huffed.

"Now, no need to get upset. I'm just stating a fact. But that started me wondering. Seems there are only three reasons to keep quiet," Rueben said darkly. "Either she had something to do with his falling, she saw something that scared her, or else she had her tongue cut out."

Celena felt slightly sick. Could it be possible that someone had been involved in her father's fall? She shook her head. That was just crazy. Then again, perhaps she ought to look at the equipment herself sometime. That might give her some answers.

* * *

Doc Harrison was just coming out of Matthew's bedroom, carrying his familiar black bag, when Celena and Rueben approached. He was a fastidious little man who wore old-fashioned shirts with cellophane collars. His hat was tilted at a cocky angle.

"Hi, Doc," Rueben greeted him. "Celena wanted to talk to you, so I'll go on in and see Matthew."

"How is he today?" Celena asked.

"Ready to bite my head off because I haven't got a magic cure that will let him jump out of bed," Doc Harrison said good-naturedly. "He's got a fever today and has some congestion in his lungs. I told Helen to watch him closely and left some medicine with her. It'll make him drowsy and disoriented, so don't let that worry you, but I don't want this developing into pneumonia."

"Can you tell me how long it will take his leg to heal?"

"Tibia fractures can take anywhere from ten to sixteen weeks, but this was an open, comminuted fracture, so I'm guessing four to six months. Possibly longer." Doc Harrison did some mental calculating. "I'll be able to shorten the top of the cast in about nine weeks. Hopefully by then, we'll be able to rule out nerve damage. Even if there is some residual numbness, he could just need more time. Some injuries take years before a full recovery is made. Any other questions?"

"Nothing medical, but Zach told Joshua that you'd said there was going to be a new lighthouse keeper. That really worried Joshua. You see, he wants to run the light when he's older. Joshua thinks if they bring in a new keeper, he won't be able to run the light himself."

The doctor looked perplexed. "Zach must have overheard my wife and me talking. We wondered if they would send out a new keeper. But we don't know anything for sure."

"I found out that Helen wants to buy the light if they close it."

"Does she now?" He looked startled. "I suppose she hopes it will bring in more customers. She's been doing whatever she can to turn a profit."

"I thought Bay Haven was doing very well."

Doc Harrison shook his head. "She's been struggling for years. That's why she started taking in more nursing patients." He glanced at his pocket watch. "Well, I'd better be off."

She watched him leave. Hadn't Lydia said Bay Haven was doing well? As Celena went down the hall, she tried to recall exactly what Lydia had said. When she reached her father's door, it was ajar, allowing Rueben's voice to come through. "She's grown into a beautiful young woman, hasn't she?"

Celena stopped.

"She's the image of her mother," Matthew replied in an uncharacteristically soft voice.

"I hope you told her so."

There was a great silence.

"Thought so," Rueben snapped in disgust. "Stubborn old fool. Won't ever tell the girl what you're really thinking. That's what caused all the problems before. Don't you ever learn?"

"She didn't want to hear anything I had to say." Although the words were muted, there was such sadness tied up in them that Celena was caught full in the chest. Still, her father had it backward. *He* was the one who wouldn't listen to *her!*

"All I can say is that since you've got a second chance, you better take advantage of it. Talk to her. You want to lose her all over again?"

She couldn't listen to any more and pushed the door open. Rueben's faded blue eyes looked startled. Celena kept her voice level. "Hello, Father. How are you?"

"For a stubborn old fool, I guess I'm about where I should be," he said grumpily.

Rueben got to his feet. "I'll be going now. See you two later."

She went to Matthew's bedside, noticing that his face was flushed and there was a sheen of sweat on his forehead. "Can I get you anything?"

"Aye. Get me out of here." The words were light but his tone was leaden, and it had taken an effort to get the words out. There was a strange welling up of fear against her ribs. Celena poured water into a basin, dipped a cloth in, and began sponging his face. The fact that he didn't object alarmed her more than anything else. His breathing was heavy and sounded raspy.

When Helen came to sit with Matthew so she could go to the light, Celena pulled his blanket up and tucked it in before leaving.

* * *

Celena and Joshua left for the lighthouse and were halfway there when Celena heard a noise. She stopped and a deer emerged. They often popped up unexpectedly, standing for a few moments like statues before bounding off, showing the whites of their tails. At the light, brother and sister took turns lugging the kerosene up. Joshua insisted on filling the tank, and after he wound the clockworks, they went up to the lantern room, then out to the catwalk. Dusk was settling and the sky was a mixture of pinks, oranges, and violets, with the last rays casting halos around a few fluffy clouds. Seagulls were making their last circles over the bay. Fishing boats would be slapping against each other at dockside. It was as good a time as any for the conversation she had planned.

"Joshua, I talked to Doc Harrison," Celena began. "It's going to take a long time for Father to get well." His brown eyes were large and solemn. "You know that I have to get back to my job. It would be a lot easier for me to take care of Father if I took him back to Maryland."

He looked puzzled. "But we have to run the light."

"Well, someone else could do that. Maybe Clint."

From the look on his face, Celena might have suggested that he leap off the catwalk. "But if we don't run it, they're going to give it to someone else!" Joshua's voice was panicky.

"You don't know that for sure. And it will be great to all be together in Maryland. You like it there," she reminded him desperately. "Remember how much fun we had there every summer?"

He looked troubled. "We can be together *here.* You said you'd help me."

"The doctor said it could take four months, maybe even six, before Father's leg heals. I don't think I can stay that long."

Joshua faced her directly, his expression distressed and his eyes tearing up. "I want to run the light when I grow up! You *told* me you'd help me run it!" His voice was accusing now.

"I don't even know if the Lighthouse Bureau will let me run it."

"Have you asked them?" Joshua stood stiffly, watching her face. When she didn't reply, he seemed to relax. "I bet they'll let you," he said reassuringly.

Celena sighed. Things had not gone as well as she'd hoped.

When Clint came, he looked in awe at the Fresnel light, with its prisms and bull's-eyes that sparkled like jewels. Celena did some admiring of her own, looking at his firm jaw, straight nose, and deep-set eyes. After a few moments they went outside, where white, frothy waves were breaking on the shore in an endless cycle.

"This is magnificent! No wonder your father never wants to give it up," he said, putting a strong, tanned arm around Joshua's shoulder. "We must have the best jobs on earth."

It *was* lovely. There was a twinkling of lights from towns along the island. In the ocean, a faint phosphorescence shining from the crests of the breaking waves created a ghostly effect. Looking out at the thin band of land that made up Fire Island, Celena said, "The island is so narrow it looks like the ocean could just wash it away without any effort at all."

"When you think about all the storms Fire Island has withstood over the centuries, it's a wonder the island's survived long enough to become inhabited," Clint commented.

"Not only survived, but become bigger," Celena said, pointing west. "I remember my grandfather telling me that the lighthouse used to be much closer to the end of the island."

Joshua looked puzzled. "You mean the island's growing?"

"Actually, it is." Celena laughed. "Fire Island is almost three thousand acres now."

"Have you heard of littoral drift?" Clint asked Joshua, who shook his head. "Well, that's the dominant ocean current. It moves in a southwesterly direction, carrying sand along with it. So it erodes the eastern end of the island while piling up sand at the west end."

Celena nodded at her brother. "It's true. The western end of the island has gotten bigger. Father has some old maps that show what the island used to be like."

Clint was interested. "Does he really? I'd love to see them."

The time passed enjoyably, and it wasn't until Joshua started yawning that Celena looked at her watch. "You need to get to bed, Joshua, if we're going to Clearwater tomorrow." He went reluctantly to the watch room where they had cots. When Celena wandered over to the windows, her skin began to prickle. In the distance, lights were flickering along the shore. Holding very still, she whispered, "Clint! Come here." When he was close, she asked, "What do you think it is? Lydia said there's a ghost."

"I hardly think ghosts would need lights," Clint said with some amusement.

"Do you think it could be rumrunners?"

Clint looked doubtful. "From what I've heard, they're farther up the coast. They'd have to be pretty daring to come to this end of the island with the Coast Guard station nearby. I'll go and check things out. I'm sure it's just a bunch of kids."

She grabbed his arm. "But what if it *is* smugglers?"

"If it is, they're probably just fishermen trying to make a few bucks on the side. They'll scatter fast." He gave her a reassuring smile. "Don't worry."

She gave him the key so he could let himself back in, then waited anxiously, watching out the windows. After a time, the lights disappeared. Celena didn't know whether to be relieved or anxious. It seemed like hours before Clint pushed at the trapdoor, making her jump. He smiled sympathetically.

"You look scared. It's all right. It was just as I thought—a bunch of kids fooling around on a Friday night." He chuckled. "You should have seen them scatter when they saw me. I bet they thought *I* was a ghost."

SIX

Each morning at Bay Haven, chafing dishes were placed on a large mahogany sideboard in the dining room so people could help themselves to breakfast. The construction workers were up early. Next to rise were the tourists, and last to eat were Joshua and Celena. Today, when Joshua finished, he went into the foyer, and Celena heard him eagerly inform someone, "I'm going to Clearwater for a tour!"

"Are you now?" a man's deep voice answered. "I'm headed that way myself."

"My sister's going too," Joshua was saying as Celena walked out. He turned to her and said brightly, "Daniel's going over to Clearwater too! We can all go together!"

"Oh! Isn't that nice," Celena replied hesitantly, feeling Daniel's penetrating brown eyes on her. Today he was dressed in tan pants and a white shirt with sleeves rolled back at the cuffs. He looked quite rugged and attractive. "Joshua, Father wasn't feeling very well this morning, and I forgot to remind him that we were going to Clearwater. Will you run and make sure he knows?"

After he scampered off, Celena turned to Daniel. "I think we got off on the wrong foot. I didn't mean to be secretive the other day. I was just caught up in my own personal issues. I've come home to a rather difficult situation."

Daniel's face softened. "Naturally you're upset about your father's accident."

It was tempting to let him think that was the only reason, but it wasn't strictly the truth. "That's part of it." She paused. "I left Fire Island five years ago because of some . . . uh . . . problems with my father. This is the first time I've been back."

"Oh, I see." Daniel looked concerned but was too much of a gentleman to probe. "I hope everything works out," he said as Joshua came running back, cutting their conversation short.

The day was drenched in May sunlight. Peonies, flag lilies, and poppies were blooming in many of the gardens they passed, and the buds of early roses were swelling. Daniel moved with an easy grace, and he and Celena talked comfortably as, high overhead, a few seagulls drifted aimlessly in the light breeze.

With its many-paned windows gleaming, Clearwater was large and impressive. Built of red brick, it had a cobblestone entryway leading up to regal white columns that marked the entrance. Barrels of petunias, marigolds, and salvia lined the driveway, and the lawns that sloped toward the beach were lined with flowerbeds that added more bright splashes of color.

Inside, the walls of the lobby were of gold damask. The deep pile carpet was a pale buff, and the chairs, tables, and sofas were creamy white. It was strikingly elegant. Daniel led the way to Gerald's office, which was heavily paneled in dark walnut and had a large number of rifles and pistols displayed on the wall. Gerald, wearing an immaculate gray suit, pushed back his chair when they entered and, smiling broadly, came around to take their hands in a warm clasp.

"I'm so glad you're here!" Gerald exclaimed in his loud voice. "What do you think so far?" He then rubbed his hand lovingly along the walnut desk with its ornately carved legs and remarked, "It's Victorian, you know. Helen has been teaching me about furniture and went with me to pick it out. Follow me."

Celena found it odd that Helen would help Gerald, considering they were more or less in competition, but she decided not to pursue what could be a touchy subject. And she quickly forgot this oddity as they began their tour.

She and Joshua were awed by everything, from the spacious kitchen to the well-appointed guestrooms, and finally the enormous ballroom, which opened onto a huge patio that had steps leading to the beach. Gerald was as proud as if he'd personally placed every timber and mortared every brick.

During the tour, Celena took the opportunity to study father and son. She decided that, except for their eyes, Daniel resembled his father very little. Gerald's face was round and red, as if he had been out in the sun too long, while Daniel's was square and deeply tan. There seemed to be deeper differences as well. While both men appeared confident, Gerald's jolly demeanor tended toward brash and boastful while Daniel's was unpretentious yet quietly commanding. And while Gerald was light-hearted, there seemed to be a curious air of vigilance about Daniel.

The towering lighthouse stood off to the west, as if presiding over the island. On their right, a sickle sweep of a cove bit into the shore, and Gerald pointed out his private boathouse, gleaming whitely against the shining blue of the water. When Celena dutifully admired it, Daniel said unexpectedly, "It's a perfect cove for rumrunners."

Although he seemed to be speaking to no one in particular, Celena sensed that something lay behind his words. Gerald's eyes crinkled with amusement. "Are you thinking of going into the business?"

When Daniel didn't rise to the bait, Celena asked, "Why is it a good place for smugglers?"

"Because the curve of the beach hides it from view, and the cove is far enough away from town that smugglers won't be seen," Daniel replied.

Gerald explained further. "You see, Celena, big ships loaded with liquor stay anchored offshore. When the coast is clear, they load up smaller boats and bring their cases to shore."

Celena was puzzled. "Why doesn't the Coast Guard do something about the big ships?"

"They're careful to anchor in international waters where the Coast Guard has no jurisdiction."

Daniel added, "It used to be that ships could stay three miles offshore without being seized, but last year, the United States reached an international agreement with other countries, and now ships have to stay twelve miles away from the coast."

"Thanks for the tip. I'll be more careful next time," Celena said.

Gerald was laughing raucously when Clint came striding toward them. "What do you think of the place?" Clint asked with a flash of that white smile as he held out his arms wide to encompass all of Clearwater.

"It's magnificent," Celena said sincerely.

Clint seemed pleased. "How is your father?"

"Not good. He has a fever and might be coming down with pneumonia."

"That was a terrible accident," Gerald commented, shaking his heavy jowls.

"I hear you were the one who called the doctor," Celena said. "Do you have any idea how he fell?"

Gerald looked at her oddly. "I thought the rope broke."

"But Father was always so careful about his equipment. Rueben said he saw someone around the lighthouse—a woman. Did you see who it was?" Was it her imagination, or did Gerald look faintly alarmed? If so, he recovered almost instantaneously.

He was saved from answering because just then, a young, anxious-looking man with a black goatee came to the patio and beckoned to Gerald. An animated discussion ensued, with Gerald excitedly waving his arms. Finally Clint walked over. He listened intently, then spoke in low tones. The young man, looking relieved, scurried away.

When the two men came back, Daniel asked, "What's going on?"

Gerald waved a hand airily. "Just a little problem. Some of these employees get into a lather about nothing, but I've dealt with it."

"I'd better be on my way," Clint said, then caught Celena's eye. "It was wonderful to see you," he added in a way that made her feel special.

After he left, Celena looked at Gerald. "I'm glad Clint was able to help."

Gerald looked dubious. "Yes. He, uh, knows a lot about the resort."

"He should," Daniel said pointedly, "since he owns part of it."

Celena was surprised. "I didn't know that."

"I'm the one who takes care of the day-to-day management," Gerald maintained, his chest puffed out slightly. "Now, Celena, I wanted to ask you about your plans regarding the lighthouse."

"That's just what I wanted to talk to you about," she replied. "Why do you want the light if the bureau decides to close it?"

"*When* the bureau decides to close it," Gerald amended jovially. "Combining the lighthouse with Clearwater will make an unbeatable destination for people planning vacations. If I print up brochures of the resort with the lighthouse, tourists will come out in droves."

Joshua piped up. "But Celena and I are going to run the light."

Gerald turned to her in surprise. "You're not really thinking about staying, are you, Celena? If you did, the bureau might decide not to close it."

Celena wanted to assure him she had no intention of staying, but that was impossible with her brother standing beside her. She said uncomfortably, "I've told Joshua I'll stay for a little while."

"It's far too soon to be thinking about expanding anyway," Daniel told his father. "The last thing you need is to become overextended." There was an edge to his voice—some sort of under-the-surface conflict Celena didn't understand.

Joshua wanted to make things perfectly clear. "Celena's going to run the light until Father gets better. Then I'll be the keeper."

"Last time I checked," Gerald replied amiably, "they weren't letting eleven-year-old boys run lighthouses."

His superior tone irritated Celena. "What about twenty-four-year-old women?"

"Surely you're not serious." Gerald smiled indulgently. "You're young and attractive, and the last thing you need to worry your pretty little head about is running a lighthouse. Besides, the bureau will want their own keeper. I doubt they'd let you run it." His smile seemed benign, but she had the feeling that something more lay behind that placid expression.

Joshua was shuffling his feet, anxious to go, as was Celena. "Well, you've done a splendid job," she said. "Everything looks wonderful."

Gerald was delighted at the compliment. "You're a woman of good taste. Say, that gives me an idea. Why don't you and Joshua come to lunch when my chef arrives in a few weeks? I'd like to put him through his paces."

"That's very tempting," Celena began, "but won't you be too busy?"

Looking chagrined, Gerald complained to Daniel, "Why does she always say I'm too busy? I'm supposed to be busy! Aren't I running the biggest resort on the island?" He turned to Celena. "Please come. It will be good to give the kitchen staff a run-through. And Daniel will come too, won't you?" He looked at his son enthusiastically.

"I wouldn't miss it," Daniel said heartily.

"Perhaps Helen could come," Gerald said, rubbing his hands together. "She'll be able to critique the food—she always has the most wonderful ideas." He turned to Celena. "Helen's the one who suggested I hire Ethan. Top-notch advice. He's a hard worker. A bit solitary, mind you, but he does a thorough job. It was a shame about his wife drowning."

"Yes, it was a terrible thing."

"Rather odd, isn't it, that she went out in a boat by herself when she was scared of the water?" Gerald remarked. "Didn't know how to swim."

"I didn't know that." Celena was about to make a further comment, but Joshua had had enough.

"Can I go to the beach?"

"Why don't we all go?" Daniel suggested, but Gerald begged off, saying he had business to attend to.

On the beach, Joshua started digging a trench to connect two small tide pools, so Daniel and Celena walked along the shoreline. Birds scattered in a vast gray, brown, and white cloud, screeching their disapproval of the human interlopers. Celena and Daniel continued until they reached a rocky outcropping. Other than the call of the gulls and the rhythmic slap of waves on the beach, there was no sound at all in the great expanse of salt-scoured air and bright light. Celena picked her way down the steep slope to the water.

"Come here," she said to Daniel, "I want to show you something. When the tide is right, you can see mussels here. They grow in clusters on the reefs." Stepping into the water, Celena reached out and tore one free. Using her fingers, she spread the cottony threads that had held the mussel to its rock. "This is the byssus, which is spun by a gland in the mussel's foot. It uses those threads to lash itself in place."

"Like Ulysses to his mast."

Celena smiled. "That's right. Once he picks a spot, he doesn't move but stays put for life." She turned the shell over in her hand. It was nearly six inches long. "This is an old one," she declared, bouncing the mussel in her hand. "They grow quickly in the beginning, some more than three inches their first year. After that, they don't grow as fast. Have you got a pocketknife?" Daniel reached into his pocket and handed one over. She shoved it through the hinge and there was a tearing sound as she pried open the shell.

"He's orange!" Daniel said in surprise.

Celena looked at the mussel that was as brightly orange as a pumpkin. "It makes him unique, don't you think? Different from oysters and clams."

"Are mussels related to oysters?"

"Yes," Celena replied. "But oysters are rather pedestrian. An oyster wouldn't dare be orange. Another amazing fact you can astonish your friends with is that a mussel doesn't have a brain. No heart or lungs either. He's mostly a stomach."

Daniel laughed as Celena pointed out how the shellfish were clustered together. "Mussels are stay-at-home creatures, happy to munch away on microscopic plants and animals. A few have pearls, but they're not worth anything."

"How'd you learn all this?"

"Oh, my father taught me. He was interested in anything to do with the ocean." Celena threw the mussel in the water.

"Will it reattach itself to the rock?"

"No. Its byssus is broken. I took him away from the place he'd set himself down in, and now he's a goner."

On their way back, Celena talked to Daniel about Joshua's plans. She even told him a little about her problems with her father. It was amazing how quickly she had come to feel at ease with Daniel. Celena explained how she was going to take her father and Joshua to Maryland.

"I assumed you were going to run the light," Daniel said with more than a touch of surprise in his voice. "But either way, I hope you can work things out with your father."

Picking up a stray leaf, Celena tore it to bits. "At times, I still feel hurt by some of the things that happened before I left," she admitted.

"If you ever want to talk, I'm a good listener." Daniel touched her hand lightly. It was a gesture of compassion, of sympathy, and she felt a rush of warmth. "I know it can be hard to talk, but it's not good to keep everything bottled up inside."

Celena studied him intently, then gave him a slight smile. Daniel took her arm and they started back along the shoreline to find Joshua.

* * *

On their way home, Joshua decided to go to Zach's house, so Celena was alone as she went up the sidewalk to Bay Haven. Glancing up, she saw a curtain drop back down into place. She wondered who had been watching until Helen walked into the foyer a few moments later.

Celena decided to ask a question she'd been meaning to ever since talking with Ethan. "Did you know Ethan's watching the beach?"

Helen's smooth face registered no surprise, though it was there in her voice. "Why would he be doing that?"

"Apparently, Sarina told him that if she ever left and didn't come back, he was to watch the beach. Do you have any idea why she would say something like that?"

Helen's voice was chill. "Actually, it's quite possible she didn't. Sometimes Ethan has a hard time telling the difference between fantasy and reality."

"I suppose you know Ethan doesn't think his wife's death was an accident."

Helen's unruffled demeanor told Celena that she was well aware of it. "My brother lives in his own world. It's best not to pay a lot of attention when he gets these bizarre ideas." She looked at Celena with those pale eyes. "Your father was asking for you earlier. I asked Minerva to sit with him until you got back. He was rambling a bit because of the medication."

* * *

Matthew Jackson's eyes were closed, and there was a furrowed line between his brows. His face was pinched and shrunken, his chin whiskered with gray stubble. There was a faint smell of Mentholatum in the air, and his hands lay quietly atop the white sheet.

"I'll stay with him," Celena whispered to Minerva, who nodded without speaking, her eyes friendly. When Celena sat down in the chair Minerva had just vacated, it made a protesting sound. At that same moment—as if the two were intrinsically connected—her father opened his eyes. Matthew's cheeks were so flushed they were almost vermilion, and his eyes, which had a feverish glitter, had sunk back into the flesh around them.

"What happened at the light?" he asked heavily in a worried tone.

"Nothing happened. Everything's fine."

"No, it was wrong," he protested, looking anxious and confused. "The flash pattern."

Unsure what he meant, she said, "I was there, everything's fine. Are you saying it would be wrong for the bureau to close the light?"

"No, no! The light," Matthew said thickly. "It changed. I won't have it."

Celena tried to reassure him. "Don't worry, they aren't going to change anything right now. Joshua and I are taking care of everything."

He closed his eyes, but ten minutes later, he stirred again. Peering at her with an odd, vacant look, he asked querulously, "You got those prisms cleaned yet, Lena?" Her father hadn't called her that since she was fifteen. She stood to feel his forehead, but Matthew pushed her hand away grumpily, as if shooing away a pesky mosquito. "You check the oil level?" At this, Celena allowed herself a small smile. If she'd heard that question once while growing up, she'd heard it a million times. This was the first time it hadn't made her want to run screaming out into the night.

"Yes, yes." She soothed him as if he were a baby. "That's the first thing I do, you know that."

"Aye. I could always count on you." She felt a surprising trickle of pleasure at his words. His eyelids fluttered shut. Minutes ticked by. When Matthew opened his eyes again, they seemed out of focus.

Celena leaned forward. "Are you all right?"

"Don't know what's the matter with me, dozing off like that." The words were sluggish. "Where are the children?"

She stared until he repeated his question, his voice a thin thread. "The children, Elizabeth, where are they?" It took him a great effort to get the words out.

Elizabeth. He thought she was Elizabeth. Fear began rising in his eyes at her silence. She had to say something. "Uh, Tana is watching them."

"I feel strange," he said gravely. "Have I been drinking?" He made a move as if to rise.

"Oh, no you don't!" Celena cried, standing up and pressing her hands against his shoulders.

His brows lowered in outrage. "What do you think you're doing?"

"Stopping you from hurting yourself."

He glowered at her furiously. "I've got to get to the light!" He didn't seem to notice the cast on his leg, nor the sunlight coming through the window.

She thought quickly, knowing that if she didn't reassure him sufficiently, he would crawl to the lighthouse on his hands and knees. "Rueben's watching it."

Matthew stopped struggling. "Ah, Rueben. Takes good care of the light. Like my father." His voice sounded a little stronger, though his eyes were still glassy. "Father tried to teach me but I didn't want to learn. Boys are rebellious creatures." Looking at Celena, he admonished her, "Don't ever be a boy."

She raised a hand to hide her smile.

He went on. "Wanted to go to sea."

"And you did. When you were fourteen."

"Aye. Got that out of my blood. Decided I wanted the light after all. Met you." There was a change in his face. "Didn't think you'd look twice at me." Celena's mother had told her how shy Matthew had been around girls. "Your folks thought you were crazy for marrying a keeper. But you loved it. Bit of a tomboy, you were."

Celena spoke softly, "I could climb those stairs faster than you. But then, you insisted on carrying my basket up so I could knit or mend while you cleaned prisms and polished the brass."

"Free as birds. In our own world." Matthew looked at her for confirmation, and when Celena nodded, he added, "Couldn't live anywhere else. Hated cities." Celena remembered occasionally accompanying her father to New York City; he had always seemed ill at ease there.

When Matthew spoke again, his voice was thick with what sounded like sorrow. "Only time I went willingly was when Lena left." Celena felt her body freeze as her father went on. "Like cat and dog, we were. Wouldn't listen. Lost my temper." Matthew's chest moved with rapid, shallow breaths. "I went to your folks. But they said Lena didn't want to see me."

Her heart flew up inside her ribs like a wild sparrow trapped in a cage—beating its wings so hard it felt likely to leave her entirely. It wasn't possible. He *couldn't* have come to Maryland. Her grandparents would have told her. But then again, *would they?* Even as a small child, Celena had known that the relationship between her father and her mother's parents was a bitter one. Over the years, she'd learned that their high hopes for their only child had been dashed when Matthew had taken Elizabeth to what they considered a life of deprivation on Fire Island. When Celena had shown up on their doorstep, white-faced with misery and anger, they had listened to her tale of woe, nodding as if it were only to be expected. Still, it was hard to believe they had said nothing of his visit.

She bent closer. "You went after Lena?" She hated hearing the anguish in her voice.

"Oh, aye."

She trembled all over, a fine shivering. A deep, inner part of her was tingling, as when circulation is finally restored after being cut off for a time. She had to know more. "Did . . . did you miss Lena?" It was a cry from the deepest core of her, where the child that still loved him lived. Unconsciously, Celena held her breath as if she were standing on ice that had begun to crack. Matthew held very still. A tear crept out of the corner of one eye, trailing down his face. The silence was so intense that she could almost hear her heart thumping against her ribcage. Finally he spoke in a faint voice, shutting his eyes so tightly that bunches of wrinkles gathered in deep folds around the outer edges of his eyes.

"It was like the light had gone out."

Tears, thick and briny, gathered behind her eyelids, and Celena had the eerie feeling that sand was shifting under her feet, preventing her from gaining a foothold. Her thoughts scattered like a broken strand of beads on the floor, and she had a hard time gathering them in. Sitting down in the chair as heavily as if she'd been thrown there, she fought to regain control long after her father fell into a restless sleep, a deep V between his closed eyes.

* * *

That night as she rode to the lighthouse with Joshua, Celena was aware that an indefinable melting had begun—a dissolving of the ice that had entombed her for so long. It felt as if her blood was suddenly flowing again. For during the past five years, no matter how far down she stuffed it, there had always been a longing to reconnect with her father, even though Celena was not sure she could ever forgive him for ordering her to leave. Now, after being bound for so long, something inside had lightened and broken free.

By the time Celena leaned her bike against the lighthouse, Joshua had already filled the jug of kerosene and gone inside. She climbed, aware of the damp, musty odor of old stones, and found him waiting in the service room, his young face alight with eagerness. Joshua poured the kerosene into the holding tank, then pumped air into it to create enough pressure to feed the mantle above. After winding the clockwork assembly so the lens would revolve, they went up to the lantern room, which was as round and small and enfolding as a cocoon. When it was time to start the light, Joshua leaned over and touched the flame carefully to the wick, his face a study in concentration. Celena thought herself happy at that moment. She felt useful and needed, a feeling she'd missed. When the mantle began to glow, Joshua pulled back, wearing a self-satisfied smile.

The sun dropped from sight, and a tender shaving of new moon rose in the sky, almost transparent as it rode far above the ocean. A few stars bloomed beside it, the first ones of the new night. When it was time for bed, she and Joshua went down to the watch room. Her brother fell asleep quickly, but Celena lay awake with her thoughts, listening to the lapping sounds of the ocean and the occasional cry of a night bird.

Finally Celena gave up. She had to check. But first, she went to stand over Joshua, bending over to smooth his hair back from his forehead. He looked happy and utterly at peace. Climbing up to the lantern room, she looked outside and there it was: a light on the beach. A single one instead of a half dozen like the night before, and quite near the lighthouse. Celena fetched the binoculars, but they were useless in the dark. All she could tell was that the person was wearing a dark cap and either a large billowing coat or blanket. The figure began receding until he was a tiny speck, then disappeared altogether.

It took a long time for Celena to fall asleep.

* * *

The next morning was Sunday. Although Celena had planned to hurry back to Bay Haven to get ready for church, she took time to look around the lighthouse, hoping to find some clue as to the identity of the late-night visitor, but there was nothing. Joshua had scoffed at her worries that Father might object to him going to church with her, so Celena put that out of her mind. Matthew was tired and feverish when they stopped to see him before leaving for Sunday School, but at least he was not disoriented any longer. Celena was sure he remembered nothing from the night before.

During the following week, the doctor came out regularly, since Matthew had developed pneumonia. Matthew spent most of his time sleeping but had a few visitors, most of them friends from the Lighthouse Bureau. On Friday morning it rained in earnest, rushing straight down and bouncing back up, with great forks of lightning splitting the sky, followed by gigantic bellows of thunder. During the storm, Celena tried to read but often found herself staring at nothing. It still caused a warm glow inside her to think that her father had actually gone after her. In the middle of the afternoon, the clouds broke apart, and Celena flung down her book. Perhaps a walk along the beach would help order her thoughts and release some of the restless anxiety that would not let her be still.

Everything shone wet outside, with trees, fences, and even the road glistening. The beach was nearly deserted as she walked idly along. All reality seemed blurred, and the distant sounds were subdued by a faint white mist blowing in from the Atlantic. The ocean was still angry after the storm, boiling against rocks and sending streams of spray high in the air. There were a few black clouds scudding by to the north, but the sky was a glorious azalea color in the west. With her eyes on the tall, graceful tower that reached far into the deep blue sky, Celena crossed to the wet band above the tide where the sand was hard-packed. As the gray waves washed in, they ended in a creaming curl that withdrew before it touched her feet.

Going to her favorite spot, Celena sat taking in the sound of the waves and the scent of the ocean. She had been happy in Maryland, Celena told herself. She had. Still, there had been an underlying emptiness that prickled at unexpected moments. Ever since the revelation that her father had gone after her, there had been a luminous warmth in her bones—a restoration of sorts. And, as clear as if it had been outlined in silver, there was the realization that something new could begin. Peace hung in the air like smoke, and she listened to the roar of the incoming waves as if it had secrets to tell, feeling that she was in a cocoon, getting ready to burst free. Celena had almost forgotten what it was like to have the ocean as her backyard, and a sense of oneness with the island filled her to overflowing.

She looked up to see a woman headed in her direction. As she drew near, Celena recognized Lydia's blond hair, curvy figure, and carefree gait. Celena stood to meet her.

"Enjoying the beach before you leave?" Lydia asked brightly.

"Yes. Soaking it all in. I wanted to ask you something. There's been someone around the lighthouse the last two nights. I wondered if you knew who it was."

"You can't say I didn't warn you."

"I don't believe in ghosts."

"You're a Mormon—you believe in spirits."

"Not the same thing. But if you and your friends are getting tired of being out late, you can stop," Celena said bluntly.

Lydia was not taken aback in the least. "Believe me, dear-heart, I've got better things to do at night. There are plenty of live men around to keep me company. I don't need dead ones."

"Are you telling me you don't know anything about it?" Celena was skeptical.

"Oh, I know *all* about it. It's the ghost of a bloodthirsty mooncusser who wants to take revenge on whoever runs the lighthouse." Lydia pointed a scarlet-tipped finger at Celena and grinned wickedly. "That means *you*. Good thing you're going back to Maryland."

"I may be going back, but not because you or someone else is trying to scare me. By the way, I found out that Bay Haven isn't doing too well, but you told me the opposite. Why?"

Lydia wore a little cat's smile, smug and sly. "I simply said there were no worries. If you made a wrong assumption from that, don't blame me." Lydia waved a hand airily. "Besides, we'll do fine once the tourist season hits. And when mother gets the light, we'll have so much money we'll be able to wallpaper the place with it."

"The lighthouse isn't going to be sold," Celena stated with more conviction than she felt. "I've talked to both Rueben and Clint about it."

Lydia arched an eyebrow. "Maybe they didn't talk to the people who know what's going on, like Mother did."

"Helen had no right to call the Lighthouse Bureau and tell them Father was permanently disabled." Celena clenched her fists in outrage. "There's a chance he might recover just fine."

"There's a bigger chance he won't. Besides, Mother found out something interesting when she called—that the Fire Island light has been put on the 'not vital' list. And with your father out of the picture and you leaving, there won't be a keeper. That should be enough to make them put the light on the 'close down' list." There was a slight change in Lydia's expression. "But since you're leaving, what do you care? By the way, does your brother know you're not going to stay and run the light?"

"I haven't told him yet," Celena said wearily.

"Exactly what *are* your plans?"

"I already told you. I'm taking Joshua and Father back to Maryland as soon as Father can travel."

Lydia put on a self-satisfied smile as she looked over Celena's shoulder. Celena whirled around.

Joshua was standing there, ashen-faced, his mouth hanging slightly open. Celena was frightened by the look of naked horror and betrayal on his face.

"You lied," her brother choked out. "You *told* me you were going to stay." Celena reached out for him, but he backed away. "You *lied!*" he repeated unbelievingly, his eyes enormous with hurt. "You said you'd come and help." The pain in his voice made her cringe. Then, in an instant, Joshua's look changed from hurt to fury. "I'm not going and you can't make me." With that, he turned and began to run.

"Joshua, don't go!" Celena cried. "Let me explain." She ran after him, but he was more agile than she was in climbing the dunes. Reaching the boardwalk, he yanked his bike upright. Once more, Celena called to him to stop. She got close enough to see the gleam of tears on his cheeks before he gave her one last baleful glare and began pedaling away furiously.

SEVEN

By evening, Joshua still hadn't returned to Bay Haven. Nor was his bicycle at Zach's house. Alone at the lighthouse, Celena went to the catwalk to watch for him. In the west, scarlet-stained clouds threw a pinkish sheen on the ocean. Joshua's absence from his beloved light made it clear just how profoundly wounded he was.

The next morning, the mist was rising from the water as Celena extinguished the light and raced to Bay Haven. But when she threw open her door, Joshua's bed had not been slept in. Celena peeked in her father's room. No Joshua.

Matthew saw her, and when she didn't enter the room, grumbled, "Disappointed I'm still here?"

She walked in. "I thought Joshua might be here."

Looking confused, Matthew said, "Isn't he in school?"

"It's Saturday."

He shook his head. "I've lost track of time. Open the curtains, will you? Helen keeps it like a morgue in here." Once again, Celena noticed the bare wall and wondered why Helen had left it that way. Brushing the thought away, she noticed that Matthew's congestion was better, but he was still frail and prone to bouts of coughing.

"Is there anything I can get you?" Celena asked. When he looked pointedly at his leg, she added, "Besides a new leg, I mean?"

"If you can't do that, you're no good to me at all!" His voice was crusty as ever, but Celena could hear the dry humor behind it.

Smiling slightly, she said, "I'll be back later."

Celena went to the phone in the foyer and dialed Zach's house. Doc Harrison answered. "I don't think he's here. The boys had a sleepover last night, but I think Joshua got up early. Zach would know. Hold on." Zach came to the phone and confirmed that Joshua had already left.

"Do you know where Joshua was going?"

"No, but he was acting really weird." Zach sounded distressed.

"What's the matter?"

"That's hard to explain, but if you happen to see Joshua, tell him I'm looking for him."

* * *

Celena was riding along Lighthouse Promenade when she saw Tana in her front yard wearing a wide-brimmed straw hat, attacking a bush with long-handled pruning shears.

Straddling her bike, Celena asked, "Have you seen Joshua?"

"Not today. Why?"

Celena quickly explained, then added, "I wanted to ask you something. Lydia told me that the bureau would be more likely to close Fire Island if I didn't stay. Do you think that's true?"

"That girl has a big mouth," Tana grumbled, "but I have to agree with her on this one. Not having a keeper would definitely be a deciding factor if the bureau really is considering closing the light. Especially when they know it's going to be months before your father recovers."

"And there's a good chance he might *not*." Celena watched a butterfly flit by erratically. "So, even if I did stay, Father could still lose the light in the end. Besides, the bureau might not let me run it while he recuperates."

"A face-to-face chat with them would clear that question up fast enough, but the bureau has a firm tradition of loyalty to keepers and their families." Tana was definite. "They're very good about letting lights stay in the family, as long as you pass their inspections."

Celena was anxious to get on her way. "Thanks, Tana. I'm going to keep looking for Joshua."

"Have you checked the docks? Rueben's there—he might have seen him."

Celena headed there, biking through town. In front of the fresh-fish market, she had to veer around a couple looking over bluefish and flounder lying on a bed of ice. At the dock, the sharp odors of fish, wet burlap, and lumber filled the air. On a post in the harbor, an osprey watched for fish. She found Rueben sitting on a bench, working on his nets.

She had no time for preambles. "Have you seen Joshua?"

He shook his head, looking faintly amused. "Ran out on his chores, did he?"

Celena recounted what had happened. "If I could just talk with Joshua, I think I could make him understand. Right now he's upset and can't see any side other than his own."

"Yeah, *some* people are like that," Rueben replied sardonically.

She looked at him sharply. "I suppose by that, you mean me."

Rueben changed the subject. "How did it go at the light last night?"

"Good. But someone was down on the beach again with a light. Lydia says it's a ghost."

"Probably my Aunt Margaret," Rueben deadpanned. "She does that a lot."

Celena told him about Clint and how he had scared a group of kids off, then said, "Rueben?"

He squinted up at her, his face shaded by his brimmed cap.

"You'd tell me the truth wouldn't you?" she asked uncertainly.

"If it suited my purposes."

"Do you know if my father came to see me after I left?"

The net fell from his hands. "Oh, Celena. Of course he did."

Her eyes filled with tears. "Why didn't you tell me? All these years and you never said a word," Celena said accusingly.

Rueben looked at her. "What was there to say when you refused to see him? When you wouldn't take his calls?"

"What calls?" But from the disconcerted look on Rueben's face, Celena knew exactly what he meant. It was as if a bomb had exploded in front of her, with the pieces falling to earth around her like shrapnel. Feeling furious and betrayed, she walked to the other side of the dock. Boards creaked, and she knew Rueben was standing behind her.

"My grandparents never told me he called or that he came," Celena choked, her throat feeling like it had rusted through.

"But they must have!" Rueben sounded incredulous. "Each time Matthew called, they told him you didn't want to talk to him. He wrote too, but all his letters were returned. Matthew didn't say much, but I know it tore him up inside."

So he had written too. Celena put her hands on a piling, holding it as though it had become a necessary part of her, an extension she could never relinquish. It all fit. It explained so much. Why her grand-parents watched every day for the postman. Why they always had to check the mail before she did. And why, especially in the beginning, they jumped whenever the phone rang. Celena had overheard enough to know they were bitter beyond belief at Matthew.

Finally, Celena turned. "I should have guessed, but I had no idea. It never occurred to me they would do something like that."

"Are you okay, Celena?" Rueben asked, looking more than a little upset himself.

Although she felt stiff with shock, Celena replied, "I'll be fine." Then, walking carefully, as if she had forgotten how to do it properly, she started toward her bike. "If you see Joshua . . ."

"I'll hang onto him."

* * *

Celena pedaled down Broadway, stopping in Tillman's, then Bigelow's Drugstore. She was passing Jere's Café when Daniel came out, so she pulled over, bumping her front tire against the wooden sidewalk. "Have you seen Joshua?"

"No, I haven't. What's up?" Daniel asked.

She was too worried to dissemble. "Last night he overheard me telling Lydia that I was taking him and Father to Maryland. He got pretty upset and ran off."

"Where have you looked?"

"At Bay Haven, the docks, and along this road. I was just going back over to the lighthouse."

"I'll look along the beach," Daniel said.

* * *

It wasn't until later that Celena realized she hadn't asked Daniel to help. His offer came as a matter of course, and she wondered at the unexpected sense of friendship that had allowed her to confide in him without a second thought.

At the outskirts of Saltaire, Celena rode on a path between patches of sea oats interspersed with clusters of holly and scrub oak. Once she'd dreamed of walking this path with Sam at her side, but she determinedly pushed those thoughts aside. She wasn't going to let him ruin a place he had never been.

A pair of white herons streaked across the sky. Nearby were dense thickets of beach plum with masses of white flowers that would turn to a cherry-sized purple fruit in September. The only sound was the soft murmur of the ocean and the occasional warble of a catbird or call of a marsh hawk. Her heart gave a great leap when she saw a figure in the distance, but by the time she reached the outbuildings by the light, it had disappeared over the dune line. Her bike fell, and as she ran, spiked strands of beach grass brushed her legs. At the crest, she stopped.

It was Ethan. He had found a rock to sit on and was facing the ocean, wearing the shapeless coat he favored. Water gurgled around the rocks that lay in crevices near the water's edge. She called out, and Ethan's round face split with honest joy at seeing her. Solid and muscular, he wrapped his arms around her, lifting her off the ground easily. She was gasping by the time he set her down.

"I hope my ribs survived that," she said breathlessly.

Ethan's whiskered face broke into a big smile as though she'd told a great joke.

"Have you seen Joshua?" she panted.

In a flash, Ethan reverted to his old manner. Leaning forward to peer disconcertingly into her face, he answered, "No. Have you seen Sarina?"

Celena sighed. "Ethan, Sarina's not here." She thought he might argue, but Ethan simply looked thoughtful, as if considering some weighty issue.

"Can evil get into the air—like fog?" he asked seriously.

Startled, she replied, "It doesn't work that way. I think evil comes from people."

Ethan nodded. "There are bad people around. I can feel them sometimes." He went on musingly. "It can be bad not to know where the evil is coming from."

She hardly knew what to say. "Why do you think there are bad people around?"

"Sarina said there were."

"Last night someone was walking around the light. Was it you?"

"I'm watching the beach."

Celena felt relieved. So, it *was* him. He looked around suspiciously, as if the dune grass could hear, then whispered, "Ever since you came back, everything's changing. They're all around."

"Who's around? You don't mean ghosts, do you? I don't believe in ghosts."

"They don't care if you believe or not," he stated flatly as the breeze blew his long hair about. "There are bad things here. I thought you could help, but I don't want you to go where Sarina is." He paused, then added, "Sarina is angry." His words had an ominous ring.

A shiver ran down her back. "Why would she be angry?"

"Because they killed her," Ethan said bluntly, seeming surprised that he had to state something so obvious. "She didn't want to die."

Celena felt helpless. Apparently, Ethan had become so obsessed with Sarina's death that he had lost touch with reality. Instinctively, she knew Ethan would never be at peace until he could accept that his wife's death had been an accident, but how could she convince him?

Far out on the beach, the surf gleamed whitely. Gulls wheeled over the coastline, flashing their white wings in the sun. Feeling disconcerted, Celena left Ethan sitting, watching the breakers hurl themselves upon the rocks and shatter like broken glass. What *had* happened the night Sarina had drowned? All Celena knew was that Sarina had gone out in a boat and the next day her body had washed up on shore. But if what Gerald said was true, why had Sarina gone out alone in the boat?

As she climbed the dunes, the lighthouse filled the horizon, a black-and-white sentinel standing as tall, proud, and shining by day as it did by night. The air smelled salty-fresh as Celena followed the well-worn path to the front of the keeper's cottage. It was a sturdy, unpretentious house, with a singular charm given by the towering lighthouse to which it was connected by a short corridor. Honeysuckle twined around the fence, smelling like the breath of heaven in the summer. A gull shrieked overhead. When she looked up, the bird had perched on the high-pitched roof and was staring down at her with its head cocked, as though trying to remember a question it wanted to ask.

When she was little, Celena loved nothing better than to sit on the porch swing in the cool of the evening, playing with her dolls. Sometimes, after dinner, she sat there with her mother in the soft, fragrant night, secure in knowing her father was tending the light and all was right with the world. In summer, shaded from the late sun, mother and daughter would sit on the porch and shell peas or string beans, the pauses in their talking punctuated by the slight thunk of vegetables as they hit the bottom of the tin bucket as the two worked away the afternoon.

Celena dug into her pocket for the key as the house seemed to embrace her and draw her in. Although most people didn't lock their homes on the island, the keeper's cottage was connected to the light-house, and both were government property. She moved carefully in the thick, dusty shadows. There were many of Matthew's things here, and for some reason, Celena could think of her father more quietly here, with less pulling and tearing. His raincoat and woolen coat hung on pegs. An extra lantern that he often used was on the table. She could sense his presence—the father who had been so harsh and unyielding her last year on the island, and the man who had been altogether different when she was younger. How had the change occurred? Were problems between children and parents, as Rueben had said, a rite of growing up? And would it be possible for her to bridge the gap? For after she'd left, her bitterness had become a glass wall—hard to see until she put out her hands and then it felt impenetrable.

Celena went down the enclosed corridor to the light. At the bottom of the stairs, she cupped her hands and called, "Joshua! Joshua, are you there?" There was no reply. But would he answer if he were there? Celena climbed the winding steps, but no one was there. She thought about how often she had climbed through the trapdoor to find her father polishing the glass slabs that made up the huge Fresnel lens. A hook on the wall held Matthew's Lighthouse Service jacket and another held his cap, adorned with the lighthouse crest stitched in silver and surrounded by gold leaves.

Outside on the railed catwalk, the gusting wind, blowing straight off the Atlantic, nearly knocked her off her feet. A few people walked along the beach, but all of them were in couples or groups—nowhere was there a solitary boy. The door took a bit of tugging to open against the wind, and once inside, Celena ran a hand along the brass railing that encircled the great lantern, examining the glass prisms set in brass that were surrounded by other triangular prisms. She thought of the miles of brass and glass her father had polished and how she had, under his direction, cleaned the soot off those same prisms. It was disturbing to think a stranger might invade this room. Would they ever know, could they ever understand, how her father and grandfather had given their lives to this light? When Celena thought of Gerald and Helen, her eyebrows drew together in annoyance.

Her mother had always said—whenever Celena complained about being a slave—that it was not just up to her father to keep the lighthouse, but it was the responsibility of everyone in the family. Elizabeth had solemnly told her children that a lighthouse keeper held a sacred trust, for his job could mean life or death to people aboard schooners, trawlers, liners, and freighters, as well as the fishermen and lobstermen that made up most of the population of Fire Island.

It was still a struggle to get it into her head that her father had come to Maryland after her. Not only that, he had called and written. For years, Celena had believed he had cut her off without a second thought, and now, in a single moment, history had been changed.

Pulling out a battered tin box, she flipped the clasp back and pushed aside the rags used for cleaning the prisms to reveal the large shells that were laying on the bottom. They had been there as long as she could remember. There were mussels, several cat's paw shells that had five toes each, a number of scallop and slipper shells, and her favorite, red scalloped shells. She picked up the largest mussel, and as she handled the rough, craggy exterior, she recalled how she'd told Daniel about mussels. It came to her that her father was rooted to this island—this light—just like this mussel had once been lashed to its place on the rocks. Matthew's byssus was just as strong as this mussel's had been. It would take a crowbar to pry him away. With a deep inner trembling, Celena suddenly realized what would happen if she did manage to tear her father loose from Fire Island. Closing the box, she started down the stairs.

* * *

Celena went down the hall and, turning right, walked into the front parlor. She had a need to touch the things her mother had touched and to walk where she had walked. Celena remembered how, in the months after her mother's death, tensions had risen with her father. Celena had refused to back down on anything, whether it had to do with the Church or not, and her father would let nothing go. The very air had been fraught with friction until quarreling had become a way of life. And even though she had known it was wrong, Celena had felt powerless to alter the vicious cycle. How strange it was that now those memories were the ones with an air of unreality and that those of previous years, whose recollections were pleasant and filled with joy, seemed more genuine.

Celena had been afraid the house might seem empty and cold, but the very air was bursting with memories. For her, voices were as much a part of the house as anything, and everywhere she turned, she could hear them: Joshua's young treble, her father's deeper tones, and her mother's soft replies. Her father had always been a man of few words. It was her mother that had been the voluble one. Celena smiled, remembering how, when her mother laughed, it sounded like running water. Suddenly, Celena had the feeling that if she were to call out right now, her mother would answer.

As though searching for evidence, Celena continued to wander about. Fragmented scenes—those that had remained like cloaked figures at the edges of her mind—rushed in, filling the empty rooms. A night in winter. She, Joshua, and her mother seated around the fireplace, safe and snug as the wind howled outside while her father kept watch at the light. Her mother's knitting needles making soft clicking sounds, silenced only when she unwound more wool.

Or a summer evening, when the sunlight stayed late, allowing her father to remain home longer. Sometimes he would flip through catalogs or magazines such as the *Lighthouse Board Report* or *New England Historical Quarterly*, but more often he would just sit, watching, listening, and sharing the space with his wife and children. When it was time to go to the light, Matthew would reach out his hand, and, with a small, contented smile, Elizabeth would squeeze it, looking into his eyes a moment. It was a sort of rite. Then he would go.

Celena touched the rocking chair, recalling the time her father had rocked her when she had the measles. Later, he had done the same with

Joshua. Another time, when she had felt unwell, Matthew had wrapped her in a quilt and taken her to the lighthouse, carrying her up each step simply because she had wanted to go with him. At the time, Celena had not given a thought to the effort it must have taken to carry a child up all those stairs.

There was the hearth where she and Joshua would line up the pieces of penny candy their father always brought back from his trips to Long Island. The end tables now held electric lamps, but Celena's mother had told her about trimming wicks and cleaning smoked-up lamp chimneys. What a delight it was, Elizabeth had said, to simply pull a cord or flip a switch to get light. In the lighthouse, Matthew still used lamps, for although the generator provided electricity for the house, it did not extend to the lighthouse. Celena had never heard him complain.

Going upstairs, she opened the door to her parents' bedroom. Celena's throat had a lump when she touched her mother's Book of Mormon on the bedside table, its satin ribbon marking a spot. How could her father bear to leave her mother's things out? To see them every day? Then again, how could he have put them out of sight? Celena had expected to be awash in tears upon entering this room, but instead there was an unexpected feeling of peace. The air seemed cottony soft, yet it contained a strange sense of urgency that flowed from some unknown source. Thoughts came to her, uncomfortable ones. Her mother had not wanted her to stay away for five years. Nor did she want Celena to go away now. There were promises she expected her daughter to keep. Tremulously, Celena realized that it was the easiest thing in the world to make promises. What required strength was following through.

On the cherrywood dresser, her mother's hairbrush still lay in its accustomed spot. Celena picked it up, feeling the smoothness of the handle. How could a brush last longer than the woman who had used it? Once again, she felt a special warmth inside to realize that her father *had* come after her. He *had* called. And written. The bitter-sweet pang of that knowledge was almost as sharp as when she'd first heard it. She could still hear her father's haunted voice, saying that her leaving had been like the light had gone out. For a lighthouse keeper, there could be no greater catastrophe.

Though Celena sat still, her mind and emotions were kept busy, as if being fed from some outer source. How strange life was, following a kind of seamless brushstroke arc as it stretched languidly from birth to death. Sometimes it flowed smoothly. Other times it soared or plummeted from the hills and valleys that made up life. Perhaps it took time to be able to look back at life and understand more fully what had happened and why. Celena sat for a long time, her thoughts whirling. When she finally rose, Celena held her head high. Peace and surety had soaked into the marrow of her bones leaving no room for uncertainty. Picking up a towel, Celena carefully wrapped something she had taken from the lantern room. It had to be protected so she could show it to her father.

Before leaving, Celena paused at the threshold to look back. The softness in the air was still there. It seemed to cling to her, making her heart tranquil and calm. Suddenly, Celena knew where to find Joshua. She closed the door.

EIGHT

Without even thinking, Celena set off down the trail. It was almost as if she were being led. On this part of the island, everything was hushed. Golden rays of late afternoon sun fell on the iron fence that guarded the small cemetery, causing the intricate pattern on the main gate to be thrown in detailed shadow on the sunny gravel pathway that led away from it. The gray headstones in their neat rows were worn by the weather. Some were crumbled around the edges from age and sea air. Others had moss where they turned their backs to the sun. Evidence of neglect was in the overgrown bits of lawn and in the weeds, which were lush around the fence lines. Many of the great stone statues and urns seemed to sprout from deep grass, telling of descendants too far away to tend the lots.

Joshua was sitting cross-legged beside his mother's grave, head bowed, hair mussed. Celena sat down silently, pushing aside her sack and sitting close to her brother, who accepted her presence but did not turn or speak. Nearby, two willow trees brushed the grass with long soft fronds. Words almost seemed out of place in the hushed atmosphere. After a while, Celena didn't feel the bumps in the ground anymore. It was as if somebody had lifted her up off the ground to cradle her in quiet, invisible arms.

When Joshua finally spoke, his voice was small but resolute. "I want to run the light." By the look on his face, Celena knew he could not imagine living in a place that wasn't made up of equal parts land, sky, and sea. "Father wants the light too. I . . . I wanted to run it for him until he got better, to make up for me making you and Mama go away."

Celena jerked as if he had touched her with a bare wire, shooting electricity through her. She managed to stifle her first impulse, which was to cry out that he was wrong. Somehow, she knew instinctively that he would never accept anything superficial. Joshua lowered his head again. An occasional tear splashed on the overgrown grass. It was a moment of portent, and Celena felt an overwhelming responsibility to say the right thing.

"You didn't have anything to do with Mama going away," Celena said quietly. "She just got sick. And I left because . . . I got angry." It was only half the truth, but all she could manage.

"I heard you and Father arguing about me," Joshua countered, his young voice soft and sad. "Mama talked to him about me too. I tried to be good. But Mama died. And you left."

Celena's heart physically ached. Had she ever truly considered what her leaving had cost her brother? "None of what happened had anything to do with you," she assured him, but when Joshua refused to answer or look up, Celena knew he was unconvinced. She plowed on. "Father didn't want me, or you, to have anything to do with the Church. That's why we argued." Celena put an arm around him. "And you had nothing at all to do with Mama getting sick."

"Why did she have to die?" His voice was a hoarse whisper.

Celena laid her cheek against his hair. "I'm not sure," she replied honestly. "One person told me God needed her, but I can't imagine God needing her any more than we did."

"I asked God to let Mama live," Joshua said earnestly. "Over and over. But He didn't hear my prayers."

Celena closed her eyes. A strange feeling went through her, cool and quiet as wings. Then, as though the words were written on the front page of her mind, she murmured, "One thing I've learned, Joshua, is that God *always* listens. Just because we don't get the answer we want doesn't mean God didn't hear us. Heavenly Father listens to our prayers. He loves us. But sometimes the answer is no, even though we're asking for something we want very much. And when He does say no, we shouldn't get mad. God is a whole lot wiser than we are, and we have to trust Him. Sometimes what we want may not be the best thing for us, or for others."

Joshua's voice quavered a bit as he said, "Mama getting better would've been the best thing for me."

Celena's own lips quivered, and she could not answer immediately because emotion threatened to choke her. There was a faint rustle of leaves as a slight breeze stirred them. Celena asked, "Do you know why we came to earth?"

His answer was automatic. "So we could get a body."

"That's right. We're also here to learn and to be tested. We came knowing we'd have lots of problems and trials."

"That stinks."

"Sometimes it does," Celena agreed. "But we can learn from our problems. And part of our test is to stay faithful and get through our hard times the best way we can. And Mama . . . well, Mama got done with her test sooner than most people. And she did a real good job." The last was said with a catch in her throat that made Joshua look at her. Celena struggled on. "And . . . and if we do a good job, we'll be able to see Mama again."

"I'm trying," Joshua said simply, his brown eyes earnest.

She hugged him to her. "So am I."

There was a sense of tranquility wrapping itself around them. Without really seeing, Celena gazed around the enclosure with its marble and granite markers and grassy inclines.

"Is Mama an angel?" Joshua asked.

"If an angel is someone who watches over people, then I'm sure Mama is an angel."

"Sometimes I think I feel her around."

"Me too."

"She wants you to help me run the lighthouse," Joshua said matter-of-factly.

At any other time, Celena would have smiled and thought he was trying to manipulate her. Instead, she felt a strangely warm, radiant feeling in her chest.

"I—I think so too," she said slowly. Joshua did not move—an outburst would have been out of place in that warm, peaceful atmosphere—but there was a glow on his face. She asked, "Joshua, how do you feel about the Church?"

"It's okay."

"Do you think it's true?"

"Well, sure."

"Do you want to get baptized?"

"Yes." Absentmindedly, he reached out and plucked some grass.

"I guess Father said you couldn't."

Joshua's look was reproachful. "Father said I could be baptized whenever I wanted, but I wanted to wait until you came home." Celena was stricken. She had not planned on coming back. In fact, she wouldn't be here now if Joshua hadn't called—if Father hadn't had an accident.

He interrupted her thoughts, asking, "Why are you so mad at Father?"

She hadn't realized he was aware of that. Celena picked her words carefully. "A lot of it was because I wanted to go to church and he didn't want me to."

Joshua looked puzzled. "Father lets me go and doesn't get mad. He even comes with me." Celena started slightly. To cover it, she brushed stray wisps of hair away from her face. It was then that she realized that the wild tangle of emotions she'd been caught up in ever since Joshua had asked her to run the light had vanished. Instead, there was a remarkable feeling of peace and a certainty that her mother was close.

"Joshua," she said softly. "I'm going to stay and run the light until Father can take over."

Her brother's face broke into a wide smile, but his voice was cautious. "But you told Lydia you were taking me and Father away. And that it would be a long time before Father got better."

"I know. But I've changed my mind." Joshua's eyes locked onto Celena's long enough to know that she spoke the truth, then he flung his arms around her, hugging her tightly. As they left the cemetery and drifted out into the sun, Celena felt like she was being borne up on wings.

* * *

Cycling back along the beach, Celena watched for Daniel. They were almost to Clearwater before they saw him. "Your father knows Joshua was gone," Daniel began, looking chagrined. "I stopped at Bay Haven to see if Joshua had turned up, and Matthew demanded to know why. He's pretty worried."

"You'd better go see him," Celena told Joshua. "Since it's so late, I'll go back to the light right now. Ask Minerva to pack us something for dinner, and you bring it when you come."

He was off like a streak.

"Where did you find Joshua? He looks pretty happy for someone who ran away." Daniel looked at her closely. "And actually, so do you."

The radiance had stayed, and Celena held onto it like it had been sent from the plenitude of heaven. She took a deep breath. The air was sweet with the scent from a huge lilac bush that stood nearby, heavy with fragrant purple blossoms. "I've decided to stay and run the light. That is, if the bureau will let me."

Daniel's eyes warmed with approval as though he knew what a tremendous decision it had been. He put a hand on her arm, and without thinking, Celena laid her hand on top of his for a brief moment. Her response to his touch was stronger than she would have expected—a sudden rush of warmth that was startling. Slightly flustered, Celena was suddenly conscious of how attractive he was and of her own dishevelment, with hair that was loose and wild. Trying not to be obvious, she made an attempt to smooth it.

When he noticed, she gave up. "My hair's a mess today."

Daniel tilted his head slightly. "It looks like a halo." When she smiled wryly, he asked, "What changed your mind about staying?"

How could she explain? After a pause she said, "I went to the lighthouse, and while there, I thought about how important it was to my father and to Joshua. Then I looked around my home, and there were so many memories." Celena's throat grew tight. "I had the strangest feeling. I was alone, but it felt like I wasn't. It . . . it felt like my mother was there." Celena paused to watch two sparrows picking about the dirt. "I suppose that sounds silly."

"Not at all. I think it's entirely possible." Daniel sounded definite.

"Then suddenly, I knew where Joshua was. I went to the cemetery and he *was* there—at my mother's grave. We talked, and . . . and it was almost like I wasn't the one talking. And all the reasons why I didn't want to stay just fell away, leaving me with the most incredible feeling of peace. And suddenly, the decision was made. I was going to stay."

Daniel nodded understandingly, his brown eyes warm. "I'm sure you're doing the right thing, Celena." He squeezed her hand. "And it's certainly good news for me, although my father won't be too pleased."

Celena didn't dare look at him, afraid that the warmth she heard in his voice would be on his face. "Neither will Helen," Celena added, unable to suppress a mischievous smile. She moved toward her bike. "It's getting late. I'd better get to the light."

Daniel eyed the sack dangling from the handlebars. "What's that? Would you like me to take it back to Bay Haven for you?"

"No. It's something I was going to give my father, but it'll have to wait. Would you stop and tell Rueben and Tana that I found Joshua? They'll be worried."

"I'll go right now. See you later."

* * *

The following morning, Celena and Joshua hurried back to Bay Haven to change into their Sunday clothes. After a quick good-bye to their father, they were off. The congregation was singing the opening hymn when they slipped into a pew beside Tana and Rueben. After opening exercises, Celena told Rueben and Tana that she'd decided to stay.

"I knew you'd come through," Rueben said. "You've grown a lot."

"You *and* your father," Tana said, her eyes bright. "Did you know that after his accident, your father asked for a blessing?"

Celena was speechless, but Rueben quipped, "Later that afternoon, I saw a few devils wearing winter coats."

* * *

During Sunday School, Celena heard a familiar voice answer the teacher's question and turned to see Daniel sitting in the back. She was both surprised and delighted, and after class, she threaded her way to him. "Brother Roberts." She smiled, holding out her hand. "What a surprise to see you here!"

He shook her hand firmly. "It shouldn't be. I've been a member since I was nine. My father was baptized here on Fire Island when he was young. But don't tell him I told you." Daniel smiled wickedly. "He likes to keep his membership a great secret."

As they walked down the hall, Celena asked, "Is your mother a member?"

"She was converted when I was little. My mother, sister, brother, and I were all baptized together. She's remained active, even though it was hard when my parents got divorced because some people looked down on her. Since she's remarried, it's been easier."

He certainly seems to take his parents' divorce calmly, Celena thought. "My mother and I were baptized together too," she said as they made their way outside.

"What about your father?" Daniel asked.

"He didn't join. When we were looking into Mormonism, all of us went to church together. Then he heard some slanderous stories and stopped going. When my mother got sick, he turned against the Church completely. After Mother died, he and I started arguing a lot. He didn't want me to have anything to do with the Church."

"By the time he was an adult, my father wasn't interested in the Church either," Daniel said. "But he never had a problem with my mother taking us."

As they walked, bees hummed industriously as the smell of flowers drifted about on the June breeze. "Where does the rest of your family live?" Celena asked.

"My older brother stayed in Virginia to farm, and my mother and stepfather are nearby. My sister moved to Delaware after she got married." The smell of savory pot roast was in the air as they walked into Bay Haven. Daniel loosened his tie. "When something smells that good, I can change in two minutes flat. See you in the dining room."

* * *

Celena changed, then went to see her father. There was a pinched look around Matthew's mouth, and his eyes spoke of pain. Apparently, today was one of those bad days he occasionally had. Joshua was there already, and he turned to her and said, "Last night I told Father why I ran away. He wasn't mad, though." Her brother seemed anxious for her to know this. "He was glad when I said you were going to stay and run the light."

Celena stepped closer and was taken aback by the raw emotion displayed in her father's blue eyes. He swallowed hard, then choked out, "After all that's happened, Lena, it's good of you to stay. I'm grateful. Clint wanted me to retire, but I'm not ready." Years before she might have expected more, but Celena could sense how much was contained in those few words. The use of her childhood nickname also touched her.

Matthew whispered, "What about your grandma and grandpa?"

"I'll call them and explain," Celena assured him. "Don't worry, it'll be all right."

Sensitive to the emotion in the air, Joshua asked softly, "Can I go to the lighthouse tonight?"

"It's a school night—you won't be able to stay," Celena replied.

He made a face. "I know, but I can come for a while, can't I?"

"I suppose. Go hang up your clothes so they won't be wrinkled for sacrament meeting, and then we'll go eat."

After Joshua left, Celena reached into the sack she'd brought. "I've got something for you."

When she pulled out the mussel shell, her father looked at it, blinking. "Is that the one—"

"That was at the lighthouse? Yes. I still remember when we got it. You told me all about mussels—that once a mussel had picked a place to live, no other spot would do. That the mussel would lash himself in place so he could stay there all his life." Matthew nodded, his eyes on the rough shell. "I wanted to keep the shell here as a reminder." Celena made room for the shell on the dresser, then came back to Matthew's bedside.

"There's something I wanted to ask you. Did you come to see me after I left Fire Island?" For some reason, she needed to hear it from him when he was lucid.

He looked into her light brown eyes steadfastly. "Aye."

Something in her heart softened like a spreading pool of melting snow. "And you called? And wrote?"

He nodded, then looked away, the expression on his face strained.

Celena tried to swallow down the sadness even as she whispered, "I didn't know."

Matthew's eyes turned back to her, questioning.

"I never told Grandma and Grandpa that I wouldn't see or talk to you. They didn't tell me you'd called. I never saw any of your letters."

As comprehension dawned, Matthew's lips grew tight and thin. His face flushed and a muscle in his jaw jumped. It was apparent a battle was raging within. If he had been well, Celena had no doubt she would be covering her ears. She still felt angry herself. Her grandparents had taken her in, clucking like sympathetic chickens at her plight, never letting on that her father had tried to contact her. Still, Celena *had* placed the blame for her exile squarely on her father's head, knowing they already had bitter feelings against him. Was it really so surprising that they had returned his letters and refused his calls?

A feeling of heaviness and loss hung over her, an aching for how different the years could have been. So much pain avoided. But it was not fair to blame her grandparents entirely. Telephone lines ran both ways, and she had neither written nor called her father.

Celena leaned over and put her hand on Matthew's arm. "I'm going now." He nodded almost imperceptibly. Right now their relationship was tentative and fragile, but given proper care, it could grow. It could not be a continuation—they could never take up where they had left off—but they could build something new.

That evening after sacrament meeting, Joshua changed quickly and rode his bicycle to the light by himself. Because it was such a lovely evening, Celena decided to walk. As she did, she wondered again if it were possible that someone had seen her father fall. But if so, why hadn't they summoned help?

When she neared the light, Joshua waved his arms wildly from the catwalk where he had been watching for her. She joined her brother inside, and they played backgammon. She lost the last game, and when she sent Joshua back to Bay Haven, he grumbled that Celena was being a sore loser. Lighting a lamp, Celena read for a while and was about to go to bed when she checked the beach. She inhaled sharply. The ghost was back. Someone in a billowing coat was carrying a light, walking to and fro below, as if to taunt her. She wondered if it could be Ethan, but this didn't seem the kind of thing he would do. Celena went onto the catwalk, but fog had begun to wisp its way onto the island and obscured her view. The figure was eerie in the whorls of white.

Cupping her hands around her mouth, Celena shouted, "Ethan, is that you? What are you doing?" Her words seemed to quiver on the air, and she wondered if Ethan or whoever it was could hear her well enough to understand. Why was someone trying to frighten her? Perhaps it was Lydia. If so, Lydia would soon learn that it would take a lot more than this to scare her away. Moonlight flooded the catwalk and silvered the ocean as she stood at the railing, the wind tousling her hair. Finally, the figure turned toward the ocean and went down a scrubby bluff.

When Celena finally lay down in her cot that night, she lit a candle and left it burning fitfully beside her.

* * *

In the morning, the sky over the Atlantic was streaked with rose and gold, tinting the water and gilding the edges of the waves that curled in over the gray sand. Celena took time to clean the prisms, and by the time she got back to Bay Haven, Joshua had already left for school. She poured a glass of juice, lathered several biscuits with blackberry jam, and took a tray to the porch. It was a beautiful morning, and her spirits rose to meet its beginning. Celena had feared that the peace she felt about her decision to stay might fade, but it was as strong as ever.

After spending some time with her father, who was drowsy from his medication, she returned to the light. As she polished the brass and cleaned windows, Celena made plans. Her first step would be to talk with the Lighthouse Bureau. Rueben might be able to help her there. And she wanted to talk to Clint, for who would be better to advise her than the mayor?

That afternoon, Celena went to the docks when the ferry was due in and talked to both men. Clint offered to go alone to talk to the Lighthouse Bureau on her behalf, and while Rueben agreed that having the mayor of Saltaire speak to the bureau was a good idea, he thought Celena ought to go herself. Rueben felt it would give the bureau more confidence in Celena if they could meet her in person. Knowing that many of the men on the bureau knew Rueben, Celena asked him to go with her and Clint, and he agreed.

* * *

That evening, when Celena walked in with his dinner tray, Matthew leaned over and put something into a drawer before commenting, "Dinner's early tonight, isn't it?"

"Just a little." She put a pillow behind his back. "You look like you're feeling a little better." He nodded. They talked a while, then Celena left to have her own dinner. In the dining room, Lydia and Helen were talking fiercely, their heads bent close together. When Celena walked in, they fell suddenly silent, their words practically hanging in the air like birds hovering in a stiff wind.

She was sure Joshua had announced her plans, but to make it official, she said to Helen, Lydia, and Gerald, "I've decided to stay and run the light until my father recovers." Their eyes fixed on her. Questioningly? Accusingly? Warningly?

Helen Montgomery's face seemed to sharpen and drain of blood all at once. "But he's not going to be able to run the light again! That was a terrible fracture."

Joshua began to squirm, but before he could speak, Celena said, "We think he'll recover just fine."

Lydia scoffed, "You don't know any such thing."

Gerald objected in his boisterous voice, "A nice young lady like yourself shouldn't be running that old light. You should be at home, taking care of a husband and babies."

The man was a dinosaur. "I'm not even married," Celena retorted.

"And you never will be if you stay cooped up in a lighthouse," he shot back. "That's no job for a woman."

"Is that so? Well, Joshua has a book you ought to see." Celena turned to Joshua. "Right?"

Her brother's grin split across his face. "I'll go get it!"

She put a hand out to stop him. "*After* dinner."

Gerald was not one to give up. "You know I want the light for my resort. What if I made you an offer you couldn't refuse?"

What was he saying? "Surely you're not suggesting money would change my mind about staying. My father is the keeper, and I'm going to run the lighthouse until he recovers."

"I see," Gerald said softly, studying her with an expression she had never seen before. Celena felt suddenly chilled, and in spite of the warmth of the room, she shivered.

"Besides," she added, "it's not up to me whether the light is put up for sale. The Lighthouse Bureau will decide that."

Clint walked in just then. Lydia's face lit up, and she patted the empty seat beside her. Celena knew that look. It appeared whenever an attractive man was in Lydia's vicinity.

"Sorry I'm late," Clint apologized, then took the chair next to Lydia.

"We forgive you," Lydia simpered. "Celena just told us she's going to run the light." She turned to Celena. "But dear-heart, what about your job?" There was no mistaking the way Lydia was watching her. Her heavily made-up eyes were darkly intent, almost scheming.

"I've already called my boss. Mr. Weatherby assured me I could take an extended leave of absence."

Dinner was served and, although the food was delicious, it proved to be an uncomfortable meal. Roasted chicken, scalloped potatoes, and tender new peas should have relaxed everyone, but no one was at ease, including Celena. No one seemed willing to drop the topic of the light-house. As opposing opinions continued to fly, Celena felt her determination rising. Beyond taking care of the light, she had been given a second chance to fulfill her promises and feared that if she failed to take advantage of that opportunity, it might not come her way again.

In a voice encrusted with ice, Helen said, "I agree with Gerald. I think the Lighthouse Bureau should appoint someone who has more experience."

"My father taught me how to run the light," Celena replied curtly.

"Actually, experience won't matter if the bureau decides to close it," Helen asserted coolly. "And the severity of Matthew's injury could very well make the decision for them. Especially when they know he'll be out four to six months, possibly even a year. Isn't that right, Clint?"

"I'm sorry, Celena, but Helen's right," Clint said reluctantly. "It's going to take a long time for your father to recover, and that could very well influence their decision."

"This is all conjecture," Celena stated flatly. "As far as I'm concerned, the Fire Island light is not going to close. My father is the keeper, and

I'm going to see that he *stays* the keeper." Joshua's face lit up with a triumphant grin, and at the same time Helen stiffened further—if that were possible. Her face seemed to harden, like concrete does without changing outwardly, and Celena knew the older woman detested her for standing up to her.

"I know you want the light to increase your business," Celena said to Helen. "But what does your husband, Mr. Montgomery, think about it?" It was a speculative question, and she was curious as to how Helen would respond. A steely glitter appeared in Helen's eyes, and Celena had the feeling that if Helen could have spat, she would have. Why did Helen dislike her so much? Surely there was a reason behind such a strong antipathy.

Helen then answered coolly, "He approves of anything that would increase business." Her words were reasonable, yet there was something behind them. Celena wondered if Helen had even told her ocean-faring husband about her plans to buy the light.

Lydia grinned roguishly at her mother. "This is interesting. You, Celena, and Gerald all want the light. I wonder who will win?" Trouble was humming in the air and seemed to be coming from many directions. There was something here. Something she didn't understand.

Gerald asked, "How did things go last night at the lighthouse?" Celena studied his ruddy face. It was a face that invited confidences. Yet he had made his intentions regarding the lighthouse very clear. Could he have something to do with the ghostly light? She glanced around the table. It was possible that someone here had tried to scare her last night. If she spoke out, someone might react in an unusual manner and reveal themselves.

"Last night there was someone on the beach, near the base of the lighthouse. Lydia told me that a ghost has been haunting the lighthouse. Has anyone seen it?"

Joshua cried out, "I did! I saw it!" But no one else spoke up. So the ghost had not been seen by as many people as Lydia had intimated.

Celena added, "The person was carrying a torch and wearing a blanket or a big coat."

"It's called a shroud, dear-heart," Lydia said playfully.

"I thought I'd put an end to that," Clint murmured. After he explained to the others about the group of kids, there were murmurs of amusement. The mysterious visitor had been explained.

Celena wasn't so sure. "I don't think it's kids. It might have been the first time, but lately, there's only been one person. But there's something else. Rueben saw a woman leave the lighthouse either just before or after my father had his accident. He couldn't see who it was. Does anyone know who it might have been?" There was a heavy silence.

"Ah, well, lots of people go to the light," Gerald said.

"It seems rather strange that no one's mentioned being there," Clint said thoughtfully.

Celena pursued it. "I wondered if the person had seen anything."

"Just what are you getting at?" Lydia asked suspiciously.

"I'd like to know more about how the accident happened. My father always checked his equipment carefully. His fall seems a little strange, that's all."

"We already know what happened," Gerald said. "The rope broke. Ropes *have* been known to break." It was unlike Gerald to be sarcastic, and Celena noticed Clint looking at Gerald strangely.

"Celena's father was badly injured," Clint said sharply. "Naturally she's curious about how it happened." Celena remembered that she had thought about looking at the equipment her father had been using when he fell. She'd have to do that. Surely she'd be able to tell if the rope had broken or if another part of the equipment had failed.

Gerald stopped Celena as she was leaving the dining room. "Daniel's got a monster of a headache. I wonder if you would be able to take him a dinner tray? He wasn't hungry earlier, but I bet he could use a bite now." When she hesitated, he added, "I need to discuss some business with Clint, or else I'd do it."

Lydia overheard. "I'll take it, Gerald. I'm sure Celena needs to get to the lighthouse."

Gerald smiled pleasantly. "That's very kind of you, Lydia. But I know Helen depends on your help after meals."

"Oh, Mother wouldn't mind," Lydia said quickly.

"I'm sure she wouldn't, but I know you'd hate to leave it all up to her and Minerva." There was a note of finality in his voice as he turned to look expectantly at Celena.

Amused at his deft handling of Lydia, Celena replied, "I'll be glad to."

Lydia was not done, however. Her face had changed, becoming malevolent. "Since you're going to stay and run the light, you might as well know there's someone else that wants it."

"I can always count on you to be the bearer of good news."

"Clint wants it," she said. "But don't tell him I told you."

Celena was tempted to laugh out loud. "You've got it wrong. Clint is going with me to the Lighthouse Bureau so *I* can run the light."

Lydia smirked and turned away. This had to be a game she was playing. Yet, as Celena carried the tray upstairs, she wondered. Lydia had to know that Celena would ask Clint about this, so there had to be something in what she said. But if it *was* true, why had Clint never mentioned it?

NINE

"Room service," Celena called out gaily.

"Come in." Daniel's voice sounded tired. He had settled deeply in a chair by the window with his head against the back of the chair and his long legs sticking out in front. He looked so vulnerable that for a brief moment, Celena wanted to reach out and smooth the line between his eyes away.

"I expected Minerva," he said.

"I can go get her," Celena teased lightly.

"Oh, no, I just meant—"

"I know." Celena pulled the small table over to him before he could protest and then uncovered the plate. "You'll enjoy this."

"Thanks. I told Father I wasn't hungry, but he doesn't know how to take no for an answer."

"I don't either, so eat up. I'm not leaving until it's all gone."

He smiled slowly. "You'd better sit down and help me, then."

She took a chair and regarded him solemnly. "You look rough. Do you get many headaches?"

"No. But when I do, they usually knock me out." He looked at the chicken and potatoes sadly. "It looks wonderful, but I don't have much of an appetite."

"If you tried just a little, it might help you feel better." Celena was again struck by how attractive he was, even when grimacing. "Just a few bites," she prodded.

After Daniel said a quick blessing on the food and took a bite, she asked, "How long have you been here at Bay Haven?"

"About two months. Our rooms at Clearwater should be ready by the end of the month." Daniel picked up his roll. "Does Father know you're going to stay and run the light?"

"Everyone knows now. Your father and Helen weren't very happy, but Joshua was, and that's what counts. By the way, Lydia just told me Clint wants the light too."

"Tell him to take a number and stand in line." When Celena smiled, he went on, "Seriously, I think it's great that you came back to help your father."

Celena felt a twinge of guilt. "I didn't come back out of the goodness of my heart," she said glumly. "I only did it because of Joshua and . . . and a promise I'd made to my mother. And, as you know, I had no intention of staying."

"But when you realized how important the light was to your brother and father, you put your life on hold to help them. There aren't a lot of people who would do that. And then again, sometimes we do the right thing because others encourage us." He looked at her meaningfully.

Celena was startled. His words showed an uncanny understanding.

Daniel continued. "I remember you saying that it felt like your mother was with you. I think it's very possible that your mother did come back—to prompt you to make the right decision."

She smiled tremulously, remembering how the thoughts had come, liquid and formless. She'd tried to fulfill her promise regarding Joshua, and though she still wasn't sure what her mother had in mind when she had asked Celena to promise to have empathy for her father, things seemed to be moving in the right direction there as well.

"It may not be easy," Daniel said.

"I know. Things were pretty bad between my father and me before I left."

"It sounds like you had a tough time." Reaching out, Daniel clasped her hand. His fingers were firm around hers, and there was strength and reassurance in his grasp. Celena was glad to cling to the comfort he offered. Suddenly, she found herself telling him about her father's ultimatum all those years ago. Even now, Celena remembered how that moment had felt—like she was spinning so fast that she was thrown clean off the planet, torn violently away from everything she knew.

"I'm sorry, Celena," Daniel said in a low voice when she finished. "That must have been very hard."

The pain of it was with her still. "Yes, it was. But I shouldn't be bothering a sick man with my troubles." She smiled weakly and stood up to go. As she did, Celena pushed the chair away and it groaned for her.

"Don't go just yet," Daniel said. When she hesitated, he added, "I don't want you leaving when you're feeling like this." When she sat down, Daniel went on. "I don't know Matthew very well, and although I've heard he can be a little cantankerous at times, I have to say I'm surprised he told you to leave. I've seen him at church occasionally. Maybe he's changed."

Celena recalled something Rueben had once said and repeated it. "Going to church doesn't make you a Christian any more than standing in a garage makes you a car."

Daniel laughed. "You're right of course."

Celena felt the old bitter feelings rush back. "He never tried to understand how I felt about the Church. What kind of a father would throw his daughter out of the house? Especially when I'd already lost my mother!"

"I wish I knew what he was thinking. But he'd recently lost his wife. He probably felt like his life was turning upside down."

"So was mine. Because of *him.*" Her words were quiet but full of bitterness. Once, Celena had thought her anger would never be quenched, and for a long time she didn't *want* it quenched. For it was only when she was angry that the hurt could be held at bay—the hurt of feeling unloved and unwanted.

Daniel was watching her. "You've still got a lot of strong feelings about what happened, don't you? They're going to hold you back, you know. You can't move on until you can free yourself from the past."

Suddenly she was embarrassed. "You're right. And here I thought I was doing so well at forgiving."

"Forgiveness is like an onion."

"Because it stinks?"

Daniel gave her an exaggeratedly stern look. "Are you trying to make this difficult?"

"If I can. No, I'm kidding. Go ahead." In a singsong voice, Celena repeated, "Forgiveness is like an onion, because . . ."

"Because you can forgive on one layer, only to realize there are more layers underneath."

"Which means more work."

"You're a quick study."

"At least I'm good at something." Celena stood. "Thanks for the vegetable lecture. I'm sorry to talk so much when you're not feeling well. Now you know everything about me."

"Hardly. But I'd like to know more."

Pleased, and feeling a warmth she wasn't sure how to handle, Celena said, "Joshua will be wondering where I am. I hope you feel better in the morning."

"I'm sure I will. Good night, Celena."

She wondered at herself. She'd always been a private person, even with Sam, yet it seemed natural to talk to Daniel, and somehow, Celena knew her feelings were safe with him.

* * *

Celena woke to a lovely June day with the lightest of breezes blowing off the opalesque water of Great South Bay on one side and the deeper blue of the Atlantic on the other. The night had passed uneventfully. Before going to Bay Haven, she wanted to take a look at the equipment that had caused her father to fall, even though everyone insisted it was just an accident. She looked in the assistant keeper's quarters for the rope and bosun's chair, but the equipment was not in its normal spot. It wasn't in the keeper's quarters either. Celena stopped at the dimly-lit storage shed where the only light came through cracks in the boarded-up windows in the loft. A table in the middle of the room was crowded with assorted tools and fishing nets. Along the sides were coils of rope, a broken dinghy, lobster traps, barrels, and crates, but the bosun's chair and ropes were not there. A ladder led to the loft, but no one would have bothered to take them up there.

The equipment wasn't in the paint locker either. The small, square shed held nothing but partially-used cans of paint, turpentine, and a wide assortment of wire brushes, sandpaper, paint brushes, and rollers. A stack of old buckets stood in one corner.

When she arrived late at the boardinghouse, breakfast had been taken away, so she went to the kitchen. As she entered, Helen jumped slightly, her face pale and startled. The older woman's face was so drawn, Celena wondered if she were ill. Minerva moved a pile of dishes from counter to sink and gave a friendly smile before getting on with her work.

Helen collected herself and, while wiping her hands on a towel, said, "I talked with Ethan this morning. Apparently you're filling his head with some nonsense about Sarina coming back."

"I think you misunderstood him," Celena replied placidly. "*He's* the one who's been telling *me* that Sarina is around. I just asked him if he'd been around the lighthouse at night."

"Why would you ask Ethan?"

"Because he's always there," Celena said with some exasperation. Did Helen not know anything about her own brother? "Like I told you the other day, Sarina told him to watch the beach, and he's doing just that."

Helen looked at Celena disapprovingly. "Ethan's gotten worse since you came back, and it's because you're accepting everything he says as if it were true. I learned long ago not to indulge him in his fantasies. If you do, he just gets worse." Her words were clipped as she wrung out a dishcloth in the sink. "Ethan has never accepted Sarina's death. He's come up with all sorts of crazy ideas to cope with her being gone. You're not helping him by going along with his delusions. He needs other people to help him understand what is real and what isn't."

"All I'm doing is listening," Celena countered. "Ethan needs a friend. He's very disturbed about Sarina's death—he thinks she was murdered."

Helen's blue eyes were cold. "That's one of his more outlandish delusions. If you were really his friend, you'd point out what is real and what isn't."

Celena was losing patience. "I don't think I'd be helping Ethan by telling him that he's wrong."

"He *is* wrong a lot of the time! When Ethan starts to let his fancies run away with him, I help him stay grounded, but you're confusing him by acting like his fantasies are real." Helen looked at her stonily. "You keep saying someone is around the light at night, and that's convinced him that Sarina is haunting the beach. That's why he's watching. He thinks he'll see Sarina."

"Ethan was watching the beach long before I saw anyone at the light," Celena said brusquely, then decided it was pointless to pursue the matter. She turned and left, too annoyed to get breakfast, but she did find it curious that Helen was so disturbed by Ethan's behavior. Why was that?

* * *

During the week, Helen often seemed distracted, but that could have been due to a sudden influx of boarders. Meanwhile, Celena and her father were settling into the strange ritual of learning how to talk to each other. Some days they were able to talk easily. Other times Celena felt like she was tiptoeing on eggshells, afraid to mention the past because their deep emotions were still too close to the surface. Celena set an appointment with the Lighthouse Bureau, hoping the meeting would put an end to speculation that the light was going to be closed.

On Sunday, Celena and Joshua walked to church with Rueben and Tana. Rueben told jokes the entire way, and when they arrived, Celena was pleased to see that Daniel had saved seats for them. After a hymn and a prayer, the speaker, a slight man with a short, gray beard, went to the pulpit. When he said he wasn't going to take much of their time, Rueben leaned toward Celena. "There's a sure sign of trouble," he whispered. "A person's idea of time changes when they get behind a pulpit. Religious people only work from a prospect of eternity and that's what we're in for now."

Frowning, Tana tried to shush him, but Rueben was on a roll. "What this man needs is a change in perspective. His talk would be shorter if he knew the audience was going to beat him for the same amount of time he spoke." Daniel tried unsuccessfully to stifle his laughter while Tana dug her elbow into her husband's ribs.

After the meeting, they walked to Bay Haven. Daniel excused himself while Tana and Rueben went with Celena and Joshua to see Matthew. Her father looked happy to have company and surprised Celena by asking Joshua, "What did you learn in Sunday School today?"

"They talked about Moroni, that general you like."

Matthew coughed and asked quickly, "What else?"

"We learned about the stripling warriors. They were young but had so much faith that not one of them was killed in battle, even though they had never fought before!"

"They had been taught by their mothers that, if they did not doubt, God would deliver them," Matthew recited solemnly. Celena looked at him in astonishment. Discomfited by her reaction, he quickly said, "Joshua's mentioned that one a lot."

"It's one of my favorites," Celena said. "I think the next verse says, 'We do not doubt our mothers knew it.' It reminds me of Mother. She had such a strong testimony."

"One of Elizabeth's gifts was great faith," Tana said musingly.

Rueben spoke up. "Did you know, Joshua, that everyone is blessed with certain gifts? Take your father, for example. He has the gift of being stubborn."

Matthew snorted. "Better than being a pompous goat."

"Says the old windbag."

"That's enough, children," Tana said rolling her eyes. "A fine example you two are!"

Joshua giggled, then assured her, "It's okay. They're funny."

"Funny!" Tana spoke to Rueben sternly. "Sometimes I think your sole purpose in life is to serve as a bad example." She picked up her scriptures. "I think it's time the goat and I went home."

* * *

That evening, Celena and Joshua brought trays in and ate dinner with their father. Then, just before going to the light, Celena returned to look in on him. He was asleep. Celena still shivered to think that she'd nearly wrecked everything at their first meeting. Even now, she had the feeling they were skating on thin ice, each being careful lest they break through. Time was needed for something solid to build between them.

* * *

The next morning, after taking care of chores at the light, Celena decided to go see Clint. It was late spring, and the fresh new leaves, the birdsong, and the gentle sunshine all seemed to offer a promise. Did this pleasant feeling come from spring fever or from a lightening of the burden she'd carried for so long? Hope was in the air, and not just in the songs of the mockingbirds and warblers.

The dock for the ferry extended far into the bay, its boards brown and splintery. The smell of fish and seaweed mingled in the air. Celena had timed her visit well—the *Sea Siren* was nearly in. She waited as people began streaming off the ferry. At the top of the gangplank, Clint's eyes lit up when he saw Celena. Yet he did not rush his customers, taking time to wish them a good day and answer their questions. Celena wondered if he noticed how the women lingered. Clint was so attractive he must make them feel faint.

When Celena said she wanted to talk, he invited her to ride the ferry to Long Island, explaining, "Once we're under way, I'll be free."

"I'd love that," Celena replied, pleased. She wandered around topside as gulls soared and darted in the air—graceful to watch but raucous to hear. Her shining hair fell freely over her back, blowing gently in the breeze.

Clint came to stand close by her at the railing, his interest in her clear. "I'm so glad to see you, Celena." She looked out over the bay where sunlight was sparkling on the water and dozens of small boats were taking advantage of the beautiful day. When he noticed the direction of her gaze, he asked, "Why don't you let me take you out on my boat sometime? It moves a little faster than this ferry."

Celena smiled. "I'd like that." It did sound fun, but she couldn't imagine when he'd have the time. "I don't know how you do it all— run the ferry, be the mayor, and help with Clearwater."

"I really don't have much to do with the resort. I invested in it, but Gerald is the one who manages it all. All I do is give him a few ideas, things that might persuade people to spend an extra day in Saltaire. I told Gerald he ought to rent boats as well as put up some little cabins to rent. Clearwater is going to dramatically increase revenue for the city. With a bigger tax base, I'm hoping we can build new roads, fund a park, and take care of other things on my 'wish list' for Saltaire."

"I think you got involved in Clearwater just to help Saltaire," Celena declared.

"Having a first-class resort is always something I've wanted—but it's also just what the city needs," he conceded. "Now that Clearwater is about to open, I predict a bright future." Although Clint was speaking of Saltaire, his eyes were on her.

To cover her confusion, Celena decided to move on to the purpose of her visit. "Last night Lydia told me you wanted the lighthouse. Is that true?"

"Yes, in a way, I do want the light." Seeing her surprise, he led her to seats in the middle of the ferry. "Let's sit down."

Her voice was a little unsteady. "Why haven't you said anything to me?"

"It's not quite what you think," Clint said firmly. "I don't know why Lydia put it like that. Frankly, she has a way of twisting things that makes me think she enjoys upsetting people. My only interest in the light is that it be preserved. During the past thirty years, the Lighthouse Bureau has decommissioned a number of lights. Unless someone buys them, they inevitably fall into disrepair." He looked at the black-and-white lighthouse almost reverently. "I don't want that to happen here. If the bureau does happen to close it, I'd like to have the light designated a historic landmark. The lighthouse plays too big a part in the history of Fire Island to let it crumble away." His voice was earnest. "It must be preserved as a legacy for future generations."

Celena was delighted. "You're absolutely right. Of course, they're not going to close it for a long time, but when they do, it *must* be preserved."

Clint's gray eyes caught hers. "I hope running the light isn't going to be too much for you. Would it help if the bureau had someone run it temporarily until your father recovers?"

"I'm managing just fine," Celena assured him. "Joshua is a great help."

While the ferry was docked at Long Island, Clint had to go ashore briefly. Celena amused herself by watching a great blue heron. The bird was sitting on a pole, and it spread its sleek wings, probing them with its long beak. With quick jabs, the heron groomed its feathers, stretched out its curved neck, then settled into a brooding squat. It was still sitting there, blinking its eyes sleepily, when the *Sea Siren* departed.

When Clint returned, he flashed that brilliant smile. "Miss me?"

"Oh, did you leave?" Celena said innocently.

"I can see I need to work at making myself indispensable."

As they walked around the deck, Celena asked, "Do you see much of Ethan?"

"No, that one keeps pretty much to himself."

"He misses Sarina," Celena said. "Did you know that Sarina told him to watch the beach if she went away?"

Clint raised his sandy eyebrows. "I hadn't heard that. But then, Ethan's always coming up with all sorts of crazy notions. Good thing he's got Helen to bring him back down to earth. He appears harmless, but I've always had an odd feeling about him."

"He doesn't think Sarina's death was an accident."

"A lot of people feel the same way," Clint answered dryly.

Celena looked at him closer. "What do you mean by that? Did the police find evidence of foul play?"

He pressed his lips together slightly. "The evidence was inconclusive. The detectives and examining doctor ruled it an accident. But there were rumors."

"What rumors?"

Clint appeared to be debating whether to say anything or not. Finally he relented. "I guess it won't hurt to tell you. People say that Sarina got tired of living with somebody like Ethan and wanted to leave, but he refused to let her go. Supposedly, she was trying to escape the night she drowned. Some say that Ethan went crazy when he found out Sarina was leaving and, either intentionally or accidentally, swamped the boat. And Sarina couldn't swim."

Celena was aghast. "Ethan would never do that. He loved Sarina."

"I'm sure he didn't mean to hurt Sarina. It was probably just an accident. But several people saw Ethan walking along the beach that night, soaking wet. He was disoriented and talking crazy. And Ethan was the one who found her boat on the shore. He rowed it over to the dock, but when he told Rueben where he'd found it, a couple of men said they'd searched that area several times and the boat hadn't been there." The ferry's motor shifted, and she looked up, startled to see that they were already pulling up to the dock. Clint said, "I hate to leave on such a terrible note, but I have to get below."

It just wasn't possible, Celena thought. Yet, if the rumors were true, they could explain Ethan's eccentric behavior. His mind could have become unhinged by such a terrible accident. As she thought, she watched Clint tend to his passengers. He was polite and charming to young and old. Celena had to admit she enjoyed being with him. In spite of the disturbing information she'd gleaned, Celena felt a good deal better when she left the *Sea Siren* than when she had come.

* * *

As the week progressed, her father became noticeably stronger. As his need for painkillers decreased, Matthew became more alert. Celena enjoyed their time together but spent many of her free hours cleaning the light and outbuildings in case the Lighthouse Bureau made an unannounced inspection.

Celena's days had fallen into a pattern: Each morning she would return to Bay Haven, see Joshua off to school, visit with her father, then go back to the light and take care of chores there. She had a few hours to herself in the afternoon, then after dinner she'd go back to the light. Sometimes she and Joshua ate with their father; other times they went to the dining room. That week, Celena asked Ethan again if he was the one walking around the lighthouse at night. He was emphatic in his denial, and Celena felt her questioning did more harm than good when Ethan vowed to watch the beach even more carefully.

After dinner on Sunday, Celena and Joshua rode their bicycles to the light under the golden rays of a waning day. A stray current stirred leaves as they parked their bikes, and a squirrel paused to chatter at them from a nearby pitch pine tree. After they did the preliminary work, Celena left Joshua in the light and went to the generator building. It was the one place she hadn't searched for the missing equipment.

Celena was elated to see the bosun's chair and rope flung in a corner. The light was failing though, which meant she'd have to take everything outside to get a good look. Gathering everything up in her arms, Celena turned and was startled to see a man standing in the doorframe. Because of the dimness, it took her a moment to recognize

Ethan. He wore rough brown corduroys that had been patched at the knees.

"What are you doing?" he asked, peering at the tangled mess. She explained, and once outside, Ethan hunkered beside her, his hair in his eyes as he watched her examine the pulley system. There were no separations or cracks in the metal, and the wheels were set firmly inside their metal casings. The bosun's chair was also intact, the rope firmly secured to triangular steel rings which were bolted firmly to the chair. Celena picked up a measure of rope, running it through her hands. It appeared in good order. The second rope was also in good condition, except for a puzzling fraying at the top.

When Celena nimbly rewove the section together, she gasped. The top edge was cleaner and more even than it should have been. Someone had simply pulled apart the strands to give the impression of fraying. This was not a worn rope that had frayed and torn apart, leaving uneven, broken strands. This rope had been cut. Celena dropped the rope as if it had turned into a snake. It wasn't possible. There wasn't anything at the top of the light for the rope to rub against—nothing that would slice through as cleanly as this.

Ethan looked at her curiously. "What's the matter?"

In a daze, Celena answered shakily, "The rope's been cut. *That's* why my father fell."

"Who cut it?" Ethan certainly had a way of getting to the heart of the matter. Who indeed? She had the odd sensation that swampy ground had opened at her feet. Who would have done such a thing? And why?

"I don't know, Ethan." Her voice sounded hollow. As he helped return the rope to the shed, Celena thought about the woman Rueben had seen. She was the one person who might be able to provide some answers. "Ethan, Rueben thought he saw a woman around the lighthouse the day my father fell. Did you see anyone that day?"

Shuffling his feet, he answered nervously, "Sarina said there were bad men." He looked everywhere but her face as he began clenching and unclenching his fists. "There's bad things here. *Bad* things. Sarina doesn't like it." Suddenly he turned and hurried away.

Lost in thought, Celena shut the door. When she reached the top of the light, she could not remember going inside and climbing the stairs. She was glad Joshua was staying the night. She also knew exactly what her brother was looking for when he kept glancing out the windows. It was almost bedtime when Joshua went rigid and pointed a finger. Celena went over. There was someone down there all right, holding a flickering light and trailing back and forth—coat billowing in the breeze.

"Zach said it's an old mooncusser that got drowned when he went out to salvage a ship."

"You don't believe that, do you?" Celena said more heartily than she felt. "There's no such things as ghosts. It's just someone fooling around. Say, why don't we play a game?"

"Okay."

As they went below, Celena wondered if it was Lydia out there. This seemed the type of game she would find appealing. But if it wasn't Lydia, then who was it? And what was he trying to do? Scare her away? Celena grimly thought that if the "ghost" was trying to frighten her and stop her from running the light, he or she didn't know her very well.

* * *

On Monday, Celena took special care in dressing. It was important to make a good impression on the members of the Lighthouse Bureau. After a final glance in the mirror, Celena went to see her father. Matthew looked stoic, as usual, but his jawline was tense. And though he told her not to worry, Celena noticed that Matthew's eyes were anxious and that he kept running a hand through his gray hair.

Lydia was working at the registration counter in the foyer. "I'd wish you luck," she said, "but since I don't want you to keep the light, I won't. I'm not a hypocrite."

"Ah, but are you a ghost?"

"So, you're still being haunted?" she replied with a strange look that might have been innocent or not. "Well, I'd get out if I were you. Say, would you and Clint like to go dancing sometime with Daniel and me? You could get Rueben to watch the light for you. Daniel and I are going dancing tonight on Long Island." Her eyes sparkled in anticipation. "He's a divine dancer—so light on his feet. We can't wait for the grand-opening ball at Clearwater."

"I didn't know you two were seeing each other," Celena said before she could stop herself.

"Oh, yes." Lydia smiled archly with a toss of her smooth, blond hair. "If you want to go, just let me know."

A few moments later, Rueben and Tana arrived. Rueben looked stiff and uncomfortable in his suit, the buttons straining across his middle. He had shaved, even though it wasn't Sunday, and his gunmetal gray hair was combed and slicked down with pomade.

"You're a picture today," Tana said, admiring Celena's glossy hair and trim, midnight-blue suit with gold buttons. "You look very professional, very capable. You'll do fine."

Although the morning sun was rising high in the tender vault of the sky, it had not yet burned the dew off the grass. Thunderheads that would sweep in late in the day were still only white marble puffs at the margins of the sky, solid and silver-lined.

As they walked along, Tana remarked, "I'm glad Clint agreed to go with you. As mayor, he has a lot of influence."

Celena nodded and said, "I don't doubt that at all." Clint was so dynamic, he could have gone into politics in a big way if he'd chosen. It was easy to picture him as a congressman or senator.

"By the way, I knew you'd want to go to the grand-opening ball at Clearwater, so Rueben will be happy to watch the light for you that night," Tana said

"Wait a doggone minute," Rueben roared. "Don't I have a say in this? I thought I was going to cut the rug with you!"

Tana laughed merrily. "Do you really think your knees would hold up for dancing?"

"If they can do lighthouse stairs, they can do the Varsity Drag!"

"Let the young people have their fancy new dances. The only drag you're going to be doing that night is hauling yourself up to the watch room." When Celena protested, Tana firmly said, "It's all settled."

They stopped at the corner, and Tana straightened Rueben's blue-striped tie. "Okay, you'll do," she said, giving him a peck on the cheek and turning to Celena. "I've got to get to work, but I'm sure everything will be all right. I've been praying." She gave her a quick hug.

As they walked toward the dock, Rueben said, "Last week I called my friend who works for the bureau. It was his opinion that having a ready buyer for the light could sway the bureau's decision. And both Gerald and Helen have contacted them, saying they'd like to buy it."

That wasn't good news. And now that she had Rueben alone she could share her own disturbing news. "Yesterday I looked at the rope and bosun's chair to see if I could tell which piece of equipment failed. The pulleys were sound. So were the steel rings on the chair."

"Matthew did always keep things shipshape."

"But the rope had been cut."

Rueben stopped in his tracks. His leathery face looked shocked. "Cut? Are you sure?"

"I am. The equipment was all in good shape, even most of the rope. It wasn't worn or even frayed, except slightly, near the top. But when I looked at the fraying more closely, I realized it was too clean to be from repeated usage. Besides that, the location of the fraying doesn't match up with anything sharp or rough on the light or the equipment." She let him digest that in silence for a few moments. "We both wondered why the woman you saw at the light didn't speak up. Maybe this is why. Perhaps she saw something. Or perhaps she *did* something."

Rueben shook his head as they continued. "This is awfully hard to take in. Are you *sure,* Celena?" When she nodded, he asked, "But why would someone try to hurt Matthew?"

"I've thought about that. Perhaps Father had an enemy. Or maybe someone thought that by getting him out of the way, they could get the light. After all, if the Fire Island lighthouse didn't have a keeper, the bureau would be much more likely to close it."

They walked along in silence for a while. Then Rueben said, "If the rope *was* cut, then whoever did it means business. And that means you—being the new keeper—are the one they're going to set their sights on next. Maybe it's not a good idea for you to run the light."

Celena looked at him in exasperation. "And who was the one who wanted me to stay?"

"That was *before* you found that rope."

TEN

At the dock, a fisherman was unloading his catch. The fish slipped over one another like water from a cupped hand, their scales flashing with a rainbow sheen like oil spilled in a puddle. Clint was waiting for Celena and Rueben. Where Rueben looked ill at ease in his suit, Clint looked like an ad for a menswear shop—suave, sophisticated, and disarmingly handsome.

"Good morning, Rueben, Celena," he said, offering his hand to steady Celena on the gangplank. They took their seats while Clint went below to get the *Sea Siren* under way.

On the ride over, Celena asked Rueben, "How is your grandson?"

"Will's not doing good. And you need to be rich to get good medical help. I've been able to help out a little from my fishing and what the Lighthouse Bureau pays when I substitute for Matthew, but it's like throwing money into a bottomless pit."

Celena asked after his other grandchildren, then the conversation turned to other topics. Before long they reached Long Island, where Clint hired a cab to take them to the bureau. When they arrived, they were directed to a utilitarian room that held only a long table and chairs. Five somberly dressed men sat across from Celena, Clint, and Rueben. Celena wondered which one was Helen's cousin. The men all knew Matthew and offered their sympathy. The head of the bureau, Joseph Rennicke, a portly man with a receding hairline and neatly trimmed gray beard, thanked them for coming and asked Celena about Matthew's condition and prognosis.

"Although it's too soon to know whether there will be permanent nerve damage or not, Dr. Harrison feels there is a good chance my father will recover completely." Celena looked at the men. "I asked to meet with you to find out what your plans are for the light and to ask you to allow me to run the light during my father's convalescence. Mr. Rueben Wyatt and Mr. Clint Paxton have come to speak on my behalf."

Rueben stood first. He told the board that Celena had been trained by her father, who had been the Fire Island keeper for nearly thirty years. He testified Celena was knowledgeable and competent and that he had been present the first night she had run the light and that Celena had executed every procedure in a proper manner. Rueben concluded by asking if they had any plans to close the light.

Looking somber, Mr. Rennicke replied, "It is a matter of record that some lights have been decommissioned. Because of the need to generate cost savings, we are evaluating all lights along the eastern coast. Because we have received a number of inquiries regarding Fire Island, we have been assessing this light in terms of efficacy and fundamental need, but have not yet reached a firm decision."

Clint went next. Tall and confident, he pled Celena's case. He ended by saying, "All of you know that lighthouse keeper is a demanding job and might question whether a woman has the necessary stamina." He smiled genially at the men, including them in a brotherhood. "To ease your concerns, you might consider allowing Celena to run the light in partnership with either Mr. Wyatt or myself." Clint took his seat.

Celena was dismayed. She didn't want to be a part-time keeper. Rising on somewhat shaky legs, she said, "Though Mr. Paxton's suggestion has merit, I would urge you to consider me as a full-time keeper. As a child, I grew up helping my father clean the prisms, trim the wicks, polish the brass, keep weather records—in short, take care of everything inside and outside. My father taught me all there is to know about the lighthouse. Since my return a month ago, I've been solely responsible for running the light, with the occasional assistance of Mr. Wyatt and my brother Joshua, who plans to take over the light when my father retires." She glanced at Rueben, who gave her an encouraging smile.

"My father is very precise and thorough in running the light and has taught me to be the same. Your inspectors will find everything in order when they come. All I'm asking for is the chance to run the light until my father recovers." Flushed, Celena sat down. As the men began murmuring, several gave Celena looks of approval.

"Well said, Miss Jackson," Mr. Rennicke declared. "While we were told that Mr. Jackson had sustained a permanent disability, this is apparently not the case. We will discuss the matter and call you with our answer in a few days."

* * *

Rueben was jubilant as he, Celena, and Clint walked down to the dock. "If they had any plans of closing Fire Island, they would have said so. And they were dead impressed with you, Celena. You did a great job."

Celena was less sure. "I was hoping they'd give us an answer today."

"They have to act like big shots," Clint drawled. "But I'm sure they'll let you run it."

"Just make sure you've got everything shipshape," Rueben advised. "They're sure to send out an inspector soon, and you know they won't tolerate a speck of dust anywhere."

When they arrived back in Saltaire, Clint walked to the boarding-house with Celena. Lydia was sorting mail at the reception desk, and when she saw them, she turned the full wattage of her smile on the mayor. "Hello, Clint. Did you save the day as usual?"

"Celena deserves all the credit. She was magnificent."

Lydia's mouth drooped. "There's a note on the table for you, Celena. It's from Daniel."

"See you later, ladies," Clint said as Celena went to get the note that lay beside the telephone. Daniel wrote that he hoped the meeting had gone well and that he would talk to her tomorrow, since he wouldn't be at dinner that night. He was looking forward to seeing her and Joshua for lunch tomorrow and reminded her to bring their bathing suits.

* * *

When Celena went to tell her father about the meeting, Matthew's head was bent over something. He beckoned her in with one hand while sliding whatever he had been holding under the sheets. A sock covered the toes that protruded from his cast. She was pleased to see that he had some color in his face.

"Did they make a decision?" he asked eagerly.

"Not yet. Mr. Rennicke said he'd call in a few days." Celena sat down and smiled wryly. "There's going to be a lot of disappointed people if the bureau decides to keep the light and let me run it."

Matthew snorted. "Aye, that's the truth. A lot of people don't want to see me leave this bed except in a wheelchair, and they don't want to see you running the light either."

"Gerald would love the lighthouse to be one of the featured attractions at Clearwater."

Matthew's face hardened. "What *doesn't* he want? The man's insatiable—with an ego to match. To hear him talk, he constructed the Taj Mahal over there with his two bare hands. Now he wants the light. What's next? The Statue of Liberty?" In a heated voice, Matthew went on, "The bureau knows how important the Fire Island light is. They're not about to close it."

Her father was so certain, yet the bureau *was* closing down lighthouses. Celena didn't want to argue, so she replied casually, hoping to lighten the mood, "You sound pretty sure."

"I *am* sure. Just like you were when you went and got tangled up with the Mormons."

It was as if the years had stood still. In an instant, Celena was on guard—all of her senses on alert. Not wanting to damage what had been developing so tenuously between them, Celena willed herself to reply calmly, "I *believed* what they said was true."

"You were gone from the first meeting—didn't even give yourself time to think things through," Matthew said grimly. "You were always so impulsive. Wouldn't listen to a thing I said. It wasn't logical."

As if logic ran the world one minute of any day. His words rankled, but much of what he said was true. At times when she'd be reading the Book of Mormon, the Spirit would swell up so much that Celena thought she might burst with it. The gospel had brought her a joy so real she could breathe it in like air. But Celena could no more explain it to her father than she could measure sky and weigh air. Fortunately, years had taken the edge off the defensiveness she used to wear like a shield, and when Celena spoke, her voice was calm and even.

"You're right. I felt the Church was true from the start. I knew it then and I know it now." Celena's words weren't mutinous or defensive. She was simply stating a fact. "But you didn't have any right to judge me," she added in a slightly sharper tone. "You didn't know anything about the Church. You didn't even try to understand the doctrine."

"That's not so," Matthew replied stonily. "I went to the meetings. I heard what they said. At first I thought they made a lot of sense, but I was worried about you. You didn't know enough to answer any of my questions, yet you were still bent on joining them, no matter what I said."

Celena was slowly becoming angry. "I was eighteen—old enough to make up my own mind. It wasn't right for you to try to stop me. Then you had to start talking with people who hated Mormons. Their stories were nothing but slanderous lies, started by people who hated the Church, but you believed them." Celena was blazing now, her face red, her earlier restraint gone. "You wouldn't believe me or Mother or the missionaries, but you believed the nutcases!"

"It wasn't that I believed them," Matthew shot back, his blue eyes chill. "I just wanted to check out both sides—find out what was true and what wasn't. And I *did* talk with the missionaries and Elizabeth. It was *you* I couldn't talk with. You always got so huffy, spouting off and saying I was against the Mormons." His voice was like flint.

"If you weren't against the Mormons, why did you insist on telling me every single bad thing you heard about them? You never had anything good to say."

"All I wanted was for you and Elizabeth to slow down—not rush into anything. But you were determined to force the Church down my throat. There was no respect for what I thought. Whenever I tried to say anything, you brushed it aside. You wouldn't listen to your own father."

"And you wouldn't listen to me!" Celena cried, seething with resentment. He was a stubborn man, her father, but she could be stubborn too. "I tried to tell you that those stories weren't true and that they came from people who hated the Church."

"But didn't you ever ask yourself *why* they hated it?" Matthew's eyes were penetrating. "That's what didn't make sense. If the Church was so good and true, then why were they so against it?"

"Satan has always tried to mislead people, ever since the Garden of Eden. He doesn't want people to have the truth, so he turns them against the Church by spreading lies. Look at Jesus. He only did His

Father's bidding, yet Satan led people to believe that Jesus was just a mortal. Satan twisted the truth so much that the people came to hate Jesus—who was perfect and without sin. They even had him crucified. Jesus, the *Son of God!*" Celena's voice was high and trembling.

Matthew was silent as he ran a hand through his gray-brown hair. "You've got a point there. I hadn't ever looked at it that way. But back then, I had a lot of questions, and with your mother sick, no time to get answers. I didn't want you baptized until I could get to the bottom of it."

"And you didn't trust *me* to get the answers," Celena retorted bitterly. "It was Mother that finally convinced you to let us get baptized!"

"That's true enough." Her father looked at her with a level gaze. "Elizabeth was sick, and I didn't want her fretting about anything. But talking about the Church with her and with you were two different matters entirely. To you, there was no talking without you getting on your high horse and looking down your nose at me. Mormonism broke up our family."

Fresh anger boiled up in her. "It wasn't Mormonism, it was *you!*" Celena snapped. "You and your bullheadedness!" She stood there, trembling all over and waiting for him to explode.

Surprisingly, he answered quietly. "You could be right. But I was only trying to watch out for you. At the time, I couldn't make heads or tails of the Church. Not until . . ."

Celena waited, but he was like a clam that had closed its shell. Lost in thought, he never finished his sentence. Whatever he had been about to say was locked inside him now, so, sighing, Celena bid him good night, and quietly slipped out.

* * *

It took her a long time to fall asleep, but when Celena opened her eyes the next morning, it was from a sleep so long and deep she might have been drugged. During the night, a misty fog had drifted in over the dunes from the ocean, and wisps of it still hid the water. But now that the sun was up, the mists would soon burn away.

Celena and Joshua went to eat breakfast with their father. Surprisingly, there were no lingering feelings from last night's argument. Matthew even joked about how it had been like old times, but they were both aware of the difference. Though last night they had opened old wounds, their plain talk had begun to purge and wash bitterness away, where before, their arguments had only deepened wounds. While they ate, Celena kept one ear tuned for the telephone and knew her father did also.

He seemed on edge, and once he thumped his cast irritably. "If I had a hammer, I'd soon have this off!"

After breakfast, Celena packed a bag to take to Clearwater. Early June was blooming full and green across the island. Joshua was excited to be out of school. Along the road, dogwood blossoms had burst into white magic, and the delicate scent of apple blossoms laced the breeze. One moment Joshua was running ahead to capture a butterfly, and the next, lagging behind to watch a beetle.

After passing through Clearwater's glass doors, they saw Daniel. He looked fit in navy pants and a pale blue shirt. The pretty receptionist with the long blond hair gave Daniel a second look as he ushered them to the patio. Pots of bright red petunias lined the patio, and the round tables were shaded by colorful umbrellas. Gerald was facing away from them but turned at their footsteps and strode over to enclose Celena's hands in his large ones, smiling at her and Joshua as if their presence was the best treat he could ask for.

He glanced round the resort. "Looks fabulous, doesn't it? Now that everything is nearly done, Daniel and I will be moving in tomorrow. While I was waiting for you, I had a great idea. Boats. We ought to rent out boats!" His voice was eager. "I think our guests would love it."

Celena smiled at him uncertainly. Hadn't Clint mentioned the same idea? Gerald went on enthusiastically. "It'll go along great with my idea for building some little cabins here on the east side. I've gotten some bids, and it can be done quite reasonably. What do you think?" Gerald's ruddy face looked boyishly hopeful.

Daniel was disapproving. "We need to look at the numbers before you do anything major." There was a steeliness that told Celena they had gone over this before. "Establish yourself, build your customer base, *then* expand. You don't want to stretch yourself too thin. Besides, shouldn't you ask Clint?"

For an instant, something like resentment flashed in Gerald's eyes. Then it was gone, and Celena wondered if it had actually been there at all. "You're never going to get anywhere in life if you don't take risks, my boy," Gerald said genially. He then turned to Celena and spoke to her. "The grand-opening ball is a week from Saturday. Is there any chance of you coming? I suppose Joshua's too young to run the light by himself for one night?"

"He is," Celena said, ignoring Joshua's scowl. "But Rueben's going to watch it for me."

"Oh ho! That's wonderful news!" His face was alight. "It's going to be a fantastic night for dancing—the ball of the century."

His words conjured up an image in Celena's mind of Lydia and Daniel dancing. Had it been an unforgettable night when the two of them had gone to Long Island?

Gerald glanced at a waitress who stood waiting nearby. "Let's sit down and see what the chef has for us today."

They went to a table that had been set with linen napkins, china, and goblets. The meal was impressive. They dined on scalloped potatoes and poached sole with grapes. Joshua carefully moved his grapes to the side of his plate. For dessert, there were chocolate-painted éclairs with chocolate gelato inside. From the patio, Celena could see the white froth of ocean waves as they curled inward. People were scattered about, either walking along the beach, playing in the surf, or sunbathing.

"So, are you enjoying Fire Island?" Celena asked Daniel.

As was often the case with people who were not natives, Daniel had learned a great deal about local attractions in a very short time. He'd been to the campground at Watch Hill and the William Floyd estate, which dated back to the 1700s. "I've also heard about a place called the Sunken Forest," Daniel said.

"It's a great place—a maritime forest," Celena replied. "In some places you can't even see the sun because of the trees and thick canopy of vines overhead. Normally trees don't grow near the ocean because the salt kills them, but in the Sunken Forest, the tall, secondary dunes protect them."

Joshua looked excited. "Celena, can we go there?"

"Sure," Celena replied easily.

"Do you want to come too?" Joshua asked Daniel and Gerald. It was too late to pinch him, but Celena gave her brother a burning look. "What did I do?" he asked in confusion.

Celena blushed as the men looked at her. "Oh, nothing," she said faintly, resolving that the instant they were alone, she would wring his neck. She nailed a smile on. "We'd love for you to come."

"We'll look forward to it," Gerald said, beaming with pleasure.

Daniel spoke up. "Joshua's been telling me all about the mooncussers, how they would board wrecked ships and sometimes kill the survivors in order to claim the ship's cargo."

"I imagine the mooncussers were mighty unhappy when the government built the lighthouse here," Gerald commented.

Celena answered, "Even with the light, there were still so many shipwrecks that the government started a life-saving service and offered the mooncussers jobs—rescuing people instead of killing them. Eventually, that organization merged with the Coast Guard."

"Still, there were bad mooncussers that tried to get ships to wreck by lighting lanterns or bonfires, so they would think they were someplace else," Joshua said.

Celena explained, "Captains know where they are because each lighthouse has its own distinctive flash pattern—to distinguish it from nearby lights. Fire Island flashes once every sixty seconds."

"I saw it change once," Joshua announced casually.

Celena looked at him in surprise. "But the pattern is preset. It can't change."

"It was only for a little while."

"When was that?"

Joshua was vague and unconcerned. "Oh, a while ago."

"Did you tell Father?"

"Yes." Suddenly Joshua looked excited. "Maybe it was the ghost!"

"Joshua! There aren't any ghosts." Celena laughed.

Her brother looked mutinous. "Are so. Just like Lydia said! You saw it yourself!"

Gerald looked amused. "She told you there was a ghost at the lighthouse?"

"Someone's been coming to the lighthouse at night, waving a light around," Celena said.

Daniel's expression changed to one of concern. "Do you want me to come and take a look around? Maybe you could give me a tour of the light. I've always wanted to see inside."

"You're welcome to come, but it's not a ghost, just someone being very annoying."

"Maybe I'll come tonight, if that's okay," Daniel offered. "And if a ghost does come, Joshua and I can go down and catch it."

"I'm going to have a sleepover at Zach's, so if it does come, you'll have to catch it yourself," Joshua replied spiritedly. Everyone laughed, then he asked his sister, "Is it okay if I change into my bathing suit and go down to the beach?"

"Yes, after you thank Mr. Roberts for the lunch."

"Thank you for the lunch," Joshua said politely. "It was great, except for the mushy grapes."

"Joshua!" Celena hissed.

Gerald bent toward Joshua, and in a conspiratorial whisper, confessed, "I didn't eat mine either." Looking vindicated, Joshua stuck out his tongue at Celena before running off.

"How is everything at the lighthouse, besides the annoying ghost?" Gerald asked.

"Fine. But I did find out something rather unexpected. I examined the equipment my father was using when he fell and found out that the rope had been cut."

Both men looked a little uncertain. "But that's what everyone thought had happened," Gerald said. "I suppose it rubbed against something and broke."

Shaking her head, Celena replied, "No. The cut was at the top of one of the ropes, where it connects to metal braces on the catwalk. There's nothing there for it to rub against."

Gerald was watching her intently, but it was Daniel who said, "I don't understand. If the rope wasn't rubbing against anything, then how did it get cut?"

"There's only one way," she said gloomily. "Someone had to cut it."

"But that's impossible!" Gerald exclaimed, the words fairly bursting out. "Who would do such a thing?"

Daniel was also incredulous. "That's a pretty serious allegation, Celena."

Feeling miserable, she absentmindedly folded a napkin as carefully as if it were a present. "I know, but I don't see what else it could be."

"The rope had to have been frayed or worn before Matthew ever started painting," Gerald stated emphatically. "And it simply gave way when he put his weight on it."

Daniel was more suspicious. "Did your father have any enemies?"

"Not that I know of."

"If what you say is true, he's got at least one," Daniel said grimly. "I'd like to take a look at the rope, if you don't mind. I hope you're mistaken about this, but if you're right, we need to take the rope to the authorities."

Gerald pushed his chair back. "I hate to leave, but if you'll excuse me, I have to get back to work. Need to build my customer base, you know," he said with a meaningful look at Daniel.

"Thank you for the lunch," Celena said. "It was wonderful."

"It's been a pleasure, Celena. Please come back anytime." The words were perfectly polite, but Gerald's voice seemed to lack some of its usual cheeriness.

As he departed, Celena and Daniel opted for a walk along the beach instead of a swim. They went to where the sand was wet and dark and didn't slide as they walked. Taking off their shoes, they ambled along, leaving the imprints of their feet behind to be filled in by the next surge of water. Here and there the sand was garnished with brownish-green seaweed. Little sandpipers played their endless game of tag with the surf, never quite allowing the water to touch their feet.

They found Joshua bending over a tide pool. His tanned legs were bare, and he'd stripped off his shirt. Celena and Daniel hunkered down, studying the sea life at their feet. Tiny bits of seaweed festooned the edges, and a hermit crab scuttled along the bottom. A small starfish inched across a protruding rock. Looking closer, Celena could see barnacles, their feathery arms waving in the water as they snagged the tiniest forms of plankton.

Celena and Daniel went a short distance away to sit on some flat rocks. The sea was shimmering in front of them and a fresh, stiff breeze was blowing, not enough to chill them, but just enough to keep the sun from being too warm.

"How are things coming along with your father?" Daniel asked.

Celena chose to misunderstand. "He's recovering slowly. Not fast enough for him, of course, but he's regaining strength."

"I think you know what I meant."

Leaning over, Celena drew designs in the sand with her forefinger. "Actually, things are going much better than I thought they would." She looked out over the ocean, watching the progression of the waves, ever changing and never ending. "It helps to know that he came after me. And that he wrote and called. Still, I've spent the last five years thinking that my father didn't care about me. That he'd tossed me away and forgotten about me. It's strange, but even though I know differently now, it's hard to change my old way of thinking."

"It can't be easy to erase all those years of believing that he'd cast you off without a backward glance." Daniel sounded like he understood. "But now that you know what really happened, you can get over those feelings."

Celena felt dispirited. "But just because he tried to contact me afterward doesn't excuse how he treated me the year after my mother died. Especially when he threw me out."

"You're still bitter."

"With good reason. That was a *terrible* thing he did!"

"It was. But it did happen five years ago. You can't change what happened back then, and neither can he." Daniel sounded earnest. "It's hard to get over something that hurt you so much, but I think you want to. After all, you came back despite everything that happened. Plus, you agreed to stay on the island and help your father and brother. I think you're amazing."

She felt embarrassed yet touched by his praise. "It's been hard at times, but actually easier than I expected," Celena confessed. "Father is different in a lot of ways. I think we're starting over. It's just . . . hard to forget what he did. How do I forget the past when it's part of me?" Celena's voice sounded like somebody lost.

"You don't have to forget," Daniel said solemnly. "Just forgive. They're not the same thing. You're always going to remember—you do have a brain, after all. But you can choose to forgive and move on."

"I'm trying. And failing at times. When I first got here, I—I lashed out at him."

"That's one of the problems with anger—we need to get it out, but we have to be careful not to hurt people in the process. It's not good to hold on to anger, because it will poison you. But I think you're forgiving and getting over it. I can see that in you already."

Daniel stood and reached a hand down to pull her up. There was reassurance and strength in his grasp. For a moment, Celena wanted nothing more than to cling to the comfort his hand offered. Then she shook herself. *Slow down,* she warned herself, remembering Sam. Yet she was already aware of Daniel in a different, more intense way. Caring seemed to flow from him like honey. There was something indefinable about Daniel's manner that caught her attention, a kind of goodness— a deep, clear aura of security that Celena found comforting.

* * *

That evening, when Celena went to her room, she noticed something lying on her bed. It was two twigs, each with dried red berries that had been tied together with red wool. Despite its simplicity, there was something about it that raised the hairs on the back of her neck. Celena took it to the kitchen where Minerva was ironing. She had stretched a linen shirt over a fabric-sheathed clothes board and was dipping her hand in a bowl of water, then sprinkling it over the material.

Celena held out the red-tied twigs. "Do you know who left this on my bed?"

Minerva eyed it with something akin to fear as she clutched the iron. "I sure didn't. Helen has a bunch of them things, but I don't want anything to do with them."

"Why? What is it?"

"It's an amulet. I think they are to protect a person or bring good luck, but it's all some kind of voodoo, if you ask me." Minerva's dark eyes looked disturbed. "You can ask Helen about that. Shoo now— and take that thing with you!"

"Is Helen all right?" Celena asked. "The last couple of days she's looked ill."

"Overwork, I expect," Minerva said smoothly. Celena felt there was more but didn't pursue it. In her room, Celena looked at the amulet.

What did Minerva mean by voodoo? Black magic? What magical properties was this amulet supposed to have? The twigs were well aged, the berries dried to a deep maroon color. Who would have left such a thing in her room? And why? Was it meant to scare her? Maybe she should ask Daniel what he thought. No, she told herself, she didn't want to become dependent on him, no matter how kind he seemed. It would be better to sort this out herself.

As she held the twigs, Celena was gripped by a sense of warning. Perhaps that's what the amulet was for—to warn her that perhaps she ought to back off and go home. After all, danger was afoot; that much was clear after having discovered the cut rope at the lighthouse. But she had committed herself to staying. So much had changed from when she'd first stepped off the ferry. She put the amulet on her dresser. There were more serious questions and problems than this bundle of twigs. Such as who it was Rueben had seen at the lighthouse. What had the woman been doing there? Why hadn't she spoken up? It all seemed much more sinister now in light of the rope being cut. Who could have done such a thing? Looking again at the twigs, Celena wondered. Someone was being prompted to malice, but who?

ELEVEN

Evening shadows were beginning to change the landscape when Celena reached the lighthouse. Daniel was waiting at the base, his hand on the rough, whitewashed tower as he looked up at the dizzying height. "In case you were wondering," Celena said, "it's one hundred and sixty-eight feet tall."

Daniel smiled at her easily. "Actually, I *was* wondering that."

He followed Celena to the generator building. "The rope I was telling you about is in here," she said. She opened the door and saw that even though the chair was there, the rope was gone.

"That's odd."

"What?"

"The rope's gone." She thought for a minute, then relaxed. "Oh, it's okay. Rueben wanted to take a look at it. He must have taken it home with him."

"I hope that's it."

"Yes. I'm sure that's all." She smiled and clapped her hands together. "So, let's get you that lighthouse tour."

Daniel smiled at her. "Lead the way."

After getting the kerosene, Celena unlocked the door to the keeper's cottage. "Our home is on the left, and the rooms on the right used to be for an assistant keeper, but we haven't had a live-in one for years." They went through the corridor to the base of the light where the dark was cavernous and the air damp, then up the spiraling stairs to the service room where Celena filled the tank. "Lighting the lamp isn't difficult," she said, cranking the weights, "but the clockworks have to be wound every four hours. An alarm clock comes in handy so I can get some sleep."

Daniel climbed through the trapdoor into the lantern room and looked in awe at the huge, oblong light in the middle of the floor. "It looks like something from outer space!"

"It's a first-order Fresnel lens," Celena informed him proudly, "with a visibility of twenty-one miles." She lit the spirit lamp, warmed the kerosene flow, then lit the mantle. All that was left was to release the mechanism. It was gratifying when it all worked and the great lens began to turn. "The Lighthouse Bureau has a handbook that gives very detailed explanations on how to do everything, even trimming wicks and adjusting lamps," Celena explained. "The only thing we can use to clean oil off the lens is spirits of wine."

"Good thing you're a Mormon, else you'd never be able to convince people why you're always running short," Daniel teased.

Celena rolled her eyes. "Everything has to be done just so. They're real sticklers at inspections." They went out on the high parapet that encircled the lantern room. In the distance they could see summer cottages at Kismet and the clustered houses of Saltaire. Several white steeples rose among the lower rooftops.

"Talk about a bird's-eye view," Daniel said appreciatively. "This is a little different from where I grew up."

"What did your father do when you were little?"

"What *didn't* he do?" Daniel sighed. "He was always coming up with all sorts of crazy, get-rich schemes. It was either feast or famine, and most often the latter. My mother hid money away during the good times. That helped tide us over when my father's plans fell apart. I can relate to your situation with your father. I started fighting with mine in my late teens, but it was all one-sided. My father's too easygoing to fight."

Celena could see that. Quarreling with Gerald would be like fighting the wind.

"My father was addicted to the idea of being rich. He'd risk every-thing." Daniel's eyes clouded over. "I got so mad and frustrated that finally I had to go, even though I hated leaving my mother. She's happy now that she's remarried, but I stayed angry at my father for a long time. I wouldn't have anything to do with him. Then one day, he called. We started talking and found out we could have a relationship again."

"My father is kind of the opposite of yours. He drove me crazy because he was so careful and conservative. But things started working out for your father, didn't they? I mean, he's got a great job now."

Daniel wouldn't meet her eyes. "I suppose so," he muttered. Clearly there was something here. Why the strange unhappiness? Although Gerald tended to be boastful, he was so personable and charming that Celena had no doubt he'd make Clearwater a great success.

As evening came on, all traces of blue slowly evaporated from the sky. They went inside and continued talking. From time to time they looked outside to check for the ghostly light.

"I thought at first that it might be Ethan walking around the light," Celena said. "He told me he's watching the beach because his wife, Sarina, told him to."

"But didn't she die a long time ago?"

"She drowned two years ago, but Ethan doesn't believe her death was an accident. He thinks someone killed her and that Sarina came back to haunt the person that did it."

Looking startled, Daniel asked, "You don't think there's anything to it, do you?"

Celena was hesitant. "Ethan's always been paranoid, but I think *something* odd happened that night. Some people think Ethan might have been responsible for Sarina's death."

Daniel was unconvinced. "He's a little slow, but he seems harmless." As he said it, he looked out the windows again. "I guess your friend has taken the night off. I'd better go." Celena walked downstairs with him.

"Thanks for letting me come." Daniel smiled, then suddenly gave her a quick, unexpected kiss on the cheek before stepping out in the darkness.

Celena held a hand to her cheek for a moment. As she went up the stairs, the flashlight sent odd shadows leaping about the walls as though they had a life of their own. Celena tried to rid herself of a sudden strange uneasiness. Was it coming from being alone or from the way she was beginning to feel about Daniel? She went back onto the catwalk. The beach was glistening like shiny metal under the bright moon, which cut a wide path on the ocean. The night was still, and it seemed like everything and everyone was asleep. Suddenly, a flickering light appeared. A ghostly figure came closer, then walked slowly back and forth. Celena groaned. If only Daniel had stayed a little longer, he might have been able to go down and find out who was behind this!

* * *

On Wednesday morning, she and Joshua rode back to Bay Haven in good time. At the sideboard, Joshua made a sandwich of toast, eggs, and bacon to take with him to Zach's house. Joshua was in high spirits these days, happy to be able to stay at the light every night he wanted since school was out. Celena helped herself to oatmeal and juice, joining Lydia who sat at the table nibbling toast.

"Have a good night at the light?" Lydia asked, watching her from underneath heavily-shadowed eyelids. Was there something faintly sly in Lydia's question, or was Celena just being overly sensitive?

"It went fine," Celena said, stirring milk into her oatmeal. "It was a nice warm night, wasn't it? Perfect for a stroll along the beach."

"How should I know?" Lydia shrugged. "I was in bed early. I heard you went to lunch at Clearwater yesterday. Was Daniel there?" When Celena replied affirmatively, a look of displeasure briefly curtained Lydia's face. Then she brightened. "Daniel asked me to help him move today."

It was none of her concern what Daniel did, Celena reminded herself, keeping her emotions from showing. Instead she asked, "Did you go into my room last night and put an amulet on my bed?"

"Why would I do that?" Lydia asked, a half smile curving her lips. "You're getting spooked, aren't you? I would be too if I thought someone had tried to kill my father."

"That news is traveling fast. Who told you?"

"Mother."

Celena was guarded. "I never told Helen."

"Gerald did. He's her spy. By the way, what makes you think the fall wasn't an accident?"

"I could tell by looking at the rope. It was a clean cut."

"Isn't it a little peculiar that you're the only one who thinks something suspicious is going on? Gerald, Ethan, Doc Harrison, and Rueben were all there after your father fell, and none of them thought it was anything but an accident."

"I imagine they were too concerned about my father to think about *why* he fell. But enough of that. I wanted to ask you about Sarina. Were Ethan and Sarina happy together?"

"They were married, dear-heart. Of *course* they weren't happy."

"Did you know Sarina was scared of boats?"

Lydia's catlike eyes narrowed. "No, but I didn't know her very well. Why are you asking all these questions?"

"I want to find out what happened when Sarina died. Ethan's still so disturbed about it. He thinks she's come back."

"Maybe she's the ghost at the lighthouse," Lydia said flippantly.

Celena ignored that. "Ethan says that Sarina is angry because her death wasn't an accident. He keeps talking about bad men and needing to watch the beach. Do you know what he means?"

For just a second, Lydia lost her usual confident look, staring at Celena with what almost looked like fear. She recovered quickly however and, after taking a breath, said crisply, "I have no idea. You'd have to have a certificate in crazy to understand my uncle Ethan, so don't ask me."

Just then, the sound of raised voices came from the parlor. Lydia raised her eyebrows, intrigued, then went to the door, shamelessly pressing an ear against it. Her green eyes were dancing when she turned back and whispered gaily, "There's a bang-up argument going on!" Helen's voice was now recognizable. The other voice was male, but his words were indecipherable. It seemed a long time but was probably no more than a few minutes when all became quiet. Lydia cracked the door open to peek out.

"The coast is clear."

Feeling disquieted, Celena took her dishes into the kitchen. It was so unlike Helen to have a scene in public. Who had she been arguing with, and over what?

* * *

Later that morning, Gerald came down the stairs carrying several boxes. For once he was dressed casually, though his clothes were still far nicer than what most people wore on moving day.

"Do you need any help?" Celena asked.

"Thanks; but we're nearly done. Lydia offered to help, and she and Daniel are over at Clearwater now, putting things away. This is the last of it."

Back in her room, Celena changed into a yellow blouse and, leaving her door open so she could hear the telephone, sat down to read. When the phone did ring, her book hit the floor as she jumped up, but when she ran out, Helen had already answered it. She held out the receiver to Celena, who took it with slightly shaking hands.

It was Mr. Rennicke. Soberly and without preamble, he said, "We've reached a decision. First of all, at the present time, the Lighthouse Bureau has no plans to decommission the Fire Island light. We have discussed your desire to run the light, keeping in mind the outstanding service your father has rendered over the years. This gives us great confidence not only in him but in whomever he deems capable and trustworthy of running the light during his recovery.

"Since you received training from your father, have recently demonstrated knowledge of the light and all responsibilities relating to it, and are held in high regard by two reliable men, Mr. Wyatt and Mr. Paxton, we feel it would be improper to install a new keeper at this time. Even though Matthew's recuperation will take some time, we have no reservations about having you continue to run the Fire Island light until your father is able to resume his duties, or until the doctor knows if Matthew has sustained permanent damage. We assume Rueben will remain as your backup."

"Yes, he will, and thank you!" Celena cried.

"We will be sending out an inspector soon, then once every three months, as usual, to monitor the light. If you need assistance in any way, don't hesitate to contact us. We hope your father will have a smooth and complete recovery. Please keep us updated on his condition."

"I certainly will. And, Mr. Rennicke, I want to assure you that the light will be in good hands," Celena said fervently.

A smile seemed to come into his voice. "We have no doubt of that, Miss Jackson."

Celena felt light-headed with triumph. This must be what it felt like to drink champagne—a lot of it. She jumped up and down, punching the air with her fists and whooping with joy. Minerva peeked around the kitchen door, smiling widely when she saw it was Celena.

"I got it!" Celena exclaimed. "They're going to let me run the light!"

Helen was behind the counter. Her face looked cold and her voice was the same. "When they come out and inspect, they'll soon realize they've made a mistake."

Celena struggled to maintain her self-control. This woman wanted to upset her, and she was not going to let her succeed. "My father taught me how to run the light. I can take care of it just as well as he can."

"But for how long?" Helen said frostily. "Until you have another argument and run away again?" Minerva gave a small gasp and ducked back inside the kitchen.

"What happened back then is none of your business," Celena said simply. Turning abruptly, she went down the hall.

Her father had heard the noise and was sitting up, looking as if he was getting ready to leap off the bed. "What was going on out there? Sounded like a cat was getting scalded."

Celena laughed. "That was me. The Lighthouse Bureau called."

"And they turned you down."

She ignored his teasing. Anyone could see that his face was alight. "They're going to let me run it!"

Matthew eased back, his usual somber expression returning. "I told you. Don't know why you were so worried," he said grouchily.

She looked at him with one raised eyebrow. "Then why do you look so relieved?"

"Just glad some cat didn't get hurt."

* * *

When Celena called Daniel, she was pleased at the genuine delight in his voice. She decided to go to the ferry to tell Clint the good news and stop at the post office on her way back to tell Tana. Before she left, she also called Rueben, so she could share the good news and ask him what he'd done with the frayed rope from the lighthouse.

Rueben, like her father, pretended he'd never had any doubts about what the bureau would decide, but when questioned about the rope, he said he hadn't made it out to the lighthouse yet to look at it, so he certainly hadn't taken it. Celena felt uneasy about this but told herself she was being paranoid. She hadn't really looked very hard for it the other night. Clearly she just hadn't left it where she thought. Outside, birds were chirping in the trees, and the morning was lovely and clear—warmer too, with the coming of summer. At the dock, Celena waited impatiently for the *Sea Siren* to arrive. When it did, Celena ran up the gangplank and impulsively flung her arms around Clint.

"Mr. Rennicke called, and they're going to let me run the light!" she blurted. "Thank you so much for coming with me!" His arms were strong as he held her close. When she pulled back, he touched her cheek affectionately, a tender gesture that momentarily unsettled her. As he looked at her, Celena knew he was amused by her quick confusion and the warm color in her cheeks.

"All the credit belongs to you. You won them over completely. I had no idea you were such an influential speaker." Clint smiled, his teeth flashing white against the deep tan of his face. "We should celebrate. Have you had lunch yet?" When she shook her head, he said, "Great, let's go to Jere's Café. It's a light day—let me just tell the crew they're going to be on their own for the next run."

Jere's was crowded, but they found an open booth. After the waitress took their orders, Clint asked, "What's the latest from Doc Harrison?"

"He let my father sit in a chair yesterday. Still, he said we shouldn't look for improvement in terms of days, but rather weeks."

Clint nodded, then said, "Did the doctor say anything else?"

"No. But I found out something rather unsettling about my father's accident. Actually, I'm not sure I can call it an accident anymore. I examined the rope and chair he was using to paint the lighthouse when he fell, and it looks like the rope had been cut."

Clint craned his neck toward her in surprise. "Cut? You mean it rubbed against something and gave way?"

"As far as I can tell, it didn't rub against anything. The cut was at the top, where it connects to braces on the catwalk. There's nothing there for it to rub against."

"What are you saying, Celena?" There was a tightening in his voice, a tension.

She shifted uncomfortably in her seat. "Somebody had to have cut it."

He leaned against the back of the booth, looking visibly disturbed. After the waitress brought their plates, he said cautiously, "Surely there has to be another explanation."

Celena shrugged helplessly. "I'd like to believe that, but I can't think of anything else."

Clint sat still as if he were digesting the news, trying to make sense of it. "How can you tell the rope was cut?"

"Because the rope wasn't frayed. When a rope breaks because of wear and tear, it frays and the strands will be of varying lengths, because they don't all break in the same spot. There should have been long and short fibers on each end of the break. But the strands were perfectly even all the way across."

Clint listened attentively. "This is incredible. We've got to get to the bottom of this. Have you called the police?" When Celena said she hadn't, he replied, "If you want, I'll go with you to the Ocean Beach police department tomorrow. It's too bad Saltaire doesn't have its own police station. Though I guess it's good that we haven't got enough crime on this island for each town to have its own station." He took a sip of water, then looked at her grimly. "I can't imagine someone doing such a thing. Matthew is so well-liked. It must have been some lunatic."

"Or someone who wants the lighthouse."

His gray eyes were alert, and there was an urgency in his voice that hadn't been there before. "You mean . . . Helen or Gerald?"

"I don't know what to think," she said miserably, hating to blame anyone for something so horrifying.

"There's no use speculating."

"Has anyone else seen the rope?"

"Not yet."

"Well, I'd hate to see rumors flying on this one."

"Have you told anyone else about the rope?"

"Rueben, Daniel, and Gerald. Apparently Gerald told Helen, who told Lydia."

"Lydia? The town crier? The whole island knows, then. You know, it could have been someone on the island. To be safe, you shouldn't trust anyone."

Celena smiled slightly. "What about you?"

"Not even me."

She was about to speak when the waitress came by. Clint ordered apple pie a la mode, then continued. "Celena, I know you want your father to keep the light, but if the rope really was cut, then you could be in danger. I don't like the idea of your being involved in this." He took her hand. "I can run it until your father gets better—just to keep you safe."

His offer was tempting. But just in the weeks she'd been here, circumstances had changed. *She* had changed. How could she leave when she and her father were slowly rebuilding their relationship? And what about the promises she had made to her mother?

"I appreciate that, Clint. I really do. But I need to stay."

"You know Celena, you look fragile and easy to intimidate, but you're not."

"Good thing. I think someone tried to scare me the other night by leaving some kind of voodoo thing in my room. Plus, the 'ghost' was at the light again last night."

"Not again!"

"Daniel was at the light, watching for the ghost. But he left just before the so-called ghost came."

There was a speculative look in Clint's eye. "You don't say? How long was Daniel gone before the 'ghost' showed up?"

"I don't know. Five or ten minutes."

After paying for their lunch, they walked outside. Clint squeezed her hand in parting, and Celena went down the street to Tillman's.

* * *

Elaine Tillman's son Billy was out front, shucking corn in a barrel as he watched the old-timers play checkers. Elaine was at the counter, helping a couple pick out picnic items from a small refrigerated case. The back door was open, and Celena could see Elaine's oldest son, Jeremy, on the back porch, breaking up wooden shipping crates. Celena stopped to look at a display of perfume. When Elaine had wrapped up a slab of cheese in waxed paper and rung up the couple's purchases, she walked over to Celena.

"I've marked that one down," Elaine said, pointing at an amber bottle with a round gold top. "Sarina bought that one by the gallon, but nobody else really cares for it."

Unscrewing the top, Celena took a cautious sniff. "Did Sarina come in here a lot, then?"

"Oh, yes. Buying this, ordering that. Spending money like there was no tomorrow." Elaine shook her head as if the memory were beyond belief. "You never saw the like. I often said she couldn't have come by that much money honestly." Celena looked shocked, which was all Elaine needed to keep going. "I figure she and Ethan were doing a little rum-running."

"But I thought she was afraid of the water."

"Sarina? Who told you that? Why she was always going out and—"

A loud voice interrupted. "Hey! What do I have to do to get some service?" A chubby, dark-haired man was standing at the counter, looking impatient.

"Showing me your money would help," Elaine retorted. She whispered witheringly to Celena, "Tourists! Think they own the place."

Celena frowned slightly as Elaine walked away. Gerald had said Sarina was afraid of the water. Apparently she wasn't, but why had he said that? And where had Sarina gotten her money? She would have to ask Ethan.

Celena wound through the store to reach the post office, which was in the back. Tana was excited to hear the good news and clasped her hands together. "I'm so glad, Celena!" She wanted to know how Matthew had reacted, and they talked until a woman came in. Celena was about to go when Tana exclaimed, "Oh! I almost forgot! That part for the generator finally got in. Your father ordered it before his accident. Let me get it." Tana bustled away and returned with a cardboard box. "I figured it had to be something important since the company sent Matthew a telegram to let him know the shipping had been delayed."

"I don't remember Father getting any telegram."

"Oh, it came the day Matthew fell. I knew he was anxious about that part, so when Helen told me she was going to the light, I asked her to take the telegram to Matthew. I was sick that afternoon when I found out that he'd fallen."

Celena stared. *Helen* had gone to the light. And not said a word about it, not even when Celena had asked. But now that she was in the possession of such a clue, Celena didn't know what to think. She spoke in a high, tight tone she didn't recognize as her own.

"So Helen went out to the light that day?"

"In the morning. And by the way, how is Helen doing? I saw her the other day, and she looked like a ghost. She's probably working too hard." Tana's round, pleasant face was concerned. "That deadbeat husband of hers ought to come home once in a while and give her a hand." Tana handed her a stack of mail. "Don't forget that. There's a magazine in there your father will enjoy."

"Thanks."

Helen had to have been the one Rueben saw leaving the light-house. But why hadn't she said anything, and just how significant was that omission?

Elaine Tillman's raised voice came floating to the back of the store. Walking to the front, Celena saw Elaine scolding Zach Harrison, who was holding a magazine. Joshua stood beside him, looking alarmed as Elaine continued to rebuke Zach.

"I've told you over and over not to look through the magazines without paying for them."

Zach's round face looked contrite. "I'm sorry. I forgot. It's just that my mother was feeling down today, and I thought if I could find a joke to tell her, it might cheer her up."

Elaine looked at him doubtfully. "Your mother seems to get down in the dumps a lot."

"Yes, ma'am. I try to get fresh jokes for her whenever I can."

"Go talk to Rueben then, or else get your father to give you the price of a magazine. Customers don't like to buy them when they're all worn."

"I'll do that. Thanks for the suggestion," Zach said respectfully, putting the magazine back carefully. Joshua gave Celena a small wave, then followed his friend out the door.

"That Zach is one slick talker," Elaine said, her voice a mixture of disapproval and admiration. As she went back to straightening shelves, Celena noticed a tall man with a broad back by the display of fishing tackle. It could only be one person. She called out and Ethan turned with a start, the alarm on his face disappearing when he saw Celena. Seeing Ethan smile was a remarkable sight, for his smile was as huge as himself. Today he wore rough work clothes and a cap pulled down over his bushy hair. He was holding a packet of hooks.

Celena asked, "Going fishing?" Ethan nodded happily. Standing next to the rack of toys, Celena idly pulled out a small football she thought Joshua would love. There was no price tag, so she took it with her to the counter to ask Elaine. Ethan went with her.

"Say, Ethan," Elaine said. "You bought one of these a few months ago, how much was it?"

"Fifty-seven cents."

Elaine's rather ordinary face lit up when she grinned. "He never forgets a price. I'd hire him in a minute, but he keeps turning me down." Ethan smiled shyly. Celena understood; a store would be too confining, and dealing with people too difficult.

As he paid for the hooks, Celena asked, "Where are you going, Ethan?"

He looked around quickly before answering in a low voice, "Down to the beach."

It was the perfect opportunity. "Great, I'll come with you." Celena paid for her purchases and left them behind the counter to pick up later. The afternoon had turned gray with an incoming storm. Celena loved a day like this when the sea took on the grim look of the sky and rolled landward endlessly in mountainous corrugations. Ridge after swelling ridge hurled itself upon the rocky shore and broke with a crash, sending white spray high in the air.

They went to their favorite spot to get out of the worst of the wind. Sitting in the sheltered rocky fortress, Ethan looked as though he was waiting—for what? Probably Sarina. Sea birds careened in the wind, sailing and diving in their wild play, alighting at times on nearby rocks. The birds had little fear, since Celena and Ethan sat as still as the very stones themselves.

"Gerald told me that Sarina was afraid of the water. Is that true?"

"She didn't like the water but wanted a boat," he said. "Clint found one for us to buy."

"Where was she going the night she died?"

"I don't know. Something was wrong." His voice was unhappy, brooding. "Sarina always told me before she went anywhere. Always. But she didn't that night." Ethan's brown eyes were troubled. "When I got home, she wasn't there. The boat was tied up. She'd told me that if she ever didn't come home, I was to watch the beach, so—so I did." Ethan stuttered in his emotion, the words coming out in a near frantic tumble. "But she wasn't there. When I got back, the boat was gone." He looked at Celena entreatingly, as if she could make it all come clear.

"She must have come home while you were gone and taken the boat."

"No." Ethan's shaggy head shook violently. "Sarina *always* told me before she went. I went looking. A long time. I saw her boat. It was snagged offshore. I swam to it, but she wasn't in it." Celena remembered that Clint had mentioned that Ethan had been wet. This would explain why. Ethan went on, his voice toneless. "They found her on the beach the next day." It was clear he was still having trouble comprehending how such a thing could happen.

Celena wished she could help. "I'm so sorry," she said, feeling sick. "Did Sarina say anything, even in the days or weeks before she left, to give you an idea of where she might have gone?"

Ethan thought hard. "No, but she was different. More happy. Excited."

"What was she excited about?"

Ethan's brow furrowed as he tried hard to remember. "I don't know. She was just happy. She wanted to buy a house."

"A house? Did you have the money for a house?"

"I don't think so." Ethan looked confused. "Sarina took care of the money. She said everything was going to be all right."

What had Sarina meant by that cryptic statement? Celena could not suppress a shiver. Everything had *not* been all right. "Oh, I meant to tell you, I heard back from the Lighthouse Bureau," Celena said. "They're going to let me run the light."

Ethan's face instantly became alarmed. He rose and began twisting his hands. "No, Celena, you can't! Sarina said there were bad men. She can't rest because they killed her. You shouldn't be here." Looking as if he needed an outlet for his unexplained panic, Ethan suddenly strode away. What did he mean by bad men? Could he mean smugglers?

There were too many unanswered questions. What had Sarina meant by saying everything was going to be all right? Why wasn't everything all right then? If only she knew where Sarina had gone that night. And what was this talk about buying a house? Did she mean one for her and Ethan, or one for herself after she had left the island?

* * *

After retrieving her things from Tillman's, Celena went to Bay Haven. When her father had finished grumbling over the inordinate amount of time it had taken to receive the generator part, Celena said, "Tana said she gave Helen a telegram to give you the morning you fell. Do you remember seeing her?"

"No, but then there's a lot I don't remember about that day."

Later, Celena decided to stop and look for the rope again, but that meant she'd have to miss dinner. She was putting a sandwich, fruit, and a few cookies in a bag when Joshua found her. "Can I come to the light later? Zach invited me to a cookout on the beach with his family." His eyes were anxious. Clearly, he worried that Celena might not be able to manage without him. She assured him it would be fine, then told him the bureau was going to let her run the light.

She waited for a scream of joy, but all he said was, "Why *wouldn't* they let you run it?"

"Never mind. I'll see you later." Celena tucked her hair under a wide-brimmed hat and, instead of riding her bike, walked through town, then across the dunes which were shadowed in the late afternoon. After a while she turned inland, going up a scrubby bluff and following the trail, which became a dirt track. She wondered again what Sarina had meant by telling Ethan to watch the beach. But the part that sent shivers down her back was Ethan saying Sarina couldn't rest because she'd been killed. Even after two years, his wife's death was still hanging heavily on Ethan's mind. If she could find some answers, it might help put his mind at rest.

Suddenly, Celena felt like she was being observed. She looked about uneasily. What had alarmed her? It was hard to say. A rustle sounded in the grass behind her, beyond the thicket. Celena turned her head quickly, but no one was visible. Was it a deer, perhaps, foraging in the thicket of blueberries? That must be it. Yet she felt uneasy.

Picking up her pace, she continued, and once again, there was a slight noise behind her. She turned sharply but it was gone, whatever it was. Celena was hoping to hear the snort of a deer as it emerged from the brush and bolted away, but there was only silence and a prickling at the back of her neck.

There was no need to be frightened, Celena told herself. Yet, in spite of all reason, she *was* afraid. An uncanny sense of danger seemed loose in the increasing dusk. If someone was following her, he stopped when she stopped, and started when she did. Celena uneasily wondered what would happen if that were reversed.

Celena started out again, trying to shake off the disturbing thoughts, but gasped when there was a small sound and a rabbit ran in front of her. Had the rabbit caused the sound or been frightened by it? For a few moments, Celena stood utterly still and listening. Then, sweating and cold, she hurried on. She was still minutes away from the lighthouse when she glanced behind her once again. A man, darkly silhouetted against the ocean, came out of the brush. He was headed straight for her.

TWELVE

In the same instant that Celena turned to run, a man's voice called, "Celena? Wait a minute." It was a familiar voice and she stopped, heart pounding as he approached, his body long and angular.

When Daniel saw her, he exclaimed, "What's the matter? You're shaking."

"I thought someone was following me on the trail. Was it you?"

"No, I just came over the dunes." He clasped her briefly, patting her back and murmuring comfortingly. "Tell me what happened." As she explained, there was a quivering in the pit of her stomach. "I'll go take a look," Daniel said.

He was back in a few minutes. "I didn't see anything. Come on, I'll walk you to the light." Had she only been imagining things or might something have happened if Daniel had not come along? Clint, Rueben, and Ethan had all hinted at danger, but she had not taken them seriously. But now . . . Did someone on the island mean her ill? Then again, quite possibly it had been nothing at all.

"I'm sorry," Celena apologized. "I must be letting things get to me, what with the rope and the amulet."

"What amulet?"

"Someone put an amulet in my room. I'm sure it doesn't mean anything." She brushed it off.

"I'm not sure about that. Could be that someone is trying to frighten you."

She shivered slightly.

Daniel changed the subject. "How are things with your father? Have you forgiven him yet?"

Celena was annoyed. "You make it sound easy, like flipping a light switch. It's a little more complicated than that."

"It doesn't have to be. Your father hurt you, but he tried to make things right. It's up to you whether you decide to forgive him or not." His tone was so light and matter-of-fact that it was impossible to take offense.

"I'm trying, but sometimes when I'm alone, I still feel upset. It wasn't just him ordering me to leave. It was the whole year before I left. All he did was criticize me. He'd say the most awful things about the Church, but if I tried to defend it, he'd say I was being defiant and insolent." She turned her head so he couldn't see the unexpected and aggravating tear that trickled down her cheek.

"That must have been very hard. I'm sure you did the best you could," Daniel said gently. In a gesture free of self-consciousness, he reached out a finger and gently wiped her tear away. He did not belittle, discredit, or sympathize falsely, and because of that, she felt drawn to him. Daniel continued. "Just remember, all of that is in the past. When you start feeling upset now, tell yourself you're going to let it *stay* in the past."

She looked at him. "Is that what you do?"

There was an element of melancholy in Daniel's wry smile. "We're members of the biggest club there is—children who've had problems with their parents. But there comes a point in everyone's life when you have to forgive your parents. It took a while for me to grow up enough to stop holding them to impossible standards *I* set, and to realize they were human and made mistakes just like me. When I left home and started seeing more of life, I began to realize that my father wasn't the ogre I thought he was and that there were a great many fathers that were far worse. Once I accepted my father, warts and all, I began to get along with him a lot better."

Celena looked at him in admiration. His shrewd observations were like wiping the fog off a mirror to see what was really there. "You're a better man than I am, Gunga Din."

"That's not to say I never get upset and frustrated. I do, believe me." He looked at Celena. "If it seems too hard for you to forgive right now, just think of it as letting go. You'll get through life a lot easier without carrying around excess baggage like bitterness and anger."

Daniel continued gently. "Forgiving is something we all have to do if we want peace of mind. And it's not just our parents we'll have to forgive." Celena looked at him in wonder. She had the uncanny feeling that Daniel Roberts could read her heart like a passage from a play—that he could look at her life and see it clearly in ways that she could not. It was strange, but suddenly she found herself telling him about Sam. As she did, Celena was amazed to realize that the pain that had been there in varying degrees for so long was now gone.

When they reached the generator building, Celena said, "I want to look at the rope again, but I'm not sure where I left it."

"I thought Rueben had it."

"No. It turns out I was just absentminded. Do you want to help me look for it?"

"Sure."

The two searched the generator room, then the other buildings, but to no avail. Finally, Celena sat down in front of the generator room and pressed her fingers to her temples. "The rope's gone."

He stated the obvious. "Someone's taken it."

"So there wouldn't be any evidence," Celena said flatly.

"Actually, this *does* give you evidence," Daniel said. "It proves that someone *did* cut the rope; otherwise there would be no reason for someone to take it."

Celena stood and tried to process this information. This whole situation seemed so unlikely. She shook her head. As they walked to the light, Celena said, "I found out who was at the light when my father fell. Helen."

"What was she doing there?"

"She went to deliver a telegram to my father."

"Strange she never mentioned it, but then, Helen's always kept to herself. And lately, it seems that her mind is someplace else entirely."

So, Celena thought, she was not the only one to detect a change in Helen Montgomery. Both Elaine and Daniel had noticed.

Daniel went on. "Have you talked to Helen about it?"

"Not yet, but I plan to. I can only come up with two reasons," Celena said. "Either she's protecting herself or she's protecting someone else."

"Lydia?"

"Helen would do anything to protect her daughter."

"But Lydia wouldn't try to kill your father." Daniel sounded positive, but Celena didn't think he knew Lydia as well as she did.

"I also found out that Bay Haven isn't doing very well financially," Celena began. "Lydia was hoping they'd get the light to bring in more money. If there's one thing Lydia likes better than men, its money."

Daniel laughed, then turned serious. "I don't like this," he said shortly. "Someone is desperate enough to try to kill your father, and now you're next in line. Have you thought about that?"

"No, but thanks to you, Rueben, and Clint, I will from now on, thank you."

He grinned. "You're funny, you know that?"

"I'm always funny when I'm in mortal danger."

"There you go again. Have you thought about leaving the island?"

"And hand the light to Helen on a silver platter? Forget it. I just talked the Lighthouse Bureau into letting me run it! Besides, Joshua and my father are counting on me. The light means everything to them." Celena paused. "Besides, if someone really is targeting the keeper, then anyone who runs it would be in danger. It wouldn't be fair to put someone else's life at risk just so I can be safe."

"But I'm worried about you. I hate the thought of you being in danger."

"Me too!" Celena smiled briefly. "But I really don't believe I'm in danger. We don't really know that someone cut the rope to get the lighthouse. Maybe someone has a grudge against my father. Or it could have been a crazy tourist. Perhaps it was even a rumrunner."

Daniel's face tightened. "Have you heard anything about smuggling around here?"

"Just the usual, that rumrunners are around." Did something flicker in his eyes? Celena couldn't be sure. But there was a tenseness in Daniel that hadn't been there before.

"If you happen to hear anything specific, would you let me know?" There was a curious tone in Daniel's voice.

"Sure," Celena agreed, "but why are you so interested?"

"I wouldn't want anything to interfere with the grand opening of Clearwater. It means a great deal to my father. Hey, I wanted to ask you if you'd like to go on a picnic next week. Say, on Tuesday?"

"Only if you'll let me bring the food—and only if you keep in mind that it won't be like that fabulous lunch we had at Clearwater."

"Who wants mushy grapes anyway?" He grinned. Then he added, "Actually, I'm not interested in the food, only the company." He looked at her steadily, then, leaning forward, kissed her lightly before walking away.

The tingling Celena felt in her chest troubled her. She wasn't ready for a relationship. Besides, sometimes she had the feeling Daniel was like deep water; it was hard to see beneath the surface to what was really going on in his mind. Was it just her imagination, or was there something he wasn't telling her?

* * *

The next morning, the air was clean and fresh with the wet scent of earth and new-growing things. Joshua went on to Bay Haven while Celena stayed to update the record books. At lunch time, Clint appeared and asked if she wanted to go to the police at Ocean Beach.

"I've called them, but the rope is gone," Celena told him regretfully. Clint was clearly astonished as she went on. "Someone had to have taken it. Last night, I was on my way to look at it again when I ran into Daniel. When we got there, the rope was gone."

There was a speculative look in Clint's eyes. "Where was Daniel?"

"On the trail to the lighthouse."

"What was he doing there?"

Celena was startled. "What are you getting at?" Clint shrugged, then reminded her about their upcoming boat ride before hurrying back to the ferry.

* * *

On Thursday afternoon, a police officer came to the lighthouse to question Celena and take a look around, but without the rope as evidence, there was little he could do. Thursday night no shadowy figure came to the beach to trouble her, and Friday was uneventful—until vandals struck.

Celena discovered the damage Friday evening when she opened the door to the generator building. The work bench had been tipped over, buckets of parts dumped, and everything that had been neatly hanging on the wall was now thrown to the floor. Anything that could be easily broken had been. As a final touch, sand had been thrown all over the floor. There were several dents on the generator that provided electricity to the keeper's cottage, but it had not been seriously damaged. Fortunately, the vandals had not tampered with the tank of kerosene. Celena wondered if this was simply a prank or if someone was upping the ante in trying to scare her away.

There was no time right then to clean up the considerable mess, but after breakfast on Saturday, she notified the police of this new mysterious occurrence. Then she and Joshua began working on cleaning it up. Celena felt a smoking curl of anger as she and Joshua sorted nails, bolts, and nuts, swept up glass, and picked up and put things away. It took all afternoon.

Joshua came from behind some barrels. "Look Celena," he said, holding up some rumpled fabric.

She shook it out. "It's a coat. What's it doing back there?"

He shrugged. The coat was too big to have belonged to her father. It looked like the one Ethan wore. How had it come to be here? An idea hit her. The person who came to the lighthouse at night wore something that billowed. Could this be it? As Celena folded the coat, there was a faint scent of fish, reminding her of Rueben. Was this his coat? If so, why had it been hidden here? Maybe he had misplaced it here and then it had gotten displaced by the vandals. She shrugged. It probably wasn't anything. She laid the coat aside and got back to work.

* * *

On Sunday morning, she and Joshua hurried to Bay Haven as they always did to get ready for Sunday School. Celena finished first, and when she went into the foyer, Lydia was there, dressed in a smart red-and-white dress that showed off her curves.

"Are you coming with us today?" Celena asked pleasantly.

"I almost wish I were," Lydia said, looking glum. "Anything would be better than going with Mother to visit Aunt Janet and Uncle LaVar." Then Lydia brightened. "Remember last Monday when you were eavesdropping?"

Celena was stung. "*You* were the one with your ear to the door!"

"And you were right by my side," Lydia said complacently. "Besides, how else are you going to find out what you want to know? I found out who mother was arguing with and why." When Celena remained silent, Lydia smiled conspiratorially. "Don't tell me you don't want to know, dear-heart. I know you're bursting." She paused dramatically. "It was Gerald."

"It didn't sound like him," Celena replied doubtfully.

"Of course not. But you've never talked with Gerald when he's been drinking. Nathan Gibbs just got back in town, and Gerald is as jealous as he can be." Lydia voice was animated. "Can you believe it?"

Celena wasn't sure exactly what it was she was supposed to believe. "Who is Nathan Gibbs and why would Gerald be jealous?"

"Don't you remember? He's the contractor who built Clearwater. He's been gone for a while overseeing another project. He fancies mother and it drives Gerald wild since he wants Mother for himself."

Celena was shocked. "But your mother is married."

Lydia's green eyes looked at her contemplatively. "I guess it doesn't matter if I tell you. My parents are getting divorced. Mother filed the paperwork long ago, and it'll be final soon. And already she has two men interested in her." Lydia smirked. "Like mother, like daughter."

Celena excused herself before she got too nauseated and went to her father's room. She was taken aback to see him in a wheelchair, his cast sticking out in front, resting on a metal extension.

"Where did the chair come from?"

"Helen brought it in. And yes, Doc Harrison ordered it."

"That's wonderful! We'll be able to take you outside, get you out of this room."

"Aye, it's about time," Matthew said vigorously.

"Joshua and I are going to church now." She mischievously added, "Maybe next week you'll feel well enough to go with us." To her surprise, there was no brusque rebuff. She smiled. "I'd better find Joshua. See you later."

Celena found Joshua, who looked grown-up in a crisp white shirt and dark pants, and they walked to church. They say by Ethan, who was by himself on the back row. Burly and solid, Ethan was wrapped in a black overcoat despite the heat of the day. He smiled widely in welcome. After the opening prayer, someone dropped into the seat beside her. It was Daniel, dressed in a blue blazer and gray slacks and smelling of some kind of piney aftershave. Again, surprised by how comfortable she felt with him, she set her misgivings from their last encounter aside and enjoyed the feeling of having him near. Celena was glad she had worn her best dress—lilac with gray trim. When they divided for classes after opening exercises, Joshua went off with Zach. Ethan showed signs of bolting, but Celena kept him close. After the closing prayer, she opened her eyes to see the back of Ethan's coat going through the door. She sighed, then walked outside with Daniel, where they found Joshua and Zach waiting.

"Would you like to come to Bay Haven and have lunch with us, Daniel?" Celena asked. "Minerva said we're having fried chicken and pound cake with strawberries for dessert."

"No sensible man would pass up a chicken dinner," Daniel replied solemnly.

Zach's dark eyes were wide. "That sure sounds good! My mother didn't come today because she was tired. I'll probably have to make myself a sandwich."

Joshua looked up at his sister. "It's okay if Zach comes, isn't it?"

"I think so." Celena looked at Zach. "Unless you'd rather have peanut butter and jam."

Zach was anxious to reassure her. "Oh, no, chicken is just fine."

The boys dashed off, and, as she walked along with Daniel, Celena told him about the vandalism. "It could be kids, but I wonder if someone did it so I'd look bad when an inspector came. I wouldn't be surprised if it was Lydia."

Daniel was unsure. "How would she know when the inspector was coming?"

"That's the glitch in my theory. Maybe she was just hoping to get lucky."

"Someone could be doing it just to frighten you."

Celena suddenly found herself feeling all too curious about what Daniel's feelings for Lydia might be. She remarked casually, "Lydia went to visit some relatives, so she won't be here for lunch." Out of the corner of her eye, she watched Daniel.

"Is that right?" His interest seemed minimal, telling her nothing. She'd have to try again.

"Did you have a good time last week when you went to Long Island?"

"Oh, it was all right." He sounded indifferent. Possibly going dancing with Lydia had not gone well. She couldn't help smiling slightly at the thought.

When they arrived, Matthew joined them in the dining room, sitting in his wheelchair at a corner to accommodate his leg. It was a pleasant meal, though Celena felt sorry Clint couldn't enjoy it more. He rushed in, gobbled his food, and ran out, explaining they were shorthanded at the ferry.

Late that afternoon, Daniel, Joshua, and Celena went to sacrament meeting. Afterward, Rueben and Tana joined them as they headed back for Bay Haven, saying they wanted to visit Matthew. After Joshua ran on ahead, Celena noticed that Rueben was carrying a small sack.

When she asked about it, he paused a moment before replying. "I offered to bring the sacrament to your father."

"Wait a minute," her brow furrowed. "I thought the sacrament was only for members."

"Well . . . that's right."

It took a full minute for his answer to sink in. When it did, the breath went out of her in a whoosh. She began to stutter. "But what . . . when . . . Really?"

Daniel was astonished as well. "This *is* a surprise." He put an arm around Celena and squeezed. "What great news!" Still too staggered to speak, Celena had to remember to breathe. It *was* wonderful news, but somehow, the joy was shot through with pain.

Tana understood. Sympathetically, she said, "We didn't think it was our business to tell you. He should have told you himself. But I think he was embarrassed after how he used to act toward the Church and all."

Celena remained torn between joy and indignation. "But I've been here five weeks! And during all that time, he couldn't tell me he joined the Church?"

Rueben coughed apologetically. "Matthew's always been a stubborn cuss. To tell the truth, I think he was worried about how you would react. After all, you two used to argue day and night and in between about the Church. Now, he has to eat his words, and that's a hard thing for a proud man to do."

Tana laid a hand on Celena's arm. "I think his asking Rueben to bring him the sacrament today was his way of telling you."

"But Joshua never told me either." Celena's voice began to quiver as she remembered how they'd talked in the cemetery. Of course, he *had* said that Father was going to church.

"I don't think Joshua has ever given it a second thought," Tana said. "He's just a young boy."

Tears began rolling down Celena's cheeks. "But Father hated the Church. What changed his mind?"

"It started out slow-like, with Matthew asking a lot of questions and coming to church occasionally," Rueben disclosed. "But his decision to be baptized was like a bolt out of the blue, real sudden. One day he came to ask about being baptized. I could tell that something big had happened, but Matthew never would tell me what it was."

They paused in the foyer, and Tana handed Celena a handkerchief. Daniel squeezed her hand as they went into Matthew's room. Joshua was already there. Celena watched her father surreptitiously, but he did not glance her way as the sacramental prayers were given. After visiting a while, Rueben and Tana left. Shortly after that, Daniel said he had to go as well.

As they walked to the door, Daniel said, "I'm looking forward to our picnic."

"Me too. I'll meet you at Clearwater on Tuesday," Celena replied. He smiled into her eyes and left.

When Celena walked back to the bed, she asked her father in a quiet voice, "Why didn't you tell me you were baptized?"

Matthew shifted, looking uncomfortable. "I didn't want to make a big deal out of it," he said gruffly, not meeting her eyes.

Celena said tremulously, "You should have told me."

Joshua looked from his sister to his father, feeling but not understanding the tension. "I'm sorry you didn't know. But it's okay, isn't it, Celena?" Joshua asked.

She inhaled deeply, blinking rapidly. "Yes. It's all right. I just don't like secrets, that's all."

Joshua took his sister at her word and began talking about their plans to go to the Sunken Forest in a couple of weeks. Then he asked his father, "Do you want to come? You've got a wheelchair now."

Something in Matthew Jackson's face softened. "I'd like to, but I doubt I could manage it, son."

Joshua turned to Celena. "What about Zach? Can he come?" When she agreed, he was emboldened by his success and pressed for more. "Can I go to Clearwater's opening ball?"

Matthew looked stern and disapproving. "And leave your sister all alone at the light?"

"Actually, I'm going to the ball," Celena said. "Rueben's going to watch the light."

"I see," Matthew said. Then, turning to Joshua, he said, "You planning on taking a girl?"

Joshua looked disgusted. "Yuck."

"You can be my date," Celena told him playfully.

Her brother's brow wrinkled doubtfully. "What do I have to do?"

"Dance with me at least once."

He considered it a few moments before deciding it was something he could manage. Then Joshua asked his father, "Did Celena tell you that someone was chasing her at the beach?" Her brother paid no attention whatsoever to Celena's livid glare, adding informatively, "And someone left a voodoo magic thing on her bed."

Rising quickly, Celena took hold of her brother's hands, pulled him upright, and pushed him toward the door. "I think you've done enough damage for one night. Why don't you change your clothes and play for a while. *Outside.*" He frowned briefly, then scampered out.

With one gray eyebrow raised slightly, Matthew looked at her inquiringly. Celena put on a scornful smile and scoffed depreciatingly, "Kids!"

Matthew had no intention of letting it go. "What did he mean, someone was chasing you?"

"That Joshua! You know how he exaggerates. No one was following me. I got scared by a rabbit, that's all."

"A rabbit," Matthew said heavily, giving her a withering look. "Since when have rabbits become even remotely frightening?"

"This one had big teeth."

Matthew waited, his blue eyes burning a hole through her. Beginning to feel a bit flustered, Celena went on. "And that thing in my room, it was just an amulet. Helen has a collection of them, and Lydia said she—" Celena stopped abruptly. Lydia had never actually said whether she had or hadn't left it in her room.

Matthew Jackson's blue eyes were troubled, his expression grave. "Lydia came in and said there was a ghost coming around the lighthouse at night. I told her to cut out the foolishness, and then she told me someone messed up the generator building. And now someone followed you and left some crazy thing in your room? There's too many things going on while I'm lying cooped up here like a trussed chicken." Matthew's eyebrows made a pair of high angry hills, bristly and gray. His voice rose. "And you! You don't tell me nothing," he stormed. "You say you don't like secrets, but someone's been sneaking around the light for weeks, and not a word from you, by thunder!"

"I didn't want to worry you," Celena admitted.

"And I'm not going to worry when I find out things out from other people instead of you?" he roared.

Celena ground out, "Some people need to learn how to keep their mouths shut. Look, the vandalism was just a stupid prank, and I'm sure it was Lydia who left that amulet in my room, and—and—it was a *big* rabbit."

"You're sticking to that, are you?" Matthew said dryly.

"Until I think of something better."

It was an opportune time for Minerva to come in. "Dinner's early tonight," she announced cheerfully, carrying Matthew's tray.

"I'm still stuffed, but I'd better change so I can get over to the light," Celena said.

Her father would not give up. "Why don't you go on back to Maryland, just for a little while?" When Celena stood silent, her arms folded, he said resignedly, "But you have no intention of doing that, do you?"

"None whatsoever."

"You are one stubborn person."

"No. Just persistent."

* * *

The next morning, Celena stayed at the light and did all her chores before returning to Bay Haven. After an early lunch and a quick stop to see her father, who had a visitor, Celena rode her bike to the dock. Her spirits rose, and whether that came from heading to see Clint or the pleasure of a boat ride, Celena wasn't sure. Great South Bay was a shining blue this afternoon, like the sky. Men were fishing along the docks, and the gulls were keening, darting here and there for a fish head or the entrails the men tossed aside after cleaning their catch.

Clint helped Celena aboard his powerful white boat with clean blue trim—the *Raptor*. He flashed that dazzling smile of his, looking at her approvingly in her linen slacks and cream blouse. "You look terrific, Celena. Welcome aboard." Untying the boat from the dock, Clint said winningly, "It's a beautiful day for a ride, isn't it? I ordered this weather just for you." Part of Clint's charm was that he made everyone feel special.

The *Raptor* shivered with power as it left the dock. Celena shook out a scarf and tied it around her hair as the water curled away from either side of the boat in two great waves. As they headed out into the bay, the V-shaped wake widened, frothing and swirling, with spray rising high. The bay was full of activity; big white yachts slipped by, fishermen came in with the day's bounty, launches went to and fro, and sailboats crossed the soft breeze.

Celena loved the mournful cry of the curlews and how the spray misted her face. When Clint revved the motor, it was thrilling to feel the boat plane as it began to skim over blue water. This acute feeling of being alive was something she hadn't experienced in a long while. They went through Great South Bay, then rounded the western end of Fire Island, going around Democrat Point where white-crested waves were rolling in from the Atlantic. Once Clint slowed to a more moderate pace, they were able to chat companionably.

"Is it true that Fire Island is a good place for smugglers?" she asked, looking out over the Atlantic.

"We have our share, along with the rest of the eastern coast. But having the Coast Guard station on this end of the island has persuaded most of the smugglers to stay east."

"I ask because I've been wondering about Ethan. Do you think he told me to watch the beach because he's afraid of smugglers?"

Clint considered. "I don't know why he'd be afraid, unless he was doing some rum-running himself and thought they wouldn't like the competition. Poor devil. Who knows what's going on in that mind of his?"

"He told me a little more about the night Sarina died. Ethan said their boat was at the dock when he first went home. He went looking for Sarina, and when he came back, the boat was gone."

"That's easily explained. Sarina came home while he was gone and took the boat."

"That's what I thought, but Ethan said Sarina always told him when she was leaving. He also said she was happy and excited the week or so before she died. She'd even talked about getting a house, but where would she get enough money to do that?" Celena mused.

"I have no idea," Clint admitted. "But I've always felt that Ethan had something to do with her disappearance."

"But if he did, why would Ethan tell me all of this?"

"Maybe it's guilt—and he's talking about it so much because he can't help himself." Clint sounded grim. "Suppose he did have a hand in her death—even accidentally? Ethan's mind is so fragile, the guilt could have made it snap."

"Ethan doesn't have a fragile mind," Celena countered. "He's just . . . slow." Still, Celena had to admit his behavior indicated something deeper. She would ask Clint's opinion on something else. "Do you think it could have been rumrunners that tried to kill my father?"

Clint was dubious. "Why would they want to do that?"

"Lydia said that rumrunners might want to get control of the lighthouse. You know—to keep a lookout for the Coast Guard. Maybe the rumrunners thought that if they got rid of Father, they could get one of their own men appointed as a keeper."

Clint looked startled, then shook his head. "That's not very likely. First of all, even if they did get rid of Matthew, they know the bureau is going to send out someone else. They can hardly get rid of every keeper. Second, the bureau is very careful about who they appoint as keepers. They'd do a background check, and it would be all over. Only men who are in the lighthouse service, or longtime keepers and their families can run lighthouses."

"I guess you're right." Celena felt slightly deflated, then tried out another idea. "Maybe the person who cut the rope thought that if there wasn't a keeper, the bureau might decide to close the light. Then they could buy it."

"You're thinking of Gerald and Helen, aren't you? But I have a hard time believing either one of them would cut the rope. Any more theories you want to run past me?" He smiled.

"Just one. Gerald told me a big mother ship stays out at sea while little boats run the liquor in. Would it be possible for rumrunners to use the light to signal the boats to come in?"

Clint looked amused. "This is another one of Lydia's ideas, isn't it?"

"Well, yes," she admitted reluctantly.

"I thought so. But like I said before, a rumrunner would never be able to get the light in the first place. And even if they did, what Lydia doesn't realize is that in order to use the light as a signal, the flash pattern would have to be changed. And only someone who is very familiar with the light could do that. It would require an expert, such as your father."

Or Rueben. The thought flashed into Celena's mind unbidden. He knew nearly as much about the light as her father. But that was unthinkable. Or was it? Something nudged at her mind. What was it? Oh, yes, the old man in front of Tillman's. He had said fishermen and lobstermen often turned to rum-running as a way of making money from the ocean.

Clint squinted against the sun. "Another thing to keep in mind, Celena, is that most rumrunners are two-bit hustlers. No one takes rum-running seriously. Most runners don't even consider themselves lawbreakers; it's just a game of cat-and-mouse. They're not ordinary criminals, and so its highly unlikely one of them would have done something as serious as trying to hurt your father. Cutting the rope would just draw attention to them and result in serious jail time—two things they're trying very hard to avoid."

Celena had to admit he was right. She sneezed and, digging into her pocket, found it empty. "I didn't bring a handkerchief. Would you have a spare?"

"Sure, down in the hold. In the set of drawers to the right of the bed."

Going below, she couldn't remember if Clint had said left or right and began pulling out drawers. She pulled one out too far and it hit the floor with a thunk. Putting it back hastily, hoping Clint hadn't heard, she pushed at the towels and some brightly-colored material that had been stuffed at the back. She located the handkerchiefs and started above board. Just as Celena reached the top of the steps, a wave from a passing boat hit them, throwing her to the left. When Clint reached out to steady her, Celena was acutely aware of how his arm lingered protectively around her. She let go of his arm too quickly and stumbled a little. When she looked up, Clint smiled ever so slightly, as if he had read her thoughts. Celena felt a little foolish.

The late afternoon sun was low when they turned back. The wind whistled through her hair as they rounded the western corner of Fire Island. On either side of the boat, the froth looked like it had been trimmed with lace. The water moved in a gentle swell as Clint headed his cruiser toward the dock. He cut the speed and expertly idled the *Raptor* alongside the dock.

Celena pulled off her scarf, shaking her hair out over her shoulders. "Thanks for a great time, Clint."

"Believe me, the pleasure's been mine. Are you going to attend the grand-opening ball at Clearwater, or will you be stuck at the light-house?"

"Rueben's going to run the light for me. I'm looking forward to the dance."

"It'll be a big day for Saltaire when Clearwater opens," Clint said cheerfully. "I expect the ferry's business to increase by thirty to fifty percent."

Celena noticed that Joshua was straddling his bike at the end of the dock, waiting for her. Clint took Celena's hand, helping her to the dock. He held on a few extra seconds, and Celena asked impulsively, "Joshua and I are planning an outing to the Sunken Forest. Would you like to come?"

Clint's eyes lit up with boyish enthusiasm. "That sounds great. When are you going?"

"In about two weeks. Gerald and Daniel are going, so we have to wait until after the grand opening."

"Just let me know when and I'll get someone to cover for me."

THIRTEEN

The next morning, Celena noticed that the amulet was gone. Someone had furtively slipped in and taken the cross of red-tied twigs just as quietly as he or she had left it. She got ready for the picnic with Daniel, then went to tell her father she was going. After pouring him a glass of water and plumping the pillow under his cast, Celena asked, "Can I get you anything else?"

"Aye. A new leg." Matthew's expression didn't change in the slightest.

"I'll see if they have any at Tillman's." When she stopped at the door and glanced back, she saw that one corner of his mouth had turned up.

In the kitchen, she packed a lunch. She'd told Minerva her plans days ago and was happy to see sliced ham and pie set aside. After she'd finished, Celena thought about changing her blouse, then stopped. *This would not do.* She must *not* make a big deal out of a picnic.

Ethan came around the side of the house as Celena was going down the porch steps. A rifle dangled from a strap over his shoulder. "Is that yours?" Celena asked.

Nodding proudly, Ethan ran a hand lovingly along the smooth finish of the gunstock, then said, "639534."

Bewildered, Celena asked, "What does that mean?"

He seemed as surprised at her question as Celena had been by his answer and in an attempt to make things clear, said, "It's my gun."

"Where did you get it?" She must have spoken more stridently than she intended, for Ethan looked at her carefully, as if trying to discover what lay behind her tone.

"I found it," he said cautiously. "On the beach."

Celena was incredulous. "You mean it was just lying there?"

Looking anxious, he took a step away. "I need to go," he said, "Gerald wants me to paint the fence."

"I'll walk with you," Celena said, sorry at having disturbed him. "I was going to Clearwater myself."

It was a soft, sweet June day, and Celena decided it was a good time to ask about Sarina. "A week ago Elaine mentioned that Sarina used to buy a lot of things at the store. Where did she get the money?" Anyone else would have thought such a question highly impertinent, but not Ethan. He looked at her uncertainly, like a child who was unsure of the correct answer. She phrased it differently. "Did Sarina like to shop at Tillman's?"

This he could answer. "She bought lots of presents," Ethan said, his face brightening. "Gloves and shirts. A coat. Lots of fishing stuff. Even a knife! And she bought clothes for her. Real pretty things."

There was a noise ahead, and Ethan brushed his hair out of his eyes to see better. It was Daniel, walking toward them carrying a beach umbrella. How ruggedly handsome he was! The wind ruffled his thick dark hair, which was almost down to his collar. Daniel's face was alight as he looked at her, and Celena knew she had to be careful. She didn't want to become too involved.

"Hello, Ethan. Celena. Thought I'd meet you and we'd go straight to the beach." His eyes went to Ethan's gun. "Where did you get the rifle?"

Ethan glanced at Celena uneasily, and she answered for him. "He found it on the beach."

"Could I see it?" Daniel asked, taking a step closer.

Ethan's face became wary. "I got to go," he said, clutching the gun as if afraid Daniel might take it away and scurrying off in the direction of Clearwater.

"He sure didn't want me looking at it, did he?" Daniel said ruefully.

"That's just Ethan," Celena said. "But the beach is a funny place to find a gun. Do you think it could have been dropped by rumrunners? Or do they even carry guns?"

"The small ones usually don't carry guns, but the big ones almost always do."

This seemed to be a subject Daniel Roberts knew well. "You seem to know a lot about rumrunners," Celena said.

"I've heard others talking about it," Daniel replied without looking at her.

At the beach, the surf was sounding a steady beat, and a few shore birds hopped about at the edge of the water. Daniel planted the umbrella while Celena shook open a blanket. She doled out pickles onto bright yellow plates along with sandwiches of thick-sliced ham, then put the wedges of apple pie aside for later. Celena felt a lift and a swoop of joy that had its origination in the clean ocean breeze, the sunshine, and the presence of this man beside her. At that moment, Celena liked Daniel enormously and, ignoring the little voice in her head telling her to be careful, did not question the warmth she felt.

As they ate, they talked about Celena's life in Maryland and Daniel's family back home. Suddenly the air was split with the sound of a rifle shot. When Celena looked around wildly, Daniel spoke up. "Don't worry, that's just my father. He's doing some trap shooting. Come on, let's go watch." They left their basket in the shade of the umbrella.

Gerald was dressed in a neat, khaki outfit, looking ready to go on a safari. A boy put a clay target in place, cranked the machine, then held it until Gerald gave the order to release the arm.

"Pull!" Gerald shouted. There was a clank and a blur as a disc streaked into the air. Gerald took aim, and the plate fractured into pieces.

"He's a terrific shot," Daniel said. Gerald hit the next three, then missed the fourth.

"You distracted me," he complained as Celena and Daniel walked up. Gerald uncocked his rifle and, pulling out a handkerchief, wiped his flushed face. "But it's always a delight to see you, Celena! I was just doing a bit of shooting to relax."

"Father's under a lot of pressure, given the grand opening this Saturday," Daniel explained.

"We've had a few glitches," Gerald admitted, "but I've taken care of them. Like I always say, things have a way of working out."

As she and Daniel continued along the beach, they came across Zach and Joshua. The boys had fashioned chairs out of sand and were sitting comfortably, facing the blue water, which glittered as the breeze ruffled its surface. Their legs were covered with a fine layer of dried sand. Celena went to rinse off her sandals. When she returned, Joshua pointed to what looked like a small warship out on the Atlantic.

"Look at that!" he cried. "Know what it is?" When Celena shook her head, he said, "Look at the size, and the twin stacks. I'll give you a hint. It's not a six-bitter. Those are only 75-feet long and can only go around 17 miles per hour." As Celena looked at him in surprise, Joshua reported, "It's a 165-foot Coast Guard cutter, specially designed to intercept booze smugglers."

"How do you know all that?"

He hesitated, then admitted, "Daniel told me while you were washing your sandals."

"Cheater!" Celena protested, pushing Joshua out of his chair onto the sand. When Zach started laughing, Joshua tackled him. Leaving the boys to wrestle, Daniel and Celena went on, walking along the dark waterline, which was marked by broken shells, seaweed, and other debris. A mother and father and their two children were building a sandcastle, and Daniel and Celena decided to build their own. They worked industriously at their two castles, but when Daniel tried to add a turret, his castle collapsed.

When Celena laughed, he growled, "Since you think it's so easy, you do better."

"That won't be hard," Celena retorted. "It's easy when there's no competition."

When they were done, they brushed themselves free of sand, and Daniel took her hand as they strolled along. For once, no thoughts of Sam came to mind to taint her pleasure in the day. The lighthouse loomed large before them, the white bands shining brilliantly in the sun.

"How is your father's leg?"

"Hard to say, but he's getting stronger. He's so tired of being in bed that he actually likes the wheelchair. Doc Harrison is even going to bring over some crutches sometime soon."

"And how are *you* doing?"

Celena thought. Now that the pain had shrunk, she was filled with regret over what she had lost—years of being close to Joshua and her father. "Life can certainly turn out differently from what you expect," she mused.

Daniel agreed. "Too bad you can't order it from a catalog to meet your exact specifications. Whenever I was disappointed at this or that, my mother would tell me to just do the best with whatever came my way."

"Whenever I felt down, my mother would remind me that God promised us a safe landing, not a calm passage."

"Does that mean I can't get my money back?"

"That's exactly what that means," Celena said, laughing. "But you have to remember, we were the ones who wanted to come here."

"Do you think we had any idea what life on earth would be like?"

"I think we were clueless," Celena stated. "I'm sure Heavenly Father tried to prepare us, but I don't think mortality was something we, as spirits, could fully comprehend."

"Trusting little souls, weren't we?" Daniel remarked. "To come down to a big unknown?"

"I suppose so. But then we trusted Heavenly Father and knew He wanted only the best for us. So, while we're here, the trick is to *keep* trusting in Him, no matter what happens."

* * *

On Wednesday morning, the day Matthew had looked forward to for so long finally arrived, and Doc Harrison brought over a pair of crutches. The doctor cautioned Matthew to use them sparingly, warning him, "Having such a long cast will make walking awkward, and it will be very easy to fall. You must always have help getting up, and preferably, someone walking alongside you at all times."

Unfortunately, Celena's afternoon proved to be less enjoyable than the morning had been. Celena decided the fence around the lighthouse garden could use a coat of paint. She went to the shed and discovered a second act of vandalism. Someone had opened full and partially used cans and sloshed the paint on the walls inside the small shed. Brushes had been dipped in paint, then left to stiffen. The floor was thick with colors running together. Celena trembled slightly with anger as she surveyed the scene. This was no lighthearted prank. Although the building was small, the damage was total and complete—a malicious act done by someone intent on ruining her chance at passing the inspection.

She reported the vandalism to the police, but she didn't expect anything to come of it, since there was no clue as to who might have perpetrated the act. Instead of taking only a few hours to put right, like the generator building, restoring the paint locker took two full days. The inside of the building had to be emptied, scrubbed, and sanded, then painted. Celena worked hard and was glad she and Joshua had taken care of the mess promptly, for Friday afternoon, an inspector showed up. He examined everything closely, and despite his blasé manner, Celena could tell he was favorably impressed, especially with the newly-painted locker.

* * *

On the morning of the grand-opening ball, Celena was in Tillman's, trying out a new fragrance, when she heard the thumping of Rueben's cane. His face bristled with whiskers showing white against his leathery skin. Rueben waved his hand vigorously as if to clear the air.

"Smells like something died," he said, gasping for air.

"You'll take that back if you know what's good for you," Celena said, aiming the spray bottle at him.

"Don't do that!" he begged. "I'd have a whole lot of explaining to do to Tana."

"That reminds me," Celena said, setting down the bottle. "I've been meaning to ask you and Tana if you want to go to the Sunken Forest. A group of us are going in a couple of weeks."

"I'll talk to the boss and let you know. Sometimes we have babysitting duties when Hannah takes Will to the doctor. We'll come if we can."

"I wanted to ask you something else, though I doubt you'll know the answer. Mrs. Tillman told me Sarina was spending a lot of money before she died. Do you know where she got it?"

"She had a rich uncle that kicked the bucket?"

Celena paid no attention to the jest. "Before I left, Sarina was sending her family money whenever she could—from those herbal remedies she used to make. But it sounds like she was spending a lot more than she could make from that." Celena was thoughtful. "Do you think she could have been involved in rum-running?"

Rueben looked alert. "Why do you say that?"

"It would explain a lot of things. Like where Sarina got her money. And why she would get a boat when she was afraid of the water."

"Money is a great motivator," Rueben acknowledged. "But then, Sarina was a feisty gal. She wasn't afraid of anything."

"Still, twelve miles is a long way to go to reach a mother ship."

Rueben looked at her sharply. "Only big-time runners take stuff off a mother ship. How in tarnation do you know about the new international treaty that changed the three-mile rule?"

"Daniel and Gerald told me."

The old man's eyes narrowed. "I see. That's very interesting."

"What do you mean by that?" Celena said indignantly.

"I hardly thought Gerald was the type to go into rum-running. He's not the sharpest knife in the drawer, if you know what I mean. Now Daniel, on the other hand . . ."

"Daniel would never do anything like that," Celena said quickly.

Rueben's watery blue eyes looked at her speculatively. "Touched a nerve there, did I?"

"I'm just trying to figure out why Sarina told Ethan to watch the beach. He's been saying a lot of things." She summed them up, then added, "Ethan says she's angry because she was murdered."

"Well, that would certainly ruffle *my* feathers," Rueben said dryly. He looked at her closer. "Don't tell me you actually believe him? Ethan's always been a few bricks short of a full load, and that count's gone up considerably over the past few years."

"Ethan's not going to be at peace until he knows what happened that night," Celena answered.

"But Sarina died years ago! You're not going to find out anything new now. She took the boat, had some sort of accident, and drowned. Just because Ethan can't accept it doesn't mean she was murdered."

"I'm not so sure," Celena protested. "There's something very suspicious about Sarina's death—Ethan's told me a lot of things that just don't add up."

Rueben still looked cynical. "You can't rely on anything Ethan says. He barely knows what day of the week it is. You know how he is."

"That's my point exactly!" Celena declared. "I *know* Ethan. Once you tell him something, he never forgets. I wish I could find out why Sarina told him to watch the beach."

"Celena, why don't you just leave it alone? Besides, it's possible Ethan had a hand in what happened to Sarina. A lot of people thought so at the time."

Celena sighed. "Let's forget Ethan for now."

"Sounds good to me. How's your father doing?"

"He got some crutches and likes being able to get around. He's supposed to have someone with him when he uses them, but he's up by himself all the time. Father's been asking me to go back to Maryland."

"That's natural. He's worried about you."

"He got upset when he found out about the 'ghost' at the island and that I hadn't told him about it."

"What did you expect? You and he make a fine pair. You both need to learn how to communicate. He's an ornery old mule, and you're a prickly porcupine." He rubbed his chin. "But he's right, you know. You ought to go. You're getting mixed up with things that don't have anything to do with just running the light."

"Like Sarina's death?"

"That's exactly what I mean."

She shook her head. If she left Fire Island now, she might leave behind a part of her that would never come clear again. This was her chance. She had to stand firm. Celena glanced at her watch. "I'd better get going. Will you be able to manage the light all right tonight?"

"No problem. I'm an old pro—I know everything there is to know about that light." Something in his words stirred a feeling of uneasiness. What was it? It had to do with something someone had recently said . . . but Celena was unable to place it and finally gave up.

* * *

"Stand still!" Celena hissed, trying to get Joshua's unruly hair to lie flat. He squirmed until she pronounced it as good as it was ever going to get, then preened in the mirror, nearly unrecognizable in his neat black suit, bow tie, newly shined shoes, and plastered hair.

"Can I go now?" he begged. The plan was to have Joshua go over early with Zach and his parents. Then the boys would leave a little early and come back to Bay Haven for the night.

"Sure, go on. Just remember to save a dance for me."

Celena swept part of her hair up in a topknot, curling the rest and letting it cascade down her back and shoulders. Since she hadn't brought a fancy gown with her to Fire Island, Lydia had let her borrow one of her more modest ones, a dress of Nile-green satin, topped with black lace. It wasn't a perfect fit, but Celena was pleased to see it actually looked quite pretty on her. The dress was cut full, with a train and a square neck. Her only pair of black pumps would serve since they would be hidden by the length of the gown. Celena was fastening on hanging earrings when there was a knock at the door. When she called to come in, Minerva entered, carrying a gold-colored box and looking pleased.

She looked at Celena admiringly. "You look lovely! You're going to have every man in the place fighting to dance with you." She held out the box. "This is for you." Inside was a delicate corsage—two creamy gardenias accented with silver ribbon.

"Oh, it's gorgeous!" Celena cried, taking the gardenias from their nest of shredded tissue. She inhaled their fragrance, then held them out for Minerva to sniff. "Who sent it?"

"The donor wishes to remain anonymous."

"You can't do that to me, Minerva."

"Let's just say it came from someone who thinks you're very special."

After Minerva pinned the flowers on, Celena—feeling regal with her elegant corsage—went to show her dress to her father. Matthew was sitting in a chair, his leg propped on a footstool, when Celena swept into the room. Holding out her skirt with one hand, Celena dipped one way, then another, finishing the show by twirling around.

Matthew was impressed. "You'll have to beat them off with a stick." Celena laughed happily. Then, in a different voice, he asked, "Has everything been going all right at the light?"

She hesitated. "Everything's been fine at the light, but someone got into the paint locker and made a mess."

"I was wondering if you were going to come clean."

"If I didn't, you'd just hear it from your spies."

"Did you ever find out who put that voodoo thing in your room?"

"No, but it's gone now, so you don't have to worry about it," Celena said easily.

Matthew's face darkened. "You're acting like this is all a big game," he grumbled. "But I don't like any of this. First someone gets into the generator building. Now the paint locker. Your coming seems to have stirred a lot of things up. And what's this about Ethan finding a rifle?"

"My, your spies *have* been busy. All I know is that Ethan found it on the beach."

"I wish you'd go back to Maryland until things settle down."

"And who would run the light?"

Matthew looked exasperated. "Rueben," he bellowed. "Or Clint, or Joshua."

Celena put a hand on her hip. "Right. Rueben with his bad knees, Clint who's already doing the work of three men, or Joshua, who is eleven. We've been over this before."

"I'd figure something out," Matthew said. "But I can see you're as stubborn as ever."

"No, I'm just persistent," Celena said calmly, smiling slightly at this oft-repeated exchange.

Matthew shook his head slightly. Then he sighed and reached for a small, delicately-carved wooden box that was on the bedside table. It was her mother's jewelry box.

"I asked Joshua to get this from the house." Matthew opened it, lifting out a golden chain with a small, heart-shaped locket. "Thought you might like to wear this tonight."

Celena nodded, unable to speak because her mouth had suddenly gone dry. The locket had been a favorite of her mother's. As a child, she had played with it many times—opening the small heart to gaze at the tiny pictures of her father and mother taken during their engagement. Matthew opened the locket, gazed at it a moment, then held it out to Celena.

"Your mother wanted you to have this."

Celena's heart twisted and her eyes began to smart. Although what he said was true—her mother would have wanted Celena to have the locket—she knew it was equally true that *he* wanted her to have it. Her father had never shown much outward emotion, but this gesture was as touching as anything he could have done. Matthew refused to meet her eyes, and Celena suspected the reason lay in the moisture she saw welling up there.

Celena blinked away her tears. "Will you put it on for me?"

Kneeling, she held her hair up while Matthew fastened the delicate gold chain around her neck. Celena felt for the locket and opened it. Whatever was thickening in her chest started to prickle and fizz like a glass of ginger ale. Gazing at the dark-haired woman with the large eyes, and the stern-faced man, Celena felt the weighted past as well as the vast reaches of time lying before her.

"Thank you," she choked, then impulsively hugged her father. His arms came up slowly, then gripped her firmly until a great, trembling smile bloomed upon her face.

"It seems strange to be wearing this," she told him tremulously. "Sometimes I forget she's gone and think she's just stepped into the other room."

Matthew's eyes were bright. "Celena, I was wondering—" He stopped, his voice choked and gravelly. It was a few moments before he could try again. "Rueben told me once that Elizabeth can look down and see us."

"I think she can, when we have a special need."

"But not all the time, eh? He also told me that families can be together. Forever."

Her heart gave a small jump, but she kept her voice low and calm. "There is a sealing ordinance that can be done in the temple, which allows families to be together forever."

Matthew's voice turned harsh. "I don't understand that. Doesn't seem right. Elizabeth is my wife. Surely we'd be together in heaven without this sealing stuff. It would be mighty cruel of God to keep us apart after we've been married for so long."

Years ago, Celena would have been shocked at him calling God cruel. Now she just thought hard. "I'm not sure I understand it completely, but I do know there are certain ordinances that have to be performed in order to get certain blessings. They're like laws. If you obey the law, you get the blessing."

Surprised that her father was listening instead of arguing, Celena continued. "There are rules in heaven, just like on earth. For example, if you want to be married, you have to get a marriage license and be married by someone who has the proper authority. If you don't do those things, you can't get married. If you want to be married in heaven, you need to have the ordinance performed that seals a husband and wife together."

"I suppose that makes sense," he allowed. "I'll think on it." He paused, and Celena had the feeling he wanted to say something else, until he looked at the clock. "I don't want to hold you up. Looking at those pictures just started me thinking. You'd better get going."

She patted his hand, then stopped to grab her cloak, flinging it around her shoulders as she went down the steps. The red-gold of the coming sunset was breathtaking, but not as amazing as the conversation she'd just had. A strange, warm glow made her feel as though she wasn't quite connected to the earth. Before Celena had left the island, the idea of her father thinking about religious matters was as likely as someone emptying Great South Bay with a teaspoon. And now look! Her mother had to be at work here; no one else had ever wielded as much influence over Matthew.

The evening was fair and the moon was nearly full, lighting the sky as if ordered for this grand occasion. Celena knew her father was worried, but she could not leave now. Six weeks ago, she'd been given an opportunity to fulfill her promises, and she was determined to see it through. Whatever obstacles came would be faced head on. Clearwater rose up in front of her, huge and imposing, lights ablaze. Men in elegant evening attire and women in ball gowns could be seen through the windows. Celena swept gracefully down the cobblestone drive, and at the door an employee in a white shirt and black pants opened it wide, inviting her inside.

FOURTEEN

The gold and crystal chandeliers in the dance hall were ablaze with light, causing the gold leaf on the crown molding and trim to shine in ornate splendor. Velvet draperies glowed in a rich and royal crimson. The live band was bright and lively, even if they weren't a big-name dance band like Duke Ellington, Fred Waring, or Red Nichols. The polished parquet dance floor was covered with dancers; there were women in long gowns and a few flappers in short, brightly colored dresses. The men were mostly in black, though a dozen or more from the Coast Guard were wearing their smart uniforms. Later, they would be dancing the Charleston, Black Bottom, and fox-trot, which the band would intersperse with more traditional waltzes and other tunes. Chairs, quilted satin benches, and an extended buffet ran around the outside of the room, which was full of warmth, brilliant sound, and the chatter of voices.

Celena reviewed the plans she had made as she walked around the dance floor. Whenever the opportunity came, she had to be ready. Celena was near the buffet tables when Lydia whirled off the dance floor to stand next to her, breathless and laughing as she pushed her partner away, saying she needed to catch her breath. Although the majority of women were in long dresses, Lydia wore a silky, sleeveless midnight-blue dress with a low V-neck. The dress followed her ample curves and came to her knees, ending with fringe around the hem. She accepted a cup of punch from a waiter, and as she drank, her eyes followed the dancers.

"My, my. I do love a man in uniform," she purred. "I haven't seen Daniel yet, but I'm sure he'll stand out as well." She winked at a man who waltzed by, and in return, he gave Lydia a meaningful look over his partner's shoulder. Lydia stopped her perusal of the crowd long enough to look at Celena with her sly, green cat's eyes. "By the way, Daniel told me about your little excursion to the Sunken Forest. He was sweet enough to invite me. I told him I'd love it."

"I didn't know you liked the outdoors," Celena said calmly, despite the pang.

"If Daniel's there, I'll like it."

Celena decided to broach a question. "Were you on the island when Sarina died?"

Lydia made a face. "Are you still on about that? It happened so long ago!"

"Then let me ask you this. Do you know if Sarina was smuggling liquor?"

"What makes you ask?" Lydia replied carefully.

"Last week Elaine Tillman said Sarina was spending a lot of money at the store. I wondered how she got it."

"Don't ask me. Sarina didn't like me for some reason. She was *so* uppity." Lydia took a sip of punch and waved a manicured hand around the dance floor. "Dear-heart, this is a ball. We're supposed to be having fun, not talking about someone who's dead."

"You didn't answer my question," Celena persisted. "Were you here when she drowned?"

"As a matter of fact, I was. So what?"

"I want to know more about what happened. Ethan says someone murdered her."

"Ethan also thinks the moon is made of green cheese." The sparkle was gone from Lydia's voice. "Has anyone ever told you that you're a great conversationalist? No? Thank goodness." Lydia went on, sounding mutinous. "First you say someone tried to kill your father, now you say someone killed Sarina. If I were you, I'd be careful making all those accusations." Lydia's eyes glittered. "Listen to me. Ethan's not as stupid as people think, and he's certainly not as harmless as *you* seem to think. He was crazy jealous of anyone who paid attention to Sarina. One day he caught Sarina talking to Clint and went totally berserk and attacked Clint. Frankly, I wouldn't be surprised if he had killed Sarina himself in a jealous rage."

A tall blond man in uniform stopped to ask Lydia to dance. Smiling up at him, Lydia left with a wave of a scarlet-tipped hand. Just then, Celena saw Clint at the same time he saw her. He excused himself from an elegant blond in a ruby dress and came over, smiling broadly.

"I've been looking forward to this all day," he said, leading her onto the floor. Clint Paxton was a smooth, accomplished dancer, filled with an easy confidence he wore like a second skin. Celena knew they made an attractive couple from the way other people gave them admiring looks. It had been the same when she had been with Sam. Mildly surprised, Celena realized that she rarely thought of him anymore. Celena enjoyed the dance and didn't argue when Clint insisted on another, then another. When the band started playing, "Yes Sir, That's My Baby," they went to the buffet table for crystal cups of punch.

"I saw you with Lydia earlier," Clint commented.

"We were talking about Ethan. She told me that he attacked you once."

Clint looked embarrassed. "That was a long time ago."

"I can't believe he'd do something like that. I didn't know he was jealous."

"Ethan has always been unpredictable and can be possessive," Clint admitted, clearly reluctant to talk about it. "But there was no harm done. Still . . ." When she looked at him, he continued. "It worries me to see you get involved with Ethan. He's so volatile. And paranoid."

"Did you hear that Ethan found a rifle the other day on the beach?" When Clint looked surprised, she asked, "Do you think it could have been dropped by smugglers?"

"Pretty careless smugglers, I'd say. More likely it was someone poaching deer. They probably saw someone they thought might report them, threw the gun in the brush, then forgot where they'd put it. But I can check with the police and see if they've had any inquiries about a lost rifle."

Clint gave her an intense look. "You know, Celena, even if that turns out to be nothing, I can't help thinking you might be in a dangerous position here. You've talked openly about someone deliberately cutting the rope and nearly killing your father. That could be risky, because if someone on the island really did do it, they aren't going to want you to get too close to finding out what really happened." Clint suddenly took her hand. "All of this makes me afraid for you. I wish you'd back off a little."

When the dance ended, someone beckoned to Clint and he excused himself. Celena perused the dance floor, but Daniel was nowhere to be found. Joshua and Zach were with a group of friends chatting excitedly in the corner. The men from the Coast Guard seemed determined to keep Lydia on the dance floor. She flitted from one to another with her natural enjoyment of life, standing out from everyone else like fox fire stands out in darkness. Celena accepted an invitation to dance and was delighted when Joshua tapped her partner on the back. Watching his feet carefully, Joshua steered Celena around the floor while others smiled at the earnest young boy. When the number ended, Joshua heaved a sigh of relief and returned to his friends, who started punching him on the arm.

After a few more dances, Celena made her way to Tana, who was sitting with Louise and Amanda Johnson, both of whom were wearing white gloves and concentrating on balancing their glass plates while daintily nibbling refreshments. Tana's white hair was arranged in soft curls, and she was wearing a becoming gray-blue gown that fell in soft folds around her plump figure.

"If this is any indication," Tana said, sweeping out a hand to indicate the packed dance floor, "Clearwater is going to be a huge success."

"It certainly looks that way. Gerald's done a wonderful job."

"That means I'm going to have to eat my words," Tana said grudgingly. "I told Clint he needed his head examined for letting Gerald near the place, especially with his track record. But Clint always did have a soft heart. I suppose he wanted to give Gerald a chance." At Celena's mystified look, Tana went on. "Well, after that business in Chicago, what hope did Gerald have of ever getting a job?"

"What happened in Chicago?"

"Oh, dear," Tana said, looking stricken. "I've done it again. Rueben always says I talk too much." She paused and lowered her voice. "Gerald got into some trouble with the law. But that's all in the past. Clint will keep an eye on him here."

"I believe Clint helps him out a lot, gives him a lot of advice."

Tana nodded. "I'm sure he does. It pays to protect your investment. Still, I was surprised Clint talked the other owners into hiring

Gerald. I guess it's true what they say: It's not what you know but who you know. Gerald is lucky that he and Clint are cousins." Tana smiled. "You and Clint cut a fine figure on the dance floor earlier. Is there a romance on the horizon?"

Celena considered. "I don't think so, but he is nice to spend time with. Truth be told, I had a crush on Clint when I was growing up," she confided.

"Who didn't?" Tana smiled. "Fine-looking man. Smart. A real charmer. Helen wanted him, but he never popped the question." Tana laughed at Celena's expression. "You didn't know? Oh, Helen had a torch for Clint a mile high. Even though she was older. I always thought that's why she went and married someone she'd barely known a month. Then that worthless Bernard goes back to sea, leaving her to run that boardinghouse. I understand things aren't going too well there. Poor thing. Lately, Helen always looks like she's got a toothache."

Celena silently agreed. During the past weeks, there had been a troubled tautness about her. As the dancers swirled about, Daniel finally came into view. He was dancing with a petite brunette in a frilly lavender dress. Tana noticed the direction of Celena's gaze.

"That's another good-looking man," she acknowledged. "And just the right age. Get them too old and they're set in their ways. Too young and you have two babies to take care of."

"Tana! Does Rueben know you're looking?"

Tana laughed heartily. "By the way, he came by the post office yesterday."

"Rueben?"

"Daniel," Tana said sternly. "That man you're pretending not to watch. We had a nice chat, but I got the feeling he wanted to talk about something besides the weather. Finally, he started asking about rumrunners. I think he suspects Rueben and was giving me a warning."

"You're not serious."

The older woman pressed her lips together. "Maybe he doesn't like competition."

Celena looked at Daniel and the vision in lavender whirling around. "You can't think Daniel is a rumrunner."

"Why not? He's young, he's Gerald's son, and he's surprisingly well informed about the subject." Celena digested that in silence.

Helen and Gerald glided by, looking at each other as if there were no one else on the floor. Helen had her hair piled high and was regal in flowing black. Though Gerald was portly, he looked debonair in his elegant tuxedo.

Tana changed the subject. "It sounds like you're getting along better with your father."

Celena looked at her. "Says Rueben?"

Tana nodded, her brown eyes twinkling. "He told me about your conversation. I think I understand some of the trouble you've been having. Women can have a harder time than men when it comes to forgiving. Our feelings are more sensitive and we tend to hang onto things. A lot of men can forget arguments as easily as shrugging their shoulders, but it's not the same for women." She leaned closer to Celena. "There's one thing I always try to remember when I start feeling sorry for myself. Maybe it'll help you too. It's that there isn't anyone in the world who isn't broken in some way, who doesn't have some regrets, and who hasn't wondered 'what if.' The best thing to do is just go on and try to be as complete as you can."

Celena was pondering that when a smattering of applause broke out as the dance ended. She felt oddly disappointed when Daniel led the girl in lavender to the buffet table. But he suddenly broke away and walked purposefully in her direction. As her heartbeat accelerated, Celena told herself it would be nothing out of the ordinary if Daniel asked her to dance. That's what the whole evening was about, after all.

"Ah," breathed Tana when she saw him. "Look who's coming your way!" Daniel was dressed handsomely in a white linen shirt, pinstriped vest, and a black tuxedo sporting pearl buttons. Celena was all too aware of her reaction to his deep-set eyes. Daniel greeted Tana cordially but said not a word to Celena. He simply held out his hand. Celena took it, rising as if pulled upward by invisible strings. He held her at arm's length for a few moments, looking at her with such admiration that she felt a blush come to her cheeks.

Then, pulling her close, he said frankly, "You're beautiful!" Celena was inordinately pleased. Daniel hadn't said the dress was beautiful but that she was, and she believed he meant it.

As they floated across the floor, Celena said, "Lydia was right. You *are* a wonderful dancer."

"How would she know?" Daniel's face was close to hers.

"Last week, Lydia mentioned that the two of you were going dancing. She told me you were a good dancer."

Daniel looked puzzled. "I've never taken Lydia dancing. She asked me to go once, but I couldn't make it." Suddenly Celena felt light as a feather. Daniel dipped her backward and she giggled.

She lost count of the dances. Twice, three times, men tried to cut in, but Daniel cordially explained that this particular dance was a favorite of theirs and he would relinquish Celena later. After the third man left defeated, Daniel cheerfully explained that by "later," he meant the next day.

As she and Daniel danced, Celena shimmered like the heat of lightning was upon her. She was aware of every inch of herself and every inch that was in contact with Daniel—arm, waist, hand, and hip. Daniel guided her through the open French doors and onto the patio. Other couples were there, taking advantage of the balmy evening and gentle breeze. In the distance, a lighted cruiser came into view, its own faint music drifting toward them.

When the band announced a break, Daniel led her inside. Celena left him with friends so she could check in with Joshua and tell him he could stay another half hour. When the dancing started again, Clint came over and whirled her away. At one point, they nodded to Helen and her partner, a tall man with black hair. Celena looked for Gerald and saw him standing on the sidelines—oblivious to those around him. Looking vigilant, his attention was riveted on a smiling Helen, who, with her pink cheeks and animated expression, was startlingly attractive. The expression on Gerald's face was so different from his usual amiable one that Celena felt uneasy.

Clint was so graceful in his movements and so interesting to talk with that Celena was regretful when, after a few dances, a dark, rather intense-looking man politely cut in. He was pleasant, but when Celena saw Gerald and Helen go out to the patio, she excused herself. She had stewed for a week and a half over how to get the truth from Helen regarding the day of Matthew's fall, and it had occurred to her that it might be useful to catch her off guard. Celena found herself both eager for the upcoming encounter and a little fearful of what might come from it.

Helen and Gerald were at the patio railing, looking out over the ocean. "Congratulations, Gerald, on such a successful evening!" Celena exclaimed. "I was talking with Tana earlier about what a wonderful crowd you've got here tonight." Gerald's wide face flushed red with pleasure.

Celena turned to Helen, whose cheeks were still charmingly pink. Too many of Celena's questions had gone unanswered or been evaded over the last few weeks, and she hoped a direct challenge might startle Helen into giving some answers. "I found out something interesting the other day. Tana said she'd asked you to deliver a telegram to my father the morning he fell."

It was a moment frozen in time. Helen's eyes grew wide, went to Gerald for a moment, then flicked away. In that instant Celena glimpsed something—was it fear?

Gerald ran a finger around the inside of his collar, which was tight around his neck. "Ah, well, actually I'm the one who took the telegram to the lighthouse. I ran into Helen that day, and since I wanted to see Matthew anyway, I took it. Thought I'd save her a trip."

Celena saw the flaw in his statement immediately. "But Tana said Helen was already going to the light, so you wouldn't have been saving her a trip at all."

"It's all right," Helen told Gerald, laying a hand on his arm. The two of them looked at each other for a moment while Celena watched, missing nothing. They were close, these two—closer than she had realized. Helen turned to Celena. "I took the telegram, not Gerald. He said that out of a misguided attempt to protect me, but that's not necessary. I did nothing wrong. I went to the light to talk to Matthew, but when I saw he was painting, I put the telegram on the desk and left." Helen was striving to be nonchalant, but her words sounded brittle, as though they might splinter in the air. There were dark circles under her eyes Celena hadn't noticed before.

"Why didn't you say anything when I asked who had been at the lighthouse that morning?"

"It wasn't important."

"It was to me," Celena said with some heat. There had to be something Helen wasn't saying. "Did you see anything unusual while you were there?"

Looking troubled, Gerald answered for Helen, as was his wont to do. "Of course she didn't. There wasn't anything to see," he said cajolingly.

Helen's veneer of calmness was threatening to crack. "If you're asking me if I saw anyone who could have cut the rope, or if I cut it myself, the answer is *no.* Matthew was fine when I left." The color in Helen's cheeks began to flame even as the rest of her face turned white. Celena knew fury when she saw it. There was a volcano smoldering just under the surface.

Helen continued. "Actually, I seriously doubt that the rope *was* cut. You always did love drama. You make this outrageous claim about the rope being cut, but when others want to examine the rope, it conveniently disappears."

Celena inhaled jerkily. "Just what are you trying to say?"

Helen's unusual pale blue eyes had always seemed cold, but now there was fire in them as she stared at Celena balefully—flames behind blue smoke. "When you were little you always loved to be the center of attention, and now you're picking up right where you left off—with wild accusations that someone tried to kill your father."

People were beginning to stare. Gerald's already red face flushed even darker. There were beads of perspiration on his forehead as he begged, "Celena, Helen! Please! Can't we leave this for another time?"

Helen went on as if he hadn't spoken. "It's the same with your ridiculous stories about a ghost around the light. Clint was there and said it was only a group of kids, yet you insist on fabricating some mysterious phantom. And isn't it just a little peculiar that you and Joshua are the only ones who have ever seen the so-called ghost?" Helen was on the attack now. "And despite my asking otherwise, you insist on upsetting Ethan. Now you've got him believing someone killed Sarina. He's getting more and more disturbed because of you. I'm telling you one last time to leave him alone." At the moment it seemed there was a real threat behind those grimly spoken words.

"Ethan is the one who told *me* that someone killed Sarina," Celena corrected.

Gerald held a hand up for silence. His eyes were cold. "That's enough, Celena. I'll have no more of this. You've shown very poor taste to bother Helen with such matters at a dance." With that, Gerald took Helen's arm and led her back to the ballroom.

The encounter had not gone at all like Celena had hoped. She hadn't learned anything new, and Gerald was right, she had no business bringing up such matters tonight. She'd just been so sure Helen would give her some useful answers if taken by surprise.

Celena was still standing alone when Lydia came over, her arm tucked into an older man's arm. "Celena, I want to introduce you to Nathan Gibbs. I told you about him. He was in charge of building Clearwater. Nathan, this is Celena Jackson, the lightkeeper's daughter."

Nathan was the tall, dark-haired man Helen had been dancing with earlier. His hair was brushed back from his broad forehead and he had an aquiline nose, the curve giving his face a faintly sinister cast.

"You did a wonderful job with Clearwater, Mr. Gibbs," Celena said. "You must be very proud of how it turned out."

He looked pleased. "It's always nice to see one's work taken from the drawing board to reality."

Someone stopped to claim Lydia, and Celena went on. "I guess you're going to be around Fire Island for a while longer."

His sharp, angular face looked interested but slightly puzzled. "And why is that?"

"So you can build some cabins around the resort." Since he was still looking at her oddly, she added, "I think it's a wonderful idea." Celena was trying her best.

"I'm afraid you're mistaken," Nathan said. He still wore a pleasant smile, but it did not reach his eyes. "I haven't been asked about that project. Apparently, they've gotten someone else." He kept his voice well under control, but there was a certain grimness in it. "And I thought they were satisfied with my work," he added as if speaking to himself.

Celena looked at him helplessly. "Gerald seemed very happy with everything."

"Gerald? Was he the one who told you about the cabins?"

"Why, yes."

The look of irritation faded. "I see," Nathan said amiably. "I'll have a talk with Clint and get it all sorted out. It's been a pleasure meeting you." He went to the buffet table where Helen and Gerald stood. He must have asked her to dance, for he and Helen moved onto the dance floor while Gerald stood stiffly, gazing after them.

Obviously Gerald hadn't asked Nathan to give him a bid for the cabins. Why was that? Especially since Nathan was the one who had built Clearwater. Lydia had said that Gerald was jealous of Nathan—perhaps that was why. As Celena looked out over the dance floor, she saw Daniel and Lydia. Coolly beautiful, Lydia was smiling up at Daniel, her fingers pressing lightly against the back of his neck. Celena turned away. The hour was late. Joshua and Zach would have gone back to Bay Haven by now, and she needed to check on them.

As Celena walked to the boarding house, she thought again about the vandalism at the paint locker and generator building. Had they been pranks or were they meant as a warning? It seemed the type of mischief that would appeal to Lydia. If so, it was possible she had done it so that Celena would fail her inspection, which could lead to her being discharged as lighthouse keeper. That, in turn, might cause the bureau to think again about closing the light.

There was something going on, that much was clear. Celena remembered the prickling feeling she'd had near the beach when she thought someone was following her. And why did Rueben seem to know so much about rum-running? He would do anything to help his grandson, but did that include smuggling? And Daniel. It was curious that he had gone to talk to Tana about rum-running. Celena also had to wonder about Gerald. He'd seemed frank and open about wanting the light, but how far was he willing to go to get it? She knew from tonight's conversation that Gerald was not above lying. And what about Helen? She'd already demonstrated a fixed determination to get the light by calling the Lighthouse Bureau and reporting Matthew's injury, inaccurately at that, and by using her cousin to try to sway their decision. Lastly, there was Lydia. Wild and impetuous, she could be the most dangerous of them all.

When Celena opened the door to her room, Zach and Joshua, still in their black suits, were huddled together on the floor. Joshua jumped up like he had springs in his heels while Zach held one of his hands behind his back. On the floor was an envelope.

"What are you boys up to?"

"Just playing," Joshua said too quickly.

"Zach, what's behind your back?" Reluctantly, he brought his hand forward. He was holding a letter, which she took. "Where did this come from?"

Zach lifted his chin defensively. "We were playing spy."

"That doesn't answer my question."

"Um. Mrs. Montgomery's room."

"What?" Celena was furious. "That's not playing spy. I'd call it stealing. You both know better than that."

Joshua studied his shoes while Zach responded spiritedly. "Detectives do it to get information."

"You are not a detective," Celena said sternly. "And you had no right to go in somebody's room and snoop around. Joshua, you know it's wrong to read other people's mail."

"I didn't read it." Joshua looked up, seeing a ray of hope. "Zach did."

Zach took no offense at being abandoned by his partner in crime. "Joshua told me someone cut the rope and that's why his father got hurt. We thought Mrs. Montgomery might have done it because she wants the light. We were looking for evidence."

"You've been reading too many detective stories," Celena said frostily. Then she eyed the letter speculatively. "Ah, was there anything interesting in it?"

Their faces lit up and they nodded enthusiastically. Celena debated, eyeing the piece of paper. Their eagerness was palpable. She held out for a few more seconds, then rationalized that the boys would tell her what it was anyway. Sighing heavily, she opened the letter.

Her eyes widened as she read. The boys were right, it *was* informative. Folding it grimly, Celena tried to undo the damage of her example.

"Do you understand that you should *never* go into someone's room and take something without permission?" They nodded in unison. "And you realize it was wrong to read it?" The boys did their best to look penitent. "Now we have to return it," she said firmly.

Their faces fell.

It was clear their courage was gone when Joshua begged, "Couldn't *you* put it back?"

"Me? I wasn't the thief who took it." Celena handed Joshua the letter, which he looked over.

"But you read it," Zach pointed out. He had her there.

Joshua tried to be fair. "We all read it; we'll all put it back."

They tiptoed down the hall and into Helen's room. Joshua hurried to the desk with the letter. Too fast. He slipped on the rug and, to catch himself, reached out and sideswiped a floor lamp, which crashed to the floor. Celena gasped. Both boys looked scared. Quickly, Celena got the garbage can, and the three of them started picking up pieces of the shattered bulb.

"Hurry, but don't cut yourselves," Celena commanded urgently.

They were working furiously when the door opened. Helen stood framed in the doorway. Her lips were pressed tightly together, and her eyes were blazing.

FIFTEEN

In a flash, Celena spread her skirt over the letter that was lying on the floor. Helen stepped closer. Standing over them, she had the distinct advantage of height.

As they trembled below, she asked shrilly, *"What is going on?"*

Zach was the first to take command of the situation. Standing up, he said, "We heard a noise and came to see what it was." While Helen's eyes were fixed on Zach, Celena picked up the letter and, keeping it hidden in the folds of her skirt, slowly rose.

"And you found Celena here breaking my things?" Helen asked tersely.

"Oh, no, she came with us." Joshua was anxious to set the record straight.

Celena's heart was thumping uncomfortably. "We thought—" She stopped, flustered.

"We thought we ought to check out the noise." Zach, more experienced in talking his way out of sticky situations, finished Celena's sentence. "Everything was okay, but Joshua bumped into the lamp. He'll pay you back for it. But since you're here, there's something Celena wanted to ask you." Celena's eyes widened helplessly, but Zach went on smoothly, "We were talking about the Sunken Forest and Celena was wondering if you'd like to come with us."

Helen, Joshua, and Celena gaped at him.

"Mr. Roberts is going," Zach added as if tempting her.

Helen's eyes narrowed.

Although Zach had shown unusual resourcefulness at diverting Helen's attention, Celena wished he could have thought of a less painful way of doing it. Trying to ease her way inconspicuously toward Helen's desk, Celena added, "Lydia's going, and I was going to ask Ethan."

"Let me get this straight," Helen said slowly, looking at Celena with drilling eyes. "You come into my room, supposedly to check out some phantom noise. Then, after breaking my lamp, you ask me to go on an excursion?" Celena could feel the color flaming in her face.

"Yes, ma'am," Zach piped up when Celena remained mute. "It would be great if everyone could go." Helen studied the boy as though he were some new species.

Joshua said, "I think we got all the big pieces, but the floor ought to be swept. Do you have a broom, Mrs. Montgomery?" He was perfectly polite, and it probably helped that he looked the part in his suit.

"In the kitchen," Helen replied vaguely. She turned as Joshua went by. Seizing the opportunity, Celena slipped the letter between some papers on the desk. After the floor was swept, Celena sent the boys off and was about to go herself when she noticed a display of amulets on a shelf. Many of them were similar to the one that had been left on her bed.

She stepped closer to the display. "Do you mind if I look at these?"

"Of course not. I've nothing better to do at midnight," Helen replied dryly. Many of the amulets were simple pieces of twigs tied in triangles and crosses. A few were curved in circles. Most had red berries attached, and all were tied with bits of red yarn or fabric.

"These are amulets, aren't they?" Celena said, picking up a necklace of berries strung together with red thread. "What are they for?"

"They're supposed to protect the owner from evil." Helen looked at Celena. "Maybe you'd like one for protection from me." Was that a warning or a weak joke? She couldn't tell.

"Do you believe amulets have special powers?" Celena asked.

"Why do you think I collect them?" Once again, Celena wasn't sure if Helen was toying with her or not. Her response sounded like something Lydia would say, but it had none of her lightheartedness.

Celena replaced the necklace and, seeing an amulet that looked familiar, picked it up. Holding it out, she asked, "This one or one like this was put in my room last week. Did you put it there?"

Helen looked at it briefly. "I found it the other day in the foyer. I thought someone had taken it from my collection, but it's not mine."

"Where did you get them?"

"Ethan and that wife of his made them. Sarina said the gypsies often wore pieces of a rowan tree, either in a necklace or bracelet, because they offered protection from evil spirits. If you'll look closely, you'll see the berry has a five-pointed star—an ancient symbol of protection. I used to have more, but Bernard liked to take them on his ship."

Celena noticed the past tense and said musingly, "I'd heard that sea captains were superstitious." She went on carefully. "Lydia told me that you and your husband are getting a divorce. I imagine it's been hard for you to carry on here alone."

Although Helen's fingers grasped the edge of the dresser as if for support, her poise did not waver. "You do what you have to do."

Celena had hoped for confidences, but they were not forth-coming. Helen Montgomery was one of those rare women who did not talk about herself. Still, Celena tried to draw her out. "I suppose that's true. I never thought when I first came back that I'd be running the lighthouse."

Helen rallied a little. "You'd be better off not running it. You've had a lot of chances, but if you're not careful, things could get worse."

Celena looked at her in the dim light. "Would you happen to know who vandalized the generator building and paint locker?"

There was a flicker in Helen's eyes, but her voice was cool. "Earlier you accused me of attempted murder. Now it's vandalism. If you don't mind, I'd like to get ready for bed." Helen did look exhausted. Her face was drawn, and wisps of hair had escaped, giving her a disheveled look. Celena had to be satisfied with what she had learned from the letter.

Back in her room, Joshua and Zach were in pajamas, jumping on Joshua's bed. Joshua sprang to the floor when she walked in. "Mrs. Montgomery has to be the ghost! And I bet she messed up the buildings too! She's trying to scare us away so she can get the lighthouse."

Zach chimed in. "Yeah! They're going to take away Bay Haven if she can't come up with a bunch of money, and she can't find her husband!"

They had summed up the letter perfectly. It was from a private inves-tigator Helen had hired. Part of it went over things Celena already knew—that Helen had filed for a divorce and that it would be final in the next few weeks. The illuminating part was that Bernard Montgomery had gone deeply into debt and that Helen was being hounded by her husband's creditors, who were threatening to take away the boarding-house if she didn't pay up.

This, then, might be why Helen had been looking harassed and anxious lately, as if there wasn't enough time or money. Probably there wasn't enough of either of those things. The letter made it clear that although Helen had been given extra time, it was running out. Celena wondered why Helen had been given a reprieve. Was it possible that Helen had told her creditors her business was going to increase because she was going to get the lighthouse? If that was the case, Celena's deci-sion to stay must have been a deadly blow.

* * *

In spite of the unpleasant ending to Saturday night, Sunday passed enjoyably. After church, Celena and Joshua took their father outside, taking turns pushing the chair, which had a platform on the left side so that Matthew's cast stuck straight out in front. Celena teased her father, saying she was going to hire him out as a battering ram. It was a mark of Matthew Jackson's standing in the community that everyone they saw stopped to say how glad they were to see him.

The next morning, Lydia stopped Celena as she was about to leave. "Mother wants me to do some shopping. Want to go? If you're not still mad at me, I mean," Lydia said, smiling brightly. Lydia was so unpredictable it was hard to know what to make of her. At times her mischievous behavior bordered on malicious, yet other times she seemed friendly and full of fun. It was impossible to stay angry at her for long.

"Sure," Celena replied. "Just let me tell Father I'll be back later. I promised to take him out for a walk."

The sky overhead was a fresh-washed blue and dotted with small, puffed, silver-lined clouds. There were fountains of pink spirea in Mrs. Cuddy's yard next door, swaying in rhythm to the late June breeze. They passed a group of girls playing hopscotch on their driveway. The windows were open at the Yacht Club, and Celena could hear someone playing, "Meet Me in St. Louis, Louis."

"It was a divine dance, wasn't it?" Lydia purred contentedly. Celena agreed that it was, and Lydia went on. "I must have danced every dance. Daniel is a wonderful dancer, don't you think?"

Celena refused to be drawn in and replied simply, "Yes, he is."

"That was a lovely corsage you had." Lydia had her little Cheshire cat's smile back. "I hope you didn't think the corsage was from Daniel or Clint. Minerva told me it was from your father."

Celena was certain Lydia expected her to be disappointed, but she felt just the opposite. She was touched her father had been thoughtful enough to buy her a corsage. But then, he'd always loved flowers. It was an unexpected side of him. Matthew had often brought her mother flowers he had picked from gardens in town, earning him a scolding each time. It never stopped him though, and he never returned from Long Island without a bouquet from a street vendor.

This morning, the dock was full of activity—fishermen coming in with the day's catch, big white yachts slipping in silently, launches and small sailboats crossing the blue water in the stiff breeze. Elaine was outside Tillman's, sweeping the sidewalk while supervising her son, who was picking up nails from a broken keg that had spilled out its shiny contents onto the dirt. Celena went through the store with Lydia, putting their purchases in a small wire basket.

When they were done, Lydia asked Elaine, "Do you have any cheese?"

"Sorry, I'm out. My supplies didn't come in yesterday." Elaine called to her oldest son, Jeremy, who was in the back sorting apples and potatoes. "When did you say the supplies would get here?"

"They should be here anytime," Jeremy replied. "There was too much freight yesterday, and the ferry couldn't bring it all. Clint said he'd bring your stuff over this morning on the first run."

Elaine's plain face looked apologetic. "Every once in a while our supplies get held up." The girls gathered their sacks and almost ran into Tana and Rueben on their way out. The sea wind was brisk, causing Tana's dark blue skirt to flap around her legs and blowing her white hair in all directions.

"We just got back from Long Island," Tana explained.

"Another doctor appointment for Will?" Celena wanted to know. Rueben nodded.

"I hope they can help him," Lydia said sympathetically. She took Celena's bag. "Mother needs these things, so I'll run them back while you stay and chat." Lydia hurried off, the sun reflecting brightly off her blond hair.

"How did the appointment go?" Celena asked.

Tana's face was worried. "They took more blood so they could run a few more tests."

"Will didn't cry at all. He's a real trooper," Rueben said proudly. "He's always patient and mild." He laughed. "Kind of the opposite of you as a child, Celena."

"I think you're getting forgetful in your old age," Celena grumbled. When Rueben and Tana looked at each other, Celena said huffily, "Oh, come on. Tana, you tell him. I was a sweetheart. Remember?"

"I do!" Rueben gave a mock shudder, then turned to his wife. "You tell her, darling. She won't believe me."

Tana opened her mouth, then closed it. Then, in a placating voice, she said, "Look how you turned out! You're a darling sweet girl now."

Celena was outraged. "Tana!"

"Well, dear." Tana hesitated, her pleasant face troubled. "You were adorable, but there were times, if you were crossed . . ." her voice trailed off. "But your parents were very patient."

It was a shock. Celena knew she'd been impulsive at times, but she'd always thought it unfair when others called her headstrong, because to her way of thinking, she always acted in a wise and prudent manner. Privately, Celena thought she'd been almost angelic but had the uncomfortable feeling that if she said so, Rueben would laugh out loud. And Tana said her parents had been patient. Imagine. She'd been so focused on the recent past that she rarely took the time to look further back. But her father *had* been patient when teaching her how to ride a bike, running alongside, shouting out encouragement. And again when teaching her how to swim, even though her mother thought Celena too young.

Rueben broke into her thoughts. "What are you up to today?"

"I promised Father I'd take him out."

"That will be a real treat," Tana said enthusiastically. "He so enjoys spending time with you. When I visited him the other day, all he could talk about was Celena this and Celena that."

"Oh, by the way, we ran into Daniel on the Long Island Railroad," Rueben said, digging into his pocket. "When he found out we were coming this way, he asked me to give this to you." He handed Celena a folded square of paper and winked. "I must say, you've caught the eye of more than one man since you've come back. And I thought it was Clint all the way."

"Oh, hush," Tana cried, slapping at his shoulder before pulling him inside the store.

Celena unfolded the note. It was brief. Daniel wrote that he'd had a wonderful time last night and was sorry she'd left before he could dance with her again. He ended by saying he and his father were looking forward to going to the Sunken Forest and they would bring the dessert. Although Celena told herself not to make too much of it, she folded the note carefully, as though it mattered, and when she put it in her pocket, there was a small smile on her face.

* * *

After lunch, it was still breezy, so Celena tied her reddish-brown hair back with a ribbon before helping her father into his chair. When she put an afghan over his knees, he yanked it off and threw it on the floor, growling, "I'm not an invalid."

"Grouch," Celena said under her breath. A Book of Mormon lay on top of the bedside table, and she went over and picked it up. "You forgot to hide this."

"Got tired of doing that. I guess you're surprised I'm reading it," he said peevishly.

"Not at all. I saw several pigs fly by this morning."

Matthew tried hard not to smile and kept his voice gruff. "Reading it wasn't my idea. Elizabeth made me promise." He looked at his daughter. "I suppose she made you promise things, too. Elizabeth always did like to have all of her bases covered."

She sidestepped the question. "Do you like the book?"

"I didn't at first. Expected something different. But it was a lot like the Bible so I got used to it quick. Then, after a while, something grabbed hold and whenever I read it, I got a peculiar feeling. Finally, I asked Rueben about it. He told me it was indigestion."

"What?"

Matthew looked amused. "You know Rueben. Then he told me that I was feeling the Spirit." Unexpectedly, Matthew smacked the arms of his chair. "Well, are we ever going to get out of here?"

It was a sudden shift, but Celena replied heartily, "By all means, let's go. Ready?"

"Aye. I was born ready." Celena couldn't help but giggle as she wheeled him out.

Ethan had nailed boards to form a ramp over the right side of the stairs. As they set off, a gull soared overhead, squawking noisily.

"Doesn't this thing go any faster?" her father complained. "You're crawling along like a crab." Celena picked up the pace, but it wasn't enough. "Can't you go any faster?" Matthew barked, sounding exhilarated. Celena began jogging. "That's better, but I was hoping for a little speed. A snail could go faster!"

Celena began to run, her legs churning. Her father gave a whoop of delight, which Celena would have echoed had she any breath left. Louise Johnson was gardening in her front yard, wearing a wide-brimmed hat. She stared as they flew by, her mouth a round O. Celena laughed aloud with the radiance and sheer joy of the bright morning. Finally, she had to slow down.

Matthew's face was deeply flushed with exhilaration, and there was a light in his eyes as they continued more decorously along Bay Promenade. Since the ferry was in, they went over to the dock. Matthew's wheels clattered noisily over the boards as they went past a line of nets drying on wooden racks. Little waves broke against the dock pilings with repeated sighs. Clint noticed Celena and came striding over. He gave her a warm smile, then shook Matthew's hand firmly.

"It's good to see you out and about!"

"Been cooped up too long!" Matthew grumbled.

"How about a ride?" Clint nodded toward the ferry. "No charge. If you're not too tired, that is." Clint couldn't have said anything more calculated to ensure Matthew's acceptance. Clint signaled an employee to help him up the ramp, then made sure the wheelchair was secured by the railing.

Celena smiled at him gratefully. "This is very good of you."

"It's my pleasure. I like to make my passengers comfortable." With a twinkle in his eyes and a quick squeeze of her hand, Clint added, "Especially special ones."

It was restful sitting there beside her father. Celena looked across the bay where white sails flitted against the outline of Long Island, looking like butterflies. Great South Bay danced cobalt blue, and a wide, white wake frothed behind them. At times, Celena's eyes searched for Clint. One time he was talking easily to a middle-aged couple with their lanky teenage son, another time, two elderly women. Friendly and easygoing, Clint got along with everyone.

They were halfway to Long Island when Clint returned. The two men started in on their favorite topic—political instability in Europe.

"Even though France signed alliances with Poland and Czechoslovakia, trouble's brewing over there," Clint warned darkly. "I don't think Germany, France, and Belgium signing the Locarno Treaties means a thing."

Matthew gloomily agreed. "Germany's still a threat, but no one seems to realize it. I'm afraid we're headed for another bad ending."

"But wouldn't the League of Nations take care of Germany if they tried anything again?" Celena challenged. "I mean, the whole purpose of creating the League of Nations was to regulate international disputes and to protect other countries from aggression."

"Ah. The operative words there are 'supposed to,'" Clint said. "But since the war ended in 1918, many governments in Eastern Europe have become politically unstable, and quite a few leaders are jockeying for position, trying to take advantage of the situation. That Mussolini is someone to watch, especially since he picked up the reins of power over the Fascists a few years ago."

"There's a man named Hitler that sounds like trouble," Matthew added. "He's moving his way up through the ranks, and it's only a matter of time before he becomes chancellor."

"If that happens, we just might find ourselves in another war," Clint proclaimed.

Celena couldn't stand any more. Jumping up, she said, "I think I'm going to leave this lovely conversation and take a stroll around the deck."

Clint laughed. "Can't say I blame you." He addressed Matthew. "If you don't mind, sir, I think I'll join your daughter." Matthew waved them away, and they strolled around the deck before stopping at the railing. When a Coast Guard ship went by, Celena decided to try Joshua's trick.

She pointed. "Look, Clint, a six-bitter. The Coast Guard built them to catch rumrunners, but they can only go about 17 miles per hour. They're rather small, only 75-feet long."

"My, aren't you a fountain of knowledge!"

"Impressed?"

"Very."

Celena laughed. "Actually, I got that from Daniel."

Clint looked suddenly alert. "Daniel? Well, well. He certainly knows a lot, doesn't he?" A wave from a passing boat hit the ferry, sending water up the side.

"We're nearly there," Clint said, turning. Their heads were very close, and Clint leaned over and kissed her lightly. "Hope you don't mind," he said. "You're so pretty I couldn't resist."

"I'd better get back to Father," she said softly.

"And I'd better check the crew."

When Celena returned, Matthew eyed her. "Nothing more bracing than being out on the water. It's put roses in your cheeks, I see." He looked around the ferry. "Clint's done well for himself, hasn't he? It's commendable how he built this business up."

"Yes. He's amazing, all right."

After the passengers disembarked and others came aboard, the *Sea Siren* shivered with power as it started back to Fire Island. Celena and her father talked companionably, with Matthew more at ease than she had seen him since her return. It was a sure sign he was getting better.

"Father," Celena said impulsively, "why don't you come with us to the Sunken Forest on Saturday? You're doing so much better."

Matthew shook his head regretfully. "I asked Doc Harrison and he acted like I was trying to commit hari-kari. Said it wasn't a good idea to travel miles on bumpy roads." Celena hadn't thought of that. He went on. "Joshua's excited about going. Your mother and I used to take both of you there a lot. As I recall, you liked to collect leaves for that album of yours."

Celena remembered—holding her father's hand as they walked along the trails, choosing leaves with care, using sticks as machetes and slashing at the shrubbery, picnics spread under the green canopy of the forest with tree-dappled sunshine falling around them. After returning home, she'd put her leaves between pages of a book to flatten and dry before pasting them in her album. She could almost smell the paste now.

Matthew interrupted her musings. "You didn't say much about the dance. How was it?"

"It was great. Thank you for the corsage."

He frowned deeply. "I told Minerva not to say anything."

"She didn't. Someone else told me." They were silent for a while, but it was a comfortable stillness.

When her father spoke, his voice was soft. "When you came back, I didn't think you'd stay."

"I didn't plan to," Celena admitted.

Matthew looked out over the bay. "I know I made mistakes, but I didn't go too far off because you've grown into a fine, good woman."

Her father didn't turn to look at her, but that didn't lessen the impact of his words. The bay disappeared until Celena could see nothing through tear-filled eyes but a blur and a shimmer. Her hand found his and she clasped his fingers. There was great comfort in knowing her father approved of her and that he cared—and that in fact he had never stopped caring. It was all there in their tightly woven hands. The peace of it sunk deep in her bones, imbuing her with a fullness that caused her to shut her eyes briefly and turn her face to the sun to feel the sweet sunshine on her eyelids, cheekbones, and lips.

That was the moment Celena knew their relationship could be made completely right, and that it was already further along than she'd realized. She knew that once their bond had been fully repaired, it would be like a piece of fabric that had been mended—stronger than ever before and unable to be torn again in that same place. Celena suddenly felt so unencumbered she could have floated upward with only the least bit of effort. Out of nowhere came the impression that her mother was watching—at that very moment—and that she was smiling.

* * *

When they got back to Bay Haven, Matthew was tired and fell asleep quickly. It would be a good time to talk to Ethan, if he was home. Celena went to the back of the house and knocked.

"Who is it?" His voice sounded fearful.

"Celena."

The door opened, and there he stood, big and bulky—a wide smile of delight on his face. His room was in disarray, his bed unmade, clothes on chairs and on the floor, shells and pieces of driftwood covering the table and dresser. The door to his closet was open, and near the front were flashes of color.

Celena went over and touched a scarf. "Sarina loved bright colors, didn't she?" On top of the chest were half a dozen amulets. Celena picked one up. "Helen said you and Sarina made these."

"They're good luck. Sarina made that one."

She turned to him. "Did you put one in my room?"

Ethan nodded solemnly, his face innocent. "To protect you."

"Did you take it back?"

"No."

"Well, someone took it."

His frown was fierce. "I put it there to protect you!" He pointed to the one she held. "You take that. It'll keep you safe." He picked up a carved amulet. "Sarina made this. It's very powerful. See the waves?" Ethan pointed out the undulating lines. "It's made for protection on water. Whenever Sarina went out in the boat, she'd take it."

"She must not have taken it with her the night she died."

"No." Ethan's voice was barely above a whisper. "But she *always* took it when she went in the boat."

Celena hated to probe old wounds, but knew she had to find out more. "Ethan, did anything different happen that day? Anything unusual?"

His broad face was thoughtful. "Sarina was mad. When I came home for lunch, Lydia was here. They were both mad." He grimaced at the memory.

Celena was surprised. "What did Lydia want?"

Ethan didn't know.

She tried again. "Do you know what upset them?"

"No," he said glumly. "After Lydia left, Sarina told me to watch the beach if she went away."

Celena felt a faint chill. Lydia could easily have been the last person to see Sarina alive. Why hadn't Lydia mentioned her visit? Wanting to see if Ethan stayed true to his story, Celena asked, "So Sarina and the boat were gone when you got home that afternoon?"

He shook his head. "Sarina was gone. The boat was there. I went to look for her. When I got back, the boat was gone." Ethan's eyes were dark, and he kept wringing his hands. Unexpectedly his voice rose until he was practically shouting. "Sarina didn't *take* the boat. She *never* went without her amulet. *Never!*" He ran his fingers through his hair, then hit the top of the chest with a sickening thud, causing several amulets to fall to the floor. Celena stepped back. She had never seen him like this.

He groaned. "What happened to her?" The anguish in his voice was hurtful to hear. Tears began running down his cheeks. Then, as if his legs would no longer support him, Ethan sank his bulk into a chair.

Celena gave him a few minutes, then pressed on. "Did Sarina go out a lot at night?"

"Sometimes."

"Did she tell you why she wanted you to watch the beach?"

Ethan shook his head, then added, "Daniel watches the beach too."

Startled at first, Celena asked, "Do you know what a rumrunner is?"

"Someone who brings in rum and gives it to someone."

"Did Sarina ever do that?"

His brows came together and his face darkened. "No! Only bad men do that."

At least that answered the question of whether Ethan was involved in rum-running. Celena still wasn't sure if Sarina had been smuggling or not. If so, she had kept it well hidden from Ethan. It seemed clear that there was more to Sarina's death than anyone had thought. Had Sarina been smuggling that night when something went wrong? But then, if Sarina *had* taken the boat to get a load of liquor, why hadn't she taken her amulet? It would be interesting to know what had happened during Lydia's visit, too. Sarina might have given some hint, some idea of where she was planning to go that night. And if she really was planning on leaving Ethan, she might have given some indication of that as well.

To distract Ethan, Celena told him about the upcoming picnic. "Helen's coming, and we'd love for you to come too," she said encouragingly. "I know you like the Sunken Forest." Ethan didn't answer, just kept wiping his eyes. "Look, it's time for dinner. Come with me."

Ethan refused, but Celena wouldn't take no for an answer, grabbing his hand and pulling till he rose reluctantly. At the door, Celena paused to scan the room. Something was nagging at her mind—triggered by something she had seen. What was it? But Celena was unable to put her finger on it and went out, dragging Ethan with her. In the dining room, Helen was surprised and delighted at her brother's presence. She even smiled fleetingly at Celena as she fussed over Ethan, who perked up when he saw the nice spread on the table—flounder, clams, oysters, and hush puppies.

*　*　*

That night, on the way to the light, Joshua rode on ahead as usual. When Celena arrived, the door to the house was open, and it wasn't until Celena locked the door behind her that she noticed that something was wrong. Papers were scattered on the floor in the assistant keeper's quarters, and everything on the desk had been dashed to the floor. Books had been knocked from shelves and chairs overturned. Shards of glass from a broken clock glinted on the floor. Suddenly there was a high, wavering cry from above.

Joshua!

Celena rushed up the stairs. She found Joshua in the watch room. Thankfully, he was standing on his own power, no blood in sight. Celena looked about. Their cots had been turned over, blankets spilling onto the metal floor. The box that held their books and games had been overturned and the contents strewn about. Fighting a sickening feeling of panic, Celena rushed to the next floor. It was a huge relief to see that the clockworks had not been damaged. Brother and sister slipped through the trapdoor to the lantern room. Her father's lighthouse jacket and cap had been thrown to the floor and were covered with bits of glass from the shattered spirit lamp. The box of cleaning cloths had been dumped, with rags and shells lying white against the dark wooden floor. All of the candles had been systematically broken in half. But thankfully, there was no damage to the prisms or the light itself.

"Do you think it was the ghost?" Joshua asked.

"There isn't any ghost," Celena ground out.

"But who did this?"

"If I knew the answer to that, I'd be running the country."

SIXTEEN

It took a lot of daring for someone to enter the lighthouse and wreak havoc. It was also a clear indication that matters were escalating. Celena called the police and notified the Lighthouse Bureau as well. A detective came but indicated they had little to go on. It remained a mystery as to how the vandal had gotten inside. When Celena checked, her father's key was still in his drawer, but anyone could have taken it if Matthew happened to fall asleep or was out of the room, and they could have easily returned it later.

* * *

After lunch the next day, Celena was getting ready to go back to the lighthouse to attempt to straighten up the mess there when Zach and Joshua approached her. They almost looked like twins, both of them wearing striped shirts and jeans that were worn at the knees.

"Celena, can we use some of the wood that's out back?" Joshua asked. "Zach and I are going to make a birdhouse."

"We'd better ask Helen."

The boys followed her to the kitchen where Ethan was replacing a hinge on a cabinet. "Do you know where Helen is?" Celena asked. "The boys want to know if they can use some of the wood that's in the backyard."

Zach wanted to make things perfectly clear. "We want to build a birdhouse."

"That's my wood," Ethan said, looking at them doubtfully.

"Can we use some?" Joshua begged.

Ethan eyed the boys, then set down his screwdriver and went outside. They followed. There were two piles of wood against the storage shed, one with small, uneven pieces, and one with longer pieces. Ethan pointed at the pile with smaller pieces.

"You can use that."

"Great!" Zach exclaimed. "Can we use your saw and hammer? And some nails?"

Ethan strode to the shed door, then stopped. He stared at it, seeming transfixed by the shining padlock.

Celena came up behind him. "Don't you have a key?"

"No," Ethan said, scratching his beard. "It's never been locked before."

Zach sighed heavily before turning to Joshua. "Let's load up the wood in the wagon and take it to my place. We can use my father's tools—as long as he isn't home."

* * *

Later that afternoon, Celena went to her father's room. She'd put off telling him about the rope being cut long enough. Really, she was surprised no one else had told him about it yet. Matthew was standing by the window, leaning on his crutches and looking toward the light. When she came in, he swung around and walked to his bed.

"You're getting better at using those crutches," she said delightedly. Matthew snorted, then used his hands to lift his casted leg onto the bed. Inwardly she sighed. This would have been easier if he had been in a good mood. She started at the beginning, from initially being unable to find the rope and bosun's chair, to her discovery that the rope had been cut, and then its disappearance. He took it better than she thought he would, although he was angry that he hadn't been told sooner.

"Did it occur to you," Matthew groused, "that I might like to know if someone had tried to kill me?"

"I should have told you before," Celena admitted. "But I wasn't sure if you'd believe me about the rope being cut."

"Why wouldn't I?" he asked crossly.

"Some people don't."

"Idiots."

"Do you have any enemies?" Celena asked thoughtfully.

"Not anyone I can think of," Matthew replied, bemused. "Sometimes I rub people the wrong way, but that's no reason to try and kill me."

"Maybe it wasn't someone from the island. Could it have been a rumrunner?"

"Why would smugglers want to do that?"

"Could it have been someone who wanted the light? Like Gerald or Helen?"

Matthew looked astonished. "Neither one of them would cut the rope on me."

"Well, *somebody* did."

Her father was silent a time. "I've been thinking, and all I can come up with is that someone must have some kind of vendetta against me. I don't think it's any stranger, either. Whoever did it has to be on the island, because the rope disappeared only *after* you started telling people it had been cut."

"I hate to say there's more."

Matthew's face was hard as flint when she told him about the recent vandalism at the lighthouse. When he spoke, his voice was chillingly somber. "That's it, then. This has gone way beyond rabbits or amulets. I want you out of here."

"I understand your concern, but I'm staying."

"You're going back to Maryland."

Celena planted her feet and folded her arms. "Make me."

Matthew's blue eyes nearly popped out of his head. "There you go again!" he shouted. "If you aren't the most stubborn girl God ever put on earth—I might as well talk to the lighthouse as try to talk sense into you!"

She wouldn't let him rile her today. "Don't think of me as stubborn, think of me as persistent. Persistence is a good thing." Celena said lightly. "Say it—*persistent*. It sounds ever so much better than stubborn."

Matthew stared at her as if she had just exited a flying saucer, then snapped, "Doesn't do any good to talk with a crazy person."

She went on calmly. "Now, just to set your mind at ease, I already ordered new rope, and when it came, I attached it to the pulleys and bosun's chair. It's all stored away in the watch room."

"Good, you'll need that done for inspections." He looked up at her under heavy brows. "But from now on, you've got to be very careful."

"I intend to."

* * *

On Friday, Rueben came down the hall at Bay Haven. "Hello, Celena. I've been visiting your father."

"I'm glad. Now that Father's feeling better, he's getting restless. Did you remember we were going to the Sunken Forest tomorrow?"

"I'm babysitting in the morning because Will has a doctor appointment. But Hannah ought to get back in good time, so Tana and I will drive out after she's done at the post office."

"Did they get the results on Will's blood work?"

Rueben looked gloomy. "Yes, and everything's about the same. It hasn't gotten any worse, but it hasn't gotten any better either. Tana says that's good, but I don't know." He looked at her glumly. "Will's my only grandson, you know. I'm the one who taught him to bait a hook and play horseshoes. I took him for his first boat ride."

"I'm sure he'll be all right," Celena said consolingly. "Tana said he has good doctors."

Fire came into his eyes. "They ought to be for what they charge! It's highway robbery, that's what it is. Just isn't right." There was a belligerent look on Rueben's face. "But I'll come up with the money somehow."

It wasn't until later that Celena realized Rueben hadn't said how. At the light that night, Celena retrieved the coat Joshua had found in the generator building a couple weeks earlier. Maybe it had more meaning than she had previously thought.

SEVENTEEN

On Saturday, Celena put on a cotton shirt and comfortable shoes for walking. Gerald was driving his black Buick, and Helen slid in beside him. Daniel was in the back, wearing a gray shirt and dark slacks. Ethan was there also, taking up much of the back seat and forcing Daniel and Celena to squeeze together closely.

Daniel winked at her. "We ought to invite Ethan more often!"

Lydia went in Clint's car, with Joshua and Zach bouncing in the back. They followed the Old Coast Guard Road, and, as it ran along a stretch of maritime forest, they plunged in and out of dark shade in the midst of tangled trees. Helen looked more relaxed than she had in a long time, seeming almost human as she pointed out the cranberry bogs to the north—the low, creeping vines looking like thickly-matted carpets.

"Why do they call it the Sunken Forest?" Daniel asked as they drove slowly along the heavily rutted road.

"Because it appears to be lower than the ocean," Celena responded. "It isn't, actually, but seems like it because the surrounding sand dunes are so high. Some of them are thirty feet tall. Although trees usually have a hard time growing on the island because of the salty spray from the ocean, the high dunes around the Sunken Forest protect the trees there."

Helen added, "There's only one native pine on Fire Island—the pitch pine. It can grow just about anywhere because its waxy needles protect it. Holly is also resistant to salt because of its waxy leaves. Some of the American holly trees in the Sunken Forest are over two hundred years old."

They parked beneath trees where it was shadowy and cool. The air was pungently scented, filled with the murmur of branches whispering overhead. They carried food hampers to the long tables that were built from loggerhead planks. Ethan went a short distance away to scrape out a hollow for a fire, and Daniel set off to gather wood, with Lydia trailing after him.

When Daniel returned with an armload, Lydia was carrying a few sticks, laughing gaily. Celena turned away and began spreading out the tablecloths. Zach and Joshua were scrutinizing Ethan's every move. Taking a dry pine bough, Ethan broke it into twigs then arranged them on a pile of dry moss. He added twigs and showed Zach and Joshua how to stack small branches like tepee poles. When the fire was burning well, Ethan added bigger logs. The fire drew everyone like a magnet, making Ethan, who was sitting cross-legged before it, seem uneasy.

Daniel looked over the forest. "Do they allow hunting here?"

"They do now," Clint replied, "but the city council is talking about changing that."

"Too bad Ethan didn't bring his gun," Lydia said.

"I don't have it anymore," Ethan muttered. "Clint took it."

Every face turned to the mayor. "I was going to take it to the police in Ocean Beach, but when I called and talked to them, no one had reported a missing rifle."

"I wouldn't mind seeing it," Daniel said. Although his face was impassive, there was something guarded in his eyes. Celena wondered what it meant.

"Celena had an idea that the gun might have been dropped by smugglers," Clint said. "Since that's possible, I thought the Coast Guard might be able to tell us something, so I took the gun in to them at Long Island."

"Long Island? Why not at the Coast Guard station here?" Helen asked.

"They have a bigger station on Long Island—more resources to check things out," Clint replied. "Since I'm there every day, it wasn't any trouble."

Celena was curious. "But how would the Coast Guard be able to tell us anything about the gun? There's no way to know if it was dropped by smugglers or a poacher."

"Smugglers often use stolen weapons, and the Coast Guard can trace the serial number to see if it's been stolen," Daniel explained.

"Clint, I'd be interested in knowing what you find out. By the way, what kind of a rifle was it?"

"Springfield '03," Ethan answered.

Daniel's face registered interest. "Hope it wasn't an early model." When the others looked at him, he explained, "Rifles in the early models, with serial numbers under 800,000, can have defective receivers and shatter when used. Changes were made later so that higher-numbered rifles—those manufactured after 1918—are safe."

Helen voiced what everyone else had to be thinking. "You're quite an expert!"

"You sure are." Lydia's teeth flashed in an insolent, secretive smile. "How does a bookkeeper come to know so much about rifles?" When Daniel was hesitant in replying, Celena noticed that Clint was watching him with some interest. Gerald defused the situation by slapping his son on the back jovially.

"Oh, ho! Daniel takes after his old man, that's all. He's always been interested in guns, just like me. We talked about the rifle after Ethan showed it to me. It's nothing special. Typical army issue." Despite his cheerfulness, Celena, as usual, had the feeling that there was more behind Gerald's genial facade than one might think. Especially when Gerald glanced sideways at Clint, giving him a look she couldn't interpret.

Ethan was beginning to look agitated, and Helen was quick to notice. "All this talk is upsetting Ethan," she said. "Let's leave him to tend the fire by himself." Zach and Joshua were the only ones to ignore her as they busily searched for twigs to throw on the fire. Lydia strode over to the tables as if she owned the forest and seated herself on one end, swinging one foot as Celena began unpacking dishes. Helen unpacked the tuna, which Gerald carried over to the fire for her so she could help Ethan arrange it over the coals.

Lydia was always vibrant, but today there was something electric about her—with her perfect hairdo and eyes that flashed emerald fire. She flirted openly with Daniel, who was putting stones on the corners of the tablecloths.

Although Celena busied herself setting out the box of silverware, she couldn't help watching Daniel and Lydia with a twinge of jealousy. Ever since Celena had run into Daniel Roberts at Tillman's, she had been drawn to him. When inner voices of warning had risen and she should have drawn back, Celena had not. If she had been more careful, more watchful, she might have been able to pull back from the strength of the current that was now carrying her along.

"Oh, leave that," Lydia said suddenly, stopping Daniel when he started to unpack the glasses. "It's a beautiful day. Let's go for a walk in the woods!"

"That's a great idea," Clint said, reaching for Celena's hand. "Let's go."

When Helen looked across the little meadow toward Ethan, Gerald spoke softly. "He'll be glad to be alone. Come with us."

Her face softened. "I expect you're right."

In the past weeks, Celena had envisioned her and Daniel walking hand in hand to explore, but today she pushed those thoughts away and called to the boys. Zach and Joshua gamboled after them like puppies as they set out on a winding path that led through the forest. Although Celena told the boys to stay close, she might as well have been talking to the wind. Soon they were in a primeval world of green, shadowed overhead by a canopy of trees and vines. In places, the ground was damp and marshy. The growth was thick, studded with holly, sassafras, tupelo, red cedar, and post oak. Far off, Celena could see beyond the forest where the inner dune sloped downward, then back up to the main dune where dune grass, beach heather, and goldenrod grew in the swale. The surf was only an occasional distant rumble, making it seem as though the island were breathing.

There was a warm odor of earth and sun, and the air was so pine-scented that it seemed to rise up out of the very earth and seep from the rocks. If it hadn't been for Lydia's constant chatter, it would have been the most quiet, peaceful place Celena had ever been. They began to spread out, with the boys far ahead and Lydia pulling Daniel along at great speed at the front. Gerald and Helen took off on one of the side trails, leaving Clint and Celena to bring up the rear.

"I'm glad Ethan could come," Celena said. "I think he's been lonely since Sarina died."

"I'm sure he has. She was so bright and energetic. I guess it's true that opposites attract."

"Did you know Sarina very well?"

"Not really, though we'd talk a little whenever she rode the ferry."

"Ethan told me you helped them buy a boat."

Clint was modest. "I was able to get them a good price since I was buying a new one myself. Quantity discount, you see."

"Gerald told me that Sarina was afraid of the water."

He looked surprised. "I knew she didn't swim, but I didn't know she was afraid of anything. Sarina said she wanted to be able to get across the bay whenever she wanted. And Ethan planned to do a little fishing."

She tilted her head up at him. "Do you think Sarina could have been a rumrunner?"

"Not if she was afraid of the water." Clint smiled slightly. "But now that you ask, one time I did hear her talking to Rueben on the dock. She was asking a lot of questions—what kind of boats smugglers used, how they found contacts, which liquor sold for the most money, that sort of thing. I didn't pay much attention—everyone talks about rumrunners. Besides, if Sarina was planning on trying it, I doubt she'd be talking about it so openly." Still, Celena felt disturbed, not so much that Sarina had been asking questions, but that she had picked Rueben to query.

They walked on through crystal air that swarmed with birdsong. Rounding a bend, they came upon Daniel sitting on a log, tying his shoe. Lydia was beside him, looking sulky. They walked along as a foursome for a while. Then suddenly Daniel was alongside Celena. He slowed down, letting Clint and Lydia go ahead. Unexpectedly, he took her hand and darted down a side path.

As she was pulled along, Celena whispered, "Won't Clint and Lydia wonder where we are?"

"Let them wonder," he said quietly. "I'm tired of getting trapped by Lydia. She'd hog-tie me if she could."

"Then why did you invite her?"

Daniel looked at her. "I didn't. She told me *you* had." Realization dawned and he shook his head. "Never mind. Come on." His step was quick and lively. Occasionally, he glanced back to see if anyone was following. Overhead, the treetops moved in a gentle whisper, and when a breeze stirred, Celena could hear it coming from afar off. Soon they found another path that branched off and, laughing, took that.

"This is much better," Daniel proclaimed in a satisfied voice. Celena laughed at his boyish tone. As they walked, she lifted her face to the misty yellow light that penetrated the overhead ceiling of green. There was a spring in her step that didn't come entirely from the thick carpet of pine needles.

"How are things going at the light?" Daniel asked. When she told him about the vandalism, Daniel frowned. "I have a feeling you've stirred up a lot more than you realize."

"I'd like to know who's behind it. Lydia and Helen want the light." She had almost listed Gerald, but stopped in time. "Do they think they can frighten me away with their pranks?"

"Maybe it's not a prank. Everyone knows you're trying to find out who's responsible for nearly killing your father. Plus you've been asking a lot of questions about Sarina's death. If there is anything there, you might be making someone very nervous. Maybe even desperate."

"The main reason I've been trying to find out more about Sarina's death is to help Ethan—to give him some closure," Celena said solemnly.

"But Celena, don't you realize that if you *do* get to the bottom of it, you could be unmasking a murderer?" Daniel was disturbed.

"I didn't think about that at first because I thought her drowning was an accident. But I don't believe that anymore."

"So tell me the facts you have so far."

She listed off everything Ethan had told her.

"Putting it all together like that does make it sound fishy," Daniel admitted, "but do you realize that the single common denominator in each and every thing you listed, except for Elaine's gossip, is Ethan? Think about it. Can anyone else corroborate anything he said? I'm not saying Ethan is lying, but his thinking can be twisted sometimes. Besides, I'm sure the police looked into it at the time."

"The police?" she scoffed. "Do you think they would have paid any attention to someone like Ethan? To them, it was an open-and-shut case. Just an accident."

"Look, I know you're trying to help, but maybe Ethan is upset just because you're stirring up old wounds. If you let it go, he might settle down."

But Celena didn't believe that. Sarina had died two years ago, and Ethan was still very disturbed. Someone had to help him, and Celena was convinced the only way to do that was to find out the truth about Sarina's death.

There was the sound of voices, and it appeared their stolen moments together were over. "They'll certainly find us if we stay together," Daniel said in a rushed whisper. "You go that way, and I'll go over there. And when they've gone, we'll meet back here!" It was childish fun, and Celena grinned at him before dashing off. Celena followed a path that led toward a stand of trees, and when she could still hear faint voices, she plunged along a trail that had been worn by generations of Fire Island deer.

She stopped for some time before heading back. As she walked, the trail seemed longer than before. Celena looked around. Certainly she had not passed that huge post oak before, with its peculiar five-lobed leaf. Trying to get her bearings, Celena went in another direction. Finally, she had to accept that she had gotten turned around. It was frustrating rather than frightening, for although the Sunken Forest was deep, it was not endless.

She entered a dark copse, and its thick ferny groundcover made her think of the evil forests of Grimm's fairy tales. Celena was lost in her own clouded thoughts when she had an uncanny feeling—the extra sense one gets occasionally when someone, sight unseen, is watching . . . malignantly. Celena shook off the disturbing feeling. What was the matter with her? The prickling along the back of her neck was absurd. She had heard nothing. Seen nothing. It was merely something she sensed. Looking over her shoulder, she shivered and crossed to another trail. Clouds of gnats settled thickly, making her hurry on.

There was a sudden burst of sound off to her right as some disturbance set a group of yellow warblers with their bright yellow bodies darting into the sky. Celena's heart started beating unreasonably fast. Was it better to hurry along and have her movements loud enough to allow whoever was out there to track her, or would it be better to move more stealthily in hopes of escaping detection? For there was no doubt now that someone was following her. There was a rustle and crackle of breaking twigs, but when she looked back, there was nothing to see.

"Daniel?" she called out tentatively. "Clint?" There was no answer. She passed a clump of dead trees with their scraggly dry branches intertwined and went on through a stand of large sassafras trees with their mitten-shaped leaves. Here and there, ferns grew thickly in shaded spots. Once, when she paused, Celena thought there was a sound behind her and stopped, going as still as a woodland mouse after seeing a hawk swoop past.

A strange sense of foreboding warned her not to go off the trail, though she felt it might help to hide from whoever was after her. There seemed to be danger in every shadow. Celena ran into the deeper woods—a place of green gloom, where the sun barely filtered through the twisted canopy overhead. More rustling came from behind. Heart pounding, Celena ran down a path that zigzagged through scrubby brush, but vines and shrubbery enveloped the area, and there was no way to get through the green tangle. Celena turned to go another way, but it was slick underfoot, and she fell heavily, feeling the slimy mold of decayed leaves under her cheek. For a few seconds, she held still, looking out into the leafy darkness under the matted trees.

Jumping up, her heart thudding so hard it nearly shook her, Celena hurried along. When she found a narrow path, she took it, blinking in surprise when it suddenly broke out of the green canopy into sunshine. Celena inhaled sharply then looked back, but whoever had been following her had melted away as silently as he had come. She sank down to allow her heart to return to normal. There was a sudden sound, and her head jerked up to see a vast, brooding presence lurch toward her.

"Ethan!" Celena gasped, then scolded, "You truly are going to give me a heart attack one of these days!" The smile on his big face died, and she asked, "Why were you following me?"

"I wasn't. I came to tell you the tuna is done."

Looking around, Celena saw she had come out on the far end of the meadow. A small copse of trees hid the fire from view. But if not Ethan, who *had* been following her? And how had Ethan crossed the meadow so fast? Could he have been in the woods behind her and come out through that small copse? Those legs of his would carry him a long way in a short time.

He was watching her. "Maybe it was Sarina. She's angry."

Celena scowled. She was in no mood for this. "Sarina is *not* here," she said with more force than she intended. Ethan blinked at her in owlish surprise. "Never mind," she said. "Let's go back."

As they walked, Celena finger-combed the leaves out of her hair and brushed at her jeans, which had several muddy patches on them. Who was so bent on frightening her, and why? Celena was determined not to be scared away, but whoever was doing this seemed equally determined. How far the person would go remained to be seen. Then again, perhaps their intention was not just to scare. A chill ran up her back. It was if she was being swept along—a series of events moving her toward some unknown climax.

When Ethan and Celena rounded the trees, they saw Joshua and Zach throwing rocks into a small pond. Daniel emerged from the woods.

When he got closer, he asked worriedly, "Where did you disappear to?"

"I got turned around," Celena said simply. She was surprised to see Tana sitting at the tables, contentedly reading a book. She was wearing a green print dress and had on sturdy shoes that were covered in fresh mud.

"So you decided to come after all!" Celena cried with delight. "Where's Rueben?"

"We got here a while ago, but no one was around, so he went off for a walk. Where is everybody?"

"The bears got them," Daniel said jokingly. They talked for a while, then Gerald showed up.

"Has anyone seen Helen? She said she was coming back to help Ethan with the fish, but I don't see her." Just then, Clint and Lydia came out of the woods in different places, saying they had gotten separated. A few minutes later, Helen came across the meadow from the direction of the cars, carrying a large pan. There was a slight breeze, just enough to rustle the leaves and fill the air with the savory aroma of baking fish. Ethan proudly carried the fish to the table that was laden with hush puppies, slaw, and punch. As they ate, Celena couldn't help but think about who could have followed her. It was with a chill that she realized she could rule out no one. There was much to think about on the ride back to Saltaire.

* * *

They were late getting back, so it wasn't until the next morning that Celena was able to tell her father about the outing, though she omitted the part about her scare in the forest.

"Helen saved a piece of the roasted tuna for my dinner last night," Matthew said. "It sure hit the spot. I'll be glad to get this cast off so I can go fishing again." He paused, looking thoughtful. "Elizabeth always liked me to bring home a tuna."

Her mother loved seafood and had been a wonderful cook. Elizabeth had found it aggravating when her strength waned and Celena had to take over the cooking. As Celena thought about the months preceding her mother's death, she marveled that even during those days of sadness, there had been many precious moments. Knowing that their time together was short, they decided to study the gospel together—concentrating on the plan of salvation. Mother and daughter clung to the sweet knowledge that they would see each other again. That their husband and father did not share in their joy of the gospel was a hidden source of pain they avoided discussing.

"Can I ask you a question?" Celena asked her father.

"Aye. Fire away."

"After mother died, why did you become bitter against the Church?"

Matthew thought on that for so long she thought he might not answer. "That's a doozy," he finally said, rubbing his chin. "In the beginning, I wasn't against it. Everything they said made sense, and I got some questions answered that had been on my mind for a long time. But I heard some stories that made me question whether Joseph Smith was a prophet or not. Then, Elizabeth got sick." Matthew's voice became distant. "The Mormons had a lot of stories about miraculous healings, and Elizabeth became convinced she'd be healed if she was given a blessing. I agreed to it, and when the elders came, I—I made a deal with God. I told him that if He made her well, I'd join the Church."

It was painful to watch Matthew's lined face crumple. "When she died, so did what little faith I had. I felt like I'd been sucker-punched." His voice was burdened with an inexpressible, lugubrious sadness. "I couldn't believe God would let Elizabeth die—someone who was so good, someone who believed in Him." Celena was aware of that bewildered grief. So she had not been the only one to feel that terrible, bone-sucking sadness. It had lain heavy on her father as well.

To stay in control, Matthew hardened his tone. "It made me angry. I felt like the Mormons had deceived us both. All those miracles Elizabeth had told me about . . . Ha! Hoaxes. Lies. Fairy tales. I couldn't understand how you could keep going to church—the same one that had fooled your mother. I didn't want you or Joshua to have anything to do with them either—a church that talked mighty big but had nothing to back up their fine words." He jabbed a finger at Celena. "But you were so stubborn, so set on going to their meetings. It drove me wild how you talked about them day and night." Matthew stopped, his chest heaving.

Celena waited a bit, then said softly, "But all that changed. You started going to church without Rueben having to strap you down and gag you. What happened?"

Matthew opened his mouth, then closed it. It was surreal when his bottom lip began to quiver slightly. Finally he choked, "Elizabeth."

He stopped and swallowed. "I don't know how, and until now, I've not told a living soul, but Elizabeth came back." His face began working like he might not be able to go on. In a tight, strange voice, he said, "I didn't see her, but I might as well have, for I was never so sure of anything in my life."

Celena brought a hand to her throat, which ached with unshed tears.

"Remember when you told me you felt your mother's presence in the cemetery when you talked with Joshua? I never questioned that because something like that happened to me, too." The atmosphere in the room grew thick, and Celena felt a fine trembling from deep inside. "After you left Fire Island, I went to the cemetery every day. I'd begun having doubts—thinking that maybe I'd been wrong about the Church, that maybe there *was* something to it."

He glanced at her and tried to joke. "Kinda frightening, I know. Maybe the Apocalypse *is* right around the corner." He stumbled on. "I started spending more time there, talking with Elizabeth. I—I argued with her. Told her that if the Church were true, she would have been healed."

Matthew's voice trailed off. The muscles in his face twitched. "And then . . . she was *there*." His voice was thick. "I didn't see her, but—but she was *standing* right there. I didn't hear her voice outright, but it was there in my mind—sounding just like she used to."

He swallowed hard, his Adam's apple bobbing. "She told me straight out that not everyone that gets a blessing is healed and that it had been her time to go. She said there wasn't any tragedy in death, only in sin. She told me to read Doctrine and Covenants 42:48, and to talk to the bishop if I had questions. She put me in my place, all right. Said it wasn't fair to condemn the Church for *my* lack of faith. Elizabeth told me I was acting like God had broken some kind of agreement, but the only thing He'd ever promised was that He'd always be there to help."

When Matthew looked at Celena, his eyes were a brilliant blue. "Elizabeth said she was happy there but sad about you and me. She gave me a good talking to. Said it was important to make things right with you. And . . . and, your mother let me know she'd talked to you too."

Celena's tears were flowing freely, and she let them fall where they would. So, she hadn't been imagining things. When Celena had felt her mother's presence, gently urging her to keep the promises, she had actually been there. Celena took her father's hand as he went on.

"After you left, when I thought you didn't want anything to do with me, I decided to just wait it out and hope that someday you'd forgive me."

Celena's heart, which for years had been bound and shut down in her chest, broke free and soared. But she had to scold her father. "Why didn't you tell me all this when I first came back?" When he shrugged, she whispered under her breath, "Stubborn fool."

Matthew heard. "I've been called worse," he said philosophically.

They got ready for church, then set off for Sunday School, Joshua happily pushing Matthew in his wheelchair. After her baptism, Celena had dreamed many times of going to church as a family. It was bittersweet because her mother wasn't there, but sweet nonetheless.

Several times during opening exercises, Celena looked over at her father to make sure he was really there. During class, when the teacher asked when the Aaronic priesthood had been restored, Ethan slowly raised his big hand from the back corner where he sat.

The teacher waited briefly, his eyes scanning the class, then finally said, "Okay, Ethan. I like to give other people a chance, but go ahead."

Proudly, Ethan recited, "May 15, 1829."

After the meeting, Matthew grabbed hold of Ethan's coat before he could fly past. "You come and eat with us today, hear? I'm not clear on some of the dates they were talking about, and you're the only one I trust to give me the right answers." Ethan, who would have agreed to fly to the moon if it meant he could get out of there, nodded, then disappeared. Matthew asked Tana and Rueben to eat with them as well, before being surrounded by people who were delighted to see him.

Standing a little apart, Tana said to Celena, "He looks right at home, doesn't he?"

"First time he came to church, I was ready to run in case the roof started caving in." Rueben chuckled. "Your father acted like we were trying to steal his soul—glowering at anyone who looked his way. Poor Brother Martin, the Sunday School teacher, didn't know what hit him. Matthew objected to everything and kept firing questions like he was some sort of machine gun."

"In time, Matthew calmed down," Tana said soothingly; then, looking at her husband, she said, "If the Church could tame *you,* it can tame anyone."

"I had a difficult time with the Word of Wisdom," Rueben admitted. "Why, when I first stopped smoking, I would have beat up a dozen people by breakfast if Tana had let me out the door." As they talked, Joshua went past them, pushing his father, who waved languidly as they went by.

Tana tugged at Rueben's sleeve. "Come on, I told Amanda Johnson I'd drop off this cross-stitch pattern today." She said to Celena, "We'll see you at Bay Haven. We shouldn't be long."

As Celena started down the sidewalk, Daniel caught up. They chatted for a few minutes before he remarked, "I saw you talking with Tana and Rueben. You know them pretty well, don't you?"

"I've known them all my life."

"Rueben knows quite a bit about rumrunners, doesn't he?"

Celena remembered what Tana had said at the dance and narrowed her eyes, loyal to her old friends. "Everyone does. What are you getting at?"

Daniel hesitated, then asked, "Do you think he could be involved in smuggling?"

"No. For one thing, Tana would kill him."

"You can earn big money, I've heard. And from what I understand, his grandson's medical bills are staggering."

"You're serious, aren't you? Well, you can forget it. Rueben would never do that." Then, making her tone more polite, Celena asked Daniel to come for lunch. He politely declined, saying he was needed at Clearwater. After he left, Celena wondered why he was inquiring about Rueben. His questions made her uneasy, partly because, despite her loyalty and faith in Rueben, Celena wasn't sure herself how far Rueben would go to help Will. Love and desperation were powerful emotions.

Joshua had wheeled his father into the dining room where Ethan dutifully answered Matthew's questions. Helen had invited Gerald, who was his usual jovial self, and Lydia made conversation with several of the boarders. When Matthew had finished his dinner, Celena took him to his room. Celena decided it was the perfect opportunity to ask a few people about the coat Joshua had found a while back. With some luck, she might find out who had been playing ghost at the light. On her way back to the dining room, she stopped at her room to pick up the coat.

Joshua had finished and run off, and the tourists had left as well. It was perfect timing—the only ones left in the dining room were Helen, Gerald, Lydia, Ethan, Tana, and Rueben. All conversation stopped when Celena held up the coat.

"Joshua found this stuffed in a corner of the generator building," she began. "I think the person who used to come to the lighthouse at night wore this. Does it look familiar to anyone?"

No one answered. Celena went around to Ethan. He looked at the coat with interest but made no move to claim it. Tana's eyes were big behind her glasses. Rueben was next. Celena caught the flicker of some emotion in his face.

He spoke up. "That's mine. I lost it quite a while ago." Then he took the coat and held it up to his face. "The fishing smell is mine, but I can tell you right now this isn't my flowering perfume."

Celena went around the table and held the coat out toward Lydia. "I think this is yours."

"Rueben just said it was *his*," Lydia flashed, then added derisively, "Besides, it's a little big for me, dear-heart."

"But it is what you wore to go around the lighthouse at night, right?"

Lydia looked around the group. All eyes were riveted on her. "So what?" she said lightly, her quicksilver charm still evident, even when caught in her tricks. "I warned you the lighthouse was haunted. I didn't say by whom."

Rueben said, "Well if that isn't one of the most underhanded tricks—" before Tana stopped him, although her eyes were blazing as well.

Celena had to resist the temptation to pull out every blond hair from Lydia's head. "I wanted you to go home," Lydia said simply. "So Mother could get the light. We need the money." She threw her mother a defiant look. "There's no harm in people knowing we're broke."

Helen flushed deeply. "No matter what our private circumstances may be, you had absolutely no business doing such a thing. I'm deeply ashamed that you would stoop to this." Then, drawing her dignity around her like a cloak, she added, "Besides, there was no need to worry. Our reservations have doubled the past few months. We're doing better every week."

Lydia seemed untouched by the criticism. She jumped up impatiently, as if her seething energy would not let her rest. "The money's coming too slowly." With hands on hips, she faced Celena. "I thought if I pretended to be a ghost, you'd hightail it back to Maryland. You used to be such a scaredy-cat, but you didn't scare as easily as I thought. Oh, well. No harm done," she said impudently. "But just so you know, it wasn't me the first time." She took the coat and gave it to Rueben. "Thanks for letting me borrow your coat."

There was one more thing Celena wanted to know. "Why did you stop coming?"

"After you met with the Lighthouse Bureau, there was no sense continuing. If I hadn't scared you off by then, I wasn't going to." Lydia gave her a smile, one that Celena didn't trust. It was a smile that hid too much and told too little.

Helen's eyes were cool and critical as they rested on Celena. "I think we've had enough of your theatrics for one night."

Gerald spoke as he rose. "Lydia shouldn't have been playing games, but there was no real harm done." Celena looked at him, bemused, as he gathered a pile of dishes and left the room. She'd apologized for her actions at the dance, and he'd been gracious about it, yet ever since, there had been a strange tension between them.

Rueben came and put an arm around her shoulder for a quick hug. "I'll talk to you later. I'm going to go and see Matthew," he said. When Rueben left, Ethan slipped out.

Tana, however, was not finished. She was steaming, no doubt about it, and when she spoke, there was a dangerously sharp edge in her voice. "You know, Lydia, it takes a certain kind of person to act as mean and nasty as you did. I don't take it kindly when someone deliberately tries to hurt someone I care about. Since you say there's no harm in letting people know the truth, I guess it won't hurt if you explain that business in Chicago?"

"That's old news," Lydia said, looking daggers at the older woman.

"Not to me," Celena said, still put out by Lydia's tricks.

"It was just a little misunderstanding," Helen insisted.

Celena folded her arms, waiting.

"Oh, it doesn't matter if you know," Lydia said irritably. "Aunt Rose told me I could borrow her necklace, and then when I did, she forgot. Hateful old fussbudget. Can't remember anything."

"If you borrow something, you return it. You don't turn it in to a pawn shop," Tana stated grimly.

"It's no business of yours," Lydia shot back. "I would have redeemed it soon enough."

"It became my business when you asked me for money." Tana's voice was hard. "I gave you a loan, thinking you were in a bind, then found out you had stolen the necklace and were on probation."

"I *didn't* steal it," Lydia said sulkily. "And you wouldn't have found out if you hadn't read my telegram."

"Receiving telegrams is part of my job," Tana replied evenly.

Helen sniffed and began gathering dishes. "Lydia's had to pay a heavy price for this mix-up, and as far as I'm concerned, it's over." With that, she left. Looking out of sorts, Tana followed with more dishes.

But Celena had more questions for Lydia. "Earlier this week the lighthouse was vandalized. Just like the generator building and paint locker. Was that more of your tricks?"

"You can't pin that on me." Lydia's tone was malevolent. "But there is one person you should ask: Daniel." Celena was speechless, and Lydia went on, her voice taunting and malicious. "That's right, Daniel. Since you like playing detective, why don't you ask *him* a few questions?"

"Such as?"

"Such as, what is he *really* doing here? And why doesn't he ever talk about his recent past?" Lydia was watching Celena carefully for her reaction. "Go ahead and ask Daniel what he does for a living. See if he lies again. Because if he's a bookkeeper, then I'm the Queen of Sheba."

Although Lydia was not to be trusted, there was an element of truth in what she said. It was true Daniel never talked about the past few years. And why had Daniel been asking questions about Rueben? He also seemed to know quite a lot about the boats used to catch rumrunners.

"Ethan told me you visited Sarina the day she disappeared," Celena accused. "Clint said there were rumors that Sarina might have been planning on leaving Ethan. Did she say anything about that or give you any idea where she was going that evening?"

Lydia's voice was cold. "I've already told you, we weren't bosom buddies."

"But you were friendly enough to pay her a visit. Why *did* you go to see her?"

Lydia's expression turned wooden. "That's none of your business," she said coldly, then left.

When Celena visited her father, she told him what had happened after dinner. He nodded without surprise to find that Lydia had been the "ghost."

"Aye, that one was always a little minx," he muttered.

Celena also told him that Ethan had put the amulet in her room. "I guess Ethan thought I needed protection."

"He must have got that idea from Sarina. She was a superstitious woman, from what I've heard." Matthew looked at her sharply. "You don't believe in that hocus-pocus do you? I thought you Mormons were supposed to be above that kind of thing."

Five years ago, a remark like that would have irritated her beyond measure. Now, she wanted to giggle, especially since her father was now a Mormon himself. "What are you smirking about?" Matthew growled. "If you've got something to say, say it."

She answered mildly. "For your first question, no, I don't believe amulets can protect you from harm. As for *we* Mormons being above that sort of thing, I don't think most Latter-day Saints are superstitious, though some might be, the same as with any other group of people." He seemed mollified. When he began to pull the blanket up, Celena asked if he wanted his sweater.

"Aye, that would be good."

She went to the closet, but when she pulled on his green sweater, the hanger fell. As she picked it up, Celena noticed a picture at the back of the closet. It was Christ at the Garden of Gethsemane. Carrying it over to her father, she looked pointedly at the empty place on the wall. Matthew said nothing, though his mouth tightened a little in his attempt to look unconcerned.

Finally, she asked, "Any idea what this is?"

"Looks like Christ praying."

Oh, he's good, Celena thought, eyeing him sternly. "This was hanging on the wall before I came, wasn't it?" Her father grunted noncommittally, avoiding her eyes. "Did you ask Helen to take it down?"

"No." When Celena stared him down, he added grudgingly, "I asked Rueben."

"Don't you like it?"

"Yes."

"Yes, you like it, or yes you don't like it?"

Matthew looked annoyed. "Blame it all, you're getting me all confused."

"Why did you have it taken down?"

Squirming uncomfortably, he muttered, "Didn't want you going all gooey on me."

"Gooey? What's that supposed to mean?"

"You know . . ." He frowned. "Like—'Oh, you've got a picture of Jesus on the wall!'" He'd changed his voice to a high falsetto. "'This must mean you've finally seen the errors of your sinful ways!'"

Celena had a great urge to bring the picture down over his head.

Matthew continued. "I didn't want you to start pushing me again."

Celena glared at him indignantly. "When did I ever push you about the Church?"

Matthew's tanned face was incredulous. "When *didn't* you? All those anxious looks on Sunday mornings. Mentioning that my good shirt was pressed. Telling me a dozen times what time the meeting started. Saying how nice it was that the Widdison family all went *together* to church. How wonderful that the Butlers had a worthy priesthood bearer in their home. Then there was that disappointed look you always gave me just as you left so I'd know just how much I was letting you all down."

Celena's mouth opened slightly. She never realized how it had come across—how it had made her father feel. She'd been so young, and youth was so sure of itself—so positive it alone knew the right way.

"I didn't realize I was pushing you," she said. "The gospel was such a glorious thing that I wanted to share it with you. I wanted you to be as excited about it as I was."

"And I didn't fit your timetable, did I?"

Celena lowered her gaze, swallowing hard. Picture in hand, she headed for the closet. When Matthew called after her, she stopped but refused to turn around. "You're not going to put that away, then come back and give me 'the look,' are you?"

Flushing to the roots of her auburn hair, Celena replied in a small voice, "No."

She'd opened the closet door when he called again. "Will you look at that!" Matthew's voice was full of disapproval as he pointed at the nail on the wall. "That's one big, ugly, empty space there. It needs something, doesn't it? I know. Why don't you put that picture there?"

Celena didn't move. "I *told* you I wouldn't give you 'the look.' You can choose whatever you want to have on your wall."

"I *am* choosing," Matthew bellowed impatiently. "I'm sick of looking at that dang nail every day. Now cover it up."

EIGHTEEN

On Monday Nathan Gibbs was coming down the sidewalk just as Celena was about to go in Bigelow's Drugstore. She paused, and Nathan stopped to chat for a few minutes.

Inside the store, she saw Daniel and a rather tall, wiry man with glasses talking together earnestly in the far corner. Celena thought the other man looked vaguely familiar, but when she went over, the man seemed startled and hurried off.

Celena looked after him. "Who was that? I seem to have frightened him."

She sensed something hesitant in Daniel's manner, but he replied, "He's just a tourist. Wanted to ask some questions about Fire Island."

"I just saw Nathan outside. At the dance, he said your father hadn't asked him to give a bid on those cabins he wanted to have built, but I guess he talked with Clint and will be giving Gerald a bid after all. Why would your father get a bid from another contractor?"

There was a visible stiffening beneath the easy manner Celena had always admired. "He wouldn't," Daniel said shortly.

Celena looked at him blankly. "I don't understand. Gerald said he'd gotten a bid."

"He—he likes to put on a good front." There was a look of strain in the set of Daniel's mouth.

She blinked. "Are you telling me Gerald didn't get a bid?"

Again, Daniel would not answer her question directly. "Sometimes my father gets caught up with all his plans."

"So caught up that he says things that aren't true?"

Daniel looked uncomfortable. "Father just likes to talk big."

"You sound like you're excusing him."

"I'm not, but look, it wasn't over anything important."

"No it wasn't," Celena said slowly. "I know he's your father, but I don't see why you're defending him when he lied."

"Someone has to."

Celena stared. What did he mean by that? She remembered what Lydia had said. "Can I ask you something?" she started. "You came to Fire Island to help your father, but it sounds like you're just here temporarily. Are you on a leave of absence from your other job? What were you doing before you came here?"

"What's with all the questions?" Daniel retorted defensively. "I told you I was helping my father with his books, and he's been having me do other things as well. My boss understands."

He made no attempt to give details or offer any further explanation. Celena felt oddly disappointed.

Finally he said, "Celena, it's not what you think."

She bit her lip. "And exactly what *am* I thinking?"

"I—I don't know," he admitted. "I just came here to Fire Island to make sure my father was okay."

She searched his face. "Why wouldn't Gerald be okay? He's the manager of a big new resort." Again there was that faintly evasive look and silence.

"All right," she said, turning to leave.

He caught her arm, then glanced around to make sure no one else was within hearing range. "In the past, my father has been involved in some shady incidents. He gets these big ideas and sometimes it gets him in trouble." Daniel spoke in a low, urgent voice. "My father has a knack for attracting scoundrels. A few years ago, he got hooked up with some crooks. He thought he was going to make a million bucks, but they only wanted a fall guy. When their scam fell apart, they took off and left him holding the bag."

"Are you afraid something like that might happen here?"

"I don't think so." His tone indicated uncertainty. "But I wanted to make sure everything was all right. I'm not going to have him go back to prison."

"Your father's been in jail?"

"For about six months," Daniel admitted reluctantly. "Then some new evidence came to light, and they let him out. Shortly after that, my father wrote to say he'd gotten a new job on Fire Island." Celena felt shaken and a little torn. She had the feeling Daniel was more anxious than he was letting on. Had Gerald gotten in with the wrong crowd here on Fire Island? She wasn't sure what Daniel was holding back but felt he ought to know something.

Celena said softly, "The other day, Gerald was at Bay Haven and—and he was drunk."

Daniel grimaced. "Yeah, well. Actually, Lydia told me about that. He becomes a different person when he drinks—wild and unpredictable—so now he avoids it."

But *was* Gerald avoiding it? And what else was he up to? Celena needed to think, and that was something she couldn't do properly here—not with Daniel staring at her. In his own way, Daniel seemed as blindly loyal to his father as Helen was to Lydia. Helen had always been unable to see any of Lydia's faults. Was Daniel the same way? Maybe he wasn't seeing his father clearly because he didn't *want* to see.

Then Daniel took her hand. At that moment, she forgot about Gerald and became acutely aware of everything about Daniel. The clean smell of soap and water. The faint hint of aftershave. The way his hair curled a little toward the end. There was just something about Daniel that was steady and reassuring—something that made her trust him. But she had to slow down. Maybe she was reading him wrong, like she'd read Sam wrong. If so, this feeling could lead to nothing but hurt. Celena squeezed his hand, and they talked of other things briefly before she made her exit.

* * *

The next day, Celena went to Tillman's. There were a few customers, but no Elaine, so Celena went around the counter to the back door, which was open. Elaine was on the elevated porch, struggling to move a barrel. Celena hurried to help her move it into the corner.

Elaine had stopped to catch her breath when someone called, "Hello? Is anyone here?"

In annoyance, Elaine yelled, "Nope! I always leave an unlocked cash register in plain view when I leave." Before going in, she said to Celena, "Just shoot me, please."

Celena looked around. Many of the stores had wooden fences in the back, with gates in between for easy access. A few doors down, two men were talking. One of them looked like Daniel. The second man was a little taller, with sunlight glinting off his glasses. He reminded Celena of the tourist that had talked to Daniel earlier. There was an oddly secretive look about them. Their heads were close together, and occasionally, Daniel or the other man would look around furtively.

Celena went down the steep stairs. As she did, the men disappeared from view because of the wooden fence. Their voices were audible as she approached the gate.

"How did it go last night?" That was Daniel's voice.

"It was a good haul," the other man answered. "We got about thirty-five cases."

"Thirty-five!" Daniel sounded incredulous. "It's a wonder they didn't sink."

Celena's hand stopped just short of the latch. She felt a plummeting sensation far down in her stomach as the other man asked, "How are things going here? Anything new?"

"Nothing yet," Daniel replied.

"You still getting along all right with the locals?"

"Everything's fine. They all think I'm working with my father." There was a sharp bark of laughter from the other man. "Quiet!" Daniel said roughly. "You'd better go."

"Right. See you tonight."

What did it all mean? Confused, Celena wasn't sure whether to hurry away or open the gate and confront Daniel. The decision was made for her when the gate suddenly swung open.

Daniel's face showed surprise, then darkened angrily. "What are you doing here?"

"I saw you from the back of Tillman's and . . ." Her voice trailed off.

He came toward her, alarming her with the look of fury in his eyes. "What did you hear?"

"Enough!" she cried. "What were you talking about? What cases?"

It was apparent he was working hard to collect himself. Gradually, his expression returned to normal, but it was a quick change, and in those few moments, Celena's suspicion rose.

"I wish I could explain, but I can't."

"What are you really doing here?" she cried. "Is something going on with your father?"

At her words, something in Daniel's face altered. It was as if he had closed the shutters against her. "Leave my father out of this," he said stiffly.

The urge to be away from him was upon her, and she walked away briskly. Daniel caught up with her in a few quick steps, giving Celena a moment of apprehension when he took hold of her arm, stopping her.

"You can't go away like this," he said, looking earnestly into her eyes.

She looked back at him. "Why can't you trust me enough to tell me what's going on?"

Daniel let go then. It was impossible to tell what he was thinking. Despite the warmth of the day, Celena shivered. Daniel could be utterly secretive, so it would seem. In her heart, Celena trusted him, but was that trust well placed? Until she knew for sure who was behind all of the mischief on the island, she couldn't trust anyone completely. There was much that Daniel had not explained, and worse, had no intention of explaining. This time when Celena walked away, Daniel let her go.

* * *

The rest of the week passed smoothly. Yet Celena felt there was a kind of pulsing waiting—a sense of slow gathering. Something was deepening, but she could not put her finger on it. Neither did she know exactly where it was coming from, and so she was kept on edge by not knowing.

She saw Daniel occasionally, and they were somewhat aloof with each other. He would pop up on the beach occasionally and walk along with her, but there was always some restraint between them—even when he came to the lighthouse to visit her and Joshua so the three of them could play games. Whenever Celena was with Daniel, she found herself trusting him. It was only when she was alone that uncertainties came. One night, he surprised her by asking Rueben to tend the light so he could take her to Clearwater, where they had dinner.

During the same time period, Celena also saw Clint regularly. Although he was busy with the ferry, she usually saw him at lunch and dinner. One night Rueben was again pressed into service so Clint could take Celena to a Broadway musical at the Imperial Theatre in New York. They saw the Broadway musical "Oh Kay!" Celena loved the Gershwin tunes and found the plot intriguing, especially since it was about the adventures of a bootlegger in Prohibition America.

It was flattering to have both Clint and Daniel interested in her. Besides giving life a savor she hadn't felt for a long time, it had also successfully dissolved the last emotional link she'd had with Sam. And while it was true that Clint made her feel womanly and wanted, Daniel made her feel all that and more. Yet Daniel remained an enigma. Did he truly care for her or was there some other reason for his affection? With Clint, there was no guessing. She loved being with him and was proud of how others looked up to him. Still, for now, Celena was content to remain uncommitted.

On Sunday, her father decided to attend his priesthood meeting, and later, sacrament meeting. It was still too much for Matthew to attend all three meetings. Doc Harrison had continued to stop by to check on his patient, and had made an appointment for Matthew to go to Long Island soon for X-rays, which might be able to tell them whether he had sustained permanent nerve damage or not.

On Tuesday morning, Celena and Joshua went for a swim. When they returned to Bay Haven, Celena saw there was an envelope with her name lying on the side table. She unfolded the note. In tidy but uneven writing, it read:

Must talk to you. Meet me in the storage shed by the lighthouse at 5:00. D.R.

Daniel must have found out something he didn't want anyone else to know, but what? Perhaps he was finally ready to tell her what was really going on.

That afternoon, the wind picked up. Celena put on a jacket against the stiff breeze that was pushing gray clouds through the sky. The absence of the sun reminded her of the Sunken Forest. She still got a cold feeling when she remembered how someone had pursued her. How chilling to realize it was likely someone at the picnic. Any one of them could have done it.

Lydia had already shown herself fond of tricks and capable of more than deceit, as proved by the matter of her aunt's necklace.

Then again, Helen had demonstrated a deep and marked hostility toward Celena from the moment she had set foot back on the island. It was easy to imagine Helen being determined to save Bay Haven no matter what the cost.

Of course, Gerald had also plainly shown his desire to have the light. Lately, he had seemed rather remote. There was also his recently discovered prison record. His conviction made him someone to watch. Then there were Tana and Rueben. Celena could not seriously suspect Tana, but there had been enough worrisome conversations with Rueben to make Celena uneasy. Just how far was he willing to go to get money for his ailing grandson?

Ethan was another riddle. Although he was deeply troubled by his wife's death, how much of what he said was credible? Ethan had also shown himself capable of violence by attacking Clint. Then there was Clint. Unless he had some hidden motive Celena wasn't aware of, it didn't seem likely he was involved. Still, he was a very ambitious man and part owner of Clearwater. Surely he would benefit from having the lighthouse connected with the resort. Celena knew Clint was attracted to her. Was she vain to think that because of that interest, he couldn't be behind the vandalism?

It was harder to consider Daniel. He was a complication she had not expected. When Celena was with him, she was swept away by feelings she wasn't sure how to handle. Yet there were so many questions, especially about the revealing conversation she'd overheard.

When she arrived, it was dark and gloomy in the storage shed, especially with the sun hidden behind lowering clouds. When she called out for Daniel, there was no answer. Celena left the door open to allow in what little light there was. The storage shed smelled of fish, sawdust, and oil. The two side windows were shuttered, and boards covered the windows in the upstairs loft. Celena walked around idly. The table in the middle was cluttered with an assortment of tools, rope, and lengths of chain. Stepping around it in the gloom, Celena wandered over to take a closer look at a broken dinghy leaning against the back wall. Suddenly the door slammed shut, enveloping Celena in darkness. She whirled, yet with the total absence of light, she could not immediately tell if she was facing the door or not.

"Daniel?" she called. "Daniel is that you?"

The capricious wind must have blown the door shut, yet a chill seemed to reach out and touch her, a palatable feeling that there was something here to frighten her. Reaching out, Celena found the wall. Using her hands to feel along, reading it like Braille, she followed it to the corner, but when she turned, she stumbled over something on the floor. Thinking she heard a noise, she held still, but all was quiet.

Celena had taken three or four more groping steps when she heard a sound that was more frightening than anything she'd ever heard in her life. It was faint—an odd shuffling noise. A sound made by someone who was in the shed with her. Although Celena could not identify the danger, an inner part of her knew something was very wrong—and she was afraid. This was different from the Sunken Forest. There, she had been out in the open, able to flee. Here she was trapped and the danger was close at hand. For a moment, Celena didn't dare move. Instinctively she knew not to call out. Somehow she had to find the door, for she could not remain shut a moment more in this dreadful darkness with an unknown person. But where was the door—her escape—in this inky darkness?

Daniel, Celena cried out in her mind, *please hurry!* The moment he came, she would be safe, and whoever was in the building would be exposed. Then again, could it possibly *be* Daniel? Had he lured her here? If he had come inside innocently and been trapped by the sudden shutting of the door, surely he would have called out. The silence was sinister.

There was a faint scuffle as the person moved, and Celena wondered if he was putting himself between her and the door. Trying to quell her rising panic, Celena crept in a direction she hoped was away from her unseen predator. Straining, she could hear the faint sound of someone breathing—someone who might even have the advantage of having been there first, hiding inside until she entered, eyes already accustomed to the gloom. Celena jumped as cold fingers touched her arm. She pulled away so sharply that she hit her shin against a box and had to stagger to catch herself.

A husky voice whispered, so raspy and quiet she could not iden-tify whether it belonged to a man or a woman, "You're meddling with things better left alone!" Celena   gasped as a hand clamped upon her left forearm. "If only you had gone back where you came from, you would not have been hurt. You've been given too many chances to escape now."

Panicking, Celena yanked her arm away and started in the opposite direction from the threatening voice. She took three steps before running into something that caught her about the knees, and she fell, hitting her head hard. Dazed, Celena lay there for some moments, only vaguely aware of odd sounds. As she slowly got to her hands and knees, Celena heard the door open, then close. The faint smell of sulfur came to her nose.

Having adjusted to the darkness, her eyes could now make out a faint, horizontal line of light at the bottom of the door. She had her direction. Crouching, Celena stretched out her hands to feel for unseen obstacles until she reached the door. She fumbled for the cool metal of the doorknob and twisted, but it would not turn. Even using both hands, it was no use. The intruder must have locked it.

A faint crackling noise came from behind her. Celena turned to see a few small flames licking a stack of boxes piled against the far wall. Banging on the door, Celena called out for help, then looked for something to put the flames out. The fire was growing amazingly fast, curling up the sides of the dry, wooden boxes. She prayed that Daniel would arrive soon.

An old canvas tarp lay folded under the table. It was stiff from age, and from sheer desperation she threw it over the blaze, but it remained rigid and did nothing but fan the flames. Celena stamped at the edges, but the fire—fed by the dry wood of the floor and the wooden crates around it—only increased in size. Celena ran again to the door, beating at it and yelling for help.

There was no one. She looked around. Her only hope was to escape through a window. The shuttered windows in the main room were too high, so she ran to the ladder that led to the loft. Celena stacked two boxes near one of the windows and, balancing precariously, pulled at the boards that covered them. She managed to pry several boards loose, then saw with despair that the windows were too small for her to climb through. Still, they would allow her to shout for help.

Balancing awkwardly on her perch, Celena struggled to open the window. It refused to budge. Frantically, she searched for a catch, running her fingers along the edge, breaking several fingernails in the process. Even after twisting the catch to one side, the window still refused to slide. She would have to break it.

Meanwhile, the fire had been steadily growing. Her eyes were watering from the smoke, and she had begun to cough intermittently. In a corner of the loft, she found a broken oar, and after using the end to smash the glass panes, she climbed back onto the teetering boxes. Smoke drifted out of the window around her head as she shouted for help. There was a sickening, crunching sound from below as something collapsed. Her screams grew wild and tinged with hysteria, the force of them scalding her throat. Suddenly there were three figures running down the path toward the shed—Helen, Clint, and Ethan, whose long hair flew out behind him as he ran.

"Help me!" she shouted. "The door's locked!"

Helen's narrow face looked up at her in wonder, and Clint's expression was all urgency as he raced around the corner. Soon she heard repeated crashing at the door. The heat caused her clothes to cling to her body with sweat. Taking off her sweater, Celena held it over her nose as she descended the ladder into the heat and flames. Then, crouching, she backed into a corner the fire hadn't yet reached. A few more blows and the door burst open. As it did, the sudden influx of air caused the fire to shoot up and outward, expanding as though kerosene had been thrown on it.

"Celena!" Clint shouted as he stepped inside. "Where are you?"

"Here!" Through the haze, Celena tried to make her way to the door but was forced back by the crackling flames. Going to the table, she pushed it over onto its side. Then, using it as a shield against the flames, she squatted beside it and began working her way to the door, sliding the table in front of her. Once she was near the door, she stood to make a run for it but tripped and felt herself falling. She threw out her arms to catch herself, but suddenly Clint was there, catching her before she could crumple to the floor.

The next moments were a blur. Celena was conscious only of the flames and a heat that was almost unbearable. There was a roaring in her ears that was not the fire, and her vision blurred whitely, but Clint would not let her go. Carrying her, he made his way outside where he dropped to his knees, spilling Celena onto the ground. She choked and sputtered, trying to pull clean air into her lungs. Clint was coughing too, and when her gaze focused, she saw that his eyes were streaming. She became aware of Helen kneeling beside her and of pain in her hands, leg, and arms.

Ethan, a hulking mountain, was on the other side, patting her face and plaintively asking over and over, "Celena, are you all right? Celena, are you okay?"

Soon there was a mass of people milling about. Ethan dragged Celena away from the burning building that was sending fiery trails up into the air. There was no attempt made to save the building; it was too engulfed and was left to burn itself to the ground. Dazed, Celena listened vaguely as people spoke in shallow waves that rose and broke, subsided and rose again. Then Ethan picked Celena up and placed her gently in the back seat of an automobile.

* * *

At Bay Haven, Daniel yanked the automobile's door open and, scooping Celena up, carried her to her room. He laid her down carefully as others swarmed into the room, then bent and kissed her forehead gently. When Doc Harrison arrived, he shooed everyone out except Helen. He then set to work bandaging the burns on her hands, arms, and leg. As Helen bent over to dab ointment on her arm, Celena noticed that the older woman's face was white and strained.

Doc Harrison gave Celena a sedative and said to Helen, "It was a good thing you and Clint were there."

"Ethan alerted us," Helen replied. "We were coming down the trail when he told us smoke was coming from the shed." Celena was worried about Clint and asked about him.

"He was luckier than you," Doc Harrison replied. "He's got a few burns on his hands and arm, and he has some singed hair, but he'll be fine. Your burns are a little more severe, but it could have been a whole lot worse if Clint hadn't been there."

Celena closed her eyes. "I'll never be able to thank him enough." She felt drained and limp. When Doc Harrison left, Joshua ran in and flung himself at her.

"Watch the bandages, Joshua!" Helen reprimanded. Her brother pulled back in alarm. Seeing traces of tearstains, Celena reached out and pulled him close.

"I'm going to do some more investigating," he whispered earnestly, casting his eyes at Helen. Before Celena could warn against further spying, Daniel reentered. Joshua stayed close beside her as if fearing Celena might disappear at any moment.

Brown hair tumbled over his forehead as Daniel bent over, his face worried. "How are you? What did the doctor say?"

Helen answered for her. "She'll be fine. All the burns are minor—first and second degree. Her feet are elevated to prevent shock." Celena looked down. She hadn't even noticed that her feet were propped up by pillows.

"Did you tip over a lamp?" Daniel asked. "Is that how the fire started?"

"Someone came inside and started the fire, then locked me inside." Celena shuddered, remembering the dreadful crackle of the flames and the horrible feeling of panic upon finding that the door wouldn't open. Daniel seemed shocked, and a fleeting glimpse of skepticism crossed Helen's face. When Helen spoke, it was in the calm, measured tones she always used with patients.

"What were you doing inside the shed?"

"I got a note from Daniel. He wanted to meet me there."

Daniel's brows furrowed. "I didn't write you a note."

"It said you had something to tell me," Celena said. When Helen and Daniel stared at her strangely, Celena said with a touch of asperity, "I left the note on the dresser."

While Daniel went to see, Helen spoke to Joshua. "Your father is bound to have heard the commotion. Go tell him what happened and that Celena is all right." As he raced out, Rueben and Tana came in, followed closely by Gerald.

Daniel returned, holding out the letter. "Celena, I didn't write this."

"You didn't write what?" Tana asked.

"Celena said she got a note from me saying I wanted to meet her at the shed, but that's not my writing." Daniel handed Tana the note.

Rueben came over, his cane thumping on the wooden floor. His face, weathered by salt spray and the sea-mirrored sun, looked anxious. "You look like five miles of bad road," he said.

"And you look like ten," Celena replied.

Rueben's face lightened. "If you can still joke, you must be all right. That's all I needed to know. I'm going to tend the light tonight, so I'd better get going."

Gerald took his place. "Do they know what caused the fire?" he asked tensely.

"I heard there was a rubbish barrel close to the building," Tana said. "Apparently hobos often light the barrel and use it to cook with. The wind must have carried sparks to the shed."

"That wasn't what happened," Celena cried, quivering with emotion. "The fire started on the inside. Someone started it, then locked me in."

"Celena's suffering from shock," Helen said in a low voice to the others. "I wouldn't pay too much attention to what she says. The doctor gave her a sedative."

"The door was locked!" Celena insisted.

Helen searched Celena's face, as though questioning what she saw, then asked pointedly, "Then how did you get in?"

"It wasn't locked when I got there. I left the door open. Then someone shut it." Celena began to feel vague and confused. Her mind had become foggy.

"Ah, well, the wind could easily have blown the door shut, jamming it." Gerald said to the others, speaking as if Celena were not there.

"Someone was in the building with me," Celena snapped. "He or she spoke to me!" She looked at Helen beseechingly. "You were there, you saw that the fire was on the inside!"

"The whole building was on fire," Helen said. "I couldn't tell if it had started on the inside or outside."

Celena felt tears of shock and anger well up. "Why won't anyone listen to me?"

"No more questions," Tana said. "She's in shock, poor thing. Doesn't know what she's saying." Celena looked at her out of heavy-lidded eyes. She was, she found, dreadfully tired. Her limbs felt like lead.

Helen bent to take her pulse. "The sedative's taking effect, Celena. Try to sleep now." Celena glanced at Daniel. The expression on his face told her that he remained skeptical.

He saw her watching and said reassuringly, "What happened was enough to shake anyone. The important thing is that you're going to be all right. Don't worry about anything else."

She sagged back against the pillow, tired to the marrow of her bones. No one would believe that someone had actually tried to kill her. Somehow, on her own, she would have to find out who had done this. And soon, too, for one thing was dreadfully clear—whoever was doing this was done playing games. Lydia playing ghost, the acts of vandalism, even the scare at the Sunken Forest all paled next to being trapped inside a burning building and being left to die. Someone wanted her gone. But why? Was it over the lighthouse or because she had discovered that someone had tried to kill her father? Or was someone disturbed about the questions she had raised about Sarina's death? There was no way of knowing.

NINETEEN

With a jolt of body and heart, Celena startled awake. Realizing that she was in her room and not the smoky, flame-filled shed caused such relief that Celena felt slightly light-headed. Her body ached as if it had been beaten, and she felt the tension of fear as if it were a dark, thick coil squeezing the air from her lungs. From now on, she had to be on guard. There was no telling from what source danger might come. If she had been somewhat disbelieving before, it was evident now that someone on Fire Island would stop at nothing, not even murder. She had hoped that sleeping would make things clearer, but it had done nothing to sharpen the blurred edges.

The door was open, and she jumped slightly when she noticed someone sitting across the room. But it was only Daniel, his face dark with stubble. His head was against the back of the chair, eyes closed in slumber, and his long legs were stretched out in front of him. When she made a small movement, Daniel opened his eyes.

"What are you doing here?" she asked, her voice sounding faraway and fragile in her own ears.

"I thought someone ought to watch you a little closer." His statement sent a little shiver through her. Was she becoming so paranoid that even the simplest utterances had evil connotations? Yet, after what happened, who could blame her? He went on, "I slept on the couch in the foyer, and came in this morning when Joshua left."

"You probably didn't get much sleep," Celena said, struggling to sit up without using her hands. "I'd like to look at the note again. If you didn't write it, maybe we can compare people's handwriting to see who did."

Daniel went to the dresser, but after some time said, "It's not here." Celena felt a prickle of fear and started to rise, but he stopped her. "There's no need to get up. Believe me. It's gone."

Someone had taken it. Someone who had been in her room last night. Most likely the same person who had tried to kill her. The last person she could remember looking at the note was Tana, but she'd have no reason to take it. Celena's fears made her look at Daniel closely. Could he have taken it after Joshua left and while she lay sleeping?

Daniel came closer. "I think the police ought to know about this."

"I'm going to call them this morning, though if they feel like everyone else, I don't expect them to take me seriously. Did Father come to see me last night?"

"You don't remember? You talked coherently enough. Those pills must have really knocked you out." Somehow, last night's events had fogged and misted together. She seemed to recall her father walking in haltingly and bending over her with anxiety in his eyes.

There was a light knock on the door, and Lydia stepped in. She wore a tight black dress and stiletto heels that tapped across the floor. Celena suddenly realized that Lydia had been absent last night. Did that denote innocence or guilt?

"So sorry to hear about your accident. It must have been frightful!" She didn't wait for a response, but tapped Daniel playfully on the arm. "Mother told me you were here. Are you ready to go to Long Island?" Her red lips were curved in a big smile.

He looked surprised. "I'm sorry, I don't remember making any plans . . ."

Her smile drooped a little. "When you said you were going to Long Island, I suggested we go together."

"Oh, that's right. But as it turns out, the man I was going to see called me yesterday. So I don't need to go after all."

Lydia tried to salvage it. Smiling playfully, she said, "It doesn't *have* to be a business trip."

"I'm sorry, but after he called, I told Father I'd help him at Clearwater today."

Lydia shrugged. "Suit yourself. I'm not going to leave for another hour, so if you change your mind, let me know. Take care, Celena."

Turning, Lydia walked out, swinging her hips in the suggestive way she did whenever she had an audience.

Daniel looked at Celena in desperation. "You can see how it is!"

Celena could. And somehow she was pleased he was naïve enough to be uncertain how to react to Lydia's blatant advances.

He went on. "That phone call I got was from a friend who works for the Coast Guard. I asked him about the rifle Clint turned in. He told me it hadn't been stolen." Celena was surprised but didn't have time to comment when Minerva came in with a tray.

"Thought you might enjoy having breakfast in bed," she said. Daniel left Minerva to cluck sympathetically over Celena, giving her pain medication and helping her get dressed. Celena was sitting at her dressing table, attempting to brush her hair, when there was a loud knock. When she called out, Gerald entered. He seemed different somehow, oddly nervous—a change from his usual easygoing self.

"Just wanted to make sure you were all right," he said uncertainly, his eyes on her bandaged arms and hands.

"I'm fine," Celena assured him. "Nothing serious."

"Close call, that," he said uneasily, never quite meeting her gaze.

"Yes, it was." Celena waited for him to reveal the purpose behind his visit.

"Terrible accident," he repeated.

"It *wasn't* an accident," Celena cried. "No one believes me, but it's the truth."

Finally, Gerald met Celena's gaze, and she was chilled to see acknowledgment in his eyes. So, he knew as well as she did that someone had tried to kill her. What else did he know?

"Could it have been a warning?" he said faintly. Celena set her hairbrush down with a clatter, but before she could ask what he meant, Gerald continued in a quiet voice that was so different from his usual boisterous one. "Have you ever thought, Celena, about going back to Maryland? Just for a while. To be safe?"

He *was* warning her. "Why aren't I safe here, Gerald?"

"I'm not saying you aren't," he recanted quickly. "But if it were me, I'd take a trip back home. Visit the grandparents for a while." When Gerald went on to talk about Clearwater, it was plain that he wasn't going to reveal anything more. It was then that Celena came to a conclusion. Gerald Roberts was definitely hiding something. Celena marveled that she had ever thought him to be an open person. Shortly after Gerald left, her father walked in, surprisingly agile on his crutches.

"How are you this morning? You seemed kind of dozy last night."

"I must have been." Celena gave a little laugh. "I hardly remember your visit."

Matthew eased himself carefully into a chair. "Do I have to repeat everything I said?"

"Let me guess. I'm in danger. Someone means business. I need to leave."

A corner of his mouth twitched. "Are you sure you don't remember my visit?"

"I'm not going," Celena declared resolutely. "Now, can we talk about something else?"

"Like fires? Or people breaking into the lighthouse and smashing things up? Or someone vandalizing the paint locker or following you on the beach?" Matthew's blue eyes were steady. "I can go on if you want. Things have gone too far, Celena. I want you out of here."

"Fine thing for a man to say about his own daughter."

"You always could talk circles around me," he said, shaking his head. "And you still have that nasty habit of digging in your heels, even when you're scared." She made a movement, but he went on. "No, don't deny it. I can tell. You looked like you were sitting on coiled springs when I came in."

She had no answer. All Celena knew was that she could not go away. Not when she and her father were rebuilding their relationship. Not when Joshua was counting on her. Not when her absence meant they would probably lose the lighthouse.

"Have you called the police?"

"Not yet, but I'm going to, even though everyone thinks the door just got jammed. No one believes it was intentional."

"Tell the police everything you know. They'll be able to look into things."

Matthew cleared his throat and took a deep breath. "There's something I should have said a long time ago. For a while last night, I was scared I might have passed up my chance. So I'm going to say it now. It's about when you left." Celena noticed that her father's hands had tightened around his crutches so tightly his knuckles were white. How had she ever thought him unemotional? He went on. "I hurt you bad. Said things I shouldn't have and never made it right. I'm sorry."

It had come. The moment she had thought about for so long—her father apologizing. In her fantasies, there had been many endings. Sometimes she had been cold and scornful, rejecting his apology. Other times, Celena had railed at her father for hurting her so badly. A few times in her imaginings, she had accepted his apology and the world had become whole again.

There was so much Celena had planned to say. But now, inexplicably, all of the declarations and all of the pronouncements had collapsed under their own weight before they could be properly recalled to mind. And the strange thing was that suddenly, none of them was as vital as Celena had once felt them to be. In the past months, during quiet moments, she had thought about the promise she'd made regarding her father. For her mother's sake she had tried to have empathy, and surprisingly enough, Celena was the one who had benefited from it.

Celena could feel something flowing up from the very most inner part of her—clearing out the last remnants of pain and hurt she had carried for so long and transporting them to where they could be dispelled in the light and the sky and the heavens. Since her return to Fire Island, there had slowly developed within her an increased understanding—a sharpening of outlines, as when sand is washed from a shell. A deep inner peace swelled within her, filling her so completely it was nearly spilling out of her. Tears welled up, and, reaching out, she took hold of her father's hands, disregarding the pain in her own.

"I'm sorry too," Celena whispered. "I was prickly and self-righteous. I wouldn't listen to a thing and fought you at every turn."

"You were young," he said roughly, refusing to let her shoulder any of the blame. "And I wouldn't listen either. I rode roughshod over you."

She *had* been young. So young that life was something only experienced in peaks and valleys. How thin, how weak, and how transparent she had been. Life had been so intense. Either things were too slow or too fast, too prudent or too perilous. Fortunately, with the passage of years and without plan or effort, life had become more moderate.

"You were always so angry." Celena didn't say it mutinously or defensively, but as a simple fact and with more understanding than she'd ever had before.

"At life, not you."

"I couldn't tell the difference," Celena admitted, tears running down her cheeks.

"Ah." He was silent a moment. "After you left, I learned a bit about repentance. Had a hard time with that at first. After all, I had tried and felt that ought to be good enough. But I studied it out. Finally came to see the sense in wiping the slate clean." He rubbed his chin. "You and Elizabeth believed the Church was true, but everything was changing too fast for me. It never pays to make up your mind too fast." Celena had heard him say that a million times. It was his guiding star. Her mother used to say that if she wanted to know what he wanted for breakfast, she had to ask weeks in advance. Matthew went on. "I didn't like you and your mother going to a different church without me."

"But we asked you to go with us!"

"Aye, but I liked *my* church. I'd gone there since I was a baby. I didn't like those Mormon rascals coming in and sweeping you and Elizabeth away from me. It seemed I was losing everything all at once." Matthew's voice caught on itself. "Your mother was dying. I was losing you. Everything was upside-down."

In a split-second crack of clarity, Celena knew that her father had not been as uncaring as she had thought. He'd merely been struggling with enormous changes. For a man who liked to work things out far in advance and then proceed slowly, it must have been an incredible ordeal. With a rush of perception, Celena realized just how overwhelmed her father must have been. In that split second, forgiveness came as easily as water running downhill, and she threw herself into his embrace as he gathered her in his arms and held her tightly. Celena felt his chest heave with strong emotion while her tears soaked into his shirt.

Without fully realizing it, the long road between Celena and her father had groaned and shifted and rearranged itself until it wasn't any distance at all. The old anger and hurt seemed something far away—as if it belonged to someone else. When she pulled back, Matthew wiped his eyes roughly and, clearing his throat, tried to rearrange his expression back to normal.

"Thank you for talking with me," Celena said, her voice quavering slightly.

"Not exactly my specialty," he said with a grimace.

Celena smiled. "You know what they say—practice makes perfect." At that moment, there was a faint whisper, a fluttering inside, like something brushing past her mind. A warm feeling glowed within like a conduit of solace, and without a doubt, Celena knew her mother was aware of this moment, knew that this was what she had envisioned when extracting those promises from her daughter. Celena was filled with a radiant happiness—a feeling she knew would not soon fade.

* * *

Celena spent the afternoon resting. Matthew had begun eating in the dining room regularly and was there tonight. The meal of fresh clams, scallops, and flounder was excellent, but dinner was an uneasy affair. Helen was even more taciturn than usual, and Lydia was subdued, her banter with the tourists lacking its usual sparkle.

The long summer days gave Celena a little free time in the evening before she had to go to the lighthouse, and tonight after dinner, she and Clint went to sit on the porch. The swing creaked as they settled in, and Celena slipped off her shoes and socks so her bare feet could rest on the warm wood of the porch. It was lovely to sit there, breathing in the sweetness of the honeysuckle that wrapped itself around one end of the veranda.

When Clint noticed Celena looking at his hair, he reached up to feel the scorched ends. "I didn't have time to see a barber." His gray eyes crinkled as he smiled that dazzling white smile. The combination of his chiseled features and tanned face was enough to take one's breath away, even if his eyebrows were singed and some of his hair frizzled.

Her heart swelled. "I can't tell you how grateful I am for what you did. I owe you my life."

"Anyone would have done the same thing. I can't accept thanks for being in the right place at the right time."

"Are you okay? You look kind of worried."

"I am. About you," Clint admitted. "All day I've been trying to figure out who would want to hurt you. I've thought a lot about Ethan, wondering what he was doing around the storage shed yesterday."

"You can't think Ethan started the fire!" Celena cried. "He wouldn't hurt me."

"I didn't think anyone would try to hurt your father either. And from what you've told me, there's something suspicious about Sarina's death. It's just that Ethan is so unpredictable. I wish I knew exactly what happened between him and Sarina that night."

Celena was disturbed by the direction of his thoughts. She thought of Sarina's black eyes and her brilliant smile. "Ethan loved Sarina. He wouldn't have hurt her."

"Even if she was planning to leave him? Ethan can get carried away—at times he's out of control. Believe me, I've seen it firsthand."

Celena protested. "I still don't think he harmed her."

"Sometimes it's the quiet ones that surprise you the most."

The door banged, and Joshua came out. "Do you want me to run the light for you tonight, Celena? I can, you know." His face was eager.

"Thanks, Joshua, but I want to go," she said, determined to run the light in spite of her injuries and her fears. It was important to show whoever had locked her in the shed that she wouldn't be frightened away. "Run and get some cookies for us to take."

"Rueben told me he was going to escort you to the lighthouse, but I told him I'd take you and Joshua over tonight. Daniel, Rueben, and I will take turns from here on. But are you going to be able to manage the light with your hands like that? I'll be glad to stay and run it for you." His eyes were kind. "I find myself wanting to take care of you."

Celena looked at her hands ruefully, the bandages white against her skin. "It looks worse than it is. And Joshua will be there to help." She bit her lip and changed the subject abruptly. "Did you know that Gerald had been in prison before you hired him to manage Clearwater?"

"Of course. He is, after all, part of the family."

"Weren't you worried?"

"Do you mean, was I worried he'd get another scam going here? I'll admit the thought occurred to me, but it was a risk I was willing to take. You see, I've always been more like a brother to Gerald than a cousin—always watching out for him." Clint spread out his hands as if this was the simplest thing in the world. "This was one way I could help him."

"I suppose you knew Lydia had a brush with the law too."

Clint looked pensive. "I just found out. If I were you, I'd watch out for her. Lydia's a dangerous kind of person. If she got her temper up, she'd stop at nothing."

When Joshua returned, he was excited about riding in Clint's car. As they started to pull away, Celena glanced back at the boarding-house to see Helen standing at the window, a tall figure staring after them. What was she thinking? And why was she looking after them with that strange, wooden expression?

* * *

The next morning while Celena was visiting her father, Helen came in with her bag of supplies and changed Celena's bandages. After a quiet morning, Celena decided to go to her special spot on the beach. As she settled in, several pinkish-brown pelicans flew past, far more graceful in the air than on the ground. For the moment there was nothing she needed to do. Celena could simply breathe and let the peace of the island take over.

She thought about her father again. Somehow, her perspective had changed. Before she'd left the island, it was as if she were standing in front of a granite boulder, where it was impossible to see anything but rock. Then, after a few years, she had taken a step or two back and began to see other things. Now, after having taken more steps back, more was revealed—trees, flowers, grass, and all sorts of lovely things. Yet the boulder hadn't changed. It was still there. It was only because *she* had moved that Celena could see things that she had not seen or appreciated before.

A shadow fell across her and she looked up, startled. It was Ethan. His hair was wild, and for once there was no smile. Ethan's eyes were large as he stared at her hands and arms wrapped in white gauze. He almost winced as he asked, "Does it hurt?"

"A little. But it could have been a lot worse if you hadn't gotten Clint."

"I've been watching you. I thought you were going to the light. But you didn't. Then I saw the smoke." Ethan was anxious that she understand.

"A good thing for me," Celena said gratefully. "Did you see anyone around the shed?"

He shook his head, then asked, "Do you think it was bad men?"

"I think it was, yes."

Ethan looked up and down the beach, then said, "I want to show you something."

"What is it?"

"Just come." There was something in his voice that made Celena uneasy, but she followed him across the sand. The surface of the Atlantic was alight with the silver-foil dance of late afternoon sun. To her surprise, Celena realized he was taking her to Clearwater. As they approached, Ethan kept looking around uneasily. Her apprehension increased, and she could not rid herself of the notion that she was being watched, that someone was waiting for the chance to strike at her again. But that was ridiculous. She was with Ethan, within calling distance of others. Nothing could happen. Still, Celena could not shake the notion that somewhere, someone's eyes were upon her. Was someone watching, even now asking themselves, "Is this the time?" It would not be death by fire this time. But there were other ways.

Ethan led her around the back of the resort. No one paid any attention as they went in a side door. They went down the hallway and, before she could protest, Ethan opened the door to Gerald's office and slipped inside. He went to the wall that held Gerald's collection of guns.

Pointing at a rifle, he said, "That's my gun."

Celena moved closer. "You mean the one you found on the beach?" When he nodded, she asked, "How can you tell?"

"639534."

Celena stared at him blankly. Then she reached up and, taking the gun from its padded supports, turned it over until she found what she was looking for. "Tell me the number again."

"639534."

It was the number inscribed on the rifle stock. "Did you put the gun here?" she asked. When he shook his head emphatically, Celena stared at the rifle as if it might give her some answers. She hadn't even known that rifles *had* serial numbers until Daniel had mentioned it. Ethan had rattled off numbers when he had first showed her the gun, and though Celena couldn't remember them now, she was sure they were the same ones he had just given.

Celena was suspicious of many things right now, but one thing she did trust was Ethan's memory. But how had the rifle come to be here? Clint said he'd turned it in. Was he lying, or could there be some other explanation? Could Clint be the one behind everything? Whoever was doing this had to be both intelligent and knowledgeable, and Clint had both of those traits in abundance. Still, what would he gain by any of this? Besides, Daniel had already checked with his friend at the Coast Guard who had confirmed that Clint had turned in the rifle. Then how had it ended up here?

A faint illumination, a suspicion, began to form. How did Daniel know Springfield rifles with low serial numbers were defective? And why had Gerald come to his son's defense so quickly after Lydia had questioned Daniel's knowledge? Celena shivered as she recalled Daniel's clandestine meeting by Tillman's. Ethan had said that Daniel was watching the beach. And she only had Daniel's word for it that he had actually talked to his friend at the Coast Guard station. Another possibility was that Gerald had put the rifle here. If so, Gerald was either very stupid to display the gun in plain sight or else very clever, knowing no one paid any attention to his collection. It was hard to know what to think.

"Are you mad because I showed you the gun?" Ethan's voice was uncertain, like a child's—wanting to know the direction of the emotions he saw playing across her face.

"No, you did the right thing," Celena assured him, her mind working. Perhaps someone had switched rifles before or after Ethan had given it to Clint. Gerald had already said that Ethan had showed him the gun. Could he have taken it and given Ethan a different one—the one that Clint had turned in? But why would Gerald keep it? Because it was his in the first place? If so, the only reason for not speaking up was because he had something to hide. Gerald had been distinctly uneasy when he'd found out about the rifle. Then it hit her.

Rum-running.

If it was true that most guns used by smugglers were stolen, and Gerald had dropped the rifle while smuggling, he would have *had* to switch rifles so as to avoid it being traced. Then he must have put the rifle here, not realizing that Ethan would be able to recognize it from its serial number. Since Clint was not a gun expert, he wouldn't know that Gerald had switched rifles. Then again, perhaps Gerald was innocent and someone else had put the rifle in his office in an attempt to frame him. Celena put the gun back on the wall.

"Ethan, have you told anyone that your gun is here?" When he shook his shaggy head, she said, "I need you to keep this a secret. Don't tell anyone that your rifle is here, okay?"

"Can I have it back?" he asked plaintively.

"Not right now. I need to figure some things out." They slipped out quietly.

On her way to Bay Haven, Celena had to fight a desire to find Daniel and tell him about the rifle. But she knew she couldn't. What if the impossible were true and he was involved in rum-running? Or what if his father was? Celena was lost in thought when someone called out. She looked up to see Tana coming down the sidewalk toward her. The older woman greeted Celena cheerily.

"I'm just on my way home. I was about to ask why you looked so worried, then realized that would have been a stupid question."

"Oh, I'm all right."

"Uh-huh," Tana scoffed. "I've heard that before—from Rueben. He's been going around like a bear with hangnails. But whenever I ask him what's wrong, all he says is, 'I'm all right.' What a liar. Anyway, I'm going home to do some baking. I'll be bringing you and your father some cinnamon rolls this afternoon. If that doesn't make you smile, nothing will."

* * *

Over the next week, Helen changed Celena's dressings every other day, making them smaller each time. Celena did a lot of thinking about the rifle in Gerald's office but could not decide on a plan of action. On Sunday, her father insisted on using crutches inside the church, though he still used the wheelchair to get there. Daniel arrived at the same time they had and offered his services. As they walked in, he and Celena stood protectively on either side of Matthew, like wings, prepared to catch him should he falter.

On Wednesday, Celena and Joshua went with their father to the hospital on Long Island for his X-rays. After a thorough examination, Matthew asked Doc Harrison the question they had all been wondering for so long. "Can you tell if my leg is going to heal completely?"

"It's a very good sign that you've regained some feeling in your foot." Doc Harrison looked encouraged. "While there's some lingering numbness, it should diminish in time. Even if it's permanent, it shouldn't affect your ability to walk. It'll be more of a nuisance than anything else."

Joshua watched his father's face carefully to see if this was good news or not, then burst out asking, "That's good, isn't it?"

Doc Harrison smiled winningly. "Very good. We're not out of the woods yet, but we're certainly headed in the right direction. I'm pleased with the way the leg is healing." He brought out his saw, and Joshua watched in fascination as the doctor cut a few inches off the top of the cast. After washing his hands, Doc Harrison said to Matthew, "That will make it a little easier for you to sit. You'll still have to take it slow and easy when you walk, though. And not *your* kind of taking it easy, but mine. Otherwise, you'll end up with your other leg in a cast."

* * *

The next evening, Celena and Joshua went to the light early with Rueben. When Rueben said he wanted to talk with Celena, Joshua went ahead, taking the kerosene. The older man's faded blue eyes glanced at Celena's bandaged hands and looked away quickly, as if the sight made him uneasy. There was a nervous tension about Rueben tonight as his hand clutched the head of his cane.

"I talked with Matthew. He said he'd asked you to leave but you refused." Rueben looked troubled. "I can run the light. You ought to get out of here."

"We've been over this before."

"That was before the fire," he replied tersely. "And before you started digging into Sarina's death. That was something I didn't expect."

Celena looked at him curiously. "Why was Sarina talking to you about rum-running?"

He looked at her suspiciously. "Who told you that?"

"It doesn't matter. Why was she asking you about smuggling?"

"Curious, I guess."

"Could it be that Sarina knew you'd have the answers she was looking for?" Celena looked at him steadily. "Was she a rumrunner?"

"So what if she was?" A note of defensiveness crept into Rueben's voice.

"Smuggling is illegal."

"Legal and illegal are not the same thing as right and wrong."

Celena felt suddenly cold. "Rueben, rum-running is against the law."

"Doesn't mean it's wrong. Lots of people get jailed when they haven't done anything wrong. Sometimes you have to look behind the scenes to know what's going on. There could be good reasons for what a person does," he said enigmatically.

Fighting a rising sense of disquiet, Celena asked grimly, "You're rum-running, aren't you?"

Rueben's blank, leathery face told her nothing. "Anything's possible."

"You're doing it to help Will, aren't you? But what if you get caught?"

"I've already decided between right and wrong. And it's wrong to let a little boy suffer because you can't afford treatment. I'll leave legal and illegal up to the authorities." His voice was disturbingly detached.

Celena tried again. "I think Sarina was a rumrunner or else knew someone who was. That's why she was killed."

Rueben's face darkened, and there was a sudden warning in his eyes. "You're getting into things you've no business meddling with. I'm telling you, Celena, for your own good, just leave it alone. Sarina died a long time ago. You're not going to bring her back, no matter what you do." With that, he turned sharply and walked away, leaving Celena with the unsettling feeling that she didn't know Rueben as well as she had thought. Overhead, a seagull circled the lighthouse. Its shrill cry floated eerily on the wind, and another gull's distant, mournful cry answered back. Her thoughts whirled in a morass of speculation from which it was impossible to extract anything that would be of help.

Rueben was right—anything was possible. Anything.

TWENTY

Celena climbed the tower and went outside on the catwalk, even though it was unseasonably chilly. Temperatures had plummeted because of an unusual low-pressure system hovering over the area, and the ocean breeze had stiffened into a cold wind. She was glad to have her brother there. It was a pleasant diversion to hear Joshua talk about the fort he and Zach were building on the beach to use as their spy headquarters. But later, after Joshua had gone to bed, Celena was once again left alone with her thoughts. She looked out over the ocean, where the moonlight brushed the surface with streaks of rippling silver foil. The lights of passing ships twinkled, their lights all the brighter for the inky blackness that surrounded them. The last thing Celena thought as she slid into a thin, restless sleep was that Rueben had not, after all, given her a clear answer as to whether Sarina was a rumrunner or not.

* * *

During dinner the next evening at Bay Haven, Joshua related his plans for the next couple hours, which included looking at something Zach had found in the boathouse by Clearwater and seeing some newborn puppies. And couldn't he have one, please, since Father was doing so much better and they'd be back home soon? Celena listened absentmindedly, breaking off bits of toast and adding dabs of honey.

They were gathering their dishes when a door slammed. Shortly thereafter, raised voices came from the foyer. Celena held Joshua back, waiting until all was quiet before going out. But it had only been a lull. Helen was standing there, her face flushed a dark red as she faced Lydia, whose face was thunderous. With spectacularly bad timing, Gerald came in the front door. He stopped short, taking it all in— Helen, whose mouth was pressed in a hard thin line, and Lydia with her balled-up fists. When Lydia turned abruptly, heading for her room, Helen determinedly went after her. Gerald stood there looking embarrassed, his face red and round. When Joshua told Celena he was leaving, she barely noticed. It was something of a shock to see Gerald, who was always so fastidious, in wrinkled pants and a shirt that was only tucked in halfway.

"Glad to see you, Celena," he said uneasily, running a hand over his disheveled hair. "I was going to talk to Helen, but since she's, uh, busy, there was something I wanted to ask you." When he took a step or two closer, Celena could smell the liquor on his breath. "On the night of the fire, did you see anyone around the shed?"

"No, not until Ethan, Clint, and Helen came running up."

"Helen, eh?" Gerald's face changed slightly. He didn't go on, merely pulled himself upright, regaining some of the composure he usually wore like a second skin, then said, "Ah, well, I'd best be off." Celena stood looking after him, then realized that Helen was standing at the end of the hall. Helen's spine was straight as a birch tree, and her face was white and set.

"Is something wrong?" Celena asked.

Helen's hostility was palpable as she advanced on Celena. "It's you," she snapped, her usual cool sense of control gone. "Why did you have to come back to Fire Island and make trouble?"

"I came back to help Joshua and Father."

Helen laughed shortly, and there was more than a hint of hysteria in it. "You're always so helpful, aren't you? Do you actually think you're helping when you meddle with things that don't concern you?" There was a smoldering beneath the surface that hinted at explosive depths. Suddenly, Helen brought up a hand and pressed it to her temple. Emotion had broken through, and Helen Montgomery was not a woman who liked to betray raw feelings to anyone. With her silent, sweeping tread, Helen went to the front door and was gone.

She was probably going after Gerald. Something had happened. But what? Celena took her dishes to the kitchen where Minerva was washing up, assisted by Katy, a pleasant young girl who had been recently hired. Through the kitchen window, Celena saw Lydia cross the backyard. What could she be doing out there? Celena was determined to find out.

The wind had begun to rise, whining around the side of the house while heavy, gray clouds scudded overhead. There was a chilly nip in the air, but no sign of Lydia. How had she disappeared so quickly? Then Celena noticed that the shed door was ajar, the open padlock hanging on the clasp. When she opened the door, Lydia turned quickly, her eyes wide and startled. Celena stepped in, looking over the piles of unmarked wooden cases.

"What's in the boxes?"

Lydia's face had blanched alarmingly. "None of your business!" she practically spat at Celena. "Just turn around and leave. Now!" Lydia's typical gaiety was gone. Instead she was filled with a tension that gave her voice a quick, brittle quality. Celena turned as if to go, then closed the door and stood in front of it with her arms folded.

Lydia's eyes became slitted as she took a meaningful step toward Celena, who kept her face outwardly calm and unshaken. "Not smart, Celena. Get out now, while you can."

Celena stood her ground. "It's liquor, isn't it? You've been rum-running. That's why the shed was locked. Who are you working with?"

"You don't actually expect me to tell you. Besides, you'd never believe me anyway, dear-heart." Celena noticed that Lydia's face, with all its youthful prettiness, looked older and more strained than she had ever seen it before.

Celena went to a stack of boxes, touching them lightly. "I probably wouldn't. You've done nothing but lie ever since I got here. That, and try to scare me away."

"I made a great ghost, didn't I?" Lydia said, regaining some of her spirit. "I certainly had *you* going." She moved gracefully to the door, and when Celena followed, Lydia snapped, "Stay there! I'm not going to have you going to the Coast Guard. Not until I can get this moved to Long Island." The electric gleam in Lydia's dark eyes was alarming.

"Why did you get mixed up in smuggling?"

"What a stupid question," Lydia said scornfully. "I told you why when you first got here. Money. I'm not going to be stuck on this island forever. Money is my ticket out of here. And I'm not going to let Mother lose Bay Haven either, so my advice is to forget you saw anything." Her voice turned hard. "It would be a shame if you had an accident."

"Like the one at the storage shed?"

"Actually, that would have solved everything," Lydia admitted. Then she waved a hand at the boxes. "What's the big deal about a little liquor anyway? This is nothing compared to what others are bringing in. Including your precious Rueben. So stop poking your nose where it doesn't belong. You don't need to get mixed up in this."

"I'm already involved," Celena said tightly. "Even though you've been trying to get rid of me ever since I got here, I'm still here."

"For now," Lydia said, sneering darkly.

Suddenly Celena was afraid. "Were you the one who locked me in the shed?"

Tense nervousness ran through Lydia and set her hands dancing as she talked. "Why did you have to come back and interfere? Just when things were starting to fall into place! I found a way to get enough money to help Mother *and* get away from this place, then you had to come and ruin it all!" Lydia's voice cracked slightly.

Celena could sense the strong purpose that drove Lydia like a whip. Her hand went to her necklace and touched the heart-shaped locket. She had come back to the island for two specific reasons, and she wouldn't give up now.

"You've got enemies here," Lydia asserted.

"Such as you," Celena replied bitterly.

"I'm not the one you need to worry about." She looked at Celena contemplatively. "Did you ever ask Daniel what he really does for a living? I'm wondering what story he gave you."

Celena didn't want to admit he had told her nothing.

Lydia was triumphant. "Just what I thought." For a few moments, she appeared deep in thought, then seemed to come to a decision. "I hate to burst your bubble, but I've decided to tell you the truth. You know how Daniel's told everyone that he's helping his father? That much is true, but what he neglected to mention is exactly what kind of help he's been giving Gerald. They're rumrunners. Gerald had the contacts and set it all up, and Daniel came out to help run the show and put his father's plans into action."

"I don't believe you."

"What's not to believe? That an ex-con decided to make money the easy way? Or that his son, whose father taught him everything he knows, decided to take up the same line of work? You know Gerald's been in prison. You don't get a rap sheet for being a Boy Scout." Celena felt a sinking feeling as Lydia continued. "Surely you've noticed how Daniel perks up when anyone mentions rum-running. Haven't you wondered why he's so knowledgeable about it all? I've even seen him talking with members of his crew. And lately, Daniel's been doing something that's made even Gerald real nervous. I don't know what it is, but you've seen how jumpy he's been lately."

"You can't be sure of any of this," Celena said, wanting to deny that Daniel was involved. But then, even if Gerald was doing it on his own, Daniel had to be aware of it.

"Oh, but I am," Lydia declared. "I did a little snooping. I'm good at that, you know. When I found out what they were doing, I went to Gerald—told him I'd tell my mother all about it if he didn't help me get started. That did it. Gerald would do anything to stay on Mother's good side." Celena was sure of that as well. It was clear Gerald was deeply in love. Still, how much of this outpouring could she believe?

It was as if Lydia could read her mind. "There's one way to find out the truth," she said. "Go look in Gerald's boathouse. He got a big shipment in night before last. You'll find enough liquor there to keep New York City soused for a month."

Celena considered. Lydia could be sending her on a wild-goose chase, or she could even be trying to get her to walk into a trap. But then again, this couldn't have been premeditated on Lydia's part, so it couldn't be a setup like the storage shed. Suddenly Celena caught her breath. Hadn't Joshua said he was going to the boathouse? What if Lydia was telling the truth and Gerald discovered him snooping around? Pushing past Lydia, Celena wrenched the door open and ran for her bike.

It was storm-brewing weather—gray and cold, more like December than early August, with an electric quality in the air as she rode.

Drawing close, she jumped off and left her bike by a sassafras tree. There was no one in sight as she ran to the boathouse, built out into a little sandy cove. Celena thought she heard faint noises coming from inside, but they stopped as she approached. She entered cautiously to give her eyes time to adjust to the gloominess. In the silence a whisper of sound stirred from the opposite side, across the two boats that sat in the middle. Then a slight figure in red shorts and a striped shirt rose from where he had been crouching.

It was Joshua. Furtively, he motioned her over. "Celena, you've got to see this." Celena walked around the boats, staring all around her. All three walls of the boathouse were stacked high with long, rectangular wooden cases, similar to those she had seen at Bay Haven. Something inside her crumbled. Lydia had been telling the truth after all.

"Over here!" Joshua called as he stepped into the larger of the two boats. Her brother knelt and pulled up a loose board on the floor of the boat, then another. "Zach showed me this. Look!" His voice was full of excitement.

Celena went closer. "A false-bottom boat!" she gasped.

Joshua removed several more planks, revealing the hold underneath, which was filled with wooden cases. The top case had been broken into; its splintered lid lay scattered about. A crowbar was nearby. Stunned, Celena looked inside. She'd expected to see bottles of liquor, but something else was there. Something long, which gleamed dully in the half light.

Rifles.

Joshua touched one gently, and Celena commanded, "Give me that crowbar." She went to a short stack against the side of the boathouse. It took only a few minutes to pry off the lid. That case was also filled with rifles. They were wrapped in wax paper, and the stocks had a dark wood grain. Celena pulled one of them out from where they lay wrapped tightly in wooden dividers that held them firm. The metal shone dully in the subdued light. A chill ran through Celena when she saw the inscription: Springfield '03.

There was no sound except for the gurgling of water in the boathouse. She glanced outside. Darkness would come early because of the coming storm. Already it was nearly time to go to the light. Celena looked back at the rifles. How had Ethan come by one of these? Had Gerald given Ethan one of these rifles? But why? As a reward, perhaps, for helping him? That would explain Ethan's anxiety when she'd asked where he had gotten the rifle. Gerald would surely have told him to keep quiet, and Ethan wasn't used to not telling the truth.

Everything Ethan had said, which had sounded crazy at the time, was falling into place now—the bad men and telling her to watch the beach. Perhaps he didn't even know they were smuggling guns instead of liquor. Celena's heart skipped a beat as she remembered Daniel talking to the man behind Tillman's. The cases they had mentioned— were they talking about liquor or guns? Celena shivered. Lydia had sent her here, but she'd said nothing about guns. It didn't make sense.

Unless she hadn't planned on Celena opening any of the cases.

That had to be it. Lydia had assumed, quite correctly, that Celena would think the cases were full of liquor. Lydia hadn't known that Zach and Joshua were playing spy and would discover the rifles. Then again, perhaps Lydia didn't know about the guns. She'd certainly given no indication that Gerald and Daniel were doing anything other than smuggling liquor.

"What are we going to do, Celena?" Joshua asked in a small voice.

Celena peered outside. Heavy clouds made the early evening dark and gloomy. She didn't dare go to Bay Haven to call the police— Lydia was too unpredictable. She couldn't call from the lighthouse either, since telephone service had been discontinued at the keeper's cottage. The ferry was about to make its last run; she'd never make it across town before it left, and it would do no good to go to the Coast Guard station because they'd be out on patrol by this time.

"We're going to have to wait," Celena said regretfully. "In the morning, we'll go to the Coast Guard station. If no one is there, we'll take the ferry to Long Island and notify the authorities there." She looked at the mess in the boat. "We don't want Gerald to know we've been here. I'll stay and clean this up while you go on to the light-house. But be careful. Keep an eye out and if anyone is around, don't let them see you. Get things ready, and I'll come as soon as I can." Joshua ran off like a jackrabbit, looking fearfully over his shoulder.

Celena put one of the rifles aside. She'd take it for evidence in case Gerald and Daniel moved the cases tonight. She had been working a short time when a slight noise made her look up to see Helen standing in the doorway.

"What are you doing?" Helen screeched wildly. "Sabotaging Gerald's boat?" Celena scrambled out on the far side, glad there was a good distance between her and the older woman who looked so wild-eyed. "She was right! Lydia was right," Helen said, her voice full of wonder. "She just told me what you were up to."

"Me? This is not my doing. Unless I'm very much mistaken, this is *Gerald's* boat—not mine."

Looking incredulously from the boat, with its cache of rifles, to the boxes stacked against the walls, Helen exclaimed, "Lydia told me you were a rumrunner, and I didn't believe her. But now I've caught you red-handed." Her eyes narrowed as she looked at the rifles. "What are you doing? Planting guns in Gerald's boat to divert attention away from your own smuggling?"

"*My* smuggling?"

"Gerald never uses these boats. You may have taken in everyone else with your innocent act, but I could always see through you!" Helen's tone was heavily disapproving. "Lydia just showed me your stash in the shed at Bay Haven. How *dare* you store liquor on my property?"

"You can't honestly believe that's mine!"

"Who else would do such a thing?"

"Lydia!" Celena cried, fighting the urge to stamp her feet. "Your own daughter! *She's* the one who's been smuggling!"

Helen stiffened. There was a pinched look at the base of her nostrils, and she had the smoldering look of a volcano that was set to explode. "You were always blaming her, ever since you were little, for anything that went wrong." Her words came out fast and furious, and her voice rose a notch. "You haven't changed at all."

Neither had she, Celena thought bitterly. Helen had always been blind and deaf to Lydia's faults. In this respect, Helen could not be trusted at all.

There was a bright glitter to Helen's eyes. "It was too good an opportunity to pass up, wasn't it? Now we know what you were doing when you pretended to be watching the light. And why, after staying away for five years, you came running back to Fire Island so suddenly. You weren't worried about your father. You just wanted to make some fast money." Helen had to be crazy, Celena thought, chilled by the fierceness of Helen's tone as well as her words.

"Listen to me," Celena begged. "I talked with Lydia a little while ago. I found her in the shed with all those cases. Lydia admitted she was smuggling."

Helen's face grew distorted. "She didn't say any such thing. You just want to get back at her! You were always jealous of Lydia. She's on probation now because of false charges, and if you make wild accusations like that, Lydia could go to jail." Helen stopped to take a breath, her chest heaving. When she continued, her voice was pure steel. "Whether it's over my dead body or yours, I will not let you hurt Lydia!"

A prickling of fear ran through Celena. Helen was definitely unbalanced. Celena glanced at the door, judging the distance. She decided to risk it. Celena bent over and in one fluid motion, picked up the rifle in one hand and a bucket with the other, flinging it at Helen, who ducked and cried out. It gave Celena the chance she needed to run to the door. Once outside, Celena raced for the lighthouse. In the late grayness, it was as if winter had come early, with tiny wisps of fog drifting in from the ocean and curling about the beach. Twice she looked over her shoulder but did not see Helen. Celena stopped long enough to hide the gun in a thicket of green-streaked sumac at the corner of the generator building, then hurried on to the light, where Joshua unlocked the door for her.

They climbed the tower and in an excited voice, Joshua said, "I didn't see anybody when I came, but I'd better keep an eye on things." With that, he grabbed the binoculars and went out on the catwalk. Celena followed, glad for the silence that was broken only by the occasional cry of a bird and the distant crash of the waves. Her mind was going feverishly, though she tried to remain calm for Joshua's sake. Usually, nothing was more calming than looking out over the island, but tonight the scene did not seem peaceful—only threatening, as if some great force out there was holding its breath before unleashing its power.

"Celena!" Joshua's voice was sharp with fear. She looked in the direction he was pointing. A man was coming along the beach, striding purposefully toward the light.

"Can you tell who it is?" she asked anxiously.

"No. He's still too far away."

"Let me see." Celena grabbed the binoculars and, with the strap remaining around Joshua's neck, practically strangled her brother as she struggled to see. "It's Gerald," she cried. "Helen must have told him."

"What'll we do?" Joshua's voice was chill with fear.

"Nothing," Celena said, putting the glasses down. "I locked the door. He can't get in." Still, his coming was unnerving, and Celena knew she wouldn't relax until she saw Gerald walking away. They went inside, and when an unusual sound came from below, Celena went through the trapdoor to check the clockwork assembly. She was eyeing the machinery when the sound came again. But it was coming from farther below. It wasn't the clockworks at all.

Gerald was in the lighthouse.

With a cold fear racing through her body, Celena remembered that someone else had used a key the night of the vandalism. And she had thought it was Lydia. Somehow Gerald had gotten her father's key.

Celena hurried up to the lantern room. "Gerald's inside the light," she said tersely.

Joshua looked around wildly, and Celena knew what he was thinking. There was no escape. The only way out was one that guaranteed they would run into Gerald. Then Celena thought of the bosun's chair. It was their only chance. There was no time to lose.

"Joshua, you're going to have to go down in the bosun's chair. Come and help me." Celena climbed down once more to the watch room, grabbing the chair and ropes and handing them to Joshua, who pulled them up. They heard heavy footsteps and looked at each other in terror. Gerald was coming. Celena went to the catwalk and quickly attached the bosun's chair and ropes to the iron edge, thankful she had already threaded the new rope through the pulleys.

"Maybe *you* ought to go down, Celena," Joshua said in a small, frightened voice.

Celena put her hands on his shoulders. "I know you don't like it, but you've done it before and you can do it now. I have to stay and stall Gerald. I'll get you started." Going over the edge was the worst, Celena knew, and she reminded Joshua not to look down. Whether it was worse to go down in darkness when you couldn't see the bottom, or daylight when you could, Celena wasn't sure. She kept talking to her brother as he slowly let the rope out, keeping himself away from the side by pushing with his feet.

"Okay, you're set now. Don't let the rope go too fast. When you get down, go for help." Celena watched until he was nearly out of sight, then made sure the rope was lined out smoothly on the catwalk. Back inside, her nerves were pulled as tightly as racket strings, and she wasn't at all sure she could stop them from breaking. Gerald was longer in coming than Celena thought, but she was ready and waiting, standing on the trapdoor, when he began pushing at it.

He cursed, then shouted, "Let me up, Celena. I need to talk to you."

"Just a minute, Gerald. I'm adjusting the lens." Even to herself it sounded false, but it was the best she could do.

Gerald waited a few seconds, then pushed once more. Celena fought to keep her balance. "Get off the door!" he shouted. "Helen asked me to come."

"What did she say?"

"I can't talk through a wooden door." Gerald's voice was rough and impatient.

"Just give me a minute." She had to allow Joshua time to work himself down the side of the lighthouse. If Gerald came and discovered the rope . . . Celena shivered, thinking of how her father had plunged to the ground. The same thing could *not* happen to her brother.

"Be a good girl and let me up." Gerald's voice was loud, smooth, and thick, a flowery oil. "I know you're standing on the door. I could push it up, but I don't want to hurt you." His voice continued, false and coaxing. "I just want to talk with you, that's all." His words were slightly slurred. With a chill wash of terror, Celena realized he'd been drinking more.

"I'm almost done," Celena called.

She was unprepared when Gerald pushed with all his might. As she fell sideways, Gerald climbed awkwardly through the opening. Rising slowly, she decided that to show courage was safer than showing fear, but she recoiled when she saw he was carrying a rifle. Gerald straightened, staggering slightly. His face was flushed and his hair, usually so carefully combed, was sticking out in all directions. He threw her a reproachful look.

"You shouldn't have done that," Gerald said, his voice hard. Light from the revolving lantern alternately threw bright light then eerie shadows onto his face. "You don't know what you're getting into, Celena. This is serious business."

She could feel a fury in him that could easily go out of control, and she took a few steps back. His eyes gleamed in the shadows, sharp in a way she'd never seen before. He took several steps toward her, and Celena retreated around the lens.

"I always thought you were a sensible girl. Why did you have to get mixed up in this?" His voice was reproachful, his words slightly slurred. He held the rifle loosely as he advanced. "Helen told me you found guns in my boathouse! In my own boat!" Celena had never thought Gerald capable of deep anger, but she could hear it now in his voice—roiling depths that were usually concealed.

Celena would wait no longer. When the light came around to shine in his face, she darted forward, hitting him hard. Already unsteady, Gerald's arms flailed as he went over backward. Celena pulled on the rope and slipped down the trapdoor like a salamander sliding to earth. She was three levels down before she heard Gerald coming after her. Celena reached the bottom and was running down the hallway when she nearly collided with Clint, who grabbed at her to keep her from falling.

"What are you doing here?" she gasped with great, fear-darkened eyes.

His face was anxious. "I saw Joshua. He told me you needed help. What's going on?"

She looked frantically toward the stairs. "We've got to get out of here. Gerald's coming, and he's got a rifle!"

"But Gerald wouldn't hurt a fly."

"He's been drinking. And I found out he's been smuggling!"

Clint looked toward the stairs. "Gerald? A rumrunner?"

"He's smuggling guns! I found them in his boathouse. His boat has a false bottom! Helen saw them too."

Clint's face registered shock. There was the sound of pounding footsteps, and Clint quickly pulled Celena into the keeper's quarters. They hurried around and crouched behind the desk. The stone floor was chill, and the dampness seemed to invade her bones. Footsteps came into the room, then stopped. Clint's arm went protectively around her shoulder, holding her low.

"I know you're there, Celena. And I heard you too, Clint. Get up, both of you," Gerald ordered. When they hesitated, Gerald shouted, "I could shoot through the desk, but that would be a terrible shame. It's only colonial, but it does have rather a nice style."

Clint and Celena rose slowly. Gerald had the rifle pointed in their direction. His feet were spread wide apart, as if he needed to balance himself.

"Put the gun down, man!" Clint implored.

"Stop telling me what to do. I'm sick of it. I've *always* been sick of it." Celena had never heard Gerald's voice sound so cold and hard.

Clint's face tightened. "Celena tells me you've been smuggling. Is that true?"

"Lydia's working for Gerald," Celena told Clint urgently. "She's got cases of liquor stored in the shed behind Bay Haven."

"When did you find it?" Gerald asked, his voice sounding strung-up and unnatural.

"A couple of hours ago."

"Did you notify the police?" Gerald asked.

Celena dared not allow any weakness to show. Keeping her voice smooth, she answered, "Yes, and they're on their way here now."

The rifle shook slightly. "Good try, Celena," Gerald said. "But I don't believe you."

"You're not really planning on shooting us, are you?" Clint held out his hands placatingly.

Gerald's eyes were full of hate. "I only wish I could do more."

"Stop now and consider what you're doing. Think of Daniel."

Clint's words were like a red flag. Cursing loudly, Gerald cocked the rifle. He didn't take time to aim, just fired. Celena and Clint ducked as the shot went wild. Gerald stumbled awkwardly, giving Clint time to rush him and push the rifle barrel up. It fired into the ceiling, and both men crashed around the room, struggling for control. But a drunken Gerald was no match for Clint, who managed to tear the rifle away.

"Get over there," Clint demanded, breathing heavily as he motioned Gerald against the wall. Celena ran out from behind the desk to stand near Clint. "You made a big mistake, Gerald," Clint said, his gray eyes dark and angry. "You're going back to prison for sure now." When Gerald made a slight move forward, Clint raised the rifle. "I wouldn't try it. Not unless you want a hole in your chest. Celena, can you find some rope?" When she found some, Clint barked, "Sit down, Gerald, before you fall down. Celena, tie him good and tight."

"Celena, don't!" Gerald began, "Let me explain—"

"Shut up!" Clint shouted. "You've had your chance. I gave you every opportunity in the world. If you say another word, I'll shoot." He pulled a handkerchief out of his pocket and tossed it to Celena. "While you're at it, gag him." She did as directed. When Celena was finished, Gerald slumped, looking defeated.

"Good girl," Clint said. "Now, please stand against the wall." Celena looked at him uncomprehendingly. Clint swung the rifle from Gerald to her. There were gurgling sounds from Gerald as he strained to rise. "Never mind the heroics, Gerald," Clint said savagely. Then he spoke to her again. "Now, Celena—back against the wall, if you please." He was as courteous as if he were asking for a drink of water.

Celena blinked, disoriented. Clint grew impatient and signaled abruptly with the rifle. Unable to find her voice, she did as she was directed. It was then that Celena knew fully and completely, in a rush of acute awareness, that it was not Gerald she should have feared, but Clint.

TWENTY-ONE

It was surreal—Clint pointing a rifle at her. Celena could not take it in. Why had she never seen that his eyes were like a wolf's, cold and focused—missing nothing? It was as if a mask had dropped off.

"You?" Her breath hissed out in cold, pure shock. Celena made a despairing gesture. "It was you all along?" When he looked at her now, there was no softness in his eyes, but rather something unsettling—something deadly. Celena was surprised at how well he had been able to keep this part of himself hidden. Although his eyes were overly bright, Clint spoke calmly enough.

"Remember when I told you not to trust anyone? Not even me? You didn't listen. I tried to get you to go back to Maryland where you belong. But no, you had to be stubborn and stay." Visible now was the edge of steel that had always been there and which had only appeared infrequently. The strength that had always marked Clint as a leader.

"So *you're* the one smuggling liquor?"

Clint smiled lazily, that brilliant smile she had always admired. "You sound shocked. My dear, half the people on Fire Island do a little rum-running, and the rest would if they could. I was lucky enough to fall into the business. A friend of mine began making frequent visits to Fire Island. When I discovered that he came empty-handed but always left with a number of boxes, it didn't take long to figure out what was going on. He gave me a tidy sum to keep my mouth shut, but after a while, I decided to stop settling for crumbs. After all, it was my ferry."

"But didn't the Coast Guard ever search it?"

"Oh, frequently. That's why I used my own boat at first to transport the stuff. But the Coast Guard is very regimented. Once I learned their schedule, I began using the ferry. Besides, you'd be surprised at how much they trust the mayor." He chuckled. "More than once my boys loaded cases of bootleg whiskey while I stood right there, talking with a chief petty officer."

"Did your employees know about it?"

"Oh, Celena, be sensible. Do you think the cases were marked, ILLEGAL LIQUOR in big black letters? I transport supplies. They're not going to question anything."

"Is Lydia working for you?"

"That is one sharp gal," Clint admitted ruefully. "Lydia started her own operation right under my nose. I was going to put an end to it, but Lydia said she could drive you away if I let her stay. I regret that now. Her attempts to scare you by pretending to be a ghost and vandalizing the buildings were pathetic."

"How did she get into the lighthouse?"

"With my key. I had a copy made when Rueben had me watch the light."

The smell of danger was tangible in the thick musty air of the lighthouse. But even though fear ran in her veins, Celena knew she had to keep him talking to buy time. She could benefit from the fact that Clint wanted her to know every bit of it—to show how clever he had been, to preen his feathers before her like a peacock. But this chilled Celena, for it meant Clint did not plan on letting her live to tell the story.

She glanced at Gerald. Above the gag, his eyes were hypnotized like some frightened animal. "How does Gerald fit into this?"

"I hired him so I could stay in the background, yet run things the way I wanted. I needed someone who looked good on the outside and was naïve on the inside, and I got that with Gerald. You see, he's like a child. I can give him an idea and ten minutes later, he's telling someone how clever he is for thinking of it. Gerald looks like a successful businessman. It's only if you get close that you discover he couldn't find his way out of a wet paper bag without written directions. If you gave him a penny for his thoughts, you'd get back change." Clint went on, "But I needed someone loyal, and since we're cousins, there's a bond, which solidified when I managed to find some evidence that got him out of prison. Since then, he's felt a certain allegiance to me."

"Which you exploited."

"Are you kidding? If it wasn't for me, Gerald would be in a cement cell right now eating off tin plates and looking through bars. Instead, he's a big shot with a cushy job. He never even had to do any actual smuggling; I use pros for that. All he had to do was keep his mouth shut."

"I think his days of silence are over."

"Oh, Gerald will keep quiet." Clint looked confident. "If he says one word, I've got plenty of evidence to prove he's been smuggling, and then it's back to jail for him."

"If Gerald wasn't doing the actual smuggling, why does he have a false-bottom boat?"

Clint glowered at her. "Until you and your clever little brother came across it today, Gerald didn't even know about it. I had the boat specially made so my men could use it. It was also a little extra insurance in case things ever blew up. After all, who are the police going to believe? The mayor of Saltaire or a man caught red-handed with guns in his own boat?"

"Was Daniel in on it?" Celena felt ill but had to know.

Clint looked at her with eyes that were opaquely gray and preternaturally focused. "You fell for him, didn't you? A nobody. I haven't been able to figure him out, but I'm convinced he came here to keep an eye on his old man. Gerald told me Daniel went over the books thoroughly, but I've been careful. There's nothing there."

"You probably planted the idea of getting the lighthouse in Gerald's mind."

"You're catching on." Clint sounded approving.

"Why did you want the light?"

"You mean besides its 'historic significance'?" Clint laughed. "The light is perfect for my needs. One of the biggest benefits is that my crew can wait offshore, outside U.S. jurisdiction, until I signal them to come in. Do you remember when you asked if rumrunners might want the light? You could have knocked me over with a feather when you said that. You had it all figured out and didn't even know it."

"That's why you had Rueben teach you to run the light." Nothing seemed solid under her feet. "Weren't you afraid someone might notice the change?"

He shook his head. "Not likely. Everyone is so used to it that no one pays any attention. Still, there was a slight risk, and that's why I only made a minor change for a short period of time. As an extra precaution, I only used the signal for large shipments and gun runs."

"Joshua thought he'd seen the flash pattern change," Celena said slowly. "My father also said something about the flash pattern being wrong, but I thought he was just mixed up. He thought it happened the first night I tended the light."

Clint seemed amused. "I remember that night. I stopped by, remember? You went downstairs to get some maps to show me."

Understanding dawned. "And while I was gone, you changed the flash pattern. It was *your* crew's lights we saw on the beach—"

"Idiots! Since I was there, they thought it was all right to use their lights. Rueben had already asked me to run the light that night, so I'd set up a gun run. When I found out you were going to run the light, it was too late to cancel it."

"So you went down to give them a hand."

"Exactly!" Clint laughed. "Oh, Celena, I *have* enjoyed our time together. How sad it has to end."

Celena's skin went cold and clammy. She said a quick prayer in her heart and asked, "But why guns? I don't understand—"

"There's a big demand right now. A lot of countries are begging for armaments."

"Because they're afraid of another war?"

"Yep. You only have to listen to the radio or read the newspaper to realize conditions are deteriorating in Europe. With the collapse of Germany and Austria and the emergence of new states, every European country with an ounce of sense wants to build up their military in case there's a revival of Germany's predilection to prowl. Smuggling guns was an easy way to earn a lot more. The boats were already here. No sense in having them go back empty."

"So Clearwater is just a front for smuggling?" she asked desperately, fighting for time.

"Actually it was the other way around. I'd always dreamed of having a high-class resort. I tried for years to interest developers, with no luck.

They acted like I was a nobody, a second-class citizen. I vowed to show them. Smuggling provided my start and put me in contact with people who had big money." Clint inclined his head toward the door. "No more questions. It's time to go for a little walk."

When Gerald began to struggle, Clint went over to test the tightness of the rope. Celena thought about running but knew Clint would be able to aim and fire before she could get very far. She suspected he would have no compunction about shooting her down.

"Don't worry, Gerald," Clint said coolly. "We'll talk when I get back. I just hope you'll be sober enough to remember it. Because if going back to prison doesn't make you hold your tongue, you can decide now to say good-bye to your son." Gerald became suddenly still, his eyes full of loathing and fear. Clint continued. "It's funny, but a lot of accidents seem to happen around here, and whether the next one happens to Daniel depends on what you say, or rather, on what you *don't* say."

Celena felt hot, then cold—as though she had the flu. "You were the one who caused my father's 'accident'! *You* cut the rope!"

"What rope?" Clint asked mockingly. "One piece of advice, Celena: If you have a piece of evidence, try to hang onto it." Almost by way of apology, he added, "I did my best to talk your father into retiring. I had a friend in the Coast Guard all lined up, ready to come out and run the light. When I went out to the light to try again, Matthew happened to be painting. I just *knew* he wasn't going to be reasonable. I thought about how dangerous it was for him to be out there, hanging off the side of the light. Fortunately, I always carry a good pocketknife."

Celena could bear no more. With fists raised, she rushed him but landed no more than one or two blows before Clint laid the rifle on the desk and grabbed her wrists, twisting her arms behind her and causing such pain to her still-healing burns that she cried out. Up close, Celena could see how cold his eyes were.

There was real anger in his voice now. "You had to stay—the proverbial fly in the ointment," he growled. "Everything almost fell apart because of *you*." He twisted her arm farther, sending sharp pains through her shoulder. "You never stopped poking around, stirring things up. After you came back, I went to talk to Matthew again. I hoped that with a little encouragement, he might tell you to leave again. But he wouldn't hear a word against you. You almost ruined all my plans. All of the advantages in having the light could easily turn to disaster if someone else got it."

"Then why did you go with me to the Lighthouse Bureau?"

"You and Rueben backed me into a corner. I wanted to go alone so I could persuade them to put me in charge. But no, you had to come and tell your sob story, which they bought."

Celena's fear was like nausea in her stomach. Her eyes strayed to the door. Would she be able to make a break for it once they were outside, maybe slip away into the blackness? Clint caught her eye, then reached for a length of rope and tied her hands behind her back. She bit her lip to keep from crying out as the rope tightened against her bandaged arms.

"Just a little insurance," he said. "I can outrun you, but I see we've got a bit of unseasonable fog out there, and I don't want to take any chances." As Clint propelled her to the door, Celena's heart accelerated until she could feel the pulse in her throat leaping with it. His hand was like a band of steel. Gerald twisted and turned, grunting with the effort to rise, but the ropes held. Clint looked back and smiled—a thin, stretched smile.

"It's a little late to be a hero. You do some thinking while I'm gone. I'm going to introduce Celena to some friends of mine." He laughed, and the sound was chilling. Clint spoke to Celena. "Your disappearance will cause a hue and a cry, but everyone knows how you like to walk along the beach and that there are smugglers around. It will be assumed you ran into some bad ones." When he opened the door, yellow light spilled out into the blackness. Faint wisps of fog swirled as the moon stared palely though a thin veiling of cloud.

Celena cried, "Why are you doing this?"

Clint's eyes were stonelike and unreadable. "It never would have come to this if you had gone back and if you hadn't started asking all those questions about Sarina. Her death was a hornet's nest I couldn't afford to have stirred up."

It was difficult to breathe. Sounding as if she were a fish drowning in air, Celena gasped, crying now. "You killed her too?"

"I didn't have a choice." Clint's voice was chillingly calm. "Sarina recognized me when she came to Fire Island. Years ago, when I was visiting my brother in Pennsylvania, I worked with two of her brothers. They were con artists, and together we pulled off a few deals. Sarina knew all about it and thought I might be doing something similar here." Clint paused. "She was like you, poking her nose into things that were none of her business. When she found out I was smuggling, she blackmailed me. Said she'd go to the police unless I paid her to keep quiet. I did, for a while. Then one afternoon she came to the dock, demanding a bigger cut. I told her I had some money on my boat. She was wearing a scarf when she came aboard. Did you know that a scarf, when tightly wrapped, is as strong as rope?"

Celena recoiled, feeling the cold stone of the lighthouse against her back. There was a stirring of memory . . . what was it? Then it came to her—the brightly colored scarves in Ethan's closet—she'd seen them someplace else. It came to her—on Clint's boat. She'd been searching for a handkerchief when she'd seen something colorful—one of Sarina's scarves.

Clint's manner was quiet. "I dumped her body then went and got her boat and towed it out, leaving it to drift so it would look like an accident."

Her blood seemed to thicken and run cold. "There's one thing I don't understand. If you wanted to get rid of me, why did you save me at the fire?"

"It seems you've been leading a charmed life—up to now, that is. I followed you on the beach one night, but Daniel came along. Things didn't work out at the Sunken Forest either. Then, after locking you in the shed, I was forced to rescue you."

Celena could only stare at him helplessly. "You were the one who wrote the note—and locked me in!"

"Everyone thought I was a hero." His eyes crinkled in amusement. "After I set the fire, I stood back to admire it, thinking my problems were solved, when Helen came down the trail. I turned around to make it look like I was headed in the same direction she was, and just then, Ethan came running up." He grimaced. "I could hardly refuse to help with two witnesses."

Witnesses. *Joshua.* Why hadn't help come yet? "Clint—where is Joshua?"

Clint watched her with his intent, intelligent gaze. It was a look she knew well. Until now, she had not known what lay behind it. Celena had thought she knew him. Now, too late, she had discovered how wrong she had been. "He's all right. Obviously I couldn't let him go for help. I tied him up, gagged him, and set him in a thicket. When I get you to the beach, I'll go collect him so you can be together."

She stared in horror. "He's . . . he's a little boy, Clint . . . you can't possibly—"

He cut her off. "Come on, Celena. We don't want to keep our friends waiting."

Celena shrunk back, but he grabbed her arm and pulled her along. The cold wind tore at her as she walked, almost as if it were trying to beat her back from what lay ahead. Toward the ocean, thin bits of fog puffed like smoke. Celena felt light-headed—stricken with terror—but knew she had to keep her wits about her. She put a tentative foot forward, then another, as if she did not trust the ground to bear her up. Clint kept up a steady and inexorable pace. If she happened to stumble slightly or pause even fractionally, his fingers pressed cruelly into the burns on her arm. With his other hand he held the rifle. The wind-driven clouds blew raggedly across the moon's face, causing darkness to return at odd intervals. Other times the moon caused a luminous radiance that made the beach and ocean seem unreal—ethereal.

She could feel the heart-shaped locket against her as she prayed silently. Then, unexpectedly, Celena began to feel quiet and clear-headed. Even in this moment of terrible peril, she felt an inner strength. The noise of the ocean, like murmuring voices, became louder and more insistent as they drew closer. The chill night seemed terribly, unusually quiet—as if it had caught its breath and was waiting to see what would happen next. Celena looked about, seeking a way to escape, but Clint's grasp was firm, and she could do nothing except move in the direction he wanted. As she stumbled along, Celena thought she caught a faraway movement, but the gauzy fog was deceitful. Somehow she had to find a way to get away from this man—

one she had thought was her friend but who had turned out to be her mortal enemy.

The wind hushed as Clint drew her roughly over the sand. There was only the faint sounds of Celena catching her breath and the soft fall of their footsteps. Ahead of them was the familiar outline of boulders that marked her favorite spot on the beach. This evening the rocks were blue-black in the depths of the night. Knowing the spot as well as she did, Celena sensed there was something different. As the light fog shifted, Celena saw a shape that was only the barest of outlines, not entirely there. Her heart leapt up from the cold spot at the bottom of her stomach. She strained to see, but the darkness and mist obscured her view. If only that high-sailing, white galleon of a moon would shine down through an opening in the clouds!

Could Ethan possibly be watching the beach as he so often did? There was no way to be sure, and she didn't dare call out. Celena darted a glance at Clint. He was turned toward the ocean, searching for the men who would soon be arriving. Once, Clint had seemed to care for her. Would it do any good to plead? Celena knew it would not. Clint was a dangerous man who would stop at nothing. He had his world set up, and she had come along and disturbed it. In the distance, some faraway lights appeared. They were coming. She had only a few minutes.

"You're a bad man, Clint, to kill Sarina!" Celena said loudly. She hoped her voice would carry—but it felt as though she were speaking through a mouthful of cotton. He responded by twisting her still-healing arm so hard her body filled with agonizing flashes of fire.

"It won't be long now, Celena. Too bad you didn't have a chance to say good-bye."

She was conscious of her pulse beating. "They'll know something bad happened, Clint," Celena cried at full volume. "They'll know *bad men* came and hurt me like you hurt Sarina!" The lights were closer now. Soon there would be faces to go with the lights. There was one last chance. Celena had to take it. Taking Clint unaware, she jerked free and started running toward the boulders.

"Don't be stupid," Clint yelled angrily. "You'll never get away!" Celena was almost there when her foot hit a rock. With her arms tied, there was no way to break her fall, and she hit the ground hard. She was laying there stunned when Ethan came roaring out of the boulders like a grizzly bear that had been disturbed. With a flying tackle, he crashed into Clint, and both men fell. There were grunts and curses as they wrestled on the sand. Celena strained her eyes but could only see faintly as the two men thrashed about. A gunshot rang out.

"Ethan!" Her scream, high and chilling, seemed to echo forever. Struggling to her feet, Celena saw the lights that had nearly been upon them suddenly start to fade away, like cockroaches disappearing when a light comes on. Then, someone was running toward her, and Daniel appeared like some wraith out of the fog. Her body was still so light with fear that Celena couldn't feel it.

"Did he hurt you?" Daniel asked breathlessly, his face anxious.

"I'm fine. Go help Ethan!"

Daniel grabbed the rifle that had fallen and pointed it at Clint. "Give it up. Now!"

Clint lay still then, gasping for air. Groaning, Ethan sat up. Blood had soaked through his sleeve and covered his fingers as they clutched at his arm. He rose and staggered a bit, looking at Daniel, then Clint, and finally at Celena.

"Is it all right, then?" he asked, unsure he had done the right thing in tackling the mayor.

"Yes, you did just right." Although Celena spoke quietly, Ethan's broad face relaxed. Somehow he could tell there was high praise hidden in these words. Soon, men came running. Clint was surrounded, and Daniel told the men to take him to town. A few men escorted Ethan to Doc Harrison's house while others went to the light to release Gerald.

Daniel cut the rope from Celena's wrists. "When I went to Bay Haven to escort you to the light and found you weren't there, I decided to go to the lighthouse to see what was going on. On the way, I nearly fell over Joshua. He'd been in the bushes, and although he was still tied up, he'd managed to crawl out onto the trail. I notified some men at Kismet to spread the word and meet me at the beach. Fortunately, Ethan was already here."

Suddenly, Celena was in Daniel's arms, trembling. She burrowed her face into his chest to scourge away the stinging tears and felt the warmth of him. It was wonderful to feel safe after such a struggle. Daniel held on as if he were never going to let her go. Then, gently, Daniel put a hand under Celena's chin and, raising her face, kissed her. Celena was aware of her racing heart and quickened breath. In spite of the trauma she had just endured, she realized at that moment that she didn't need to avoid Daniel and the feelings he stirred in her. She felt warmth in her heart and clarity in her mind—this was a man who loved her and whom she could trust. After a few minutes, they started across the sand, with Celena leaning into his strength. She glanced back once at the light-house where the beam was flashing—true and never ending—then set her face toward Saltaire.

TWENTY-TWO

In the morning, the first thing Celena did was go see Ethan. He was looking well scrubbed, with a clean flannel shirt and his long hair neatly combed. His right arm was in a sling. Picture books were stacked by the chair, and a nearby plate held pancake crumbs and bits of egg. Helen had been busy.

Celena sat beside him. "We're quite the pair, aren't we?" she said, glancing at her own bandages. He smiled broadly, and she asked, "How's the arm today?"

"It hurts a lot," Ethan said with a frown.

"I'm sorry. I'm sure the medicine Helen gives you will help," Celena said consolingly. "Thanks for watching out for me. That's what you were doing at the beach last night, wasn't it?"

"I heard you say Clint was a bad man. I didn't know he was bad." The previous night, Celena had spent a long time with Ethan. It had been painful telling him that Clint had caused her father to fall and had trapped her in the burning shed, but the worst was explaining that Clint had killed Sarina.

"Clint won't be able to hurt anyone else, thanks to you," Celena said gently. "He's in jail, and the bad men are gone. You don't have to watch the beach anymore." Last night, Ethan had seemed bewildered by it all, but now his demeanor suggested an inner equanimity that hadn't been there before. In fact, he was more tranquil than he'd been since her return to the island. Perhaps now that the mystery surrounding Sarina's death had been cleared up, he could start to heal.

He nodded calmly. "Sarina's gone. She's all right now."

"Sarina still loves you, and you'll be able to see her again," Celena reminded him.

"I know," Ethan said matter-of-factly.

Celena didn't stay. Ethan seemed content, and she wanted to see her father. His door was open, and Joshua was there, animatedly telling his father how he'd gone down the side of the light. Her brother was flushed and excited while Matthew was pale and still. When Celena walked in, Matthew turned to her. From across the room, she could see tears standing in his eyes, making them swim with liquid blue light. Celena swiftly crossed the room, and they hugged tightly, her father making a soft, choked noise into her hair. Although a few tears of her own came, there was nothing of the past in them. No longer did bitterness lie around her heart like a glacier. It had melted, and the last of it lay dotted upon his shirt.

Matthew looked anxious. "You're all right, aren't you? Joshua said you were, but—"

"Aye, I'm fine," she said, mimicking him affectionately.

His face worked a bit. "I've been praying. With Elizabeth, I didn't get the answer I wanted, but this time I did." Celena looked at him fondly, and he went on. "Still, I've learned a few things. Now I know God hears me, no matter what answer He gives." Then Matthew's face changed, and, sounding more like himself, he chided her. "If only you had gone back to Maryland and stopped digging around, this wouldn't have happened! You're just so—so *persistent!*"

Celena grinned. "And here I thought I was being stubborn."

Matthew laughed one of his rare laughs. "You've changed," he said. Joshua smiled too, and she knew it was true. Thank goodness for the blessings of heaven, which had strengthened her and softened him. And wasn't it a miracle how forgiveness had come along so softly, without her even knowing the exact moment it had it slipped inside her heart? The promises that had brought her back to Fire Island had not only broken the shackles of the past, they had miraculously lightened her world—making it bright and full of hope.

Joshua was bursting to tell the story to Zach and left hastily, almost plowing into Daniel. Tana came in long enough to give Celena a big hug. Celena did a double take at Gerald and Helen, who looked so different from the day before. It was their faces that had changed the most. Although Helen still had dark circles under her eyes, her face was tranquil, while Gerald looked more like his easygoing self than he had for weeks.

Matthew had some questions for Gerald. "So, you didn't know about the guns, but you knew Clint was rum-running?" Gerald had the look of a small boy being scolded as he nodded.

It was apparent Daniel was still angry when he snapped, "Why didn't you *tell* me?"

"I couldn't," Gerald said. "Not when Clint had gotten me out of prison and given me a job."

"One where you had to turn a blind eye to rum-running!" Daniel spoke scathingly.

Helen spoke up in his defense, anxious that they understand. "Gerald knew nothing about Clint's rum-running until he'd been here well over a year. When Gerald found out, Clint told him if he didn't keep quiet, he'd go back to jail."

Normally, Gerald loved being the center of attention, but now he only looked deflated. "To tell the truth, the rum-running never bothered me. No one takes Prohibition seriously, and it seemed rather harmless. Like a game. But when Ethan showed up with that rifle, I began to wonder if Clint had branched out. But he wouldn't answer any of my questions."

"Why did you go after Celena yesterday?" Matthew challenged.

"When Helen told me about the guns, I knew Clint was behind it. Helen and I talked, and once she settled down, we decided to go to the police. Things couldn't go on the way they were—for either of us." Gerald glanced sideways, indicating Helen. "You see, Helen was about to break from the pressure. Finding out that Lydia had been arrested and was on parole, then her husband saddling her with debts, almost losing Bay Haven . . ."

Gerald looked at Celena apologetically. "That's why Helen fell apart yesterday. When she saw all that bootleg liquor, it was just easier to believe you were to blame than her own daughter." Celena stole a look at Helen. Tears were clinging to Helen's bottom lashes. Gerald continued. "We realized you'd be in danger if Clint found out you knew about the guns, so Helen sent me to warn you."

"So you start drinking and take one of the rifles to the lighthouse and scare Celena to death," Daniel said sardonically, causing Gerald to flush.

"I . . . well—I had a few drinks just to brace myself to face Clint," Gerald replied, his red face flushing deeper.

"When you fired the rifle, I thought you were aiming at me," Celena admitted.

"Lost my head there." Gerald shook his head regretfully. "I was trying for Clint. Guess I'd had more to drink than I thought."

Matthew's voice was hard. "Because of you, Joshua had to go down the side of the lighthouse in the dark. How did you get into the light, anyway?"

"Clint had me keep a key in my office at Clearwater. Probably to incriminate me if things fell apart." Gerald was finally showing some astuteness.

Matthew said musingly, "It's hard to believe that Clint actually killed Sarina."

"He's not the type to allow anyone to get away with blackmail," Gerald said.

"One thing puzzles me," Daniel said. "Why did Sarina tell Ethan there were bad men around and that he needed to watch the beach?"

"I've thought about that," Celena interjected, "and I realized that Sarina told Ethan those things at different times. Sarina was trying to protect Ethan. She knew he liked to go to the beach, where Clint's men worked, so she tried to frighten Ethan into staying away by telling him there were bad men. However, she didn't tell him *until the day she died* that he was to watch the beach. Sarina must have felt like she was in danger, so she told him to watch the beach if she went away, hoping that eventually Ethan would find out about the smuggling, tell someone, and have Clint arrested."

Celena looked at Daniel. "Did you call your friend in the Coast Guard about Ethan's rifle?"

"What's this?" Matthew asked. "I thought Clint already had the gun checked out."

"That was another one of Clint's lies," Celena said. "Actually, he never turned it in. Ethan found it hanging on the wall in Gerald's office. Clint switched it. You see, Ethan's rifle was one of the ones he'd been smuggling, so he couldn't turn it in, or else the Coast Guard would find out it had been stolen. So Clint took a rifle out of Gerald's office and turned that one in. Last night, I asked Daniel to take the rifle I took from the boathouse to the Coast Guard and have them check it out."

"I took it over this morning, and you were right, Celena. The rifle *was* stolen," Daniel said.

Just then, Rueben walked in, followed by Lydia. It was the first time Celena had ever seen her with no makeup. Lydia looked like a schoolgirl, young and a little frightened.

"Did everything go all right at the light last night?" Matthew asked Rueben.

"Like clockwork," Rueben said, running a hand through his gray hair. "I was happy to do it after Daniel promised me double overtime. He said that would be fine with you."

Looking flabbergasted, Matthew growled, "And since when does a bookkeeper tell you what the Lighthouse Bureau will or won't pay?"

"When that bookkeeper works for the Coast Guard," Rueben answered. He turned to Daniel. "Well, Lieutenant, catching a kingpin like Clint Paxton is a big break for you." He wagged a finger in Daniel's face. "I always knew there was something fishy about you."

"What is this?" Celena asked, looking at Daniel in surprise.

"I'm sorry I couldn't tell you before," Daniel said, taking her hand, "but I was under strict orders of secrecy. I'm in the Coast Guard." He glanced at Rueben. "But I'm an ensign, not a lieutenant. We knew there were smuggling rings operating here, and when my lieutenant commander found out I had family living on Fire Island, he asked me to come. Having my father on the island provided me with a great cover."

The breath went out of Celena in a whoosh. "Well. *That* explains a lot!"

Gerald looked bemused. "I just found out last night."

Daniel said, "My cover was blown last night when I went to Kismet to get help. I had to show the men my identification and explain about Clint."

"No wonder you knew so much about boats and rumrunners," Rueben said. "You had me worried for a while. Good thing I got out of the business. You'd have busted me for sure."

Matthew sounded surprised. "You were rum-running?"

"A little," Rueben confessed. "It was hard to quit, especially when I knew the money was helping Will. And yes, I've bared my soul to Tana—and the bishop. I have to keep telling myself that the end doesn't justify the means."

Celena said to Daniel, "That's why you never talked about what you did before coming here."

Lydia made a derisive noise. "No one ever listens to me—"

Daniel went on. "A few years after I left home, I joined the Coast Guard. When my father told me about his job here, it seemed too good to be true. So, when I was offered this assignment, I accepted it so I could find out if he was getting suckered into another scam." Daniel continued. "When I got here, I noticed that my father didn't have any real authority. The books looked okay, but there were a lot of things that didn't add up. Then you came along, Celena, and really started stirring things up."

Rueben's watery blue eyes looked angry. "Clint played us all for fools. I thought he was just interested when he kept asking so many questions about the lighthouse."

"Oh, he was interested, all right," Daniel stated grimly. "Interested in finding out how to change the flash pattern so he could signal his crew."

Rueben turned to Lydia. "Why did you send Celena to the boathouse? Weren't you worried she'd find the guns?"

Without her colored lips and dark eyes, Lydia looked vulnerable. "I sent her there because I needed time to get rid of the cases. I didn't even know there *were* guns there. Good thing Clint's going to prison or he'd kill me for sure."

Helen had a question. "Why didn't you tell me Clint was rum-running?"

"Because if I ratted on him, it would have been the end for me. Clint Paxton is not someone you want to cross. Still—" Lydia shuddered slightly. "I never thought he'd go so far as to kill Sarina. I thought she was rum-running. That's why I went to talk with her that day, but she told me to mind my own business." Showing some of her usual spirit, Lydia turned to Celena. "I was able to get rid of that shipment so there's no evidence against me—just your word against mine that the cases were ever there at all."

Daniel spoke up. "Don't be thinking you're free and clear, Lydia. There are a lot of people who can testify against you. Your probation officer will be the one to let you know what you'll be charged with."

As Lydia pouted, Helen cleared her throat and asked Daniel, "Will Gerald be facing any charges?"

"I'm afraid he will. Even though Clint was the one who set up the rum-running and handled it, my father knew about it and didn't report it. Obstruction of justice, you see." Daniel looked thoughtful. "However, it's very possible he could get off on a plea deal if he agrees to testify against Clint."

Rueben spoke up. "If that happens, then Gerald ought to be able to stay on at Clearwater."

"That depends on the other co-owners. But since he's already familiar with the resort and things have been going so well, I bet they'd agree to keep him on." Daniel turned to his father. "Do you think you can run the resort without Clint?"

"I'll help him," Helen said quickly. "I have a fair bit of experience."

Gerald reached over and took one of Helen's hands in his. Sounding like his old self, he boomed jovially, "Like I always say, things have a way of working out for the best. Now that Helen's divorce is final and her ex-husband can't run up any more bills, things are looking up at Bay Haven. Bookings there have been steadily increasing."

"And what about you, Celena?" Rueben asked. "Think you can stick it out now that you don't have ghosts, vandals, or murderers hanging around?"

"Guess I'll have to find something else to do for excitement." She smiled wryly. "At least until Father's leg heals and he's ready to take over."

Standing tall, Daniel cleared his throat loudly. "No one's asked me, but I've put in a request to my lieutenant commander to make my assignment on Fire Island permanent."

Rueben chuckled. "I should have asked you first. That pretty much guarantees Celena will be staying."

Celena blushed. "Last night, Clint told me I should have gone back where I belonged, to Maryland, but he was wrong. I belong here, on Fire Island."

Looking smug, Gerald told his son, "I always knew Celena was the girl for you. I could see the sparks between you two—you just needed time to get to know each other. Why do you think I asked her and Joshua over for lunch at Clearwater? And asked her to take you that tray when you had a headache?"

Daniel looked at his father. "So you were plotting all along to get us together?"

"The old man's sharper than you think," Gerald replied with a wink.

Celena rose, her cheeks becomingly pink. "I think I'd like to go for a walk."

"I could use one myself," Daniel said firmly. Celena took his hand, and they left Bay Haven, walking hand in hand until they reached the dune line, crossing it to reach the beach. The sun was high and honey gold, and the temperature was rising pleasantly—a change from the chill of the past few days. Near the shore, the ocean was green, deepening to gray-blue as it spread out in a vast rolling plain that reached to the horizon.

Celena felt a crisp awareness of the beauty of the island—from the towering lighthouse to the wheeling curlews to the bright ocean rolling in, wave after white-edged wave. Everything was fresh, clear, and wonderful. Possibly life seemed so bright now because such a short time ago it had been dark and menacing. The terror Celena had experienced allowed her to see the sweetness in life. Still, a large portion of her joy came from an appreciation of the man beside her. Near the beach, small shore birds ran from the breakers, then turned to chase the waves as they receded. Celena and Daniel found some rocks to sit on, and, as they looked at each other, Celena was not afraid to let her eyes betray her heart.

Celena's voice sparkled as she asked, "So, can I still call you Daniel, or is 'Ensign' more appropriate?"

"Most people call me 'sir.'"

She laughed up at him. "Like that man you were talking with by Tillman's? Was he a spy too?"

Daniel grinned. "I guess you could say that. We met occasionally so he could keep me up-to-date. He was telling me about a rumrunner they'd caught the night before." Out on the ocean, the sun was reflected in silver flashes off the ruffled water.

There was a brief pause, and then Celena mused, "You know, it was actually very good of Gerald to come to the lighthouse to warn me."

Daniel agreed. "My father doesn't usually go against the people he works with. His style has usually been to just go along with whatever blows his way. Too bad he wasn't sober enough to tell you straight out what was going on when he first arrived."

"What about his son? Does *he* go along with whatever blows his way?"

When Daniel pulled Celena to him, there was strength yet gentleness in his embrace. "Not unless it's *exactly* what I want." Celena closed her eyes as they kissed.

Then, with Daniel's arm warm and comforting around her, they walked down the beach. This was what true loving was like, Celena thought, this warm flood of outgoing emotion and knowing that in the future, the bond between them would only become stronger. Celena smiled, tightening the clasp of her fingers about Daniel's as they moved away from the shadows of the past into a bright future where they would learn more about each other—here, on Fire Island.

ABOUT THE AUTHOR

Marlene Bateman was born in Salt Lake City, Utah, and grew up in Sandy, Utah. She graduated from the University of Utah with a bachelor's degree in English. Marlene has been published extensively in various magazines and newspapers and has written a number of books. Her hobbies include reading, camping, and gardening. Marlene and her husband, Kelly, have seven children and nine beautiful grand-daughters.